Fouled in Open Play

A novel by Pat Voss

Editing by Frankie Vasquez of Olive Press Publishing
Book cover and interior design by Sofie Birkin

Library of Congress Control Number: 2026910261
ISBN 979-8-9956794-0-0 (paperback)
ISBN 979-8-9956794-1-7 (hardcover)
ISBN 979-8-9956794-2-4 (ebook)
ISBN 979-8-9956794-3-1 (audiobook)

First edition: 2026

To all those suffering in silence.
Your pain is heard.

"I realized I could only truly enjoy my life once I was honest... My secret is gone, I am a free man, I can move on and live my life as my creator intended."

– *Robbie Rogers*

Author's Note

Dear Reader,

I am thrilled that of all the ebooks flooding your algorithm, hardbacks neatly displayed in your favorite bookstore, or paperbacks available at your local library, you gave my story a chance. I am forever grateful for this. It's an honor and a privilege that you chose my work, and I hope it transports you on the memorable journey I envisioned for my readers. However, the last thing I would ever want is to evoke any trauma that makes this read an uncomfortable experience.

As my tagline on social media suggests, my writing focuses on creating captivating queer stories in not so queer friendly settings. This book is no exception, so if any of the following trigger you, dear reader, I completely understand if you cannot continue past this note. My main character's journey takes place in University Hills, potentially one of the most homophobic college settings conceived in fiction. The fictional locals have no problem dropping homophobic and transphobic slurs, especially towards students attending the rival university. In addition, there is also a mention of the underbelly of reparative therapy. Though brief, these experiences still sting my heart now as they did when I was a confused teenager years ago. I wrote the events much darker and dramatized for the novel for plot development. Please read at your own risk.

Aside from the anti-LGBTQ+ themes, my character's trauma, which is pivotal for their development, is on full display in this story. My main character is a college soccer player, so the negative stereotypes associated with that are present in this world. Besides the typical locker-room talk, this includes a hazing incident at a team retreat. Racial profiling occurs for some characters, which includes threats of deportation. There are also instances of cyberbullying, blackmail, and drug abuse. Some characters mourn the death of family members that occurred prior to the story, which include a martyr in political violence, a victim to a hate crime, and loss by suicide. If you have lost someone important in your life in any of these manners, I want to share my deepest condolences with you. Its not my intention to open old wounds.

If after reading all of this you choose to continue on, I promise not to disappoint you. This journey is a tribute to the resilience of the LGBTQ+ community. Even with increasingly misplaced hatred on the rise, we still rise and let our unapologetic selves shine through. Our community still makes space to open our hearts to love while the world showers us with hate. We are not the enemy, nor the boogeyman. We simply exist and plan to keep it that way. No political movement will change that.

So, with no further delay, I hope you enjoy this unabridged production of "Fouled in Open Play." I can't wait to talk to you again in the acknowledgements.

Sincerely,

Pat Voss

Part 1

Chapter 1

September 24, 2025

It's the moment the doctor clears me to train that I am ready to torture myself again. Call it masochistic, but any player in my position would behave the same way, especially a college athlete aspiring for his first professional contract. It's a privilege to stand on this field melting away in the aggressive heat as each agonizing second ticks by, because I suffered a lot to reach this point. From every sprint, infinite ball work sessions, exhaustive fitness plans, and a meticulous diet, my entire life condenses into one continuous soccer practice, similar to the one I face now. Soccer demands my soul so I push my body beyond its limits. Even my recovery looks like Olympic training. I convince myself every day that nothing in my life will break me, so I keep pushing. I never stop. Through loss, heartbreak, and every struggle in between, I focus everything on my success in the sport.

A tingle in my right leg reminds me of the moment I thought my career ended. A bone break this last summer kept me away from the game for months, forcing me to watch as my new team endured consecutive close losses early this season. Games I would influence over if I were healthy. That thought devoured me more with every loss, but that insanity reduced as my extensive medical care and intense physical therapy pieced me back together whole again. I stand tall now with the pitch under my feet again, my safeguards gone at last. Even with impatience causing an adrenaline overload through my system, this session seems extreme for my first practice, especially since we are a week before our first conference game.

I line up along a series of cones next to my new teammates on the far-side of the field, facing the vibrant orange and pink colors bruising the Monday evening sky. Grimaces and scowls contort their faces, with their bulging arms and legs as aggressive as their disposition.

Part of their bitterness is toward today's practice, given that no one expected to repeat this practice after preseason. They direct the other part of aggressiveness toward me. It sucks that I haven't properly introduced myself because my rehab has separated me from the group, allowing my association with my last school to create a negative stereotype for me. I thought it was irrelevant, but it would be a lie to say I didn't expect the prolonged silent treatment and childish teasing when I walked up to the field.

This school was my only transfer option, so I'll endure this for a while. However, I focus on my priorities, and my presence evoking some level of resentment is the least of my concerns. I stand on the far-right side of the line for my safety.

I adopt my runner's pose while fixating on the cone positioned twenty meters ahead. The field is in dire shape. Without the cones, I wouldn't be able to see the faded touchline under my feet, and potholes and divots litter the distance between me and the marker ahead. It's like the school has neglected the field since the end of last season.

What's even more concerning than the field is the intense heat. The scorching rays of the sun burn into me with such force that it's hard to believe it is almost fall. Even the subtle breeze grazing the sides of my skin-bald fade could not hinder the summer's blaze. It's a miracle I'm not as parched as the grass beneath me.

But I have to stay focused on the task ahead, so I take a few deep breaths, hoping to calm my racing thoughts. Stocky Coach Jack Ramsey stomps up to the top of the rusted-out bleachers across the field. He carries a black pocketbook and stops at the top step next to his large speaker. Wearing his retro square sunglasses and black Nike ball cap, he observes us like test subjects in his scientific experiment.

"All right, boys, today is a beautiful evening to restart our season before it counts. Given our recent run of results, I figured we would wipe the slate clean and repeat the Yo-Yo Test. I will integrate anyone who passes into the first team, just like in preseason." Coach Ramsey, with his raspy British accent, yells out.

"However, given that we are into the season, we are requiring a 20.1 for the passing score. If you are a starter and don't pass, don't bother complaining. Your starting status doesn't excuse insufficient effort on the field. I need to know who wants to continue after our terrible last game."

I muster the driest swallow down my throat. I know Coach Ramsey is tough, but this is extreme. A 20.1 score is for elite athletes, most of whom play professionally. This standard is insane. And with a starting spot on the line, the standards intensify. To play immediately after experiencing an injury is the comeback I need.

The thought of losing this opportunity burns worse than the sun grilling my skin. I know I can pass, especially since I am in the best possible shape given the circumstances. Still, I sowed a seed of belief in my mind to keep myself motivated. I watch Coach tap the screen of his smartphone before setting it on top of his speaker, which resembles a suitcase. Then, he scribbles in his notebook while an automated British voice echoes from the speaker.

"This is the Yo-Yo Intermittent Recovery Test level two. Participants, take your starting positions and prepare for the final instructions. The Yo-Yo Intermittent Recovery Test requires running between markers at the shown speed, with ten seconds to jog around the marker after each run. Participants must fully stop at the start marker before the next signal. The speed is low to start, but increases rapidly as the test progresses. A double signal shows an increase in speed. The first time a participant cannot complete the back and run within the timeframe, he receives a warning. The next time it occurs, the test is over, and you must record the final speed level for the twenty-meter intervals. Now, get ready to start. The test begins at speed level eleven. You have eleven seconds to run back and forth between the markers."

Coach Ramsey's line-of-sight meets mine. Even behind his sunglasses, Coach's fixation on me is clear.

"Let's see how Caleb handles his first practice here. Bold choice wearing Fox gear to practice."

I roll my eyes as I look down at my sky blue training shirt and white shorts hugging my body. It was foolish to wear my old school uniform. The University of Southeastern is the bitterest rival of Southeastern State, so it's no surprise that University Hills frowns upon any community wearing the Fox's baby blue. But I can't help it because this is the only gear I own. No one had offered a bright tan training shirt and sleek black shorts to me since I arrived. What was I supposed to do? Show up naked? Given the heat, I would consider it, but no need to draw more unwanted attention to myself. I presented myself enough for everyone to unpack.

"The test begins in five seconds."

I stride across the crunchy grass and dust, doing my best to maintain the same speed as the beeps. At first, this feels ridiculous. I could walk and still hit the beeps in time, yet I maintained a jog to stay engaged. I know conserving my energy is the key to success in this drill. That and maintaining a steady breathing pace.

The next intervals cause my time between the beeps to reduce, forcing me to increase my pace. Despite the circumstances, I maintain a comfortable appearance on the outside. My running gait mimics a marathon runner, with my large thighs resembling tree trunks, swinging back and forth on my athletic hips as I shuffle between the markers.

Once I tap the cone with my right foot before the first beep, my body weight shifts in the opposite direction, and I explode toward the starting line. I steal a glance at Coach Ramsey, hoping to receive some praise, only to realize my coach sits motionless in the stands. His face is stoic and unimpressed.

As the levels progress, soreness engulfs my body. My hamstrings burn with each forced stride, and I feel an annoying pinch in my stomach. I grasp my side during the rest moments, but the pain lingers. The air feels as thin as paper, making it difficult for my lungs to capture the surrounding oxygen. My head spins in circles, even when I am standing still.

As I glance around, I notice the others struggling, but their discomfort brings me no comfort. I push my dirty blonde hair away from my face and repeat the arduous process. Some players succumb to the heat and collapse before the finish line.

My entire body's subtle burn intensifies to soreness as I inch closer to passing. The levels of difficulty increase while my legs resist the pricks of invisible needles, and my ankles sting with each step. The sun's rays heat my body like a pot roast in a slow cooker, bronzing my pale skin. While wiping the cool sweat off my forehead, I fight for a release of dopamine to calm my mounting anxiety. Despite my overwhelming struggle, I project comfort during discomfort.

With a heavy accent, Coach Ramsey rises from his seat and screams at us.

"Keep grinding, boys. It's all mental now...purely mental!" A projectile saliva bullet shoots across my body, sending me back a few steps behind the line. I turn and see my new teammates snickering and laughing. The player with the caramel six-pack stares me down in his runner stance.

"It's all mental faggot fox."

University Hills residents utter only 'hello' more than this one. Hating the Foxes is this town's cup of coffee in the morning and a shot of vodka before bed. It's part of the Rottweiler culture since its inception, a typical by-product between bitter rivals. For me, as a former Fox and current gay man, the insult stings both ways. I understood this risk when I joined here, but hearing it only adds more anxiety to my already complicated mess regarding my sexuality.

I stare at the player shouting at me, and I'm irritated that his looks are more attractive than his lewd comments. A clean French-tipped pompadour sits on a high bald fade, and his sharp jawline cuts through any wall hiding my slight attraction. He flashes his intense white smile, and I'm not sure if he's laughing at his own dig or coping with the pain we all feel. But as soon as he lifts his shirt, revealing a chiseled torso on caramel-colored skin. The sight of him takes my breath away. It disturbs me that men can look and act like him with no guilt.

I return to my mark, shaking off his comment. As soon as I hear the beep, I dig my cleats into the ground with each stride. I push myself to the limit while racing against the clock. Once again, I jump to the line, landing in a squatting position and contorting my body as I fight to maintain balance. And then, with a burst of energy, I sprint across the starting line. Each sprint matches the rhythm of my heartbeat rattling in my chest. My voice heaves as I gasp for air, struggling to catch my breath.

As I hunch over, I steal as much air as possible, placing my hands on my knees. I peer around to compare myself with my teammates, noticing that many others remain in the test with me. The unfortunate few either lie motionless in the grass behind me or drown themselves in water while waiting for the rest of us to finish. I know we are close to the pass mark, but I can't hear the automated voice call out the levels. My mind only focuses on the beeps.

"I must say, boys, well done! Put in that effort again. Come on, lads! Keep your head!"

The same jock gives me a look-over, sizing me up. It irritates the hell out of me this time. What is with this hyper-masculine pride toward me? I am one of them now. Do they hold a grudge from last season? We played in a rivalry game against each other. I did what I had to do to help my old team win. That's in the past now, but hurt feelings still linger, beating me down as a new guy punching bag. I left USE to revive my career, not put up with this immature shit.

I take rough, deep breaths, feeling my diaphragm expand and contract before I return to my mark. There is a renewed sense of determination washing over me. Screw just passing the test. I want to win it all. I want everyone here to know my intentions this season. As each interval passes, I leap off the starting line and sprint harder to the cone, ensuring I land on the line before the beep. I run and run and run, losing all sense of my surroundings.

"Just Caleb and Romero left now. Well done from you lads!" Coach Ramsey shouts.

I face Romero, finally putting a name to the homophobe. All players erupt in cheers, all for Romero. He looks exhausted, struggling to breathe any air while hunched over. His arrogant smile contorts with discomfort. I don't think he has many runs left in him. My body is crying out for me to stop, but I tell myself to keep going. I can beat him on this run and win this contest. I walk to the starting line and wait for my mark.

Beep

I push my body forward, stomping my cleats into the dirt path toward the farthest line. My leg stretches out again, but my cleat slides. I tumble to the ground as if someone has pulled a rug out from underneath me.

Beep

With exhaustion weighing me down, I claw my way back to my feet and muster the strength to sprint toward the finish line. I enter full gut-check mode. With only a few meters and seconds remaining, I exert all my effort, launching myself across the starting line. I stick my neck out, trying to make it before time runs out.

Beep

As my feet cross the starting line, I collapse onto the grass. The soft blades act as a makeshift bed, cradling my exhausted body. I gasp for breath, rolling over to face the sun, my rapid inhales resembling a panic attack. I remain prone for a few seconds before Coach Ramsey looms over me, his presence towering and commanding.

"Romero missed the mark! Congratulations, Caleb. That's top-notch for someone like you!" He turns to face everyone else. "As if our new boy wins the Yo-Yo Test. That's a bit of us!"

His words don't register immediately. I'm wheezing so hard my lungs feel like balloons littered with holes. Time seems to stretch as I gasp for air, the oxygen draining from me quickly. Once the pain subsides, I sit up, exchanging awkward glances with everyone around me. Everyone separates into their groups, whispering and gulping water while waiting for the coaching staff.

A few players glare at me again, this time with less aggressiveness. I tap my index finger to my head and point out, hoping to engage with anyone. But they ignored me again. The group returns to its feet as Coach Ramsey signals for everyone to gather around by the bleachers. I follow, but keep my distance toward the back.

"All right, everyone, you are all free to go. I appreciate your efforts this evening. We will select the first team based on your scores and send it out in the group chat. If you stay behind, pick up the gear when you are done. And remember, since the sewer line burst this weekend, we don't have access to the locker rooms right now. You are on your own for showers. The most important practice of the season starts tomorrow, boys. Be ready for the biggest comeback season of your lives!"

Are you kidding me? No showers at all. I joke often about this school being the region's "little brother" university. But this? This is criminal. Living in University Hills makes me miss my life in University City. I stuff everything into my old red bag and clutch the rough fabric against my hands. I leave the athletic complex and step into a new environment. The university campus spreads out in front of me, with its brick academic buildings. I approach the football stadium, known as the Rottweiler's Den. The stadium is impressive, with its shiny metal accents and colorful banners. It dominates the west side of campus, showing the importance of football. Especially when compared to the soccer facilities.

I continue my walk along a brick pathway that matches the southern architectural style of the campus. The manicured trees on the luscious lawns fill the air above me with a sweeter scent than the sweat lathering my body. I came across the university's center, a bustling hub of activity and unity. The brick buildings surrounding it reflect the uniformity of the student body.

I glance to my left, where I see a mom and dad smiling for a picture with their son in front of our school fountain. The cool mist from the fountain showers them, adding a refreshing touch to the moment. It has me wishing I could have shared a similar moment like that when I moved here months ago.

But I know it will never materialize. It has been difficult to share a moment with my father since my mother passed away. He processes his grief in his work, effectively isolating himself from my brother and me. It's been my new reality since last November, but I still struggle to cope. The thought still lingers when I refocus on my surroundings.

On my right, a lively collection of Greek life members from various sororities and fraternities congregate by their wooden letters on University Row. They dance and talk to each other, their laughter contagious among everyone, as the blaring music from a speaker creates a vibrant atmosphere I expect from members of Fraternity Row.

Now ten minutes into my journey, I pass the uniform academic halls on the far-east corner of campus. I muster the courage to cross the busy street amidst the sounds of car horns and the bustling of pedestrians filling my ears. After navigating the chaos, I cross the street toward my complex.

In contrast to the striking structures behind it, my apartment complex is an eyesore. The faded blue paint peels off the exterior wood of the apartment complex, while disintegrating roof shingles float away when the wind gusts pick up.

Walking along the jagged path, I glide past the bleached and unkempt lawn that separates my building from the parking lot. Cigarette smoke hangs in the air, and unsettling stares from strangers of all ages follow my every move. Their silence uneases me, but I ignore them and hasten my pace to the apartment. Rounding the first building corner, I'm almost home.

Just before I bolt into apartment Q, I knock over a flat package once leaning against the door. I retrieve the skinny package and lodge the cardboard between my fingertips. I ignore the recipient's name on the front before I enter the cozy living room, bathed in sunlight from the windows, and toss the box onto the black sofa.

The door down the hallway leads to our small guest bathroom. It's about what you would expect from the 2000s. A barrage of ceramic subway tiles rises in all directions from the hexagonal marble flooring. The small shower stands at the bathroom's back, exceeding only the vanity's size.

My clothes peel off my rancid body as I strip down to my bare skin. I was about to shower when I heard keys jingling at the front door. I yank the towel off the rack and wrap it around my waist as I peek out into the living room. My roommate—Machi—bursts into the apartment, ripping her stained green apron from her coffee shop T-shirt and wrinkled jeans. She slams it onto the kitchen island as she storms into the kitchen. She rips the fridge door open and lets out an angry shriek. Marching to the kitchen island, she makes a loud thud.

"Hey!" I say, walking into the living room.

"Hi," Machi replies. She rustles through various snack bags and boxes with her back toward me.

"How was work?"

She slams the cabinets before facing me. A single vein bulges from her temple. Machi starts with her high-pitched shrill. Her Taiwanese accent cuts through all the silence.

"I hate when new people don't have a clue! This èrbī I was with today kept asking about the process for our latte creation…at 7:30 a.m. The line was already out the door. And this new hire cannot focus on her tasks. She just takes the food out of the oven. That's it. But she left the food station to join another girl for some nonsense during the rush. Why can't anyone understand we take orders, prepare food and coffee, smile, hand them their order, and repeat? That's it! It's easy! But then half of our afternoon shift called out, so I stayed longer to help and make the extra cash we desperately need."

I bury my smirk in my hands while Machi rubs her frown line to erase the stress of her day. I don't know how she balances a biological engineering degree and her job at Third House Coffee Roasters. She's always overworked, so my duty as a best friend and roommate is to always check in on her welfare when I can. In return, she restores humanity in me. It's draining trying to focus on soccer and concealing my sexuality here, leaving me in a constant state of emotional dissonance.

"I'm sorry," I say. Machi acknowledges me with giggles and snorts.

"What?" I ask.

"Did I interrupt something?"

"I was about to shower. What did you think?"

While she moves her finger in a circle, she asks, "Is somebody in the shower?"

A snort leaves when I shake my head.

"No, no. None of that. We could not use the locker room showers today. Facilities are down."

"Why?"

"A sewage line burst under our game field, and they turned off the water to our locker room."

"So you can't shower after practice?"

"Not until maintenance fixes the sewage problem. I came

back here to shower."

"Then why haven't you showered yet?"

"You came in angry, and I was checking in."

Machi places her hands on her hips and exaggerates her admiration for me. "So caring," she says. She glances over at the package resting on the couch.

"Did you buy another vinyl?"

"I thought it was for you."

She rolls her eyes.

"I doubt that."

"It's true. Also, I bought none of my vinyl collection. Every record was a gift."

"I'm sure they were," Machi says as she walks to the couch and examines the package.

"Besides, I know it's for you because nothing I buy fits in boxes shaped like this," she says.

"Maybe I have a secret admirer who sends me gifts."

Machi blows a raspberry before laughing.

"If you could ask them to send money, we will soon have to sacrifice food or lights here."

"Are you exaggerating or being serious?" I ask, readjusting my towel just in time to prevent my full exposure.

Machi puts a hand in the air and lets out a prolonged huff. "All I am saying is that college students should have free housing during the semester. That way, when your old roommate bails after signing the lease, I won't deplete all my savings while working a job I don't have time for."

"I will use my remaining scholarship for our living expenses."

She clasps her hands over her heart as if I had just uttered an 'I love you' to her. "So you are the perfect roommate."

I grin. "I appreciate you letting me stay with you. I would live with my teammates, but I only want close friends as roommates from now on. It's the only way I can be my true self."

"I don't blame you. It's nice having you around this hellhole. Just don't let me walk in on you showing all of your true self."

"What are you talking about?"

She gives me an incredulous look and points to my towel. "I was lucky this time."

We share a moment of laughter, but a subtle unease emerges. Images of my previous semester flood my mind. My unceremonious exit from USE was a devastating heartbreak, and dark clouds circled above me all summer. The thoughts remind me of the arduous path that led me here and the source of its turbulence. All the while trying to hold on to the last promise with my mom, I swore to keep after her passing.

"Is it obvious?"

Machi's amusement dissipates as she looks at me. "What are you talking about?"

"Will people figure out I am gay?"

Machi shifts away from the kitchen and walks around the island. "I don't think so. People will think you are straight here, and will find out. What happened at USE won't happen here."

My lips curve into a tight smile while Machi plops onto a barstool.

"Besides, I think a couple of players on your team might be gay."

"Who?"

"Romero, for starters."

"Why?"

"It's just his personality. Something's always off about him. That and he is too pretty to be straight."

I shake my head, remembering my interaction with Romero this morning. "I am sure he's not."

"Well, my coworkers believe he is. But they also believe we are a couple, so maybe I should not take their words too seriously."

"Well, I am glad they are clueless. It helps me."

"I mean, if it helps, you can sit with me at the required chapel. That would definitely sell the lie."

"Required chapel? At a public school?"

"Yeah. At first, I hated it, but I took it as a chance to be with my brother. Maybe you could use it to be with your mom."

I mull over her words. "She would love it if I went to church as often as she did."

Machi tilts her head. "It would bring a smile to her face to see you there. I bet she's smiling up in heaven now watching us."

The familiar hurt returns as I stare into the arras on the walls. Machi notices my unease and breaks the silence by pulling out a seat from under the kitchen island.

"I am sorry. I didn't mean to upset you," Machi says.

"It's okay. You didn't upset me. I have had a tough couple of years."

She pauses, searching for a conversation starter, and asks, "How was your first day? How did the test go?"

I stand. "You are looking at the champion of the Yo-Yo Test." I flex my arms, pretending to be a bodybuilder. Machi giggles at the performance.

"Congrats. To celebrate, open your mail," Machi says.

"What?"

Machi points toward the couch. "The package!"

Oh right. The package. I walk over to the couch, sit down, and lift the skinny package onto my lap. Machi follows behind me. While doing so, I glance at the legible return address in the top corner. My heart drops when I see the address.

"New Orleans?" Machi whispers. "Who do you know from there?"

I finish tearing open the cardboard, but my face drains of all color as I pull out the vinyl wrapped in plastic. I shiver longer as I stare at the familiar face in front of me. He actually made his album, and he somehow sent it to me. I'm confused how he knew where I lived, but the fear of the album's contents blurs all other questions I have. Jesus Javi. What have you done?

Machi stares at the record. "Who's this?" she asks.

Chapter 2

September 25, 2025

My energy vanishes shortly before starting practice. I forgot about the intensity of the fitness drills, and I now realize I overexerted myself. My legs feel as stiff as plywood as I walk onto our barbecued practice field. I stand alone in my invisi-ble bubble, repelling the same teammates who can deactivate it. I wonder when this hazing bullshit will end.

"All right, listen up!" Coach Ramsey shouts. "This season restarts today, so let's refocus on the fundamentals. As the boys from last year know, a rock-solid defense is my team's foundation. Today, we are practicing our defensive principles against each other. I have you already paired up. Vince, you are with Caleb."

Apprehensively, I notice that only one monster of a player makes eye contact with me, heightening my sense of competition. Vince's athleticism is a rare blend of an NFL wide receiver and an Olympic track star. I remember how Vince defends his goal relentlessly, his every move accompanied by the thud of bodies colliding. I remember how he pressed my old teammate's face to the ground before he stole the ball away. The adrenaline coursing through Vince's veins as he launched himself into tackles, like a wrecking ball slamming into concrete. But his greatest strength is his heading ability and how he connects with the ball suspended in mid-air. And now he is going against me while I wear my USE uniform since I still have received no practice gear. It's as if I'm a red flag in a bullpen.

Coach Ramsey studies us as we step onto the training grid. Vince passes me a ball up to my shins before charging at me in a sprint. I cushion the ball on the parched grass beneath my cleats, keeping the ball within my area of control.

Vince adjusts his feet, displaying Coach Ramsey's defensive principles: close the gap, keep the gap, and don't get beat. Vince jockeys as I tap the ball forward, engaging in a game of cat and mouse. I inch forward, performing a few step-overs and body feints, but Vince is unmoved in his sideways squat stance.

"Good battle, boys!" Coach Ramsey shouts from the side. "Vince, keep him in front of you. Don't over-commit!"

Vince obeys, but I'm unfazed by it. I roll the ball a few inches in front of my right foot and then tap it with the inside of my right foot toward Vince's front foot. Falling for the bait, Vince sticks his right foot out to poke the ball away.

However, I tap the ball with the outside of my right foot, sending it into the open space on the right side. Vince loses his balance and chases after me, desperate to retrieve the ball. I sprint toward the touchline to earn a point for myself. Romero seethes as I run by, and I love it. It's nice to have the hottest straight guy's attention, especially his oblivious envy for a gay guy.

I dribble the ball toward the gate of two blue cones in the

left corner of the grid, gloating a win before I have it. As I am about to score, Vince charges toward me, ready to exemplify Coach Ramsey's golden defending rule of "If you get beat, turn and kill."

He slides behind me in a last-ditch effort to dispossess me. A swift, brutal force from Vince's quads and hamstrings connects with my trailing ankle. The contact knocks me off my stride and sends me tumbling to the ground. All the air dissipates from my body when I hit the grass, my muscles tightening around the impacted areas. I lay still on the ground, fearing a familiar pain approaching. I exhale a tremendous sigh of relief when none arises.

"Great recovery, Vince!" Coach Ramsey shouts and begins clapping. "That's the fucking desire I am talking about. Well done, son!"

I peer around at everyone else, laughing at me as the latest victim to Vince's alien-like athleticism. I roll my eyes while I brush myself off, beyond flustered with everything. The amount of effort I give to be part of this team is useless given how they bully me to shit at every opportunity. Unless you pledge your loyalty to the school at birth, it's impossible to fit in.

Maybe this cliché behavior scares off any player who threatens their mediocrity. That would explain their poor record every season. I want to break the cycle, but they don't seem to care. And now this will jeopardize my plans unless I am almost perfect. My brain pounds against my skull so hard I rub my temples, unaware Vince is saying my name.

"You good?" he asks.

"For fuck's sake," I say, teeth scraping together as the words come out.

"Needs to be better from you," Coach Ramsey says.

I pick myself up and jog over to his starting spot. My mind paces, transitioning from anger to catastrophizing the situation. All the pressure to overachieve here suffocates me, especially since a future professional career hangs in the balance. If I can't excel as a player or achieve victory here, I'm screwed. And I don't have a backup plan. I try to compartmentalize my frustration, but it all erupts out of me like a violent volcano. Too early to realize it, but too late to stop it.

"Fuck this shit, man," I say.

Coach Ramsey's line-of-sight tracks me like a sniper atop a skyscraper, locking me before he takes his shot.

"What the fuck did you say?" Coach Ramsey yells.

I turn around to witness my coach seething and my teammates looking uneasy behind him. I shake my head. "Oh no. I didn't mean it."

"Do you think you're too superior for this team? Just because you played at USE? Well, now you play for us, so show some fucking respect. Change your attitude," Coach Ramsey hisses.

"No, I didn't mean..."

"You all know the rules when one person acts out. Everyone on the goal line. Suicides. Now!"

If things aren't worse enough, Coach Ramsey burns his stare into me as I line up with the others. I look around at my teammates, expecting another round of sour glances in my direction. To my surprise, they avoid my gaze altogether. No one casts an ugly glance in my direction, not even Romero. They all stare ahead. Only Coach Ramsey tracks my every movement the moment he blows his whistle. Running my brains out is not my ideal way of team bonding.

An hour later, I drag my parched body to the scorching bleachers with the last strains of strength left in me after our last drills. Each step feels like I'm trudging through solid concrete. As I settled into my seat, the intense heat seeped through my pants, burning my backside. The sun blocks my view of the coaching staff approaching us, even with a hand covering my face.

"Listen up. We want to make this quick since we know it is hot. We are still having problems cleaning our facilities, so we won't be able to get in there. The athletic department will update us on when we will use it. However, the department delivered our new gear for the season. This gear is the best I've seen. It's a positive sign for the future. You will receive your gear after the body fat test and individual meetings."

The coaches leave, sanctioning our reprieve from these intense sessions. We celebrate by returning the maximum cubic feet of air our diaphragms will take in. Shielded from the sun by the bleachers, I observe Romero conversing with a man who is his stark opposite—tall, stocky, and loose. I try not to focus too hard on him, but I can't help it. Images of Romero's physique, at least the little pieces he exposed during the Yo-yo test, still roam free in my head. They send tiny doses of dopamine through my body, something I need after another blistering practice like this. But I need to pull myself together and remember why I am here. I avert my eyes when my gaze creeps up to a stare. A tall, pale redhead resembling Conor McGregor approaches Romero and another man.

"Lad, I told you already. Amy and I are over. Why are you

caring so much?" the ginger says.

The stockier man steps forward. "It's hard keeping track, Duncan. You both are always on and off."

Romero rises to his feet. "That, and you have been waiting to get with her for months," he says.

"Thank you, Romero, my boy." Duncan fist-bumps Romero and points to the other man standing. "Andres is always burying his motives in small talk. Must run in your family. But you know what, Andres, you can have her. Be my guest. I am tired of her driving me crazy."

"What makes you think I want to get with Amy more than Romero?" Andres points at his brother.

Romero points at himself, as if this is the most ridiculous thing he's ever heard. "I am happy with my girl. Don't bring me into this."

Andres scoffs.

"Oh, please. You only like Angelica's money and connections, bro. You would have split with her if her family hadn't created that NIL sponsorship deal for you."

"Don't be mad I go after high-profile girls while you beg for Duncan's sloppy seconds."

Andres throws his hands up in protest. "Bro, I am not picking up your sloppy seconds. I have to date off-campus because you slept with everyone during your first breakup."

"That's not true. He has not slept with transgender women yet. They might be the only women interested in him anyway," Romero says.

"Fuck off!"

"You probably couldn't reach their standards," I say. I thought my tone was soft enough for only me to hear, but

Duncan and Romero laughing made me second-guess. As I look over, my gaze crosses paths with Andres's narrowed eyes fixed on me.

"What was that smartass?" he asks.

I look away, hoping to reduce the animosity everyone already has for me.

Andres spits onto the ground next and returns to his conversation. "Faggot Fox thinks he's one of us now after a couple of training sessions."

"I would rather go to the spa too if it meant avoiding you," Duncan shouts for the entire group to hear. He taps Andres on the arm as he approaches. "Maybe if you were proper big time like him, you would understand."

Duncan, Romero, and Andres turn away and exit the field, and I see this as my sign to leave. Practice drained me, but I don't need these petty remarks to make things worse. They know I was diligent in my recovery and went to the same doctors they have for my injury rehabilitation. It's annoying that I have to deal with this.

If things were different, I would not be here. I would still play at USE, humbling these assholes and winning another conference championship with individual accolades. But I have to remind myself that I play at SESU now. Not completely my doing, but I still chose this route given the circumstances. While feeling my hair swish against my temples, I rise from the creaky bleachers and hoist my bag onto my shoulder. I feel the weight pressing against my muscles. I limp out into the parking lot when a voice calls out.

"Need a ride?"

A faded red Ford Ranger, appearing old enough to vote but

too young to drink, parks in front of me. At the wheel, Vince appears to be a foil to the player who defended me earlier. The Vince I see exudes an aura of perfect posture and physique. His gaze lifts toward the sky before his hand rises above the steering wheel. Intense tattoos of detailed scripture, a city skyline, and a lion wrap around his left arm, but it contrasts with the composure on Vince's face under his black durag. Beads of perspiration drip below his hairline onto the man's otherwise pristine polo, leaving behind faint stains around his collar.

"You can't speak English or something?" he asks.

I shake my head. "I can speak English."

He shrugs. "I don't know, bro. You have spoken little all day. I just figured you had a language barrier or something." He gazes at me incredulously. "Except for the curse words."

My lips curve upward as he unlocks the passenger side door, and it swings open smoothly. I can't decide whether this is a prank, but given how depleted I am in this heat, someone driving me home would be a plus. As I step inside, the soft fabric of the gray cloth brushes against my body. The faint scent of a pine air freshener overpowers my sweat odor emitting from my soaked workout clothes, now staining his passenger seat. The familiar notes of Kendrick Lamar's "Poetic Justice" whisper from the speakers.

"I appreciate the ride," I say with a quick nod of my head. I toss my backpack beside me, settling back into the comfortable interior.

While feeling the rough texture of my hair between my fingers, I scratch the side of my head and gaze out the window, my eyes fixated on the divots carved into the practice pitch by cleat marks. The sight of the field mirrors my weary state, and I imagine the blissful relaxation that awaits me at home, picturing the cozy comfort that awaits me. However, as my attention shifts, I realize the truck is motionless.

"Will you tell me where you live?" Vince asks in his monotone voice.

"Oh shit," I stutter. "I live in the Spoiled Rotten Apartments, just around the corner on College Avenue."

"You live there? That complex is something."

"Why?"

"I remember living there when there weren't any dorms available. That place forgot the word 'and' in its name."

A burst of laughter escapes me, but nothing more. As Vince shifts the gear into drive, he smoothly pulls away from the parking lot. Though I am grateful for his kindness, I struggle to strike up a conversation with Vince, and I default to silence. He seems nice, but the vibe of the entire team is toxic. I am not sure what to make of him yet. Vince, however, ignores my social cues and rolls into the next topic.

"I didn't know some guys were living there this year. Which one are you rooming with?"

"I don't live with anyone on the team."

"Do you live by yourself? How did you afford that? I know that place is pricey, given its condition and all..."

"No, I have a roommate."

"Is he a close friend or something?"

"Yes, she's a close friend. I struggled last year with a stranger, so now I only live with friends."

"That's cool," Vince says, shifting his truck into drive and gliding along the street. "A close friend. That sounds similar to how I would consider a girlfriend as a 'close' friend."

I choose silence over formulating a response.

"I'm just messing, bro," he reassures me after a brief, awkward silence.

"I gotcha." I relax a little. Vince seems like a nice guy, or at least he's projecting as such. I appreciate his effort in trying to make conversation. A few minutes with Vince is a breath of fresh air compared to any conversation at the training ground. He bobs his head to the faint music.

"Hey, you don't have to turn that down. It's a good song," I say.

Vince nods and presses his lips, then adjusts the volume dial to the right. "I'm Vince, and..."

"I know your name. It's hard to forget the soreness in my leg."

"Somebody sounds butthurt over practice."

I stay silent.

"I wanted to give a proper introduction," he says. "My name is Vince. It's nice to have you training with us now."

I indulge Vince's icebreaker. "It's nice to meet you. I'm Caleb. I'm happy to get a second chance here."

"Your performances last year suggest a bright future here. How do you feel you are coming along after the injury?"

"So far, so good. No inklings of pain after a couple of sessions. Well before meeting you today."

Vince huffs a laugh, and it settles me a bit.

"The only problem I feel is getting to know everyone."

"Yeah, they act weird like that sometimes. I know they are treating you differently since you attended USE."

I resist saying the obvious and nod my head. I swivel in my

seat, staring at the various foliage and brick buildings standard to the university. My concern creeps in when an unfamiliar gas station and traffic light appear. "Where are you taking me?"

"They lock the front gate around this time, leaving only the back exit available. The road only turns one way. So, I'm taking you in one giant circle just to drop you off."

"Damn, if I had known, I would have just walked. Why didn't you say anything?"

"Because I offered. Just want to help you feel more welcome."

"I appreciate that."

We sit in silence until we approach the first set of speed bumps.

"Are you from here?" I ask.

"I'm from Houston, but my family and I moved here before I started high school. We needed a change of scenery after a family loss."

"You lost someone in your family?"

"My cousin, but he's a guardian angel watching over me."

I nod. "I lost my mom last year."

My answer sucks the energy out of the car. Vince utters a soft condolence, and once more, silence fills the car. Only the hum of the truck's engine fills the space until a near-ejection from the truck, hitting a speed bump, jolts the conversation.

"Sorry, I forgot about that one."

"It's all good," I say while readjusting on the seat. Vince speeds back up as a chain-link fence appears in the corner of my eye, surrounding the perimeter of the uniform brick buildings. A bright "closed" sign sits above a giant padlock in front of the entrance. "What's this building over here?"

Vince peeks out the window. "That's the humanities college building."

I raise an eyebrow. "We have a humanities college building? No one mentioned that at my orientation."

"That's because it does not exist anymore. The school is remodeling it for the new gender studies building."

"Isn't Gender Studies a humanities major?"

"You would think, but SESU's gender studies relates to the required gender-specific core. Are you taking Male Empowerment or Patriarchal Leadership yet?"

"I am not taking those courses this semester."

"Be ready for them. They remind you how this college turned into an unhinged private school."

"So where are they hosting all the humanities majors then?"

"Nowhere because the school dissolved the humanities college."

I shake my head. "That's not possible. I'm a psychology major."

"Psychology is a STEM major, but they are online, from what I understand. There wasn't enough room for classes in the STEM buildings."

That explains why I only have one in-person class this semester. We drive past the University Center toward Fraternity Row. Vince stops at the stop sign, allowing a sea of fraternity guys to walk in front of us. Three scrawny guys carry a giant X on their shoulders as they struggle to cross, each wearing a 2016 Football Conference Championship shirt.

"Should we remind them about the football team?"

Vince laughs. "No one forgets the athletic department suspending the football team after some brutal hazing allegations surfaced. The announcement shocked University Hills residents, and now all organizations are on edge, especially Greek life."

"You think more people will come to our games in the meantime?"

"I hope so. Maybe they could keep the game day traditions for us. It would be cool to see the town's tailgates at dawn, an aroma of barbecue and beer lining the streets while everyone plays cornhole and ring toss. Imagine us walking down University Row to a sea of fans just prior to kickoff. That would pump me up on game day. Maybe we'll win more games than last year because of it. No one showed up last year for us. But I would love it if we played in the Rottweiler's Den in the meantime. Wouldn't that be something? All those screaming fans, the band blaring in the stands. Just the thought of it gives me goosebumps."

"Did the athletic director mention what would happen to the stadium?"

"I don't know. It might be in the press release when the AD announced his decision."

I nod and pull out my phone to search more on the hazing story, but an ad distracts me. I click on the Reeltime post notification, and it opens to the USE men's soccer page. The social media team's recent posts include normal media photos, schedules, and action shots, all to build up to the conference season.

However, Roger Astor's photo makes my skin crawl. Just looking at his smile makes my teeth grind together. The Barbie-built bastard is already reaping what he sowed when he got his wish of me leaving the team. If I had stayed, he would never have seen the field again. The only reason the team signed him was because of his father's prestigious alumni status. It must be nice to have that kind of wealth to pay away all of your problems, or to dig up a buried past of your emissaries. I still regret folding to him, knowing his future success because of it.

Before I let my anger fixate on that memory, the truck comes to a stop in my apartment complex's parking lot, jolting me back to reality.

"Are you sure you speak English, or does your tongue not work?" Vince smiles, slinging another jab from his slingshot of quibs.

"Oh, what? I'm sorry. I'm a little tired. What did you ask?"

"What building do you live in?"

"Right. I live a few buildings down."

Vince nods, his face void of any emotion, as the vibrant anomaly booms from the stereo, reverberating through the air. The sound of unfamiliar brass and trap beats permeates the parking lot, filling the space with a pulsating energy. As Vince's truck meanders, the notes resonate, creating an intoxicating symphony. The song's introduction feels like I am flying in the sky until the first lyrics send me into freefall.

That voice. I know that voice. The sound causes me to shift in my seat.

"You listen to this?" I ask.

"Oh, this? It's not on my playlist, but maybe it is one of those smart shuffle songs. It's everywhere on social media. The start is catchy, and his raw and powerful emotions make it a hit. I sympathize with the person this song addresses because Javi spares no details of his relationship."

Just hearing Vince say his name is enough to make me nauseous. Every note of the song unlocks memories I buried months ago. That vinyl's presence revives memories. I tossed the vinyl out before the afternoon garbage pickup. I couldn't handle everything Javi had to say, especially knowing exactly what he would say. Now, in just three painful minutes, he's bringing back memories of a past life. My heart rattles inside my chest, hard enough that it could shatter a rib. I need to leave, so I collect my bag and hop out of the truck.

"Hey, thanks again," I say with an awkward smile. I throw up a peace sign and rush to my apartment as quickly as my battered body will allow. I sling the door open and collapse onto the worn-out couch. My hands, damp with sweat, shake while rubbing my face. The weight of it all trapped me in a suffocating nightmare. Why is Javi haunting me? This is behind me.

For a second, the feeling subsides, and I regain some composure. I sit up and turn my head toward the kitchen island. I noticed something shiny reflecting in the sunset's glow from the nearby window. As I examine it closer, the composure leaves as quickly as it entered.

You have got to be kidding me.

In the middle of the island, I see the autographed Javi vinyl lying there, its vibrant colors and glossy surface in my life once again. This is an illusion. It has to be. I tiptoe over to it, like a character in a horror movie about to confront some cursed entity. I examine it again, recognizing the signature scribbled across the front. Without hesitating further, I slide it off the counter and place it in the trash can.

Chapter 3

September 26, 2025

As each second ticks away, Coach Ramsey's words rattle in my brain while I pace through the stadium hallways.

"Arrive early, and you're on time. Arrive on time, and you're late. Arrive late and you're fucked."

I sprint into the treatment room inside the Rottweiler's Den, praying I have a handful of minutes left to be on time. The trainer flinches as I stare at her in the room, sentences sticking to the back of my throat through my heavy breathing. The room is the standard treatment room one would expect for Division One football players, especially one encased in the school's athletic palace.

A petite, sandy blonde woman dressed in a sleek black polo and running shorts sits on one of the five patient tables spread apart on the back wall. She jumps from the table and walks toward me across the black carpet. She pulls the clipboard off the counter, which is covered in her medical supplies, and glides her finger down the page.

"Caleb, right?" she asks.

"Yes, that's me."

She circles my name on her sheet.

"Awesome. My name is Soleil. I am the head athletic trainer who will evaluate you today. We received all scans and evaluations from your physician regarding your injury, and he has deemed you fit for full training sessions without limitations. You will undergo a series of tests requested by Coach Ramsey. Does this plan sound good to you?"

I nod my head, feeling already exhausted before all the testing today.

"Perfect! So take off your shirt for me," she says, maintaining eye contact.

I glance at her, almost sure I misunderstood. "I'm sorry?"

"I need you to remove your shirt."

Before I can comprehend the request, she holds out her hand as if this is a perfectly reasonable request, given we are the only two in this room. Her stare unsettles me, and I pass her my shirt just to have her look away. Soleil places my shirt on the table and retrieves a vintage Polaroid camera from a nearby shelf. Before I comprehend the situation unfolding in front of me, she snaps a picture of me.

"What are you doing?" I ask.

"It's a progress picture for you. I will attach it to your paperwork." Soleil removes the ejected photograph.

"I don't want that picture."

"The picture is in your folder for our records. It's not for you."

Before I object, Soleil directs me to the scale positioned by the foam rollers and workout balls in the adjacent corner of the room. "All right, I just need to take your height and weight. Let's make this quick before the next guy shows."

I need a witness because this is evolving into a Title IX

violation. I position my back against the stadiometer as instructed, feeling a slight chill as the cold metal touches my skin. My stomach flips as she stretches to place the ruler on top of my head, her fingers brushing against my hair. My body tenses when Soleil's chest brushes against my exposed torso, enhancing this increasingly uncomfortable situation. I look away and fix my eyes toward the vibrant mural of the school's acronym painted in the school's colors above the organized medical supplies. She pulls away and points toward the scale once I return my gaze.

"Step here," she says.

I follow her instructions and glance down at the illuminated digital display reading '185.' The weight means nothing to me before Soleil shouts in disgust.

"Yikes! Six feet one inch. 185 pounds."

My face sours. "Is that bad or something?"

She looks at me, forcing a smile. "It can only get better. Let's move on to the body fat test portion of today. I just need to prepare the body measurements by marking the testing sites."

In a swift moment, I transform from a college athlete into a science experiment before I can contest the matter. An uncomfortable rush of blood floods my lower body when Soleil rolls my shorts up, exposing my thighs. Her soft fingertips brush across my skin, causing goosebumps to spread across it. She draws a circle with a black marker in the center of the thigh. Soleil returns to her feet and retrieves a sleek silver ruler and a vibrant yellow measuring tape next to it. She first unrolls her measuring tape and positions the base just above my waistline. Soleil slides her finger up the tape until her fingers hover above my chest. She jams one finger into the same spot, knocking my balance before she draws another circle. She shifts her attention to my right arm, where she has me bend it at a perfect 90-degree angle, causing a slight tingle in my muscles.

With meticulous precision, she takes the silver ruler and measures the spot of interest before marking my arm. Soleil repeats the process, marking my mid-back with her hands leaving behind a trail of temporary ink lines. By the time she finishes, I'll look prepared for an autopsy.

Soleil gives me the once-over, looking satisfied with her work before retrieving the metal caliper from her back pocket. The metal glistens in the light, resembling a peculiar amalgamation of pliers fused with a tire pressure gauge. This must be the infamous 'pincher' I over-heard the players mentioning. I never understood the back-story of its nickname, but it doesn't take long to understand with a single glance. A new sense of unease creeps over me.

"Okay, now I just have to take the skinfold readings. You may feel a little pinch, but relax," she says.

I do the complete opposite. My muscles tense as Soleil, with a forceful grip, pulls a fold of my chest toward her. It takes every muscle in me not to convulse as Soleil tugs my flesh toward her. It's so difficult to remain cool when someone touches me like this.

The cold, metallic caliber on the pinches the marked area, its claws digging into my skin. She records her measurements on her clipboard before she pulls at my skin once more, moving behind me, her touch rough like tearing off a scab. I flinch as she applies the metal claws again. I try to steady my breath, but the pinch intensifies.

My composure worsens when she moves her fingers around my abs, waistline, triceps, and even my armpit. I want to scream, but I just need to stay strong for a few seconds longer. Soleil squats down, and her clammy hands touch my thigh. Her icy touch makes the blood retreat, fortunately preventing the misunderstanding that was forming earlier. My face contorts into a grimace when she jerks my skin with the most force during the test. Once she releases the last fold, I exhale a sigh of relief.

"It's okay," she says. "Just try to relax because I need to take replicate measurements."

"Gotcha," I say. I force the fakest smile possible, bracing myself for Soleil to violate me again. I roll my eyes and catch sight of Romero walking into the training room, his body suffocating under his training top. His presence overwhelms me, increasing my heart rate faster than a fresh cup of coffee.

My senses overstimulate further when he removes his shirt, his body stealing the last particles of oxygen I'm fighting to breathe in. It's hard not to savor Romero's overwhelmingly athletic physique, but I need to fight the urge while a woman's touch sends shivers down my spine. I pray only for strength to avoid an embarrassing situation. I stare toward the ceiling, reminding myself of his homophobic comments from a week earlier.

But his body obliterates the memory. His carved abs make mine appear as lumps, and his pecks glistening under the room's harsh lighting convince me he has zero body fat. But when he turns around, I follow his angry back muscles down his V-shaped torso to his rounded glutes that even a Kardashian would be jealous of. He is hotter than any spicy content creator online, not that I browse a lot of content. I do not follow any risqué creators on Reeltime, but I won't lie and say I didn't swipe past their posts on a lonely night after my breakup. It was an unhealthy way of coping. I am past that, but the thought of seeing him naked sends a shiver through my body.

"It doesn't hurt that bad," Soleil says, snapping my atten-tion back to her. I huff out a breath that masks as a laugh, and look away before Romero sees me staring.

Once Soleil finishes violating my personal space, I bolt into the stadium hallway without uttering a word to either her or Romero, and instead race to my next appointment. Meeting Coach Ramsey in his office on the opposite side of the stadium is my last task today. I walk down the hallway until I leave the athletic center and pace around the Rottweiler's Den.

As I walk around its perimeter, I look up at the sky. The steel beams seem to pierce it, and I take twenty minutes to circle the base when empty. I imagine game days are another nightmare altogether. I scan my ID once I step into the elevator and endure the slowest ride up to the top floor of the stadium. The elevator door opens to reveal a long, yet narrow hallway.

I walk alongside the floor to ceiling windows, peering out at the soccer field on my right, which currently sits below a sludge of sewage from Saturday. It's another reminder of how the department prioritizes athletics. I remember witnessing the ribbon-cutting after the stadium remodel when I toured campus last summer, two months after the athletic director suspended the football team. I assumed they would support men's and women's soccer, given our dire need for resources. That naive idea vanished when I realized the athletic department's solution for the shortage of offices for the rest of the various coaching staffs was to transform a sliver of space out of the executive suites into micro-offices with a view of SESU's shortcomings.

A football school without football.

I walk a few doors down to Coach Ramsey's office, which resembles more of a broom closet than an office. He added a few pictures of his family on his desk with a Liverpool poster on the left wall, but a clunky filing cabinet and a built-in desk limit the amount of personal touches. Liverpool's game plays on the mounted TV to the left.

"Caleb, come in!" He waves me in while muting his TV.

I sit in the only available chair, pushing my back against the wall. Coach Ramsey positions himself, leaning back in his chair while analyzing me. Meeting him mirrors that of an employee performance evaluation by my manager at corporate. His stare unnerves me, and small droplets of sweat form on my hairline.

"So here's the deal…" Coach Ramsey slides his hands under his armpits. "I'm beyond impressed."

A silence stretches for a minute following his three words. This catches me off guard, but as I replay the words in my head, the corners of my lips are the sharpest since arriving here.

"When I found your name in the transfer portal, I needed to sign you. I never expected you to leave USE, given that you had a strong season last year. Despite the risky recovery timeline for your injury, your return and current preparation delights me. This season felt like our year to challenge for the championship, but our recent run of results has made our loss column larger than our wins. Luckily, those matches were nonconference games, but we have no momentum rolling into next week. On a bright note, I have developed some new tactics to build a successful system around you."

A light shade of red spills across my face. Before I utter a response, Coach Ramsey adjusts his tone.

"I think this will be your breakout season. But the biggest insult to a player like you is mentioning your potential. Caleb, you undoubtedly possess great potential to become the conference's best. And I will demand everything from you and won't let you relax until you have nothing left. Then I'll ask for more. This semester, I'll make your life a living hell so you can master your abilities."

My emotional blaze cools down to an ember. "I understand, Coach. I am grateful to you for giving me a chance when no one else would. You can depend on me."

"Good lad. You will know where to find me. Prepare your-self for conference games. It's right around the corner."

"Yes, sir."

Coach Ramsey holds up his right thumb. "Good lad. We are fortunate to have the first bye week this weekend, so I have planned a team bonding trip. I reserved a few cabins at the university's ranch, and I hope we leave the ranch on better terms, as our opening game features your undefeated former team. The athletic department is even throwing us a pre-conference party to help motivate us for the rest of the season. We will rely heavily on you for that game, so prepare yourself."

He leans forward to stare into my soul. "Just focus on football, and you'll be fine. That and start cutting your body fat. Soleil warned me your scores were high."

I nod and swallow, feeling him tap into my hippocampus

before reaching my soul. "I understand."

"Good lad." Coach Ramsey reaches down and tosses the bag onto the desk. "Here. I figured you need this."

I ogle at the bag in front of me. A wave of relief hits me when I notice my last name, 'Thomas,' clipped to the zipper above my lucky number 8 stitched into the fabric. My idol Martin Ødegaard wears the number, and so do many other legendary midfielders in the game. I envision myself among an elite group of players one day, wearing an Arsenal kit. But this season, it's a SESU jersey.

I unzip my sleek black Nike backpack. Inside, I notice a burst of vibrant colors against the bright tan trim. I retrieve four sleeveless training tops, feeling their soft fabric slide through my fingers. The tops showcase shades of gray, black, and a striking tan, with each displaying the number 8 on the back neckline, adding a touch of style.

I peer over the remaining standard black soccer shorts and pairs of athletic socks. My fingers glide over the smooth surface of a black golf polo, adorned with a logo on the left breast and featuring a bright tan Nike swoosh on the other side. I feel the texture of the sweatpants, windbreaker, and pullover sweatshirt, admiring every detail within the fabric. Once satisfied, I place them back into the crisp bag.

"How's the kit look?" Coach Ramsey asks.

"I love it," I say, still inhaling the scent of new clothes.

"I'm glad. I reserved your favorite number for you, a fantastic football number, as a welcome present to the team when you returned from injury. Only the best wear the eight, and I think it should be you."

He watches me as I retrieve my old drawstring bag and pull

out my miniature gold World Cup trophy, feeling its weight in my hand. I keep this little treasure with me wherever I go. It's been with me through everything, good and bad. It's silly, but this is one of the most special items I have ever owned. Losing my temper is my last resort. I tuck it away in the secret pocket at the top of my pristine bag. In a smooth motion, I close the zipper, creating a soft whispering sound that seals the treasures within.

"That's quite a collectible you have there," Coach Ramsey says.

I look up. "It's a miniature World Cup trophy."

"I know, but it's rare to see the Jules Rimet Trophy. Where did you get that?"

"It's a family heirloom, according to my father."

Coach Ramsey nods. "It must be special if you have it now."

I shake my head. "It was his Christmas gift to me after my mom's funeral."

With my words, I suck the oxygen out of the room. Coach Ramsey chokes on his words, burying his face in his elbow. I watch him stare off into space, searching for a conversation starter. He clears his throat when he settles on something to break the tension.

"Anyway. I hope you like the new gear. Now that you are one of us, maybe you will stop wearing that Fox gear to practice. It's a bit of an eyesore around here."

A smile creeps back onto my face. "You don't say."

For the rest of our conversation, we discuss Coach Ramsey's vision for the remainder of the season and avoid any conversation about my mother. And I'm okay with that.

CHAPTER 4

September 27, 2025

"Come on, boys! The next goal wins!"

Coach Ramsey ignites a blazing inferno for improvement in this intense small-sided practice match. The searing heat radiates off the sun-baked field as my training squad of seven tries to outperform our opponents. Inhaling the faint aroma of dehydrated grass and sweat, I suck in another breath.

Both teams are overperforming for a training session. The ball dances across the shrunken field for 8v8 play, mirroring the chaotic frenzy of the players. This embodies small-sided games. Coach Ramsey wants us to simulate quick possession and counter-attacking plays in a matter of seconds, testing how quickly we adapt to the situation. So it's no surprise that the sounds of thunderous footsteps on dirt, shouting in every direction, and the swish of the ball echo in the air, creating a symphony of determination and passion.

I live for these moments, especially after the praise from Coach Ramsey. I aim to win, even if it's just practice. A win is the only thing that satisfies my hunger for competition. Moments after a shot sails wide of the goal for the green team, our goalkeeper, Marshall, retrieves the ball to restart the game.

He rolls the ball across the field to me as soon as I sprint into space. I position myself, preparing my preferred right foot to receive the ball.

I am a player who loves the ball at my feet. It's the gas in my tank fueling my joy. But sometimes my eagerness clouds my focus. As the ball connects with my instep, intense footsteps stomp in my direction. I turn and notice Andres, a blur of motion, sprinting toward me at full speed. With quick thinking, I step forward and pass the ball to my teammate on my right.

The moment the ball leaves my foot, a sudden jolt of pain shoots through my ankle. The force of Andres's stomp just misses the spot of the original break and sends me sprawling face-first into the ground, the impact jarring my senses. Overwhelmed by the sharp sting of pain, I find myself breathless. For a moment, I convince myself my worst fears came true, but I breathe a sigh of relief when the pain radiates from my ankle.

"Advantage!" Coach Ramsey shouts.
"Come on, Caleb. Don't make it too easy for me," Andres says as he runs away. I shift my weight, wincing as I massage my ankle. The throbbing pounds as if it's a heartbeat of its own.

Andres fist-bumps Duncan, who howls on the opposite side of the field.

"That's a bit of us! Well done, Andres, son!"

"Just introducing the new guy to the team as you would, Duncan!" Andres says. They exchange a quick, low five.

I rise to my feet and redistribute my body weight while assessing my leg. Although the knock still hurts, I won't let that stop me from playing. I still need to prove myself. I run around for a bit, easing the pain with every step. Motion is lotion sometimes.

Andres's strike of the ball whistles through the air. It lands in Marshall's muscular arms, and he wastes no time staring at me. He rolls the ball out to me with a satisfying thud. This time, however, I check my shoulder, watching Andres take off and close the distance between us. Marshall rolls the ball into space in front of me instead of to my feet. This forces me to reshuffle my feet and body toward the field, but more importantly, it buys me a few precious seconds.

Andres appears in front of me, closing the distance to just a few steps. I faint to his right, causing Andres to stretch his left leg in the wrong direction. I maneuver the ball between Andres's legs, simultaneously elbowing his lower back with my left elbow while he's unbalanced. In that exhilarating moment, I sprint forward, a surge of adrenaline numbing the pain in my ankle as I exploit the space in front of me.

As the action unfolds, our striker stands out as an inferior figure of athleticism compared to Andres. He fixates on me, so intense his eyes could burst out of his head. I notice the open space ahead, since the striker's movement prompts Duncan to lurk behind. That space is a gold mine. With everyone else pressed onto our side, Duncan is the only defender ahead of his goalkeeper. By combining quick passes and making a smart run, I find myself behind Duncan with a clear shot at the goal.

Without hesitation, I play the ball toward the striker and bolt forward. He executes a no-look pass to our center midfielder, Melvin, who glides to the ball like the wind carries his skinny torso over to receive his pass. His feet pound the ground with surprising agility, gliding out of missed challenges to keep his pass in play. As Melvin's foot connects with the ball, he directs his pass into the space where I am sprinting toward.

The ball skids across the pale grass, rolling a couple of yards ahead of me. As it creeps toward the out-of-bounds line, I dart toward it, stretching my foot to keep it in play. I push the ball within striking distance of the goal. Romero races into the open space ahead of the goalkeeper, his outstretched hand reaching for the sky.

I have a split second to decide my next move. I could strike the ball and steal all the glory for myself if I score. But that 'if I score' nags me. The voice in my head screams I should pass him the ball. I don't know why. Could it be the gay man in me that wants the hot guy to notice me? Maybe a little. There is some other force manipulating my decision-making. Either way, I wrap my foot around the ball, watching it glide across the goal's face out of reach of the opposing goalkeeper. Romero decisively scores, the net rippling in victory.

"That's the game! Well done, lads! Fucking brilliant from Caleb! Losers on the line." Coach Ramsey shouts from the sidelines.

I pump my fist downward, my excitement muffled by the chatter of my teammates heading toward the water station. Romero jogs toward me, the grass crunching under his foot-steps. His sharp abdominal definition peeks out from under his training bib, and the visual hypnotizes me. Luckily, the sun burned my skin a cherry red because my skin flushes as his arms sway in the air, and his quads slide up and down his legs. Romero steps within inches of me, wiping his French-tip blonde highlights to the side. I stand breathless in his presence.

"That's what we love to see, big time can pass the ball," Romero says. He holds out his hand up to my chest height, snapping me out of my thirsty trance. I wrap my hand around his.

"Yeah, uh...for sure," I mutter.

"Are you tired already? Well, it's good you found the best player here. You might be useful to us this year," Romero says, before he turns his back to me and walks toward the water cooler.

"That's what it is. I'm just tired," I say. "Nothing else at all." Weird, after all my work on that play, he points out that I look tired. I guess I look tired, but at least the cute guy talked to me.

I follow Romero to the water station, still processing our interaction. The losing green team collapses to the ground, their chests heaving and sweat dripping down their faces. The sound of heavy breathing reverberates around us. Andres and Duncan, with their heads hanging low and frustration etched on their faces, narrow their tired eyes toward me. It takes more energy than necessary, but I suppress a grin and lift my chin.

In a moment, Andres bows his head in disappointment while Duncan spits and curses in my direction. I try to restrain myself, but a smile creeps onto my face.

...

An hour later, Machi strides with her hands full toward me, sitting on the couch next to the espresso bar. "One large fat-free, sugar-free, taste-free, extra foam, boring vanilla latte for my large vanilla twink crusher." She places the coffee cup in her left hand in front of me and tosses a brown sugar packet next to me on the couch. "And one sugar on the side. You like it raw, if I remember, right?"

I roll my eyes as I pull the coffee toward me. "Why do you always torture me about my first time after The Cove?"

"Because it's payment for your coffee," Machi says, sipping her latte.

I give her a knowing glare, the same as I have dozens of times prior. I take a sip of my latte, the creaminess dancing on my tongue. Machi crafts the most addictive latte in this college town, so her boss rewards her with long shifts every day. She says she doesn't mind balancing the hours with schoolwork, especially since she loves the money. I am lucky to have Machi to help me settle into University Hills, and I promise to help where I can. My excess scholarship money pays the rent, but having more cash helps.

"Whatever happened to that guy?"

I almost drowned in my coffee at her question. I jerk my head around our table.

"I promise I won't out you," Machi says, softening her tone.

"Not if you scream it out to the world!"

"Relax. The new girl behind the bar is always on her phone and can't even hear when I call out an order while standing next to her. Besides, the espresso machine hisses loudly, and headphones cover every ear in this place. Nobody is listening or cares."

"How comforting."

"Fine! I will figure it out myself. You know how I am when I put my mind to something."

"I am aware."

A proud smirk forms as she glides a white pastry bag with

the company's name around a cup of coffee.

The aroma of freshly brewed coffee mixes with gooey pastries and travels across the sleek industrial shotgun house. The ambiance invites you in, with cozy vibes and stylish decor. College students and professionals from University Hills continue to work while my stomach growls at the first hint of the fragrance of the ham and Swiss breakfast croissant sandwich. But Soleil's comment about my weight lingers in my mind, so I push it away.

Machi wrinkles her forehead. "You always eat this. Are you okay?"

"I have to lower my body fat."

"Where?" Machi asks.

I flinch as she pokes my abdomen.

"Don't be goofy, Caleb."

I swat her nagging finger away, a smile curving on my face. "I can't because I didn't get the best results on the body fat test."

"You just finished training and need to eat something." She pushes the sandwich bag up to my arm.

"I am leaving for a team bonding event later tonight and will eat something there." I tear the sugar packet and shake the contents into my coffee.

"Why are you like this?" Machi asks, waving her finger in my direction.

"Like I said, I have to lose…"

"No, your coffee."

"What? I'm just adding the raw sugar to it."

"Yes, to a sugar-free latte. What kind of psychopath does that?"

"I don't know. Maybe he learned from the same psychopath using a different name at work." I point at the name tag reading "Mackenzie" on Machi's apron.

Machi straightens up in her chair. "Listen. It is hard for your people to pronounce 'Machi-Zai' and harder for me to listen to their life stories about why they've never heard of it. So, to fix my problem, I have my white name for work."

I smirk. "I guess."

"Also, why did you throw away the vinyl again?"

My eyes narrow. "Because I don't want it. Please tell me you didn't dig it out of the trash again."

She traces her finger across the edge of the table. "I did, but only because I want to keep it for myself. I shopped online for a replacement, but I couldn't find another unit for sale. That's why I dug it out of the trash. I think it's a rare collectible. We should sell it for a lot of money, especially since it's still in the original plastic."

For a woman who never batted an eyelash toward records, it would be my luck that Machi would gravitate to the one album in the world I won't listen to. Before I can respond, my phone buzzes in my pocket. I unlock it and glance at the few notifications I have received. Group chat messages, social media alters, school emails, etc. Before I even click one icon, Machi swipes the phone out of my hand.

"What the hell! What are you doing?" I shout, stretching his arm out to retrieve my phone. I reach for it, but Machi holds it just beyond me. She swats away my hand with my more aggressive attempts and keeps her body between me and my phone. "Machi, give me my phone back!"

"I spend my ten-minute break with you, and you spend it

on your phone. So rude!"

I look at her in a brotherly fashion. "Why are you like this?"

"Because I can be." She crosses her arms, burying my phone in her armpit.

I take my two hands and tickle her sides, sending her into a laughing fit. She fidgets in place, and I continue until we hear the thud of my phone tumbling onto the floor. I fear my phone screen will shatter, but that becomes the least of my problems when Machi picks up my phone.

"Oh my God. I won't be able to unsee this for years!" Machi covers her face, keeping the phone screen facing her.

"Oh shit, is it broken?"

"No worse."

"What?"

"You are so exposed." She pushes her fingers apart as if she's zooming in on a picture.

"What are you looking at?" I grab the phone before she can resist, and my face drops when I see my Discreet & Delete profile open. I knew I would regret not deleting my account after last semester. With my luck right now, I should have expected Machi studying my headless torso, peeking out from an opened iridescent button-down and jet-black leather pants in front of a dance floor. Her reading my profile back to me is the cherry on top of my embarrassment.

CT No E, 21

Have you struggled to find the one that doesn't call you every night? How about a man who can't meet your commitment and emotional needs? Look no further! Please consult your doctor if this new closeted top looking for drama-free entertainment is right for you. It may cause effects such as euphoria, attachment, loss of self-respect, and sometimes awkward exchanges in public. Avoid taking it when committed to a serious relationship, as it complicates things.

Machi rolls onto her back in the chair. "I need therapy!"

"Chill out…it's not that bad."

"Oh, the horror!"

"Would you knock it off?" I say.

"Relax, I saw nothing." Machi readjusts in her seat. "What dating app is that?"

"It's not a dating app per se," I say. My embarrassment is almost palpable.

"So, what is that app? I haven't seen that before." Machi says, pointing to the phone.

I breathe in, already expecting instant regret. "It's D&D," I mutter

"Like the board game?"

"No, it's called Discreet and Delete. It's an app only for closeted gay men."

"So, do you swipe on blank profiles or something?"

"There is no matching process."

"Then how do you see profiles?"

"It's organized by location."

"So…like a gay hookup app?" Machi asks, crossing her arms.

I slouch and drop my voice to a whisper. "Don't say it like that."

She gives me an incredulous look. "Oh, so you found an abundance of Prince Charmings already?"

"Listen, it's not like that."

"Caleb, apps like that aren't safe. You could get hurt if someone finds out about this."

"The app generates passcodes for each conversation for security."

"That's not what I am talking about. You could meet a psycho there."

A sudden commotion startles me at the front of the bustling café. Within moments, the door violently bursts open, the hinges screeching in protest. The café's scent of coffee and pastries mixes with the summer breeze rushing in. An average-sized woman entering the café freezes the chaotic scene, clad in a vibrant red sports bra and snug yoga pants. Her displeasure echoes off the walls, and her gaze pierces the staff behind the counter. "Oh, no! No! No! No! Where is Mackenzie?!" The woman locks eyes with us.

"Oh, there you are!" the woman says as she strides over to our table. She forces herself into the space between both of us, shifting everyone on the couch. Machi's smile is now erased from her face. "Mackenzie, oh my goodness, I am so glad you are here! Today, of all days, without my latte would kill me!"

"Hey, Angelica. I'm just on break…" Machi starts before Angelica explodes, almost into a manic state.

"After I finish recording today's content, I will put the final touches on the party I am hosting next weekend. My parents are going away for my father's conference for athletic directors, so we are planning the craziest party ever at my family's estate!"

"Wow, that's cool, Angelica," Machi says, flinching when Angelica grabs her arm.

"Mackenzie, you do not understand how insane it will be.

We will have a professional DJ, bartenders, and producers from MTV in attendance. All the makings of an ultimate college party. And if you can make me your insane cloud latte, I will put you on the VIP list."

"I mean, I am still on break. I'm sure Jeremy can make the drink for you."

"Hell no!" Angelica protests. "The last time he made my drink, I saw him pour the milk into my latte. I mean, who pours milk into my cloud latte?"

"Jeremy was new when he made your latte last time."

"What Mexican doesn't understand coffee?"

Machi rubs her temples. "Jeremy is a highly skilled barista with a coffee background. He used to work on the coffee plant farms with his family in Costa Rica."

Angelica stares at her manicure. "I just don't understand why he would add milk."

"Isn't a latte supposed to have milk in it?" I ask, not quite understanding the problem.

Angelica rolls her eyes at me, looking more agitated than before. "And who are you supposed to be?"

"He's a friend!" Machi interjects. "I guess my ten minutes are pretty close to being over. I can make your drink for you."

Angelica claps her hands as she refocuses on Machi. "Yay! Perfect timing. I worried my new man would wait in the car all day. Romero can be so impatient, but that Latin God knows how to take his time in bed. Uh, there is so much I have to tell you, Mackenzie!" Angelica slides off her plush chair and skips to the front counter.

Machi closes her eyes and shakes her head. A deep exhale escapes her nose. "I don't get paid enough here."

"Who the hell was that?" I ask.

She rakes her fingers through her hair, staring at the sky as she whispers. "That was Angelica Soldano. She's the biggest internet star around here, with her massive following on Reeltime. She makes campus gossip blogs. Look, I will explain later at the apartment when I am free. What are your plans for this weekend?"

"I am at the team retreat this weekend."

"Oh shit. We'll talk later."

Machi rises to her feet to save her coworkers. As she returns behind the espresso bar, my phone vibrates again, this time on the coffee table. A new message from D&D appears in my notification center, the first in a long time. My first instinct is to ignore it, since I only used this hookup app to talk to Javi. We saved our messages from last semester, which is the reason I still have the app on my phone. But since things changed between us, what's stopping me from meeting new guys?

I open my phone and scroll down to the most recent message, and my cheeks flush at the sight of a well-sculpted caramel torso illuminating my screen. I tap his profile, a slight tightness forming in my pants.

Mister E, 21

Smooth-talking, discreet bottom looking for a chill FWB with NSA. Only 18-25 send a message. Can host or travel.

The rest of his profile lacks details about his physical appearance, but it mentions his HIV-negative status. My rule is to ignore unfamiliar profiles with vague details, but the chiseled torso is hard to move past. I click on our shared inbox.

Mister E: Sup

"So smooth," I say, while I shake my head. Another bubble

emerges in our chatroom.

Mister E: How exactly can the doctor prescribe me this new drug you mentioned? I'm optimistic that this will work and cure my condition.

CT NO E: Oh yeah? What symptoms have you been struggling with?

Mister E: I just have this difficult at traction to go od-looking white tops…

CT No E: Oh well. Unsure if I can cure the gay. My doctor pre-scribed me some antibiotics years ago, but they don't seem to work.

Mister E: Haha, you're funny! Maybe it's good we have different doctors. I think I want to be prescribed a hefty dose of you…

I burst into a bright red.

CT No E: Orally right? What name do I need to put me under? I'm guessing the last name starts with an E.

"Mackenzie, you're amazing! Crisis averted!" Moments later, she looks into my eyes and heads toward the backroom. Despite the calming Lofi playlist and thick walls, Machi's shrieks are still audible.

The green dot on his profile disappears as I look at my phone. The app labels my last message 'sent' instead of 'delivered,' meaning Mister E left the chatroom. I roll my eyes, but maybe it's a sign I don't need to be glued to an online persona. I still pin Mister E's inbox to my message board, but it's too soon to entertain the idea, given that Javi and I split a few months ago.

The thought of Javi prevents me from closing the app when I return to my inbox. My lips twitch when I see Javi's message board pinned at the top of my screen. I tap on his profile, enter our shared chat passcode, and relive all the uncomfortable yet fond memories from months prior.

Chapter 5

September 27, 2025

I need to get off this bus. Right now. The promise of float-ing down the town river, campfires, and team bonding in an isolated ranch felt like a sugar rush when we boarded, but this last hour of darkness has drained me dry. I'm the last one on this bus to resist the urge to crash, but the faint sounds of tires on pavement and snoring tempt me to just rest my eyes for the rest of the trip.

I recline my window seat as far as it will go, sinking into the black leather seats before I slip in my earbuds. I reach for the phone charging cord beneath the armrest, above the button that releases the hidden desk. The TV in the headrest in front of me lights up with the same Rotti logo on each side of the bus as it connects to my phone. I swipe through the apps until I find Spotify. Then, I press play on the chill R&B playlist and relax as Kehlani sings about folding in my ears. My mind dissociates from my body in slow pieces, and I'm about to enter temporary unconsciousness as the song con-cludes. But it's short-lived when Javi's "NO LAughing matter" rings in my headphones.

My eyes fly open, and I stare at the single cover, a distorted

Polaroid image of two figures kissing in front of a white church after sunset. You can't tell the figures are kissing at first glance, but trust me. I know exactly what's happening. I press pause on the screen and release a frustrated breath. If I believed in fate, I would listen to the signs screaming at me to address the elephant in the room. But I ignore it and remember to get my life back on track. I'm in no mood to repeat the past ten months of hell.

A new notification lights up the headrest screen, and I nearly fly out of my chair once I recognize the D&D icon in the banner. I yank my phone from the charger and peer around me, praying no one saw. Vince looks asleep with headphones in his ears next to me, as are the rest of any nearby teammates in my immediate surroundings.

Once I feel the coast is clear, I open the app to my message boards. A vibrant glow illuminates my face in the darkness as I sort through hundreds of unread messages in my inbox, searching for the one person I want to talk to. I click on Mister E's torso, and a familiar surge of dopamine courses through me as I read his first message since the coffee shop.

Mister E: My last name doesn't begin with an E.

My brow furrows as I reread my previous question.

CT No E: It doesn't?

Mister E: No

CT No E: Why call yourself Mister E?

Mister E: Sound it out.

I whisper his name out slowly three times, and the realization hits me as hard as my hand smacking my forehead. Mister E. Mystery. I muffle a laugh as I think harder on the oxymoron.

Mister E: You have to love a good pun.
CT no E: Mister E is full of mystery.
Mister E: Maybe, but I need to make this part apparent.
CT NO E: What?
Mister E: I think I am showing signs of ad-dick-tion.

My phone almost slips out of my hands. What the hell did he say? I grip my phone tighter and reread his message before another pops up on screen.

Mister E: I mean, it is possible if I continue to take doses larger than those prescribed.

CT No E: I mean, yeah, I guess. Do you do drugs? I am not into that stuff.

I wait a beat before *Mister E* sends a screenshot of my profile. It takes a second to understand what he's trying to say, but once I reread my intro, I send the same facepalm emoji that encompasses my reaction. Of course, I am the drug he's referring to.

CT No E: Oh right.

Mister E: You can't fault a guy for wanting a stronger dose of you.

Now it's my turn to add some spice to the conversation.

CT No E: I have a full dose ready…just for you.

Mister E: Oh please show me my medicine doctor! Let me get a hit of that magic stick!

I feel a rush of heat flood my cheeks. The pressure is building so tight in my pants it's throbbing past irritation. My hand slides down the top of my joggers just to rub away some of the excitement.

Mister E: Don't make me beg for it.

Vince shifts his seat. My hands flail into the armrest, and

I bolt into a straight sitting position. I press the button below the chargers and pull the ejected desk across me. Vince stretches his hand out next to me before turning and looking at me. His expression remains unreadable as he takes me in.

"You good?" he asks.

"Oh yeah definitely," I say, crossing my legs under the table. "Did you sleep?"

"Not really. I was listening to an audiobook. I just had my eyes closed. It helps me visualize the story better. "

"Is that homework?"

"No. I just like to read."

"What novel?" I ask. My voice hitches as I try to sell my less than convincing acting performance. At least the teepee in my pants sinks.

"The Hate You Give."

"I've read that book. That's a good one."

Vince cocks his head. "You've read it?"

"Oh yeah. It was one of my favorite books. I still have my copy on my bookshelf."

Vince shakes his head. His phone lights up, and he darts his eyes away. "That must be nice. I used to rent a copy from our library, but it's a banned book now." Vince clicks his tongue as he readjusts in his seat. "Probably another cost-cutting measure we keep hearing about, but spending money on a suspended football team makes sense."

I cock my head. "How does that work?"

"I will never know. The only thing I know is I will keep my promise to my mother to earn a degree, even if that means this shit school."

I sigh at the mention of his mom and the contrasting

images of our maternal covenants. Vince offers his promise to his mom with the confidence that she will be there to experience every reward. Every win, goal, and even graduation when his day comes. My promise to my mother came on her deathbed, a declaration of my intent with the weight of an empty promise. Even if I leap over every obstacle, I can't share the reward with her. But I don't know if my words even offered solace. She just stared at me with her lifeless eyes and turned away to pass her last breath. That thought pierces my heart.

"You know what I mean, right?" he asks.

I readjust my posture. "I promised my mom I would make it pro when she passed."

Vince raises an eyebrow, a fresh, uncomfortable silence filling the surrounding space. He collects himself before he smiles and places his hand on my shoulder. "Well, I hope you can fulfill your promise, but you need some work after the way I defended you."

I roll my eyes and smirk at his jab. The sound of obnoxious laughter causes me to turn my head to face it. Romero steals furtive glances at me three seats behind before tapping his fingers on a phone screen. "What's his deal?" I ask, turning my head back to Vince.

Vince jerks his head around and winces. "Romero?"

I nod.

"Bad news."

I raise a brow. "How?"

"Let's just say you are safest when you distance yourself from him. He's ruthless when he wants his way with anything."

"Like how?"

"Well, for one, he's obsessed with living on the North side, which is where all the wealth of University Hills is. It drives his thinking, and he becomes crazy when he feels threatened by someone. It never works out for that person."

I nod, absorbing every word. "I will try to steer clear of him."

"You are smarter than his girlfriend. She must be blind to his motives or just doesn't care."

"Doesn't he date that gossip influencer?"
"Yeah, that is true. They are probably using each other for personal gain. Maybe that's a match made in heaven."

"Are you jealous or something?"

"No, I don't play that way."

The air flies out of me. What does he mean by 'that way?' Was I oblivious to Vince this whole time? I wonder if his eyes were not closed as he listened to his audiobook. He possibly saw me on the app texting Mister E. Please tell me he didn't see my messages. The nausea rushes to my head as I process the idea well beyond my brain's capacity. A hint of panic creeps into my voice as I press him on it. "What do you mean by that?"

"I don't play love like them, two desperate attention hoes posting fake love to shower themselves with more views. I want something more organic with a real woman. Someone who wants me, but then reminds me she doesn't need me. A boss who makes me want to act right, and would have no fear showing me the door. A real Miss Independent."

I exhale a sigh of relief. "That makes more sense."

He cocks his head. "What do you mean?"

"I thought you were gay for a second."

He studies me, his face unwavering. "Would that have

been a problem?"

I throw my hands up and shake vigorously. "Oh no, of course not. That's not at all what I meant."

"That's good because there is nothing wrong with being gay." His voice is firm as he stares at me one more time. I nod like a child being scolded by his parents before Vince rolls over to his left shoulder and closes his eyes. I sit there contemplating explaining myself further, but it's useless to try at this moment, so I let it go.

My phone buzzes again in my pocket, another D&D icon in my notification banner. I click the icon and type in our conversation's password.

Mister E: Come on. Don't be a tease.

I waste no time engaging in our conversation again.

CT No E: Sorry you just need to wait a little. On the road at the moment.

Mister E: No!!!!!

Mister E: Heading home?

CT No E: No just going out with friends for the weekend.

Mister E: Nice. Are you from University Hills?

CT No E: No I grew up in the University City suburbs.

Mister E: Oh no. Does that mean you go to USE?

CT No E: Haha, calm down. I used to go there before I transferred to SESU.

Mister E: That's a relief. What helped you come to your senses?

I hesitate for a moment before I respond, still contemplating how I want to write this message. This is still a total stranger I'm texting, so I don't want to confide too much information with him. However, I welcome a short cathartic release from this tension I still hold on to. I take a few tries before I settle on something to send.

CT No E: It's a long story, but my roommate found out about me and this guy I was seeing. He threatened to expose both of us, so we left to avoid the consequences. The guy I was with started a new life in Louisiana, and I came here.

I see three dots appear from him on the screen, probably choosing his words as carefully as I chose mine.

Mister E: That's rough. I am so sorry. Do you still talk to that guy?

CT No E: No I don't.

Mister E: Is that why you are on this app now?

CT No E: Sort of. I think this is really the only place to meet people who share similar circumstances to me. The only place we don't have to be so discreet.

Mister E: I feel that. My father is really homophobic. I am killing myself to fulfill his dreams and make him proud. My life is just an illusion to satisfy everyone but myself. But it's all I know, and I just continue the vicious cycle. If I try to be honest about this part of me, it would ruin everything I have done.

I relate too well to the challenges of having a demanding father. Before my mother's passing, my father behaved the same way. He was my intense puppeteer, yanking all my strings as I tried to navigate life. My father's belligerent tantrum greeted my missteps, scaring everyone into submission. But ever since, he's been a shadow of his former self, more detached on an extreme pendulum of grief. The burnout stage at home exhausted all his vacation time for the first months, almost to the point he nearly lost his job. Once he returned to work, he almost never went home. I saw him only a few times during my summer visit home, which I can say is a few times more than I have seen my brother.

The bus threw me into the window as it turned into a standard retreat lodge parking lot, jolting the rest of my teammates awake. I rush to type out my last message.

CT No E: Glad to know I am not alone in that struggle.

The bus screeches to a stop in front of our destination, the first sign of civilization in hours. We all gather our belongings and shuffle off the bus,the sound of our footsteps on the pavement filling the silence. We retrieve our luggage from the compartments underneath. The metallic clinks and thuds reverberate, intermingling with the distant hum of traffic.

Vince and I step inside the lodge, and I smell aged wood and polished brass waft by me, mingling with a hint of floral air freshener. The lobby, reminiscent of an old Western setting, is impeccably clean. Worn wooden floors creak under our weight while vintage chandeliers cast a warm, inviting glow.

Our collective murmurs fill the silent lobby as everyone congregates, while our voices blend together in a low hum. My eyelids are heavy, but I wait for Coach Ramsey's instructions.

I turn to Vince, who stands at attention. "Hey, do you have a roommate already?"

He looks at me, a little confused. "I do not yet," Vince says, placing his earbuds into their case.

"Do you want to room with me?"

"I would, but I can't decide that."

"What do you mean?"

"You will see."

I follow him as we walk back over to the huddle of our teammates. The group thins out into pairs after Coach Ramsey reads off his list. "Vince…you will be with Duncan. Here are the keys." Coach hands the key to Vince. "Watch him, all right?"

Vince takes the key, forcing a smile.

Coach Ramsey looks down at his clipboard. "Romero, Caleb will be your roommate for this weekend. You both are in cabin #8."

My throat bobs as I process coach's words. It takes everything in me not to grimace. Romero is the last person I want as a roommate. The absolute last. I would even take Roger in this moment rather than him, and that is saying something. But unfortunately, I have no say in this decision.

I walk up to Coach Ramsey and take my key card, but before I can ask, he's already analyzing me. "I think this room assignment will benefit you both. There is untapped chemistry between you and Romero, and I think it could help us moving forward."

I nod before turning to Romero.

"You go. I'll be up in a minute," Romero says. He turns and whispers something inaudible to his brother.

I roll my eyes as I exit the lobby, passing the last of my teammates congregating outside. I walk along the caliche pathway, each step causing a sharp burn on my shoulder as I struggle to maintain my grip on the heavy gym bag. The sound of my footsteps crunching the dehydrated soil drowns out the whispering cicadas. My phone's flashlight is my only guide, leading me into the man-made wilderness, adhering to zoning laws. My cabin is the last to appear, secluded on the north side of the campground.

As I approach my cabin, the smell of stale air mixed with a

faint hint of cleaning solution and mountain cedar greets my nostrils. I maneuver my bag, feeling the weight digging into my shoulder, and retrieve the key card from my pocket. I float the plastic device above the lock, unlocking the door.

When I step into the room, I'm disappointed by what greets me. Walls screaming for a coat of paint wrap around an interior decorated with clearance items found during a Tuesday Morning liquidation sale. Two espresso dressers placed across from each other compete with dark walnut-stained nightstands and bed frames between them. Various shades of brown pillows litter each bed, none of which match the curtains, adorned with a swirl of chocolate bark design. It's fitting this room looks like shit with all this brown.

I set my bag on the floorboards next to the queen bed closest to the door. The crisp sheets, cool against my skin, hug me as I lie down on the made bed. I retrieve my phone from my pocket. It's no surprise my phone vibrates from another D&D message.

Mister E: I guess we both need a cure for our daddy issues. Do you have any suggestions?

Unopened attachments accompany the message on D&D. Each attachment comes with a warning stating "view at your own risk" within the message bubble. As I click the pictures, there is no stopping the flood of blood surging down to my dick. Each image shows him posing in various sex positions, with his missionary pose being my favorite. He grasps one of his rounded and tan glutes in one hand while he snaps a picture of himself in the mirror with the other.

Mister E: Maybe something that can handle this?

I rub the outside of my track pants, enhancing the girth

forming below the fabric. After taking a photo of my erect penis, I tap my thumbs on the screen.

CT No E: I know just the cure…

A faint knock pulls me away from my phone. I throw my phone into my bag and readjust myself on the bed, trying to regain composure over my body. Just another reminder for me to control myself this weekend. The last thing I need is someone else outing me to the team.

I rush to the door as the knocking becomes swifter and more aggressive. The door latch screeches against its strike plate, adding an eerie sound to the chaotic scene as men in Halloween masks charge toward me. I am so blindsided that my body and brain struggle to decide between fight or flight. Sensing my fear, someone blindfolds me, blocking out the sight of my room. The blindfold feels rough against my skin, a slight discomfort amidst the chaos.

Guided by a man's firm grip, I stumble backward, my calves and heels colliding painfully with unseen obstacles, sending sharp jabs of pain through my lower body. I dig my feet into the wooden floor, but the burns add to my discomfort. The dizzying rotation disorients me, but I don't ignore the constant shoving from the surrounding people.

The nightmare persists with my hands being restrained by another pair, someone's grip tight and suffocating. I resist as hard as I can, but it is fruitless fighting hidden figures with my arms pulled behind my back. I am thrown on the bed, wracked with anger and frustration, and I experience the violating and dehumanizing sensation of being stripped. The stripping stops at my underwear, leaving me exposed.

Once the restraint loosens, I yank my blindfold off and

wobble to my feet. A sudden flood of flashlight beams blinds me, further disorienting me.

"What the fuck?" My voice carries as I shout into the crowd.

"All right, Caleb, son," Duncan says behind a Michael Myers mask with a GoPro attached. "Are you ready for initiation?"

"What are you talking about, initiation?" I ask, my lungs struggling for oxygen.

"The initiation required of every player to be a part of this brotherhood. Everyone on the team has to perform for us."

"Perform what? What the fuck is going on?"

"You are required to entertain us. Put on a show if you will. Nothing too complicated, just something that lets us know you are truly one of us."

"And not a pathetic faggot fox!" Andres says. However, I am so disoriented I can't tell what mask he's wearing.

"That's rich. I thought the football team got suspended for hazing," I say, hoping that will scare them off.

Duncan laughs at my remark. "The football team was dumb enough to haze on campus and get caught. We learned from their mistakes. And if you even think you will run your mouth to someone, who will believe you? You aren't like us. But you have the chance tonight to change my mind."

My eyes narrow, but it's hard to gauge him when he hides behind a mask.

"Believe me, Caleb, you would rather perform than try the other option." He reaches behind him, cracks a wet towel, and rolls it between his hands.

I lift my chin at his threat. "I will take my chances," I say with what little dignity remains.

"All right then," Duncan says as he snaps his fingers twice.

A man in a Chucky mask and one in a Jason Voorhees mask tackle me onto the bed. Each one restrains my arms and legs as I squirm face down. I am ready to scream, but the Jason-masked man gags me with a sock I hope is clean. Duncan holds the camera to my back while a man in the Chucky mask walks up to my waist, his hands outstretched. He digs his fingers under the elastic waistband of my underwear, staring back at me, inspecting every inch of skin. The aroused brown eyes violate every part of me, pulling down my boxer briefs one humiliating inch at a time.

"Guess this makes you the team bitch," Duncan says.

I stare at Chucky, pleading with my eyes for mercy from this nightmare. His eyes sympathize with me behind the Halloween mask, sending chills racing down my body. I think he will save me before Duncan shouts behind me.

"Team...bitch," Duncan says.

In the light-poor cabin, the five masked players chant in unison, cultivating an eerie setting. Duncan adjusts his camera's angle, casting a faint glow over my face and illuminating the scene with an ethereal glow. Once he's satisfied, he cracks the towel again, his determination as scary as his mask.

The Chucky-masked man shakes his head in disapproval, his vibrant wig swaying with the motion. However, he pulls my boxers down with delicate yet mischievous hands, his fingertips grazing against the fabric. When I feel he's ready to expose all of me, his fingers slide off the elastic band and travel down my thighs. The motion triggers my darkest nightmare, one rooted in the darkest moment of my past.

For a second, I am transported back to an unholy time in what was supposed to be a holy space. I jolt when he brushes my pelvic hairs and explode when the towel hisses just above my groin.

"All right! All right!" I scream through the sock.

All masked men pause like my spell frees them from a trance, and the Jason masked man removes the sock.

"I will do your stupid initiation."

After they release me, I pull up my underwear as the men line up in front of the bed. I squirm backward as far as the wall will allow me, mustering the strength to perform just to end this misery. I delay as long as I can while everyone watches me. "What do I have to do?"

A sinister whisper escapes from behind the Michael Myers mask. "Just entertain us for one minute. I am feeling generous tonight, so I will let you decide what to do." Duncan adjusts the GoPro above his head.

If they get mad, they can forgive me for not preparing for my hazing ritual, but I stumble upon a high school memory from back during the pandemic. Even when social distancing, Machi and I would do this trendy dance over FaceTime. It's the last trend I have ever performed since then.

"Play Blinding Lights by The Weeknd," I shout.

A cacophony of moans and guffaws reverberates from my audience. As if they are judging me on my choice right now. The speaker hums in the background, amplifying the pulsating beat of my chosen song. As I bounce on the lumpy bed, the texture beneath me adds an uneven sensation to my movements. The first chord strikes, and I dip my right shoulder, the motion accompanied by the sound of the sheets rustling as I maintain the rhythm. I cross and uncross my right leg over my left, waiting for the second piano key melody.

In one swift motion, I throw my hands straight up, the rush of air brushing against my fingertips, before bringing them back down in a circular motion twice. Bending my upper body, I feel a slight stretch in my muscles as I become perpendicular to my legs. Mimicking the act of swimming, I repeat the same motion until seconds before The W e eknd sings.

I leap off the bed, hoping to catch the crowd off guard. As I come within striking distance of Duncan, I swing my arm and prepare to grab the camera, but he dodges my attack. Losing my balance, I somersault onto the ground, a few pillows cushioning my fall. The blinding lights temporarily impair my vision when I try to stand, but the sounds of their laughter wound me harder than any punch to the gut.

I don't see who turns on the lights since I buried my face in my arms, shielding myself from the embarrassment I don't want to face. If I had paid attention to my surroundings rather than staring at NSFWs, I could have prevented this. However, I refuse to let them bully me. They may have stolen my pride, but not my dignity. Whatever sliver I can salvage of it.

I grab my phone and start typing a scathing message to Coach about my experience. I am about to press send when a realization hits me. They have me on video. If I tell anyone, the idea of my face and dance will appear on everyone's Reeltime feed, and it feels humiliating. It's not as bad as being outed, but it's a close second. The rage seethes out of me, and I fling my phone onto the mattress behind me.

The room's silence leaves when the door swings open. Romero walks into the room, scrolling on his phone, oblivious to me. Once he sees the sight in front of him, he howls with laughter.

"What?" I ask. Dagger-like aggressiveness shoots from my voice.

"You had a rough night or something?" he asks. Romero strolls by me to his side of the room, swinging his bag onto the bed.

"You could say that," I respond, still feeling shaken by the events.

He looks at me but shrugs, almost dismissing any further explanation before I provide one. "That sucks. I'm gonna take a shower." Romero grabs his speaker and walks over, giving me a million-dollar smile.

Romero removes his shirt, and the blood floods my cheeks the moment his back dimples smile at me. I throw myself onto my bed and place the pillow on my groin. Romero leaves the bathroom door cracked open, and I can't restrain myself from peeking from my bed. I can only see a sliver of Romero in the mirror. Only the upper body is visible on the portion of the mirror free of condensation. A towel covers his lower body, and I can't help but fantasize about what he's hiding underneath. I don't know if it's because I am jaded from earlier, but I crave seeing all of Romero. I'm not sure how to conceal my excitement if the opportunity presents itself.

One chime from my phone pulls my attention away from Romero. I reach into my bag and find a notification from D&D.

Mister E: Please doctor! When can you inject me with that cure?

A playful grin stretches across my face.

CT No E: When are you free to step into my office?

As soon as I hit send, a sudden realization forms after a passing heartbeat. I hear a familiar sound coming from the bathroom, one I wouldn't suspect opposite the open door. My eyes turn toward the space in front of me, catalyzing the heartbeat of the next victim in a horror film who discovers the terrifying truth.

"What the hell?"

Romero steps out of the bathroom. He freezes in his tracks when he sees my horrified expression. "What?" Romero asks.

Chapter 6

September 28, 2025

"Why are you looking at me like that?" Romero stares at me.

I swallow hard before uttering my response. I will expose myself by pointing out the sound, but I have already dealt with some bullshit hazing tonight. The anger still lingers, eating away at any composure I have over the situation. For a split second, I think I'm losing my mind, but upon closer inspection of Romero's upper body, I'm sure I found Mister E.

"That sound...from your speaker," I say, raising my finger toward Romero.

Romero shakes his head, his face losing color, then moves to his side of the room. He chuckles and flashes me another disarming smile while rubbing his forearm. I can't help but assume Romero is trying to hide his fear, so I interrogate him further.

"You're Mister E!"

"I have no clue what you are talking about." Romero tosses his clothes into his bag. He grabs his phone and presses play on his playlist.

I twist my legs off the bed and approach Romero until only

his bed separates us. "You are on the app." I press one hand deep into the comforter, while the other shakes when I point a finger at him. I shouldn't press him, but I'm not dropping this.

"What app are you talking about?" Romero glares at me with a now dissipating smile.

"You know what I am talking about."

"You sound fucking crazy."

"No, I don't." I follow his steps as he paces around, his fists tightening with every step. "It can't be a coincidence that moments after I send a message on the app, that specific chime rings out in the bathroom."

He fidgets as he looks at me, trying to construct a response.

I extend my hand. "Show me your phone."

"Why the fuck would I show you my phone?"

"Prove me wrong. What are you so scared I will find?"

Romero stares for a moment, his mouth opens, but no words come out. He instead gathers his belongings and bolts back toward the bathroom. "Even though I am off my meds, you are delusional. Accusing me of being on gay apps."

I move around the bed and block his path to the bath-room. He ignores me and tries to sidestep me, but I push my hand in front of his waist when he tries to break through. I readjust my hand and catch Romero's arm as he tries to move around me again. "I know it's you, Mister E. Just admit it. If you're clueless about what I'm referring to, how do you know it's a gay app?"

"I could ask you the same thing."

For a moment, I thought I'd overplayed my hand. Wrongly accusing Romero as Mister E is a dangerous mistake that outs myself. If I am wrong, I have handed Romero all the ammunition he needs to shoot down my comeback. A town like this hates my existence, even if it contributes to its success. Even with that risk, my instincts tell me I'm right, but it's proving to be impossible for me to figure out.

Romero wrenches his hand free from my grasp. His sudden jerk causes my hand to skid across Romero's waist, disrupting the neat fold of the towel. In an instant, the towel cascades to the ground, leaving Romero exposed. The sight of his chiseled V-cut back, shimmering with perspiration, is now accompanied by revealing his sculpted hamstrings and glutes. Every detail of his glutes is identical to what I have seen in their message thread, right down to the beauty mark adorning the left cheek. Any lingering thought that I was crazy evaporates, but now exposed Romero in a more compromising position. The anger cools into embarrassment.

"I didn't mean…" I utter, taking a step toward Romero.

Romero explodes into a fit of anger when he turns around, pinning me against the wall with his arms. "What the fuck is your deal?" His fingertips dig into my shoulders, the tops of his knuckles whitening. I try to push him off, but he doesn't budge. "Quit messing with me. I ain't gay."

"It was an accident!"

He launches his right fist toward me, delivering consecutive blows into the drywall next to my face. Even with my significant height over Romero, I shrink in his fiery presence.

"Calm down. I swear it was an accident," I protest, pulling at his wrists, but he holds firm.

Romero breathes heavily, and his eyes stare daggers in my direction. He pins me tighter against the wall, palms bruising my skin. We sit in a state of inertia, waiting for a force to send this tension ablaze again. His eyes scan my body, and I can't help but do the same. The aggressive grooves in his abs expand and contract as he breathes, and the rest of his godlike physique clenches to his bones at the height of this stressful moment. But I follow the lines of the V-shape definition down to the area between his legs, his body revealing his inner thoughts. It becomes so pronounced that it's hard to ignore, even when he looks down at himself.

"I won't say a word. We never have to think about it again." A faint whisper escapes my lips. "I can't help but think about… the hot pics you sent…playing games with me. Imagine all of you and…"

He gazes into my eyes as he loosens the grip on my shoulder. My breath quickens, echoing loudly. Romero's grip softens, and his hands glide up my neck, his touch sending a shiver down my spine. Particles of tension hang in the room, mixing with the faint aroma of cologne and lust. As Romero pulls me closer, his lips meet mine in a hungry embrace. My eyes widen, but my initial surprise gives way to a rush of pleasure. The softness of Romero's lips against my own feels like silk, which disarms me while erasing any lingering fear. My hands find their way to the sculpted contours of Romero's waist, the fire of our touch igniting a spark within me. Our tongues intertwine, a rush of dopamine pulsating through my body like an electric current surging through a live wire.

I pull my head back, panting for air to return to my breath. Arousal hangs in the room, adding an intoxicating allure to our encounter. "Shit," I say.

"It's those damn ocean eyes for me." His lips hover over

mine. He slips his tongue into my mouth for a few seconds, before he lowers himself, stroking his fingers down my body while maintaining eye contact. He breaks his gaze to peel my underwear off.

In the next moments, I feel a rush of sensations, like entering a new world. Romero's kiss gives me chills and goosebumps. My heart races, drowning out my doubts. His touch weakens my defenses, sending tingles through me. The pace quickens, leaving me breathless. I arch my back, hoping for a break, scared of the excitement. Just as I feel overwhelmed, Romero pauses, teasingly extending the tension.

"I've needed this so bad," Romero lets out.

A sinister grin stretches across his face, revealing a row of white teeth, as he moves in to make out with me. The room echoes with the sound of heavy breathing and the faint rustle of clothes as we tumble across the room, our movements fueled by a surge of hormones rather than genuine passion. Our musky smell of sweat saturates the soft fabric, which yields beneath our weight as we crash onto the bed.

Romero positions himself on top, his weight pressing down on my torso. Our lips meet in a hungry frenzy of kisses, punctuated by the occasional gasp and moan. Romero shifts his position, ensuring I slide inside him, our bodies uniting like puzzle pieces. The synergy is a dangerous side effect of our heat and friction.

My knuckles turn white as he grips the cotton sheets, his fingers sinking into the fabric. With each rhythmic movement of my hips, a symphony of pleasurable sensations floods my entire being, overwhelming my senses and my better judgment. Beads of perspiration trickle down my body, leaving a glistening trail on the now-damp sheets beneath me. The thumping of my heart echoes in my ears, synchronizing with the primal rhythm of our bodies. As a moan escapes my lips, we harmonize with the deep, guttural grunts and moans uttered by Romero, intensifying the sensory experience.

As I surrender to primal desires, the intoxicating scent of lust permeates the air, filling my nostrils. It ignites a fire within me, overpowering my rational thinking. My mind, like a canvas, paints vivid pictures of the overwhelming future, each stroke adding to the mounting pressure that engulfs me. But before the unrealized future can fully materialize, the sound of my final, prolonged grunt interrupts my mental spiral, reverberating through the room like thunder.

In that moment, a symphony of sensations floods my body to the point I quake with pleasure. I reach the pinnacle of ecstasy, my skin alive with electric tingles as I release my fluids, and a powerful wave of worrisome clarity overtakes me. I moan and wince as my body crashes back onto the bed. Both of us pant like we had been sprinting for an hour, neither one of us wanting to look at the other. Romero rolls out of bed to retrieve his towel and walks to the bathroom to resume the shower I interrupted.

For the next several minutes, I lay on the bed, staring at the ceiling while listening to Romero's music from his speaker. An impossible number of thoughts rattles in my skull. What the hell did I just do? We just do? It's risky having sex with Romero with our teammates close by. I pray to God that no one was near us. I feel like I would have heard someone if I had.

Romero lies next to me and scrolls through his phone,

his back turned toward me. Since we finished our hookup, I've watched him walk into the bathroom before and after he showered, only exchanging fleeting glances and a few brief words. It is troubling to experience awkwardness as teammates who now share a bed, naked and still in the fragrance of our horniness. He does not ask me to leave or to stay. Part of me wants to ask, but this is also my bed. He can leave if he wants.

A wave of nostalgia hits me when the beat of "NO LAughing matter" fills the room from Romero's speaker. At first, I didn't recognize the song, but Javi's voice whispered in my ears. His singing tugs at a fragile memory in my brain, and the melody replicates the same emotions from that day in Vince's truck. Except this time, I have nowhere to run to. If I leave and return, the song will end before I find my underwear. I could ask to change the song, but I don't want to talk.

The sights and sounds of that moment flood my senses, and I can almost feel the cool breeze from that Mardi Gras night on my skin. The music, once a source of discomfort, now holds a strange allure, beckoning me to embrace the memories it stirs within me. I yearn for a sense of familiarity amidst the swirling uncertainty. The music engulfs me, wrapping around me like a warm embrace, as Javi's powerful falsetto pierces the air, accompanied by the melodic interplay of the brass orchestra, weaving through the pop instrumentals.

Javi's voice, resonating with haunting yet comforting tones, provides solace amidst the unease provoked by my now complicated sex life. The sensory overload overwhelms me, triggering a flood of emotions that surge through me, releasing the memories I had tightly locked away for the past several months.

CHAPTER 7

February 13, 2025

NO LAughing matter

Javi shifts in the driver's seat next to me, our eyes taking in the Lake Pontchartrain view ahead of us. He rolls down the windows after we park, inviting a whiff of salty estuary and Cajun spices inside. The water crashes into the wooden pier, which drowns out the lively brass filling the Mardi Gras atmosphere in the distance. The sun's last rays paint the sky with hues of orange and pink, casting a warm glow across the lake. Javi's face radiates contentment as he switches the car's ignition off and strolls in his sandals toward the shoreline.

Javi's hurried steps transform into graceful strides as he leaps along the dock and dances along its edge. Pausing for a moment, he savors the refreshing breeze that brushes against his skin while I move closer. The unfiltered beauty of this free-spirited, sun-kissed man captivates me. He turns around to face me, and that smirk bends into a genuine, wholesome smile.

"Come on." Javi waves me over.

I hesitate.

"Trust me. This side of the deck is safe. You should experience this," Javi says.

His deep, mysterious eyes draw me in with their magnetic charm. A hint of a rosy tint adorns his lips, giving a touch of allure to his handsome face. I slip out of the car and retrace his path, the soft thud of my loafers meeting the ground whispering amidst the surrounding sounds. I walk over to the pier's entrance, or at least what's remaining. Only the wooden beams that connected a descending set of stairs remained, leaving a sizable gap of lake water between the concrete and the pier. I leap onto the worn deck, a lukewarm yet salty breeze hanging in the air as I land on top of the deck's worn surface.

For a second, the ground beneath me splits, and I try to adjust my balance. I slip, teetering on the edge of a fall. I flail my arms trying to prevent an embarrassing plunge into water that's seen better days. In a split second, my left hand finds Javi's, our fingers intertwining like a lifeline, ensuring our connection remains unbroken. We hold each other's gaze for a second, a pulse of energy flowing between us.

"Can't swim or something?" he asks, pulling me closer. A whimsical smile stretches across his face.

I scoff. "Sorry, I don't have extra clothes."

"Unless the tide raises the water to our knees, I am sure your shorts will stay dry," he responds. "Here. Shut your eyes and sense the experience. Live in the moment! You don't get these experiences while you are in season."

I close my eyes, but a dizzying sensation has me swaying in the water. The darkness provides more confusion than clarity, as if I'm standing in a maze without a guide. The humid air suffocates me, and I struggle to take deep, calming breaths

I need. More thoughts about my feelings toward Javi race through my head, adding to the cacophony of noise buzzing around me. A knot forms in my stomach, and my eyelids snap open. Javi must sense this because his fingers stroke my shoulders, sending a soothing touch through a tense body.

But as we stand here together, the rhythmic thumping in my chest reverberates in my ears. The rush of adrenaline surges, creating a tingling sensation that prickles my skin. I fight the urge to open my eyes, but give in to seek reassurance in Javi's gaze.

As if guided by a sixth sense, Javi opens his eyes seconds after me. We share glances that evolve into intentional stares. His cocoa eyes send warmth to my weary soul, a comforting warmth that seeps into my bones. I want to kiss him at this moment. I crave it. But a laundry list of worries blocks me from crossing that thin line. I convince myself that my feelings would cause more hurt than love, hurting myself in the process again. I exhale, surrendering to fear again, and turn my gaze toward the horizon.

...

"Hey, over here!" My voice echoes through the bustling street, strained from the effort as I flail my hands above the sea of people. The pungent scent of alcohol and vomit, a mixture of spilled drinks and intoxication wafting through the humid night air, cannot deter the celebrations around me.

Drunken locals lean precariously over the balcony above, their boisterous voices blending with the lively ambiance of Bourbon Street. Javi can't help but laugh as he finds me in the crowd, his mirth mingling with the vibrant sounds of music and laughter that envelop the scene.

"How can I get some beads here?" I ask.

Javi smiles, camera in hand. "Maybe show them your tits!"

My face lights up with a mischievous grin. I lift my shirt and move my chest from side to side, revealing my smooth, sun-kissed skin.

Above us, a group whoop with delight, their cheers echoing like a symphony of joy. Among them, a vibrant strawberry blond stands out, her contagious enthusiasm clear in her animated gestures and joyful shouts. As she raises her Jester Daiquiri, the unmistakable aroma of strawberries mingles with the rum falling out of her cup. Its reputation as the strongest daiquiri is clear in the confident grip of the strawberry blond, who savors each sip, her face displaying a mix of delight and satisfaction.

A pair of gold and purple beads twirl through the air before dropping at my feet. Javi, the ever-captivating photographer, swiftly moves his camera to frame the moment. The click of the shutter fills the air, capturing the image for eternity. The camera's mechanical whir blends with the vibrant atmosphere, adding to the sensory tapestry.

I lower my shirt, the fabric brushing against my skin, as I bend down to retrieve my precious beads. I pick them up, feeling their cool weight in my hands. With a smile, I take a refreshing sip from his jester.

"The Big Easy, huh? Is that hinting at something?" I ask.

Javi rolls his eyes. "Shut up."

We begin our walk along a crowded Bourbon Street at the height of the celebrations.

"What's up with the beads, anyway?" I ask.

"Aren't you supposed to be Catholic?"

"Well, yeah. But I have never celebrated Mardi Gras

before."

"Well…" Javi begins. "The beads represent different Christian symbolisms. Purple beads represent justice, the green is faith, and the gold is power. I'm unsure why they throw them. In high school, my friends and I would compete for the most beads. Of course, I always lose. Nobody was interested in my flat chest."

I laugh. "Times are changing. I mean, these melons got the job done." I cup my hands under my nipples.

"Yeah, sure…melons," Javi says, giving me a side-eye before sipping his daiquiri.

The first sip of my daiquiri stings yet satisfies my taste buds as vibrant partygoers speed past us. Their vibrant outfits create a kaleidoscope of colors that dance before him, each style as bold as the alcohol swimming down my throat. The street ahead pulses with energy as hip-hop, EDM, and country music sounds reverberate through the air, blending together in a symphony of beats that makes my heart race. The aroma of soul food and greasy goodness wafts from the nearby food stalls, enticing my senses and making my mouth water. As I take a step forward, I feel the buzz of excitement in the air, electrifying my skin.

"Does everyone party like this often?" I ask.

"Not if they can help it. Everyone comes to enjoy Mardi Gras in New Orleans!" Javi shouts.

"Why not mention you're from here?"

Javi pauses before facing me. "I keep my childhood private. I moved here before high school. My mom grew up here, though. I love this place, but I never imagined coming back. It's my first time returning since college."

"What's the reason you'd never want to return here?"

Before Javi responds, the deafening echoes of rapid gunshots pierce the air, shattering the once festive atmosphere. Shouts of panic and the blaring wails of police sirens drown out the celebratory sounds of laughter and joy. The acrid smell of fear lingers in the air, mingling with gunpowder. Javi's hand grips my arm tightly, urgency palpable, as he shouts. "Let's go!"

We drop our daiquiris and sprint down the first road we see. Our hurried footsteps echo through the empty streets, mingling with the distant hum of unseen city life. We race by a row of eerie, vampire-themed restaurants and shops, and our hearts pound in our chests, fueled by adrenaline, as we push ourselves toward the majestic white basilica that stands tall in the distance.

Breathless and perspiring, Javi and I stop at the fence line, our panting breaths mixing with the cool evening breeze. Javi's hands rest on his knees, pointing a trembling finger back in the direction we arrived from, his face etched with a mixture of fear and relief. "That…is the reason."

We both laugh as we pant. Sirens wail in the distance. Javi stands, showcasing his 6'2" height, fixing his hair, and patting his sleeves and pant legs.

"Is it always like this?" I say, catching my breath.

"It's always a wild time, but it usually never escalates to this."

"Usually?"

He gives me an incredulous look. "Don't worry. I wouldn't want a handsome man like you to lose that pretty face," he says nonchalantly.

Javi's admission freezes my thoughts, and my cheeks

redden.

"What?" he asks.

"Do you think I'm handsome?"

He rolls his eyes. "Don't let it inflate your ego, hetero, but yes, I think you are." He brushes his hand down my arm, and a wave of goosebumps scales my skin.

For the first time, Javi discloses an interest in me, which I suspected all along. Javi shares everything about his life with me, from his childhood in New Orleans to his life goals and plans after USE. He omits very few details even when he tries to be secretive, and he's brave enough to take action for what he desires. What deepens my attraction to Javi is his acceptance of the consequences of his actions. He's the perfect foil and a perfect match.

During the time we spent together, I learned we share interests in music, reading, and studying in coffee shops. But most importantly, I discovered he's the sunshine that was stolen from me when my mom died, and I don't want this to go dark.

I must have zoned out too long because Javi stares at me with a worried expression.

"Are you okay?" he asks.

"Oh yeah," I say. The alcohol overtakes my senses and clouds my ability to read his worry.

"What's wrong?" Javi's eyes narrow.

"Nothing. I just…I'm not sure how to tell you this."

"What?" A fierce hostility burns behind his pupils, and his glare forces me to backtrack my answer.

"No, I just mean to say that. Well, I just think that this could change things between us." I look at him for reassurance that he understands, but Javi crosses his arms and glares at me.

"Are you serious?"

"Yeah, I mean, if you are serious."

"Wow. I didn't realize you're that insecure." Javi's tone sharpens.

I cock my head to the side. "What are you talking about?"

He shakes his head and takes a step backward, almost touching the fence. "Why am I an idiot believing you were cool with it?"

His words finally sink in. I shake my head, but not the hurt in Javi's voice. "No…I swear it's not that." I struggle to piece together my thoughts.

"Don't bother, Caleb. I didn't realize this was an issue for you. It was a stupid comment, and I regret it."

"Javi, that's not it. What I said didn't come out right."

"Apparently, that's not the only thing. Honestly, I am not surprised. A man like you would suggest people like me didn't come out right. Probably better if I didn't come out at all. I could have saved myself the humiliation from my friends and family just by hiding the truth."

My neck almost snaps from shaking my head, but Javi's choppy breaths intensify.

"Look, let's just call it a night. You can Uber to our Airbnb, and I will stay with my G-mom tonight. I can grab my stuff in the morning after you leave."

I stretch my arms out to his, terrified to let something special leave my life again. "Javi, it's not like that."

Javi's glassy eyes fight back the tears.

"It was stupid, and I regret it. Just leave it be." Without thinking, I grip his shoulders and stare deep into his eyes, hoping he can see my true intentions. But he flinches, surrendering to my grip under incandescent street lighting. I watch as a few tears flow down Javi's face, his gaze avoiding mine.

"Please don't hurt me," he whispers.

That last sentence breaks me. I am not angry, Javi; I have feelings for you. All I want is to reveal my true self and express gratitude for our time shared. Javi helped me develop a healthy understanding of romance in the middle of my grief. Now, witnessing the emotional turmoil that I caused in this same person hits me hard. Harder than any sledgehammer striking my heart. The swirling thoughts in my head are fueling feelings of dread and shame. I have to show him what he means to me.

Instead of speaking, I close the distance between us and lean in closer to Javi, allowing our lips to meet with no resistance. I maintain my position for a few seconds before dragging away, my heart pounding as I gaze at Javi, who undresses me with his eyes. Both of us are mute, frozen in place. Only the sirens in the distance cut through our tension. I try to decipher his expression, worried that I may have crossed a line.

Before I can search for an answer, his hands locate my jawline, and he pulls me in for another kiss. The touch of his lips sends joy from the base of my lips to the tips of my toes. Our tongues intertwining ignites a brass orchestra within me. I hold him close to my chest, afraid to let go of this precious opportunity. I tremble at the thought of losing such intense emotions, fearful of facing the consequences. This instant reminds me of our night, a mix of sweetness tainted by my bitter thoughts.

However, I resist the temptation to withdraw, and we embrace as if the world is ending tonight.

Chapter 8

September 30, 2025

"What's your deal with Ash?" I slump against the frame of the bed when my tired eyes shift from the pages of my textbooks to the TV screen.

Machi extends her hand toward the TV while lying prone. "How can someone train Pokémon for twenty-five years yet only become a champion once? I achieved that title within a week of starting a new game. It's mind-boggling how this guy gets a whole TV series every year, showcasing his lackluster skills. I must admit, I am happy that he retired because he's overrated."

I laugh weakly, gravity pinning me to the bedroom floor. "You were not this animated back when we watched Black and White as kids."

"That's because I didn't realize he sucked when we were kids."

"Should I call the writers and demand that the main character be Machi-Zai Chen?"

"First, it's Chen Shui Machi-Zai, something my best friend should know. Maybe if you still played Pokémon with me, my profile would jog your memory."

"I need a Nintendo Switch to play the new games."

Machi reaches over to her iPad and starts clicking away. "Don't worry, I will get it for your birthday. We can both be Pokémon champions together again."

"Machi, I don't have any Pokémon games anymore."

"Don't worry," she says. "I can get the current games out now. I have put off buying them, but I want to play that generation. Maybe we can race each other over the Thanksgiving break. That way, we can be ready for the next generation being released next year."

"So much for 'saving your money,' right?" I say. My remark sparks no reaction in Machi as she taps on her iPad.

"Pokémon is always an exceptional purchase."

I want to protest, but arguing with Machi is like denying a blessing from a priest in church, especially with Pokémon. One step into Machi's room and a visual explosion of Pokémon memorabilia hit me from every nook and cranny. Vibrant posters adorn the walls, with the Unova Region Pokedex above her bookcase being the biggest. Plush toys of various sizes scatter across the shelf, with one particular toy catching my attention. It sits on the top shelf, the fifth one from the left, beckoning with its vibrant blue color and charming otter complexion.

I used to nestle Oshawott in my childish hands after my mom bought it for Christmas. It was my favorite starter Pokémon from the Pokémon White game she bought me for my birthday a month earlier. That Nintendo DS screen stayed twelve inches from my face when I wasn't in class. I could have probably sung the familiar background tunes from memory when engaging in playful gym battles.

It was during one of these gym battles when I caught Machi staring at me in the hallway. She looked down at her own Nintendo DS. Machi was new that school year, and we had always crossed paths on the bus rides and in algebra class, but she never spoke unless she was answering every question our teachers asked. I'm not sure what possessed me to leave my bottom locker to walk over to her, but I am glad I did.

When I asked her what she was playing, she showed me her new Pokémon Black game. This led to us discussing our family struggles, experiences, and our shared love for Oshawott. For her first birthday at our school, I extended my cherished plush Oshawott toward her after school on the bus ride home. The rest was history.

Machi continues, but her body tenses. "Soccer is costly. Save money because you do not make money. I know you will get a sponsorship deal this season to help pay, but I have to take out loans to get a degree. A degree my parents want me to have and…"

"Are you okay?"

"Yeah. Yeah. Yeah." Machi's fingertips tap the screen. Rapid breaths escape her nostrils with each word.

I frown. "Are you sure?"

"Shane's birthday was today."

"I'm sorry, Machi."

"It's fine. The day drains me. Since I didn't go home this year, we met over Zoom, which I thought would be better for me, at least. But the typical family shit always hits me hard, especially with the obligations as the last remaining child of the Chen family. After underwhelming my mother with my grades and refusing my father's unsolicited marriage arrangements, they silently sat at Shane's shrine. Mom would, in tears, uttered a few memories of Shane when we were kids. Dad burned the offering and offered more prayers. Afterward, I watched as they split Shane's favorite birthday cake without saying a word."

"I'm sure they recognize your successes. Believe me, it's hard to grieve losing a family member. It still doesn't register that my mom has been gone for almost a year."

She shrugs and glances back in my direction. "I know. How do you handle her loss?"

"Well, on her birthday, my father laid flowers on her grave. On the day we lost her, I had just celebrated my birthday with the people I love."

"Oh, right. I forgot about that."

A painful silence fills the room. We exchange a few awkward glances before I reach into my mind for a conversation changer. "Are you doing anything this weekend?"

"No, why?"

"Maybe you should come out with me after the Backyard Brawl game next weekend. You deserve a fun distraction."

"By watching you play soccer?" A smile curves under her pointed look. "Where's the fun in that?"

I roll my eyes, but reciprocate with a smile back at her. "You would do me a favor."

"How am I doing you a favor by watching you play?"

"You would be the only supporter there."

"Your dad?"

"He's unavailable right now. Please come."

"Fine! Don't pull my leg."

We return our attention to Ash and Pikachu, interacting

with wild Pokémon on the screen. We watch until Ash talks to the rather suggestive girl at the Nimbasa City Ferris Wheel.

"I can't believe we watched this show as kids."

Machi turns back in my direction. "What do you mean?"

"Look what that girl said to Ash!"

"So it's okay when it's guys on your gay app?"

My cheeks burn when she mentions the app, completely forgetting she found it on my phone. "It's not the same."

"I thought it was a social networking app."

"It is, but…" I lose my rebuttal in my head, but there is no point in arguing. She's right that this app devolved into a hookup app. This wasn't always the case, but I have little hope in men rebooting soon. It's cheaper to just have a quick fling without altering daily life.

Images of that night with Romero replay in my head, and I wonder if that situation is best for me now. We go about our normal lives with a little spice on the side. Well, a lot of spice given how hot that sex was. Romero and I could play multiple rounds until we're bored and just walk away with no repercussions. Plus, we share similar schedules, so it's easier to engineer some secret rendezvous.

I didn't envision a hoe phase for myself, but it's an appealing thought and can help me move on from Javi. The only risk is Angelica. Yes, I know it's shitty of me to consider this again, but my body craves him. Romero's an addictive drug, and I know I need another fix.

"It is, but what?" Machi teases.

"Nevermind."

"So it is a hookup app then."

I ignore her.

Machi drops her iPad on her nightstand before lying prone on her bed. "Ok, don't get your feelings hurt. Have you found anyone to 'talk' to on the app?"

I avoid her gaze, but my flushed cheeks give me away.

"Don't be boring. Tell me!"

I roll my eyes. "Fine," I say, retrieving my phone.

I show her Romero's profile as Mister E on the app, gripping the phone tight in case she tries to steal the phone again.

"Not bad. I can see the appeal, but it could be a catfish."

"Believe me, it's even better in person."

She stares at me wide-eyed. "You already…?"

I nod before she finishes.

"And you both…?"

I nod before she finishes.

"How was it?"

"The sex was intense and hot."

"We love that. Anything happen after?"

I want to say we lay naked on a lumpy bed while my ex's new hit single played on loop from his bathroom speaker until it died. I would say I tried to turn off his speaker, but he swaddled me so hard that he trapped me. If I had my way, I would tell her how I tortured myself with my past and my poor decisions. But I don't say any of this, mostly for my benefit. Machi would kill me for all of it.

"He just left afterwards. We haven't messaged each other since." The last part is not a lie. Romero has left my last message on read.

"Good enough to become a repeat offender?"

I nod again. "I don't see why not."

"Okay. Do you know much about him?"

I take a beat to choose my words carefully. I don't want to lie to my best friend, but I also don't want to reveal everything all at once. It's not that I don't trust Machi to keep my secrets. Quite the opposite in fact. Given that she knows Angelica, I would rather protect her than expose her. "I don't know him too well, but I see him around campus. He's in a similar situation to me, and wasn't interested in revealing too much about himself."

Machi considers this. "Are you okay with that?"

"I think it's better that way. It prevents a messy situation later down the road and helps avoid another USE predicament." Now I feel crestfallen. "I thought about him after the hookup."

Machi raises her eyebrows. "I thought you said you were over USE boy."

"Me too, but I was wrong. I thought moving here would help the healing process and force me to focus on soccer. I know he was my first relationship with a guy, but that was the worst heartbreak. Moving on is more challenging than I expected."

"I'm sorry to hear that."

I tap on the duvet's fabric. "It's fine. He's been sneaking into my mind recently. But maybe a distraction is what I need, and Mister E was fun. What do you think? Should I keep seeing him casually?"

Machi shrugs. "Well, you know I'm not a fan of hookup culture. I would rather have a man sweep me off my feet like in the movies and transport me to happily ever after. But holding onto memories of an ex is not good either. Are you ever going to tell me his name?"

I exhale a frustrated sigh.

"You know I won't. It's better you don't know because it keeps him safe."

"That's a bit overdramatic."

"I'm serious Machi."

She throws her hands in the air. " Fine. I will just figure it out and keep it to myself."

"Please don't."

She rolls her eyes, but extends her hand. "Ok Caleb. I will stop mentioning the USE boy. As long as you promise to be safe around Mister E online."

I nod and clasp my hand in hers before squeezing it. "Done."

"I almost forgot!" Machi says, releasing our grip. She reaches down from the side of her bed. The color drains from my face as Machi pulls out the pristine Javi vinyl.

"Machi, what are you doing with that?"

"I found it in the trash again! Why throw it away?"

"Because it's trash, which is the whole point of me throwing it away."

She dismisses me. "Caleb, you don't understand! This album is due to be released next month. You own this album's only physical copy. Where did you find this?"

I shrug. "It was a gift with a weird return address on the package."

This is not a complete lie, but not the full truth either. I am fully aware of who sent this.

"He sang that song that's blowing up Reeltime right now, and it sounds like your favorite style of music. You should listen to it."

I shoot her a wry smile. "I'm guessing you've listened to the album already?"

"No, I didn't. It's still in the plastic."

I look over to the vinyl and confirm Machi's statement. Javi's beauty still leaves me awestruck. She slides the record over to me. "Machi, I really don't want it."

She glares at me. "Just take a listen. I promise you will love it. If you don't, I will keep it for myself and have a collection just like you."

"Why not just take it now if I don't want to listen to it?"

"Because it was your gift, listen to it first. I'm already going to your soccer game and helping you out. The least you could do is listen to an album once for me."

I roll my eyes. "If I listen to this, will you stop hounding me about it?"

Machi crosses her arms. "Yes, and I'd better not find it in the trash again."

A heavy sigh leaves me. "Fine."

"Thank you! I want a debrief later."

"I have to listen to it now?"

"Yep, so you better get to it! I'll meet with my study group later." She claps in an overdramatic fashion and ushers me out of the room.

I drag my body across the hallway to my room with the vinyl under my armpit. Brushing my body across the desk, I squat in front of my bookcase. I run my fingers through my tiny collection of vinyl on the far left of the middle shelf, both Kehlani and Rihanna placeholders for memories locked away in my mind. I tear off the plastic wrap, exposing the pristine condition of the album.

My eyes scan over the cover, an amber-tinted Polaroid of Javi leaning against the observer tower, his silhouette outlined against the backdrop of the evening city skyline, while the faint scent of newly printed ink and paper reaches my nose. I remember that day in the park when I snapped that photo, yet I invite my nostalgia in microdose. I flip the cover around and admire the back, a simple blacked-out Polaroid with his signature in the right corner of the photo. A cursive haiku in white ink appears in the middle:

Falls In love For once
NO LAughing matter For me
The church Queen of caves

I steal an uneasy breath, pinpointing the story in every song, especially identifying his pattern of naming them. I pull off the sleeve, revealing the dark and light blue color-melt record. However, my fear restrains me. Even without Machi forcing me to, I need to listen to him.

Yet, I have exhausted all my brainpower thinking about Javi, reliving every pleasant moment and obsessing over the bad ones. If I listen to this, the songs will trigger me until I am on the verge of a mental breakdown. Once he releases his album next month, I will confront this then.

For now, I can bullshit a review for Machi. It's easy to recall the events that took place and Javi's taste in music. I slip the sleeve onto the vinyl and place it on my bookshelf.

Chapter 9

October 2, 2025

Rivalry Week is the perfect time to introduce myself as a Rottweiler. It is the most important time of the year for everyone involved in sports. For us, the Backyard Brawl originated from a family dispute in the early 1900s and has grown into a fierce rivalry between Southeastern State and the University of Southeastern athletics. This always guarantees bedlam on the field, even when the match lacks competitiveness.

The USE men's soccer team has consistently outperformed SESU by winning the last seven games with a 20-3 aggregate scoreline. In addition, the USE Foxes are the three-time defending conference champions and were the runner-ups in last year's NCAA tournament. They are a team with an obsessive winning culture. I know because I was there.

But in soccer, anything is possible when facing rivals, and the SESU campus believes this year will produce a different scoreline. The university is so confident that it threw us a season kickoff party in the heart of University Hills.

It's hard to imagine having a dull experience at a bar with a bunch of college guys, but leave it to the SESU athletics' donors to make the impossible a reality. Balloons, streamers, and banners in the university's colors fill every corner of Buster's Run—the town's most popular bar. A tower of tarps hides the iconic bar and booze, and plain white tables and chairs occupy the dance floor. Paper mache soccer balls and Rottweiler-colored napkins adorn each table with corny yet encouraging signs.

"Go Rottis Go!"

"Rotti pride till I die!"

"Growling like a Rowdy Rotti!"

I'm not sure why the athletic department felt this kickoff event for us should have been this cringy. The whole venue transforms into a kid's birthday party put on by soccer moms. The parents, alumni, donors, and department staff seem to enjoy themselves, though. Most of their shouting, laughter, and clinking glasses fill the room with their intense cologne, perfume, and booze.

Vince and I stand in the bar's far corner next to the karaoke stage. Our matching black team polo shirts and khaki pants contrast with the men in sharp black suits and cowboy hats with their dates in elegant gowns surrounding us. We clutch our water bottles in our hands while they hold ranch waters and beer in theirs. I zone in and out of the conversation, which highlights a history lesson about the university's glory days. The time the football team went to the College Football Playoff. The time the football team won the conference. Our starting quarterback was a first-round NFL draft pick.

A football school without football.

I glance at the group directly in front of us. Romero sips his water bottle, appearing as bored in his conversation as I am in mine. He steals a quick glance in my direction and, unsurprisingly, grins once he sees me staring. This interaction is our new normal since that night in the cabin. We exchange a few words in person and leave everything unsaid on the app. It frustrates me not to yank him away from his conversation before I peel off his clothes in the bathroom, a fantasy that dances in my head more often than it should. The desire still eats at me as if it skipped lunch, but I restrain myself. At least for now.

I laugh at the end of the donor's story I wasn't paying attention to, and excuse myself when my phone rings in my pocket. The corners of my lips tick upward when I see the state police caller ID. I skip past everyone along the taped-off bar, share another side glance with Romero, and jog to the patio straight ahead before answering the phone.

A flat but husky Essex accent jolts through the phone's speaker. "Arsenal have done it again." My father's tone is as lifeless as ever, and I can't tell whether he's amazed or dejected by our favorite soccer team's game.

"I know it's incredible or dire if my father calls me about it."

A faint sigh buzzes in my eardrums. "It's the latter this time."

"I'm sorry to hear that. I didn't see the game yesterday."

"Well, I will spare you the pain. A worthless first half. A person suffering from paraplegia passes the ball better than our lads. They spend millions of pounds on their Gucci and Ferraris, but they play like Tractor Boys. I just worked a triple shift just to suffer at home. I should have slept the moment I came home, but wasted my time instead."

I sigh. "Maybe take some time for yourself, so you don't

decompress to a terrible Arsenal game. I am closer to home now, so we should schedule some time together."

"Ah, don't be daft. The Gunners are one of the few things I look forward to nowadays. It gives me a chance to talk shop with you, like the good old days. Besides, we're too busy right now."

"I know, and I am glad you called. I was getting worried there for a bit."

"I've been a busy lad. Been working more to get through this year. That's all I can do now. I hate being at the gaff alone. If I stay here too long, I'll be a few sandwiches short of a picnic."

"What about Joshua?"

"Your younger brother lives with his girlfriend's family now. He still blames me for the whole situation, so I didn't stop him."

"I'm sure that's not it."

"When the words leave his mouth, I am positive that is why he left. He blames me for her passing."

My smile tumbles down my face. The word stings its venom deep into my psyche, the same way as the first time I found out.

"He and her family. I loved your mother, and I never knew she was so depressed. I thought she just needed space. If I had known…" His voice cracks before the whimper.

"Dad, it's okay. I know."

I won't say my father made our lives easy either. The fights were brutal between my parents during my mother's last few months with us. He was absent more often while working hard for promotion, but his bosses overlooked him constantly.

When he was home, he would blow off steam on us. Not physically, but verbally. There wasn't a day without a screaming match between family members.

If it wasn't my dad and mom, it was Joshua and my dad. They are clones of each other, even down to their combative spirits. My mom always tried to manage the situation with my father to maintain our safety. My brother and I were her priority, and she fought to keep us safe. And through the worst arguments, she kept us safe and never left us. So I can say with confidence that my father is not the reason she's gone. It's sad to see him not realize it.

He exhales deeply while I peer out into the parking lot, watching large passing cars fight for the skinniest parking spots. Some cars give up and merge onto the main road, heading as far west as I can see before the setting sun swallows them into the horizon.

"Did you have time to look at the game schedule I sent you?"

"I haven't looked. Like I said, I finished three bloody shifts this morning and just turned on the game. We are working through a staff shortage and increasing chaos, so I am heading to bed after this. I'm sorry, but…"

"I get it." My father disappoints me again, but I disguise it well.

"Our finances require me to work impossible hours to stay afloat. Hopefully, this extra effort will lead to something good for once. I need it."

"I hope so too."

"I promise I will make a game once I can get back on my feet."

"I understand."

A long, uncomfortable silence draws out, only our breathing is audible through the phone.

"You still carry that trophy around with you?" he asks.

"Yes, I keep it with me all the time. Rarely leave the house without it tucked away in my bag."

"At least you got some use out of it."

"I wanted to treat your gift with the love it deserved."

"Don't get soft on me. My drunken old man gave that to me out of spite when I left England. Blabbering about how I will never experience joy as a Yank when I leave. I almost threw it out if it weren't for your mother. She wanted to keep that as an heirloom for you. I figured since she was gone, you would have tossed it."

My mouth dries up at the cynicism in his voice. Why on earth would he tell me that? I want to cuss him out, but I hear the whistle on his TV through the phone. A relief I didn't know I needed.

"All right, son. I'm hopping in the shower and fixing my breakfast before heading to bed once the match ends. Love you."

"Love you too," I mutter, unsure how deep that sentence goes.

My iPhone beeps, echoing from my ear before I slide it into my pocket. My words feel light, holding as much as the dry air brushing my cheek. I guess this means you aren't coming tomorrow, but no surprise again.

I take no time reflecting and return inside to the vibrant crowd engulfed in conversation. Only a few seconds pass before a booming shout from Coach Ramsey cuts through the chatter, causing everyone to scatter in different directions like a well-practiced fire drill.

I sit next to Vince with the rest of my teammates. As we settle into our seats, the casual and relaxed atmosphere of the meet and greet falls into a hushed silence, and we turn our attention toward the podium at the front of the room.

"How are you feeling?" Vince whispers.

"Fatigued." I look at him with heavy eyes that feel glued to my face. My conversation with my father tightened a knot of nerves in my stomach.

Vince shifts his attention toward me, revealing his infectious smile. "That's typical of new players after a few weeks. You're doing well, especially since you are starting tomorrow."

This brings a smile to my face. "I was excited to see our names on the board in our best positions, so I guess we are doing something right."

"Yes, sir! I look forward to seeing it play out in the season, especially with how bad our field is. The field is a patchwork of rough, uneven terrain, with new divots scattered across the once-manicured grass. It looks untouched for years. And even the..."

A bulky southern man dressed in a black suit and a bright tan tie walks up to the podium. "Good evening, everyone. I'm Bill Soldano, your athletic director. I'd like to express my gratitude to our donors, campus administration, and university board members who are here today. And let me say, this is an exciting time to be a Rowdy Rottweiler!"

The audience explodes in deep howls and applause.

"Our men's soccer program has been a major focus for us this year, and a special project I am overseeing. If I'm honest,

I'm not familiar with winning a soccer match, but I know how to build championship-winning programs. Every program in our school's history has done it when I oversee their progress. Given my family's fresh interest in the sport, I want to focus on this team.

When I took on this role, my top priority was hiring Coach Jack Ramsey as our head coach from our rivals. I'm thrilled with the progress we've seen so far, and we have high hopes for this season, especially now that we're part of the new American South Conference. As many of you know, my department and I made history last year by signing one of the biggest deals in our school's history to become a founding member of this conference, which helped broker a deal to sell exclusive streaming rights to ESPN to broadcast all our home games this season."

Everyone applauds.

"Now, with all these blessings the Lord is showing this way, let us remember what makes this school the best there ever was. When you put on that jersey tomorrow, I want you to encapsulate the rottweilers' spirit. You are one of Buster's boys, so show all the powerful qualities of loyalty, protectiveness, and strength that will help you succeed in the conference this season. Stay loyal to those who support your success, including teammates, coaches, classmates, and fans. Protect each other on the field during challenges.

And as it's written in Ephesians 6:10, 'Finally, be strong in the Lord and in the strength of his might.' Our university motto is 'Pro Ecclesia, Pro Amerigo.' For the Church, For America. So it's only right that we invoke the Lord's good name to help us on our journey this season. I was actually in church thinking about this, but our rival, the University of Southeastern, ended up in the Western division instead of our Eastern division. I feel it was God's plan to separate us, so we host them in the first conference championship here. Maybe we'll win if I keep going."

The donors laugh while the team sits in silence.

"I'm kidding, boys. You are a better team than your winless record suggests. Personally, I think the soccer facilities are to blame for our record. We are well aware of the dire condition of the soccer complex, and we are taking steps to address this issue. This year, we will begin the much-needed repairs. Instead of searching for off-campus facilities to host games this season, we have identified a short-term solution. The university is cooperating with the NCAA's investigation into the football team's hazing allegations, as you may know.

The NCAA has already suspended the team for this season, pending the final report. The president and I want to emphasize that hazing is unacceptable. The lack of a football season is difficult for the University Hills community and SESU. However, the city council and I have agreed to secure additional funding and improve the state of your facilities, which eases our financial losses.

With the upcoming World Cup being hosted by the US in the coming years, I believe it is in the university's best interest to increase the visibility of both the men's and women's soccer teams. Therefore, I propose that both teams use the Rottweiler's Den for this season."

Chapter 10

October 3, 2025

I ogle at my camera screen, capturing the moment of my first official match as an SESU player. The transformed Rottweiler's Den, a horseshoe of four-storied tall bleachers wrapped in a cocoon of steel, reminds me of the grandeur of modern soccer stadiums in England. The stands, in the school's proud, bright tan and black colors, present a stunning visual contrast against the blue sky. Sounds of excited chatter fill the air as students fill the stands, their voices echoing off each tier of bleachers.

In the North End, a massive student section scrapes the back of one goal up to the rafters, creating an electric atmosphere that allows fans to be right on top of the action. The smell of cut grass mixes with the aroma of fresh paint, tingling my nostrils and creating a sense of anticipation. The pitch itself is a luxurious sight to behold with its vibrant green color, a feast for the eyes compared to the absence of quality on our practice field. Playing on such a high-quality surface is a dream come true for me.

It's a miracle to play in the stadium this season, given football's issues, so I don't take this privilege for granted. A sense of excitement and gratitude overwhelms me, and it sets my mind right for tonight. This feels more than just a match. I pull my phone closer and review my panorama to capture the perfect first Reeltime story post at SESU, one that will etch into my memory forever. After splicing my videos and pictures together, I tag the Rottweiler's Den geolocation before hitting the 'post' button.

I turn and follow my teammates, all dressed in our matching black suits with bright tan ties, into the 1000-square-foot party atmosphere at the back of the tunnel. As I tiptoe, fierce cologne and athletic wraps fill my nostrils, mingling with the faint aroma of foam rollers. The thumping bass of the rave music reverberates in my chest, blending with the excited chatter and occasional roar of testosterone-fueled shouts. The sea of half-naked bodies undulating to the rhythm creates a kaleidoscope of movement and energy.

Once I navigate through an animated crowd, my eyes land on my new locker, a crisp black kit hanging inside, the number eight pressed against the fabric, the same color as my tie. I throw my bag into the cubby and assess all my gear for tonight. I peel off my coat jacket and lay out the black warm-up top across my chair, exposing the 'SESU' letters colored on the front, similar to the number on the back. My fingers brush against the fresh Nike cleats, whose vibrant colors match the home kit.

At the top of my locker, I gaze up at my last name, written in all caps, the same name that graces the starting lineup board. It's all the motivation I need for my smile to spread across my face, and my cheeks tingle with the warmth of accomplishment. Everything is perfect. The pulsating music and the surge of caffeine coursing through my veins pale compared to my excitement and anticipation.

I peel off the rest of my clothes down to my underwear and observe the men scattered across the floor. Their bodies contort and shift as they balance on foam cylinders or stretch out over a heated game of soccer-based tennis. Each one of them looks as crazy as a bull rider atop an angry bull, the anticipation building, but the gate remains closed. Once the gate opens, chaos ensues, and everyone focuses their attention on us.

I reach over to my bag and shuffle through my toiletries until I pull out my replica trophy. I kiss the trophy and lock it in the cabinet in the right corner.

"Love and miss you, Mom. I hope you are okay up there and watch over me tonight. Send me a sign letting me know you got me?"

No sign from above came, but that didn't stop me from completing my pregame routine.

After slipping on my shorts, I sit in my chair and wrap my shin guards with pre-wrap. I cut the bottoms off my soccer socks and slid them over the tops of my legs, pulling them high enough that the game socks cover the white base socks I train in. My training socks feel more comfortable than the standard game socks. I tighten the laces of my cleats last and pull up video highlights of Martin Ødegaard searching for inspiration. It's monotonous but superstitious.

Most of my success on the field comes from my preparation for it. After about an hour of analyzing their skills, Coach Ramsey walks through the door and over to the dry-erase board. He grabs the first marker available before he scribbles the starting formation on the board.

"Pay attention, boys. When we regain possession, let's keep the game fast-paced. For this, I need Vince to play past the holding mids by passing forward in between lines, into this area," he says, circling the space between the defenders on the screen.

"Once Caleb receives the ball here, Romero can cut in from the wing. And Andres should make a run off the big donkey center-back's right shoulder as Caleb drives forward into the space. It's important to note that the right-back ball watches and lacks speed in covering. If we can attack quickly, they won't be able to recoup in time to stop what's coming at them."

He circles Vince's and Duncan's names. "In defense, it is important that you two keep us organized in the back. Communicate with everyone to ensure the defensive blocks are tight. They can have the ball as much as they want in the back, but as they inch closer to our half, we have to engage them. Both of you boys must have the awareness to trigger Andres and Caleb to press."

He writes one last word on the whiteboard before he circles it. Then, he turns around to face us. "For today's game, I need you to remember this one important word," he emphasizes while he points to it. "*Discipline.* You must stay focused and composed in this game. Discipline and a killer instinct will lead us to victory. They will aim to dominate possession and exhaust us. Stick to our defensive formation until we spot our opportunities. Let's channel our energy into pressing. Keeping possession of the ball will conserve energy. To succeed, our game plan requires everyone to be disciplined. When we make them panic and lose unity, that's when we strike. Every pass, header, and shot must be purposeful and confident. Show them no mercy and give our all. Remember, they were concerned when they faced us last year. They only won 1-0 twice, but they lost some talented players from last year."

I shiver when Coach Ramsey's gaze locks onto me, his intense eyes penetrating my soul. I see he's focused on me because he knows I want this win as badly as he does. Revenge is all I have on my mind.

"Discipline is key. We need to bring our absolute maximum intensity to this match. Make a powerful statement and captivate the crowd in the opening minutes. Let's show the conference that SESU has arrived, and we're here to win! Tonight, we can't afford to hold back. Let's leave no room for doubt and take no prisoners, lads." He grabs his chair, lifts it, and slams it into the ground three times. "Let's fucking go!"

The locker room erupts into a frenzy of shouts and cheers. Duncan raises his fist in the room's center. We all rush to gather around him. "All right, lads, on me."

We huddle together as a team, our voices echoing with excitement and determination.

"Family on me, family on three," we chant, our words vibrating the surrounding room. Fueled by adrenaline, we explode out of the locker room, our footsteps echoing against the walls.

We line up in the tunnel, just steps away from our opponents. With his whistle wrapped around his left hand, the referee stands in front of the captains, ensuring both teams are ready. The roar of the crowd envelops the stadium, a symphony of cheers and chants that reverberates in my ears. As I step onto the field, the bright lights blind me for a moment, illuminating the sea of cheering fans. The announcer's voice lingers in the air, blending with the sounds of the crowd, instigating a cacophony of excitement and anticipation.

"... and your Southeastern State Rottweilers!"
The fans sway and twirl to the lively beat of the marching band's rendition of the school song, their cheers drowning out any doubts about whether University Hills would support their soccer team. A prickling sensation jitters across my skin as I absorb my surroundings.

We walk out of the tunnel with eager anticipation, taking in the sight of the Rottweiler-costumed performer emerging, leading Buster XII out to the field. The crowd erupts into a frenzy as their beloved mascot twirls on his leash. He sits down on the touchline, and the fans mute themselves moments later. The University ROTC color guard steps onto the field, pre-senting the United States flag. Some of my teammates bow their heads, while Vince places his hand over his heart. There is an eerie hush before the band plays the national anthem, and the American flag appears on the jumbo screen opposite the student section. I place my hand over my heart while its familiar melody whistles in my ears, but I inhale and exhale for a prolonged minute to soothe my thoughts.

The thunderous applause echoed through the stadium when the anthem finished, engulfing me in a wave of sound and emotion. The Rottweiler mascot retreats with Buster XII to their lounge area at the side of the field, their departure marked by cheers and applause. Following cherished athletic traditions, Greta VII, the women's mascot, takes center stage, her trainer guiding her toward the tunnel. The fans shower her with love and adoration, just as they did for her male counterpart.

The stadium falls silent as Duncan calls the starters to huddle left of the center circle.

"Boys, come in!" he says.

Duncan positions himself at the heart of the huddle, taking charge as he gives assertive instructions and shares his own unique brand of motivational wisdom. I interlock my arms with Romero and Andres, facing the passionate home supporters.

The fans extend their hands with the iconic Rotti's fist gesture, a hand with a curved index and pinkie finger, while the middle and ring fingers sit on top of the pulled-in thumb. With a sense of discipline, they stand tall, resembling soldiers at attention. A percussionist strikes the snare drum twice, followed by four rapid beats, building anticipation in the air. Then, on the seventh beat, the band ignites the fight song, prompting the fans to sing along with fervor and thrust their Rotti fists toward the field.

Go on our rowdy Rottis.
Roaming the South fierce and true
Aloof from others' transgressions
But they fight against the crude!
Come on, our fighting Rottis
Fearless heroes for you and me
I would fear if they came running
Right from good ole SESU!

"On my mark!" Duncan says. We sway to Duncan's chants

and echoes in unison. I follow the lead, but I'm unsure how to follow.

"One team..." Duncan shouts.

"... for eternity!" the boys respond.

"One dream..."

"...a champion's ring!"

"One theme..."

"... leave a legacy!"

Duncan positions himself at the center, lowering his body into a squat on his heels. In unison, the fans interlock their arms, mirroring our movements. They sway from side to side, following the rhythm of Duncan's slaps on the ground. As they move, their deep murmurs reverberate throughout the stadium, resembling the growl of a gravel-voiced Rottweiler.

WOOF, WOOF, WOOF, WOOF, WOOF

CHAPTER 11

October 3, 2025

Five minutes into the game, we wasted no time asserting our dominance over the Foxes. Despite our all-black uniforms absorbing the scorching evening sun, we run across the pitch in a controlled yet chaotic manner. Coach Ramsey delivers his orders with a commanding British accent, leaving no room for misinterpretation. We control the game, but struggle to score despite our efforts. However, the fans amplify the energy within the stadium.

We get our first sniff of a goal when I intercept a loose pass just inside the opposition's half of the field. Without hesitation, I dash into the open space ahead of me, gliding past defenders with the ball glued to my right foot. I feel so fresh and pain-free, as if I had never suffered an injury in my life. I slalom around the field until I reach our opponent's 18-yard box, where a formidable wall of bulky defenders blocks my path. While assessing the situation, I scan the field and spot Romero on my right, but he's surging forward into an offside position.

Luckily, Andres cuts inside from the wide area, display-ing his eagerness to receive my pass. I deceive my defender by feinting right, which shifts the defender's weight. Then, I thread the ball through an opening in the defense. Andres sprints toward the ball, wrapping his right foot around it. The Rottweiler emblem on Andres's jersey becomes visible below the neckline when I see him strike the ball into the top corner of the net, triggering thunderous celebration throughout the stadium. Finally, a deserved reward for our efforts.

We waste no time celebrating, aware that USE is still one of the best teams in the country. The game is still there to be won. An opportunity for a counterattack arises a handful of minutes later. Vince exemplifies his aerial strength when he heads the ball away from the danger of the opponent's corner kick. Taking advantage of the loose ball, Romero transitions from defense to offense and charges at the unprepared defense. While he leads the charge, I extend my stride into the space off his left shoulder, my words dancing at the back of my throat.

"In space. Now!"

Romero gazes upwards and sends the ball ahead of me, but it curves outward into the corner. I adapt my run to retrieve the ball, shifting it onto my front foot, preparing myself to face the approaching defender. The muscular opponent in front of me cannot stop me again, when my confidence and talent unite to produce one of my finest displays of skill.

While inching forward with delicate touches, I engage in an intricate game of cat and mouse with the defender. I tempt the defender with the ball, waiting for the perfect opportunity to make my move. Then, I perform a series of step-overs and body feints, further enticing him. However, this time, the defender remains unfazed and resolute. Undeterred, I scan the field for a potential backup plan. I spot Andres, who replicates the same run that led to the opening goal just minutes ago.

In sync with Andres, I dribble the ball with my right foot, just outside the left corner of the box. The defender matches me stride for stride, blocking my view ahead of him. I pretend to pass the ball and instead step over it, shifting the defender off balance again, and pushing the ball past him into the space ahead. Without hesitation, I strike the ball with all the force a once-broken leg can generate.

The ball grazes the trimmed grass just millimeters above the ground as it veers sharply toward the inside of the post. The goalkeeper adjusts his position, extending his body and stretching out his hand. However, I know he dives out of courtesy because he's in no position to stop this shot. As the ball finds its mark, the net emits a satisfying crackle, while gravity pulls the goalkeeper downward.

A surge of euphoria and delirium courses through my veins, electrifying my senses as I absorb the exhilarating moment. The sight of my teammates abandoning the bench and sprinting toward me, their faces filled with pure elation, fills me with an indescribable joy. The roar of the crowd, deafening and triumphant, reverberates in my ears, adding to the crescendo of emotions. As I race toward the corner, my heart leaping through my chest, a weight lifts off my shoulders, as if someone released me of my burden. A sigh of relief escapes my lips before my smile etches my face.

Before my teammates close in from all directions, I form USE's trademark Fox fist, a copy of SESU's minus the thump extending outward, feeling the cool breeze brush against my fingers. The crowd erupts in jubilation when I tap the outer part of my left hand against my wrist, the sight of my karate chop animated on the stadium's screen. In this triumphant moment, I shed my old self, transforming into a Rowdy Rotti.

When the celebrations ease, I blow a kiss into the air—a tribute to my mother when she attended a game when I scored a goal. I picture her face when I was a kid. The blood would rush to her cheeks as she would catch it in the air and pump her fist, leaning on my father for support. She never changed through middle and high school, but last season everything changed. All because I told her the truth about me. She would meet my same salute with a bleak expression before she would turn away to avoid my gaze. She would later stop showing up altogether. Part of me wonders if she is turning away in heaven now. The referee steals my time to contemplate it with two whistles for us to return.

...

The referee blew his whistle to start a second half unfamiliar to the first. USE, true to form, showcases their possession-heavy style of football, the ball gliding more smoothly from one player to another, unlike in the first half, creating a mesmerizing dance on the pitch. We maintained our consistency in defensive structure and executing the traps that Coach Ramsey outlined on the whiteboard during our pre-game session.

I snatch Vince's defensive header, my footsteps pounding on the grass as I charge into the opposition's half. I deftly play the ball into the open space the moment Romero bursts past his defender, my cleats scraping against the turf as the top of my cleat elevates the ball into the air. Romero cushions the ball with his instep and carries the ball to the corner with electric pace. He wraps his foot around the ball when he's a couple of feet from the corner flag, sending the ball into a dizzying twirl. Andres sprints toward the goal and looks hungry for the taste of a goal. He lunges forward, stretching his left foot toward the ball, the impact sending an echo to slice the tension in the stands. But his effort falls short because the ball veers three feet wide of the back post. I clasp my hands to my face, bewildered that he cannot score again.

The crowd erupts in a symphony of cheers and applause, with their collective excitement creating a wave of energy that ripples across the entire pitch. Inhaling the freshly mown grass, I lock eyes with Romero as he jogs back to his starting position. With a quick thumbs-up, I try to convey my support and gauge where we are in our own lives, hoping for some response. Romero ignores me and instead turns to focus on the USE goalkeeper taking the goal kick. My face contorts into a grimace, my muscles tensing as I shift my gaze toward the ball sinking down toward me.

A tall strawberry blond man races toward me in my peripheral vision. I grimace at his chiseled features, accentuated by the floodlights, radiating his aura of opulence, which he works so hard to project. I ignore him and leap off the ground, and focus on the ball on a collision course with my forehead. A whiff of Dior cologne is my only warning before his arm crashes into my hip, destabilizing my balance midair.

Fortunately, my back collides with the grass instead of my leg, my breath rushing out of me faster than the air out of a balloon's end. I turn my head and glare at the sight of his meticulously groomed hair and pearly white veneers. All I want to do is beat Roger Astor's pampered ass for everything, not just this cheap shot. The referee shows a yellow card, but it hardly justifies the excruciating pain I am in.

Coach Ramsey detonates in an explosion of rage. "Are you serious?! What do you mean that's a yellow card?! He's clearly trying to harm the player. There's no intention to actually go for the ball. That deserves a red card without a doubt. It's a red card all day long. *All day!*"

Roger walks over to me and gives me a tense pat on the arm. "Keep this up and I will hit you where it hurts…again," he whispers.

"Fuck you, Roger!" I scowl, gritting my teeth. But the words come out as a faded whisper.

Roger smirks as he steps away from me, jogging past Romero.

"Better luck next time, roomie!"

His cocky grin boils my blood all over again, the same way it has ever since I met that prick. That entitled shit has everything going for him, the same way he had everything going against me at USE. But I can't change that now. I snap out of my tangent when Soleil runs over to me. "You okay? Where is the pain?"

I clench my jaw, unable to utter a word. I try to point to my back, trying to restore oxygen to my lungs.

"Are you pointing to your leg?"

I shake my head, but rub my right tibia anyway to check. Much to my relief, no pain throbs from the healed break. She helps me sit up, still regaining my bearings.

"Did you hit your head? Any headaches or migraines?" She moves her fingers around, observing how my eyes dart around in their sockets, following her instructions.

"I don't think so," I say as soon as my forehead mimics my

heartbeat. I see Coach staring at me, and it unsettles me. "I think I just got winded. "

Soleil nods and pulls me to my feet, offering support as the referee directs us off the pitch. As I look up, I see Vince and others huddled around Coach, who is offering concise coaching points. I steady my breathing as I walk toward the touchline, but my head and body aches are sharper with each step.

Coach Ramsey walks over when the referee blows his whistle for the play to continue. I turn and face the field. "Is he okay to play?" he asks, staring at Soleil. She glances sideways at me but affirms Coach Ramsey. "All right. You can return after the next dead ball. Tell Romero and Melvin to rotate back into the press. Start demanding the ball more…"

I acknowledge the instructions, but they fade away as if carried by the wind. The only thing that sticks in my mind is the throbbing pain receptors that assault my cerebellum. Nagging soreness after Roger's low blow is uncharted territory for me because I never get injured. Well, at least in games. This is the best time to speak up, but I suppress the pain, aware of the high stakes of the match. My father drilled his principles of adulthood into me from a young age, his main one being to overcome pain rather than succumb to it. In hindsight, I should have questioned this, but my father is a police officer, so there's no use arguing.

"You got that?" Coach Ramsey asks.

"Yes, Coach," I say. Even though the bulk of the information flew over my head, I am ready to compete again.

As the referee waves toward me on the touchline, my first few steps mimic a runner with an ankle weight on my feet.

Despite the discomfort, I do my best to fake miraculous healing as the game continues. At first, it was a few steps in and out of space, but nothing too extraneous. The game inches closer to conclusion, and the bright realization occurs that we are minutes away from a win. One so historic, I feel the fans shake the Rottweiler's Den stands, ready for a party.

As the celebration continues, Vince wins the ball and passes it to our lean midfielder, Melvin, who takes his lengthy frame forward into space with one touch and fires a pass in my direction. Although the ball bends a few inches away from me, I take a few limp steps into the space of its path. The unbalanced center-back closes the gap between me, looking as eager to hurt me as Roger did. I sense the danger earlier and strategically stick out my foot to let the ball hit my sore ankle, redirecting it toward a charging Melvin.

While Melvin regains possession, I dodge contact with the defender and hobble into the created space. This allows Melvin, Andres, and Romero to operate ahead, creating opportunities for our team. However, the USE player read our tactics and reorganized its defense, blocking off almost all options. Melvin plays the ball to an isolated Romero, who is facing two defenders. I move over to support.

"Play me!" I scream at him.

Romero ignores my pleas and takes on the defenders ahead.

The two defenders crash their bodies onto his, knocking Romero off balance and freeing the ball from his control. Somehow, the ball ricochets in my direction, whether from a deliberate pass from Romero or an unsuccessful dribble, and rolls across my body.

In a split second, I push the ball forward using the outside of my left foot, creating sufficient room for my now unsteady run-up. I plant my weak ankle and strike the ball with my "weaker" left foot. The ball soars through the air like an unidentified flying object, dancing and defying the laws of gravity. It curves beyond the goalkeeper's grasp, ultimately colliding with the back of the net.

I dash to the closest corner flag, repeating my celebration like a dance routine. I turn around to greet my teammates, all but one partaking in the camaraderie. Romero walks toward the center circle, picking at the tape wrapped around his wrist. He turns around and glares at me for a breath before jockeying back to his staring position. A hint of confusion brushes across me, but it blows away in an instant by the surrounding stimulation.

Looking back, I was oblivious to the brewing tension between us, but I would discover that part later.

Chapter 12

October 4, 2025

"To the boys...Thank you for showing those wankers from USE whose boss. Cheers, lads!"

We raise our shot glasses, the clinking audible amidst the cacophony of blaring electronic sounds and bass-bumping beats, and we swirl the shimmering liquid. With a brief inhale, I bring the glass to my lips, the pungent aroma of tequila slapping my nose. The liquid burns my throat, with hints of oak that make me wince and grimace, my face contorting in discomfort. Duncan's voice pierces through, his hoarse post-victory shouts blending with the pulsating beat at Buster's Run.

"Now, let's find some post-game muff."
I shake my head while Duncan stumbles over to Vince along the towering bar that was once covered at the banquet. He throws his right arm around Vince's shoulder to catch his balance and readjust his posture. He takes a sip of his beer in his left hand and puffs out his chest.

"We must emulate Vince here. He is a beast on the pitch, and a shagger in the sheets with this manhood." Duncan darts his hand above Vince's crotch, and Vince reacts as if he made physical contact, despite the near miss.

Duncan shifts his drink into his right hand and wraps his arm around me. "And to Caleb, my boy. You need to get a bird tonight after winning the game for us. Shagger like you deserves a good pump tonight."

I clink my glass to Duncan, which releases Duncan's grip on my shoulder as he chugs his other drink, then I maneuver over to Vince.

"Our fearless leader right there," Vince jokes. "Stumbling over to Amy with his broken English accent and lack of motor skills."

"Kinda sounds like Duncan when he's sober," I say, letting out a laugh as we clink our glasses together and take a sip of our cocktails. We both migrate away from our teammates at the bar onto a crowded dance floor sparkling under the disco light.

Calvin Harris's "This Is What You Came For" reverberates against the walls. My eyes shift toward the bar's entrance, drawn by a sudden movement from a breathtaking woman emerging in the doorway.

Her shiny bob cut sways as she closes the distance. Her smooth, light complexion glows under the dim lights of the bar. I am shocked at how she walks with confidence while she scans the room. As blaring music plays and glasses clink, she moves with subtle poise in her jet-black pumps. The polyester blend hugs her curves, accentuating the graceful silhouette she always hides. Machi sees my hand when I wave in her direction and approaches us, clutching a shimmering gold purse tightly against her stomach. The faint scent of her citrus perfume wafts toward us.

"Hello, Mr. Superstar," she says, winking at me.

"Well, hello there. My name is Caleb. It's so nice to meet you." I reach out my hand in her direction, a goofy smile etches across my face.

"Haha, hilarious." She swings her arms on her hips.

"What are you doing here? You never go out."

"I thought I would make an exception to celebrate your excellent game. I saw it live today."

"Who are you, and what have you done with my roommate?"

"Oh, shut up. Don't ruin it."

"Fine. Can I get you a drink?" I ask, raising my glass to my face.

She doesn't hesitate. "I'll take a Manhattan…and an introduction."

I almost spit the contents of my drink back into my glass. I forgot Vince was standing next to me the entire time during our conversation. There is a glint in his eye while Vince stares transfixed at Machi. She avoids his gaze playfully.

"Oh. This is Vince," I say.

"How are you?" he asks, stretching out his hand.

She looks up. "I'm better now." A tight smile forms on her face as she slips her hand into his. They linger for a moment with their greetings, and I realize what's happening.

"I am going to get those Manhattans. Be back in a bit," I say.

I weave into the pulsating crowd, their bodies swaying as they bellow the lyrics of Garth Brooks "Friends in Low Places." The bar is a stark contrast to the team's pre-conference banquet held here just days ago. Youth and psychedelia encapsulate the inviting atmosphere that embodies University

Hills' party spirit tonight, and there is a free-spirited euphoria that intoxicates my surroundings. I receive several celebratory shoulder slaps as everyone opens a path for me to the bar.

After I reach the left corner of the bar, I take in the rich native woods and the subtle fragrance of different beverages from the town's most extensive assortment of alcohol stored in a massive, striking old-world bookcase behind the bar. Buster's Run boasts four massive flat screens above, stretching across the impressive 44-foot frame, showing a mix of sporting events, music videos, and classic show reruns.

A tall brunette behind the bar walks in my direction. I place my order and turn for my eardrums to absorb the country music, mingling with the sound of laughter and conversation. Above the dance floor, a giant disco ball twirls, casting shimmering lights across the room. The recreational area next to the bar is bustling with activity, with patrons engaging in lively conversations, the clinking of pool balls, the thud of darts hitting the board, and the nostalgic tunes of old-school arcade machines. Some exit out of the sturdy access door leading to the sprawling patio, offering a view of the bustling parking lot beyond.

This is when Angelica and Romero enter the bar, holding hands. Angelica, dressed in a simple white T-shirt and Daisy Dukes, focuses her phone on taking selfies with Romero. Romero holds onto his black cowboy hat that completes his total black vaquero outfit as he navigates through a crowd of dancers. They split in the middle of the crowd as he heads toward the opposite side of the bar, and Angelica gravitates to a group of Tri Sigmas near the patio, wearing similar outfits to hers.

He stands there alone, guarded and oblivious to his surroundings. He blew off our celebrations in the locker room, and the petty me wants to leave him to drown his sorrows in cheap beer. But one look at his long face has me second-guessing. Romero shows no signs that he's a danger to himself, but I misread my mom's situation before. I shuffle over to him and lean against the solid wood, observing Romero's profile from the side.

"Hey, so glad you showed up. You have been missing all the fun," I say, keeping a lighthearted tone.

"Been busy," Romero says, looking around at the bartenders.

"Busy?" I force some surprise into my voice.

He rolls his head toward me. "That's what I said." The sharpness in his tone pops my facade.

"Too busy to celebrate?"

"Something like that."

"Too busy right after the game?"

"No shit."

"Then what about during the match?"

Now he glares at me. "I just didn't feel like it."

"You didn't want to celebrate beating our rivals?"

"When a teammate steals your goal, it's hard to be animated."

"What are you talking about? I never stole your goal."

"I had a clean strike on goal until you swiped the ball from underneath me."

I shake my head. "I thought you passed it to me. The ball was away from you when I struck it."

He shakes his head as he signs the bill.

"Are you actually upset over this?" He ignores me, and I try to hide my irritation, but the alcohol pulls my thoughts out of me. "Or are you mad I helped break the losing streak against USE while you sat on the bench through most of it?"

He glares at me as if I had jabbed him in the stomach. "If I sucked Coach's dick as hard as you, maybe I would be in the game longer." He sips his beer.

"I think sucking dick's more your thing."

Romero spits half his beer back into his glass.

We both turn when the crowd serenades "Sweet Caroline," except replacing those words with *Faggot Foxes*, and the next line of *winning never felt so good*. Romero points at me as he walks toward the crowd. "I dedicate this song to you."

I roll my eyes, returning to face the bar. My drink couldn't have arrived sooner, because I inhale my cocktail when the bartender sets it in front of me. I'm ready to bolt as I grab Vince and Machi's drinks, but Angelica struts toward me, ignoring Romero's drink offering. She locks her eyes on me, nearly pinning me to the spot.

"Well, hello there, Mr. Superstar!" she says. Romero's surprise covers his face while watching Angelica interact with me. "Romero and I talked about how you two are killing it together on the field a minute ago. Two SESU stars on the field is a stroke of luck for this team."

Angelica's face lights up. "I have an idea! Let's capture the moment." She pulls her phone above her head, capturing a selfie with Romero and me. After typing a caption, she shoves her phone in my face. I lean back to read her post.

@the_angelica_soldano: When stars collide…

"Oh, wow. You already have over a hundred likes," I say.

"Oh, absolutely! I've built quite a substantial fan base,

which is just one benefit of being an internet sensation. I can detect a rising star. Your name is on everyone's lips around campus, and they all want a piece of you. It's fortunate that I'm the one who gets to share this moment with you, rather than those thirsty girls over there." I follow Angelica's gesture, directing my gaze toward the group of five blonde Tri Sigmas in colorful Daisy Dukes who are staring at us.

"Oh, that reminds me. Let me tag your profile." She hands me her phone with the post that has already reached 1,000 likes. I do as she asks and hand her the phone back. Romero's agitation covers his face when I look up. "Perfect. And your drinks are on the house tonight. My uncle owns this place and went to the game today. He's a fan of yours now. Also, there is something I need to ask you."

I furrow my brow and turn to Romero, who shares a confused expression toward his girlfriend. Before Angelica can finish, Romero walks between us, grasping my shoulder.

"Actually, Angel baby, I need to talk to him real quick. I will text you when I'm done," he says.

Romero pulls me away from Angelica, leading me toward the patio. Vince looks my way, raising his thumb with an uneasy look. I returned the gesture, realizing I had forgotten their drinks at the bar. I mouth the word 'sorry' before Romero and I maneuver through the standing patrons to the picnic tables. Once we reach the patio exit, we turn the corner and continue walking for a few hundred feet past closed shops. We duck out of sight by shielding ourselves by moving past the two dumpsters. After a quick glance around, Romero finally addresses me.

"Whatever Angelica asks you, say no," Romero says. I recoil

when his accusatory finger is inches from my iris. "I mean it."

"What are you talking about?"

"I am talking about my girlfriend who is trying to use you for something."

"What do you mean by that?"

"I'm not sure because she never mentioned this before." Romero rubs his head and exhales while I collect myself. "Whatever it is, just say no."

"Why?"

He creases his brow for a prolonged exhale as he tenses. "Because Angelica is only out for herself. She probably needs you as a source for her gossip videos, or worse, set you up with one of her brainless followers. And believe me, both are terrible options for us. It's worse when they force us into the same spaces more than usual."

I narrow my eyes. "Is that a bad thing?"

"Yes, it is!"

I cock my head. "What the fuck is wrong with you?"

He shakes his head while his erratic breathing increases. His words tumble out of him. "I don't want Angelica to know about us, and having you around her all the time will expose us. That relationship is everything to me, but nothing to me while you are a thing I need and…God, I need my meds."

"Romero, you are overreacting. We don't spend any time together outside of soccer. Besides, you have ignored me ever since that night in the cabin," I say in a calm tone, but more cautious with every move he makes. "We don't need to change anything."

Romero scowls at me as he paces back and forth in the skinny alley.

"Change arrived the moment you showed up. The moment we had sex. The moment you became the talk of the town. I'm addressing this compromising position instead of my pro scouting opportunities because of it."

"I assure you, if you are on a winning team, you will get scouted," I plead.

He stops cold in his tracks. His face twists as if I said the most offensive slang right at him. "Is that so? If that's the case, then why the fuck did you leave USE?" he growls.

I open my mouth, but only air flows out between my lips. Romero scoffs. "Exactly. Don't bullshit me about the game we are playing to win."

I sigh for a few exhausted seconds. "It's not like that."

"How? You won a conference title already and played for a national title last season. Yet you left."

I contemplate my next words to build a picture I am content with. "I left because of who I am."

He furrows his brow. "What does that mean?"

"I joined SESU because I needed an environment where I could only focus on soccer."

"Why here? Why University Hills?"

"Because I had to hide myself here."

"Hide yourself from what?"

I tilt my head, eyes narrowed. "What do you think?"

Romero rubs his face, looking down at the ground like a detective discovering fresh evidence. "Then why are you on D&D?"

I shrug. "Just a long, complicated story," I mutter.

We exchange another brief silence as we hear footsteps approach and walk past the dumpsters. Romero exhales and examines me while the music at the bar shifts from country to house music. He loosens his posture, as if he had released the weight off his back. "Complicated how?"

I rest against the wall, studying him. Maybe it's the moonlight, but he's acting strange in this new light. "I started hating myself for what I couldn't control, and let it affect me."

He nods. "I understand that."

I side-eye him. "Which part?"

Romero shrugs as he looks down at the ground. "I struggle with being gay too."

I glare at him. "No, you don't."

He clicks his tongue. "Ok, fine. I'm not gay because I like girls too, but I struggle to control those feelings also."

I can't tell if he's being vulnerable with me or if he's playing me. I know we sent countless NSFW messages through D&D and even explored his body in the most unconventional manner possible. But his reputation raises a bright red flag, and this filters all my observations about him. The only thing I am confident about is how embarrassed I feel knowing I have seen Romero naked before seeing his naked truth. "I guess that's good, right? It can't affect you as much."

He shrugs. "Not necessarily."

"What does that mean?"

"That night at the cabin to start."

"What about it?"

The palpable tension fills the air between us. But this feels more sultry than sour. I think he senses it too, because a grin stretches across his face. Our eyes meet, like they did before we messed up the cabin bed. I feel the arousal shifting blood down my body. "That night has been playing in my head on repeat, and it distracts me from everything in my control. But you know what bothers me the most?"

He steps closer to me while surveying the surroundings. His lips come within inches of my face as I swallow. He rubs his fingers across my denim jeans, pushing against the bulge ballooning below the fabric. Romero's eyes are hungry for lust, and I can't say he's alone. With one glance at that compressed, sculpted torso hidden behind his tight dress shirt, the air feels paper-thin around me. I suck in a breath.

"What…?"

"That you have been fucking my brain so hard…" A perfect smile shines behind his parted lips, the same lips that hover inches from my left ear. "…my body desperately craves that feeling."

I nod as he applies more pressure to my tender area, which swells to its fullest capacity. Panting replaces once-steady breathing. "Maybe we shouldn't. We can't get into trouble." Deep down, I know this is wrong, but Romero has me at his mercy. There is only one thing I crave so badly.

Romero slides his hand down my pants until he's stroking my dick. "I will go crazy if I don't."

Before I can respond, he pulls my face closer with his free hand, pressing our lips together. Initially, I reciprocate by entangling my tongue with his, and my arms slide down his waist. I bathe myself in endorphins, but my rationale twists the faucet shut.

I pull away. "Should we do this here?"

"I can't help it. I'm horny for you right now," Romero says, breathing erratically.

"What? You can't control yourself?"

Romero smirks as he lowers himself to his knees. He grabs my crotch and rubs, a sticky residue already staining my underwear. I resist the urge to fight. "Yes. I can't control myself. I like what I like."

Romero delicately traces the throbbing in my pants with his fingertips while his other hand presses against my chest, causing me to freeze in place. His eyes, desperate and mischievous, blend into a dangerous weapon that pierces through my armor against him. We remain in this position for a few moments while my heart rate elevates, awaiting his initiation. Romero never breaks eye contact as he unfastens my pants with his right hand, slipping it beneath my underwear to reveal my erect penis.

"Why fight it?" he whispers.

With his left hand, Romero guides me against the wall before squatting down to my waist. I squirm when he performs oral sex on me. His tongue slithers all around my penis as he covers every inch, sending a warm jolt across my body. His mouth vacuums out the inhibitions from me, leaving only desire for this moment. I bite my lip as he twists and grips my cock. His force is so intense that it rocks my balance. He finds his rhythm that keeps my body clenched between the plateau and orgasm stage, a heat wave burning from my head to my toes. I control my body's stimulation until my eyes find his alluring glance. Romero sucks and pulls to where my pelvic muscles contract.

"Oh God…" I whisper, releasing the climax. I gasp at the same time I hear a nearby shattering sound.

"Romero! Are you over here?" Angelica shouts.

Chapter 13

October 5, 2025

We freeze at the sound of Angelica's voice.

"Romero? Are you back here?"

I yank my dick away from Romero and stuff it down my pants as I turn my back toward an emerging Angelica. Romero throws both hands on the ground, unable to control his gag reflex.

"Oh, my God! What happened?" Angelica pounces toward Romero.

"I um…" I stutter.

"He threw up and dropped his ring," Romero says, staring at me. The fire that was once in his eyes is now extinguished.

"Yeah. We were talking, and I just started throwing up. Romero found my ring," I say with limited conviction. I pat the right side pocket facing Angelica while pulling up my zipper. The pant's fly zips shut before she steps between us.

"You poor thing! Thank goodness my man was here to help," she says, rubbing Romero's back like my mother used to when I had a rash on my arm as a kid. Romero rises to his feet, and they both share a passionate kiss. The sight makes me nauseous.

"You know I am a team player," he says. His eyes soften a touch, but I still see the whites of them.

"You are! Good thing you helped just before we headed to the mansion. I can't have anyone looking sick at the biggest party of the semester! Our Uber just arrived to take us there!" She flashes a grin in my direction. "Come on, superstar! The party needs you as its man of the hour."

I look toward Romero, whose scowl unnerves me. How does he flip a switch from devouring to despising me so fast?

"I don't know," I say, shrugging.

"Come on! We have to celebrate."

She clutches my arm and pulls me toward the Mercedes S-Class parked by the bar patio. Angelica yanks me into the Uber, placing me on her left side. The scent of freshly cleaned upholstery battles with the brewing tension between Romero and me in the air. The driver starts the engine, and a low rumble vibrates through the car as he pulls out of the parking lot. Our car's tires hum against the asphalt, turning left onto Highway 26, creating a steady rhythm that balances the sound of Angelica's rapid typing.

"What do you think of this one?" Angelica asks.

I turn to her, but she holds her phone out to Romero. He points at the phone before glancing at me. Without moving his stare, he wraps his arm around her.

I roll my eyes and ignore them both.

While stewing over Romero's erratic behavior, I stare out the window and watch the buildings explode with details in the familiar darkness of the night drive. The car turns right onto the roundabout for North State Highway 123, just ahead of the bronze rottweiler that marks the city center. The luxury engine rumbles softly as the car cruises past the sprawling botanical gardens and park.

Even at night, the blooming flower center radiates vibrant pinks and purples under the floodlights, unearthing the same beauty as SZA sings about life's struggles in our twenties from the speaker. I can't help but empathize with her. The trails twirl away from the park center, starting around the well-maintained grounds before being swallowed into darkness. The full moon reflects off the rippling body of water as we drive by, the night sky free to express itself without a cloud interfering. A tinge of envy prickles me the more I think about it.

The overwhelming scene floods my senses for a few miles until we ascend toward a tunnel covered in a tapestry of flora. The road stretches out into complete darkness for the last minute of the song on the radio until we emerge at the top of a rolling hill. This view paints University Hills in its own Starry Night. Rows of Tudor homes sleep on the outskirts of the towering University Hills Baptist Church, driving out the most historic marker in our rural downtown. The rustic main buildings surrounding the church still buzz from late-night activity, radiating a hint of light in otherwise total darkness.

The car's headlights shine on the towering oaks shielding a secluded lookout tower connected to the steepest garden trail. I catch sight of it for a second before a dramatic shift in scenery after the park's fence line. Wide stretches of dried wild grass replace the blooming flower buds with towering pine, oak, and mountain cedar trees sparsely spread out across the hill. We startle the white-tailed deer and jackrabbits awake, and their swift movements create a blur of motion once the car's beams uncover them in the night.

The Uber pulls up in front of a magnificent gate towering over us, one that I am sure costs my father's entire retirement fund to make. Stucco pillars anchor the two crafted espresso-stained wood pieces that spread between, each door littered with intricate iron finishes. In all caps, the words *North Side* spreads across the top.

"We are here!" Angelica says, wrapping herself in Romero's warmth while his icy stare fixates on me. It's almost like he wants to snarl at me, like a guard dog to a trespasser.

The enchanting barriers swing open, revealing a scene that affirmed every notion I had about the town's wealth. Angelica sits up a few seconds after the Uber's wheels connect with the smooth asphalt. We arrive at Angelica's residence, the largest Mediterranean-style mansion in the neighborhood. A vast, drought-tolerant lawn grounds the property, and dozens of majestic Italian cypress trees line the gravel patio. The driveway winds its way around an exquisite Old World-style marble fountain, reminiscent of those found only in the Northern Italian countryside. The driver parks his car in front of the iron gate, which blocks the smooth, plastered castle-like structure that exudes neoclassicist symmetry, carefully calculated ratios, and undeniable elegance.

We step out of the car, and the muffled sounds of a DJ remixing Rihanna's Super Bowl audio greet us outside Angelica's home. I see a line of students wrapping around the mansion as if this were the town's most popular nightclub.

Angelica notices my gaze. "What do you think, superstar?"

"This is one insane party," I say. My eyes beam, taking in the scene around me.

"I settle for nothing less," she says as she sticks her proud chin out.

I feel Romero creep up beside me.

"It's too bad not everyone will get in. Only people I find worthy will come inside," Angelica says. Her words feel cold as she fixes her hair. She turns to me, her expression void of any emotion. "Would you like to join?"

I hesitate as I look at Romero, who looks just as confused as I do. "Would I have to do something?"

She laughs. "I was hoping you would ask. My mother needs a new model for her luxury clothing line, and she asked for you."

"What?" Romero asks, his eyes bulging out of his skull.

"Me?" I say, pointing my finger at my chest.

She nods at me. "My father has approved everything and cleared it with the lawyers. Let's just say, you will see some hefty paychecks in your future, Thomas. If money were a problem before, consider all your problems solved. All I need is an answer from you."

I stand there, stunned into silence as I realize what is happening here. Angelica's family is offering me a modeling deal. And knowing how rich her family is, this is going to be more than anything I imagined. This money solves all my financial problems and my family's. It may not amend my relationship with them, but it could atone for my mistakes in our family's demise. Even the parts I kept secret from them.

A howl of excited shouts diverts our attention toward the party as it shakes the mansion on its foundation.

"So, are you in superstar?" Angelica asks, not disguising her clipped patience. I make sure not to waste any more of her time.

"You've got yourself a deal," I say, unable to hide the excitement.

Angelica struts forward with a giddy step, her heels clicking across the driveway, and I take my first steps behind her. Romero's hand swings forward and impedes my path. I look at him, watching his skin burn a scalding red.

"She likes to enter on her own," he growls.

"Why?"

An annoyed expression crosses his face, as if I had asked him a stupid question.

"Ok, fine."

Angelica opens her front door, hearing a serenade of applause before the door shuts.

"What's wrong?" I ask.

Romero remains unmoved, but his chiseled face radiates in the moonlight. I reach for him, but he pushes me aside and marches in feverish steps toward the mansion.

Chapter 14

October 5, 2025

I regret taking part in this stupid drinking game when Brian Johnson sings 'Thunder' for the fifteenth time, but secretly, it's what I want right now. The intricate electric guitar chords and emphatic drum beats screech from the speaker, assaulting my ears. I bring the tallboy Toxic Tonic can to my lips, feeling its dampness and stickiness. The smell of the malt liquor and carbonated fruit punch nauseates me as it wafts up to my nose, but I force myself to drink.

The liquid flows down my throat like scalding hot asphalt, burning my esophagus. My stomach bloats with the fizzing carbonation, but I continue to chug my drink while waiting for my cue to stop. The word 'Thunder' never leaves Johnson's lips. The rest of the party watches in awe and amusement, their eyes fixed on me, fingers pointing in my direction.

"Chug! Chug! Chug!"

By the time I stop drinking, I'm thunderstruck.

The alcohol infuses itself into my body and overtakes my nervous system, helping me numb my overstimulation. At one moment, manic thoughts of my modeling deal surge through my brain. I envision looking my best on social media while thousands of likes and comments bombard my posts. I was surfing on the highest wave until the emotional tide ripped my vibe from underneath me, sending me crashing into a fit with Romero.

The whole situation leaves me confused. One minute, we are kissing so hard we need a second to breathe. The next, he's seething at me, and I have no clue why. The last thing I need weighing on my conscience is another person mad at me for something. So only ten seconds after Romero storms off, I walk after him to clear the air. I see him talking to Angelica in the foyer outside the kitchen when the security guard sends me through.

Romero stops talking when our eyes meet and pulls Angelica into an overdramatic kiss. The scene nauseates me more, but it's when he stares at me that the malice stings me. His eyes reminded me of how our situation would be nothing but messy. It will be nothing of substance. Maybe before, I would have been stronger to walk away from this unscathed, but it hurts worse after my streak of pain and heartbreak. So with this level of emotional volatility, I decide to drink—a lot.

Romero and Angelica are not in the foyer when I stumble out of the kitchen this time. The stained hardwood floors sway side to side where they once stood, catching the light from the glowing chandeliers above with their rich colors and grain. The grandeur of the space appears intricately designed with beams stretching into the ceiling, but I can't stabilize myself to analyze my surroundings. I lean up against the textured walls, hoping they absorb me like the pulsating beats of the DJ's booming music coming from the next room.

I gaze out the tall windows on my right, capturing the stunning view. The windows reveal an endless pool, its shimmering water reflecting the distant town's glowing lights. Its beauty lures me in, but half of the men's and women's soccer teams jump into the pool.

In the moments I stand here, most of the party's attendance moving about the foyer, their footsteps echoing on the hardwood floors. Every room reeks of mingling scents of perfume and cologne, and the unmistakable aroma of alcohol overruns from the hundreds of red solo cups being clutched tightly in the hands of flirtatious college girls and eager guys around me.

Once I regain my balance, I walk toward the French doors, swaying as if I'm on a tightrope. Someone taps my shoulder, freezing me in my place. Piercing hazel eyes meet my own. "You rode over with Angelica, right?" she asks.

"Yeah, I did," I say. Dizziness overtakes me again.
"Oh, I thought I recognized you before," she says, biting her finger.

I drunkenly laugh. "I'm glad you could make that connection."

"Don't worry, it wasn't hard. But I am hoping something else is," she says. She adjusts her tank top, exposing more cleavage.

"Oh…that's, um…" I dart my eyes toward the scenic oil painting dangling on the wall. "Man, these drinks hit you, don't they?"

"Oh yeah. Fruit punch is lethal. I finished one earlier," she says. "Good thing you hold the ball better than your alcohol."

"Oh, um…" I regret swinging my hand behind my head because it throws off my balance.

"I guess I am talented like that."

She brushes her finger down my dress shirt. "Are you talented at anything else?" Her hands and lips inch closer

A familiar hand and a monotone voice wrap around my shoulder. "There you are, bro."

Relief consumes me as I see Vince stand by my side, still wearing the same clothes from the bar. "Hey, there you are! You want to head over to…um…"

"I got you." He waves toward the young woman. "Good to see you, Amy."

"Vince, you buzzkill," Amy says, adjusting a stray clip of hair behind her ear. As Vince shifts me away, she waves in my direction. "Good to meet you. I hope this isn't the last I see of you…"

Vince guides me toward the pool. A snicker leaves his mouth. "So you left with Amy?"

"No, I left with…I just met her." I slur the words between my teeth.

"I would avoid her when Duncan is around."

"Why?"

"She and Duncan are toxic together, but miss playing games with each other when they are not. "

"Really? Why?" Gravity crushes me harder.

"It's complicated, but it's better not to join a love triangle with those two. Only Romero and Angelica would be worse. Just try to stay away from your teammate's girlfriends."

I swallow a lump in my throat. "Ok, I will try to avoid them. Thanks for saving me." I place my hands on my knees.

"Are you okay?"

"Why aren't you drunk yet?"

"We said we were doing a dry season together this year. I guess some players don't hold their word to high standards," Vince says.

"Funny," I say, pointing to the cup in Vince's hand.

"Oh, sorry. I mean, some players can't hold their liquor." Vince takes a sip before patting me on the back.

"I also want to stay sober for this girl I'm trying to talk to." A gust of wind slaps me when we step onto the back porch overlooking the infinity pool. I grab the side of the door as my momentum pulls me to the side.

"Who?"

"I'm not trying to be weird, but I think your roommate is beautiful and I want to get to know her. I'm trying not to act like a fool," Vince says.

"How gentlemanly of you." I rub my hands on my face and take a step forward.

"I'm trying. Do you know where she went?"

I exaggerate a shrug. "I don't know. Machi never goes out, so I don't know where she will go. Maybe she left?"

"No, we came together, and I promised to take her home." Vince peers into the surrounding crowd. "Will you just chill here a minute while I find her? It will just be a second."

"Sure," I say, swaying to the dizziness in my brain.

Vince darts back into the house as I slump on the French doors. I press my hand against its sturdy handle, trying to orient myself, when my eyes catch movement in the hot tub across the patio. Romero almost swallows Angelica as he passionately kisses her while the rest of the group scrolls on their phones.

I can't tell if it's the alcohol or the sight of them that's upsetting my stomach, but it takes all my strength not to spew. First, I replay all the moments of the past few hours. I played one of the best matches of my life since my injury last summer, and a sponsorship deal of a lifetime fell out of the sky into my desperate arms.

However, I keep recycling the thought of me making out with Romero behind a bar without a care in the world. That connection thrills me in all the wrong ways. He hits every hedonic hotspot in my brain, leaving me craving him more after each moment. He's a drug I can't kick.

So watching Romero and Angelica's embrace triggers a withdrawal, and irritable agitation prickles through me. It pisses me off that he knows how to push my buttons, and I'm tired of it. I peel off the door and stammer toward them, while the alcohol impairs my judgment as much as my motor skills.

I'm a few feet away from igniting a confrontation when someone shoulder-checks me into vertigo. A thick, posh accent hisses in my ears. "Watch it, Thomas!"

I recoil toward the hot tub. Roger almost knocks me in, but I balance my center of gravity just inches from the bubbling water. Most of the hot tub occupants look up from their screens at my stumble, except lip-locked Romero and Angelica, blissfully unaware of their surroundings. I turn to square up to Roger, smirking as if he's proud of his fragile masculinity.

"What the fuck are you doing here?" I slur.

"Trying to enjoy myself."

"How did you get in?"

He gives me a sly grin. "Angelica's an old friend. Our families run in the same circles. I'm always invited to her parties.

I'm surprised she let someone like you in here."

I throw my right hand to my waist. "Like me?"

"Angelica only invites boujee guests, so you must have begged to walk in here."

Now it's my turn to grin. "She actually begged me to join. The same way you begged me to leave USE."

His eyes narrow. "You were supposed to be gone if my memory serves correctly."

"If my memory serves me correctly, you told me to leave the university. Your entitled ass forgot to specify where."

He forces a laugh. "You're a better comedian than footballer, Thomas."

"Better to be good at something than nothing at all, Roger. Tonight certainly didn't reward you any favors."

"What the fuck are you rambling about?"

I waltz toward him, the liquid courage numbing all my fears. "You are just as lousy a blackmailer as you were a room-mate and..."

Roger scowls at me as he interrupts. His finger jabs into my chest. "I wouldn't piss off the man who holds the keys to your downfall. Keep talking and see how fast I unlock that trapdoor."

I wave my accusatory finger in his face, finishing my thought. "...and just as lousy a footballer. Even worse than me."

Roger pushes me so hard that the ground feels pulled from underneath me. My feet skate a few feet across the cement before I plunge deep into the hot tub. The water coats every inch of my body in bubbling warmth. The alcohol and water join forces to paralyze me, and I can't help but drift from my consciousness for a brief second.

Vince yanks me out of the hot tub, the boiling water cooling as it drips down my hair and clothing, and we take off in the opposite direction from the chaos. Angelica's shriek cuts through the music, and everyone races toward the commotion. Everyone in the hot tub, excluding Romero, is gawking at her, pressing their phones right into her face. The image fuzzes as the chlorine stings my eyes, but this is the least of my concerns. My stomach flips inside me.

"I don't feel so good," I whisper.

My mind must be toying with me because I hear Machi's voice shouting amongst the crowds of people forming. She appears still in the same cocktail dress she wore at the bar, locking her eyes on me. She takes one look at me and pulls me away from the unfolding scene, ushering me away like secret service agents would a president in imminent danger.

"Help me get him to the bathroom!" she says to Vince.

Vince follows her orders and guides me into the half-bathroom just before the foyer. Vince lifts me and carries me across the mansion, my shoes dangling as they scuff the floor.

My eyes roll up into my eye sockets, allowing gravity to force me to the ground. The alcohol brewing in my stomach crawls up my throat, and I have little defense against the vomit volcano about to erupt. I don't see the moment we enter the bathroom, but I feel Vince adjust my limp body before I spew everything within me into the toilet. An unpleasant cocktail of gray water and vomit splashes onto my face.

"There, there, Xiōngdì." Machi strokes my damp shirt. "Let it all out."

I regurgitate most of the alcohol out of my system after a

few agonizing minutes. A cold shiver shoots down my body.

"I know you were worried about your body fat test, but anorexia is not the answer."

Vince laughs. "Damn, she's a savage."

"You should see her when she's upset with me." I wheeze while my head dangles over the toilet bowl.

Machi's gentle stroke strengthens into a smack on my back before she turns to Vince. "What happened to Prince Charming over here?"

"Mr. Lightweight had one too many Tall Boys and felt he should cannonball into the hot tub."

"Roger shoved me," I protest before dry heaving.

"Roger? Like USE Roger?" Vince asks.

"Why is he here?" Machi asks.

"Angelica invited him," I say between the vomits.

"I wish someone had caught him on video shoving you. It looks like you soaked Angelica and Romero tongue-deep in their make-out session," Vince adds.

Machi furrows her brow while tapping her fingers on my back. "How mad was Angelica?"

"She looked pissed. I don't know how he will escape the online brutality of her followers," Vince says.

"That's what I was worried about."

"Oh shit. What's our plan?" Vince says.

"I don't know."

I want to respond, but I hug the toilet instead, listening to the vomit fall out of my mouth rather than my words.

"Easy, homeboy." Vince stretches outward to prevent me from drowning in the toilet water. "No need to lose a friend now."

"You lost someone, too?" Machi asks with an unbreakable poker face.

"Yeah, I did a while ago. Close family member."

"Same here."

I expel the last fluid ounces of alcohol in my system and prop my body against the wall. No one says anything for a while. I focus on numbing the pounding headache, and Vince and Machi glance at each other in a flirtatious sort of way. It could be the alcohol distorting my vision, but I see some chemistry building there. I interrupt their connection by struggling to stand up. Machi and Vince catch me before gravity pulls me back to the floor.

"Maybe it's time to get you out of here," Vince suggests.

"You play rough, don't you?" I say.

"You're a little fruity when you're drunk, huh?" Vince pulls me up.

"You don't know the half of it," I mutter.

"What's he talking about?" Vince turns to Machi.

Machi reaches into her pocket and grabs her phone. "He's weird when he's drunk. I'm ordering an Uber to sneak us out of here. We should be back home in thirty minutes."

"Where are we going?" I ask, slumping into Vince's side.

"Home, big man. Somehow, without being seen," Vince says with a hint more concern than comfort.

"I think I'll be fine. I'm better now," I whisper in a hoarse slur.

Machi peeks out of the cracked door. "Your popularity just skyrocketed at SESU after the game, but you humiliated Angelica at her own party. We've got to get you out of here before she figures out it was you." She whips the door open.

"We can't let anyone find us."

"I'll take him," Romero says. We recoil as we all face Romero, standing stoic while soaked in pool water.

"We're good, man. We've got it covered," Vince says.

"Yeah. Don't worry about it," Machi agrees.

I say nothing.

"I overheard you guys need help to get him out."

"We already have it covered," Vince says assertively.

"I also overheard you don't want Angelica to retaliate after your mishap tonight. It would be a shame to reveal that her new model ruined her party."

"Her what?" Machi gives me a dubious look.

"She hired him to be a model, but if she finds out, I'm not sure how long that will last." Romero dangles his phone in his hand, a picture of Vince yanking me out of the hot tub. Vince's eye twitches.

"What do you want? We are not dealing with your bullshit again," Vince barks.

"It won't be messy like last time," Romero says.

"I'm sure Amy will be relieved. That way, she and Duncan don't break up again over an affair that never happened."

"Give it a rest, Vince. If you let me talk to Caleb, we can work something out that satisfies everyone."

Air flares out of my nostrils. Are you fucking kidding me? I am nearly inebriated, and now he wants to speak to me.

"You good with that, Caleb?" Romero crosses his arms and stares like he has all the time in the world.

Everyone's gaze turns to me. Part of me wants to prolong the silent treatment as payback for his handling of our situation, but I have him right where I have wanted him for some time. I want to debate my thoughts further, but drunken thoughts impair my clarity. "Yeah, that's fine."

"Are you sure?" Machi asks. Her dubious expression almost makes me reconsider, but I reassure her. She hands Romero the apartment key. "Leave it on the kitchen counter," she says with an edge in her voice.

"Just give us some time alone and enjoy the party. Here is some money for an Uber." He dangles a few bills in Machi's direction. Machi slaps the cash from Romero, sending the bills floating to the ground. She pushes past him without acknowledgement, and Vince untangles me and follows close behind her. Romero turns to them. "If you want to get on her good side, just give her free coffee for the rest of the year. Those cloud lattes are her favorite."

He shifts his focus back to me.

"Let's get you home. It's time we clarified things," Romero says.

He walks past me toward the white Honda waiting for us at the gate. I follow, and it's not until I reach the passenger side door that I lose the ability to walk. But it's not the alcohol disorienting me. It's the satellite transmission from a radio host booming from the stereo. His voice is smooth and rich, like the shot of whiskey I gulped earlier.

"All right, coming hot to you with a brand new single from the rising master of the romance ballad. Following his solid debut "NO LAughing matter," here's "For me" from R&B's biggest star, Javi, on University Hills' popular music station."

Chapter 15

January 20, 2025

For me

The aroma of my coffee envelops the space, its rich scent mingling with the comforting aura the café exudes. A bustling espresso bar sits in the middle of the hexagonal room, while tables clutter around each corner of the café. My project partner and I sit next to the floor to ceiling windows with a mesmerizing view of the coffee roaster machines in action.

Vibrant green philodendrons hang from shelves above us, and various animal hides cover the stained concrete floor, which adds a rustic touch to the space. Jazz beats whisper from the speaker closest to the bar, but it's muted by the grinding of the machines and various conversations. It's a different study environment for me, but I let Javi pick the place since I missed the first couple of weeks of class. It was the least I could do since he's helping me catch up.

I sip my mug, the coffee's warmth tingling across my taste buds, like rekindling a soft fireplace in an old hearth. The foam flower on top dances on my tongue as I savor the creamy latte. I set my mug down on the delicate china, its clink echoing softly. The circular coffee table sits empty beside our coffee mugs, its surface reflecting the cups floating on the plush cowhide rug below. Across the table, Javi's eyes gleam while he waits for my verdict.

"You're right. This is good," I say.

"I told you!" Javi says. He stretches his hands and raises them above his head. His fingers brush against his curly, high-lighted hair.

As he moves, the golden astrology earring in his left earlobe glimmers in the light, casting a subtle shine. Two large brace-lets clamp onto his forearm, one solid and imposing, the other adorned with intricate chain links. The cool metal presses against his skin, a weighty reminder of his unique style. He's very attractive, and I'm sure he's aware. Javi readjusts himself in his seat and scoops up his camera, that time traveled from the '70s.

"Besides, I had to lure you to a study session." Javi positions his camera over his latte and croissant, but captures enough of the surroundings to create a Polaroid fit for a coffeehouse catalog.

"I was worried I would complete this project by myself," Javi says, stowing his camera in his bag. "Given your absence last week."

I shake my head while retrieving my cup. "I know." I tilt the mug up to my lips and drain the rest of my coffee. "Anyway, how did you find this place?" I ask before I slurp the last drop of that dark chocolate and espresso.

Javi looks down at his textbook. "I scroll through Reeltime when I am bored out of my mind. According to this page, I'm constantly scrolling to yearn for a social reward that ignites the release of dopamine and oxytocin, creating a pleasurable rush within my ventral striatum." He fiddles with his golden chain-link necklace, which conceals a precious pendant of Our Lady of Guadalupe.

"Smartass." I open my textbook to the assigned chapter while Javi pulls out his laptop.

"But seriously, I have uncovered many hidden gems in the area on social media since I moved here. It's sad how University City is amazing, but USE is terrible. I would rather study here than on campus."

"USE isn't that bad. It's better than Southeastern State," I say.

"I guess. Even at SESU, I would force you to come here for this project."

"Why?"

"Because I enjoy treating myself when I have difficult proj-ects to work on with difficult people," Javi says. His eyes stay glued to the page. A faint smile appears as he adjusts all nine rings on his fingers, except for the bare left index finger.

"I'm easy," I say, lifting my head.

"Oh, really? What about ignoring my calls and texts?"

"I didn't recognize the number."

"And my emails?"

"I was just busy."

"Sure. Whatever hetero." Javi clicks the keys on his computer.

"What did you call me?"

"A hetero?" Javi stares at me as if this is common knowledge.

I stare back with a blank expression. "Heterosexual?" Now I look confused, not sure what he's getting at.

"Your people?"

"My people?" I say, pointing my thumb to my chest.

"You know, straight white men. They always find terms to label…" He pretends to cough. "…marginalize people. So, as a man of various minorities, I feel obligated to return the favor, just to level the playing field. Thus, you are hetero."

"Why do I sense today I will learn about my sexuality instead of personality?"

"Well, your sexuality seems to drive you hetero," he says, flapping his hand in front of my blue with white trim Adidas tracksuit.

"Forgive me for being a student-athlete and the side effects it brings me."

"Athlete, sure. Student remains to be seen." Javi winks, dis-arming me to the point where I feel more playful.

"So you call this what?" I point my index finger at Javi's outfit.

Javi's outfit catches the light when he stands, creating a dazzling display that ties together his paper-thin white long-sleeve shirt, the outline of a white tank top visible underneath. His rings reflect off my Apple Watch, making it seem dull in comparison. His accessories clink as he moves, a subtle reminder of his presence. A bejeweled black leather belt wraps around Javi's jet-black cargo pants, and his thick-soled dress shoes click against the floor under the table.

Javi moves his hand from his chest down his torso. "This is gay excellence."

I roll my eyes. "If you say so. Which part would you like to focus on, your excellence?"

"You write out our transcript, and I will put together the

presentation."

I agree and retrieve my notebook from my bag.

For twenty minutes, I engage in intense studying. I scribble down notes from Javi's textbook while he taps on his keypad and cursor to create our presentation. Faint echoes of conversations and the espresso machine hum surround us, but my focus remains uninterrupted.

That is, until Javi taps his palms on his laptop and clicks away on his screen, causing me to steal glances at him. The glances become stares as the minutes tick by. His tapping turns into head-bopping, synchronized with the rhythm of his project. The head-bopping progresses into a few musical notes that escape from his throat, adding a touch of spontaneity to the otherwise focused atmosphere. I can't help but laugh.

"What?" Javi focuses on me.

"Nothing. I was laughing at you."

"Why?" Javi scoffs.

"Because you are so extra. It's distracting."

"Would it help if I dropped to your level?"

I glare at him, but he shrugs it off.

"What can I say? It's the Capricorn in me." He points to the sea-goat earring dangling off his right earlobe. I nod, not knowing much about astrology. "What sign are you?"

"Scorpio."

"Oof," Javi says, rolling his eyes.

"What?"

"You don't know what that means?"

"No."

Javi crosses his arms and leans back. "It means you are well-hated in the astrological world."

"Oh," I say, shoulders tensing so hard they are almost touching my earlobes. I didn't realize that the stars also hated me. Add another group to the list.

"Don't worry. I fuck with Scorpios. I think people misunderstand them."

"If you only knew," I whisper.

"What's that?"

I flinch as I say "oh that's cool you like Scorpios."

"I'm sure." Javi rotates his laptop, and I'm pleasantly surprised when he unveils the most aesthetically pleasing presentation I have ever seen. "What do you think of this?"

"It looks great," I say.

Javi smiles. "And therefore, I fuck with Scorpios like you, minus the elusive, over-emasculated jock personality."

"What do you mean, elusive?" I ask, cocking my head.

Javi laughs and taps a few keys on his keyboard. "What do you call disappearing for the first week of the semester with no heads-up?"

I drop my pen on my notebook and stretch back. Before I can stop myself, my words fly out unfiltered. "I call it attending my mother's funeral!"

He stops typing and looks at me aghast. "Are you serious?"

I nod. The silence is palpable while Javi stares at me. The twinkle fades in his eye as he clears his throat. He closes his laptop and rises to his feet. "I am so sorry. I did not mean…"

"It's okay. I told no one outside of who knows besides you." "I did not intend to put you on the spot like that."

"I just don't want to talk about it."

"I understand." He nods, tapping on the table, and avoiding my gaze for a moment. After the moment passes, he packs up his laptop.

"Are you leaving already?" I ask.

"Well…kinda. I may have hidden the full truth about why I brought you here. Today is the farmers' market, and I wanted to look around for a bit. It was a study break, but I can go. I don't mean to make this more uncomfortable. We can work on the project another day."

"Okay," I say.

Javi nods as he finishes packing the rest of his belongings. He swings his satchel over his neck. "It was nice finally meeting you, Caleb. I'm sorry for your loss, and I hope I didn't do too much today."

We fix our gazes on each other, no words flowing between us for a second before Javi walks to the exit. He takes a few steps before something possessed me to speak up. "Wait, Javi."

He turns around, wearing a hopeful expression.

"Can I come along?"

Javi smiles and nods at my question.

I turn around and throw my notebook into my bag, hiding the smile creeping onto my face. I can't explain it, but there is a cozy aura around him that draws me in, and I want to stay close.

I throw on my backpack and follow Javi out of the towering barn doors. He rushes out to the parking lot across the street and scans the surrounding brush area with his black satchel wrapped around his shoulder. The sunlight kisses his face when he turns toward me. I will have daydreams about that image for a while. His charm is infectious enough to woo anyone, including a closet case like me. I walk alongside Javi in the parking lot.

"Have you been to a farmers' market before?"

"No, I haven't."

Javi pulls my arm in his direction, and I don't resist. "You are in for a treat. This is one of the best in the city."

We follow a group of people down the walking path in the grass and stumble upon the town's bustling market, a vibrant sensory overload akin to a lively country festival. Before our eyes, the scene unravels, a vibrant display of booths decorated in a kaleidoscope of patriotic reds and blues, each overflowing with local treats and charming keepsakes.

A mélange of scents surrounds our senses as the aroma of fresh produce mingles with the fragrant essence of handmade soaps, candles, and jerky products, depending on where you turn. The residents, dressed in an eclectic array of attire, showcased their individuality, ranging from elegant Sunday best to the casual garb of athletic wear, overalls, and the timeless charm of cowboy hats.

In a far corner, a harmonious blend of Christian gospel and the rhythmic strumming of an acoustic guitar reverberated through the fairgrounds, seamlessly merging with the energetic beats of indie punk, creating a mesmerizing soundscape that soothed the bustling crowd. Javi takes out his ancient Polaroid camera once again and snaps a picture of the event as we walk down the market.

"What's the deal with that camera?"

"Any reason for the interrogation?" Javi asks.

"I can't ask questions after revealing my personal shit?"

"Ok, damn. I didn't know we played that card." He lines up his Polaroid camera in the booth ahead of us.

"It is also my attempt to get to know you, I guess," I say.

"I was teasing you, but I don't mind the questions." Javi retracts his vintage Sun 660 instant camera from his face and holds it out to me. "My G-mom had this for many years and discovered it while cleaning her house. Before I was five or six, she had a company restore it and then gave it to me. It was the first gift I recall receiving from her, and I have been using it ever since." He waves the image back and forth before handing it to me.

"Your G-mom?"

"That's my grandmother's nickname. She basically raised me and my love of vintage art forms."

I examine the photograph and understand the sentiment. His picture captures the essence of the crowd better than any social media post on Reeltime. The boy swinging between his mother's and father's arms as the family walked away from us feels real in this picture, as it was moments ago. It doesn't look forced like pictures on social media.

"It feels authentic," I say. "The images feel raw to me. It doesn't look like the pictures you see often on social media."

"That's the point. Polaroid photography forces users to capture the genuine moment as it is happening while embracing the imperfections that occur. Each photo must be intentional, with limited shots. Also, replenishing film is expensive right now. The best part is that it creates a nostalgic experience with a physical photo."

I nod and study the picture before handing it back to him.

"Anymore questions for me hetero?"

Yes. So many questions I want to ask. How did you come out to your parents? Do they accept you? How did you become comfortable being out? Are you single? But instead of asking what's on my mind, I need to phrase a question that could encompass everything I'm thinking. "You're different from everyone else."

"Not a question, but okay."

I smack my head when Javi looks away, hoping to slap some sense into me.

"And Caleb, you can say it. It's not a disease, at least not one you can catch."

My brow furrows. "What?"

"You can say gay, hetero. I promise it won't hurt you," Javi says, teasing me.

Shit. Be cool. Maintain your composure. I scratch the back of my neck, searching for an inoffensive conversation starter. "I don't mean different as in gay, but as unique," I say. "I was curious how you found yourself. Since we are project partners and walking through a farmers' market together."

I think it works because Javi relaxes. "I'm not sure I have yet. I find myself caught in an endless cycle of discovery and struggle. On certain days, I wake up and love myself just the way I am. But on other days, I struggle and wish I were someone else. It would be so much easier to be straight, growing up in a country with people who look like me. My life would have been simpler if I had had a functional upbringing. But these struggles help me find my solace. My sexuality, like my Latino ancestry, is an important part of who I am, and I embrace it. The process just continues in an infinite loop."

"Does everyone know about your constant self-discovery?"

"Just people in my life, at least the few that stuck around."

"I'm sorry," I say.

"Don't be. It's a symptom of life." Before I can respond, Javi points behind me. "Look at that over there!"

He points to the 'Vinyl Vineyards' black and gold tent. Javi speed-walks toward the heavy-duty party tent so fast that I am chasing his dust cloud to the entrance. As I walk in, I notice long tables lining the tent's perimeter, adorned with full wooden crates filled with vinyl records in various conditions, ranging from rough to pristine. In the far left corner, Javi comes into my view.

"What a cool shop for a market." Javi scans the crate as I walk over to his side. "Do you have vinyl?" Javi asks.

"No. I don't even have a player." I press my finger between the crevices of each record.

"You are missing out on an underappreciated musical form. My G-mom got me into them when I was younger. She had this enormous collection in her garage. She could probably fit every crate in this tent."

I study each vinyl record, each sleeve crackling between my fingertips. The first box contains a fraction of the hundreds of vinyl records lining the shelves spanning across multiple decades. I meet Javi's dark, cocoa eyes, the intensity of his energy palpable, enveloping my attention. Javi's presence is a magnetic force that draws me in, diverting my focus toward him rather than the crate in front of me. I turn away before Javi can see the reddening above his cheekbones.

"I guess I am missing out."

He nods and moves over to the crate next to me, examining the contemporary R&B records.

"Your G-mom knew how to nurture your vintage aesthetic, didn't she?" I ask.

"That and so much more."

"What happened with your mom?"

He gives me a wry expression. "I think we learned not to discuss our mommy troubles today."

A sly grin forms on my face. "Fair enough. Let's talk about something else."

"For sure. Do you collect anything?"

"Sort of."

"What do you mean?" Javi asks, browsing the aisles behind me.

"I guess I like to collect mementos from important moments in my life."

Javi turns to face me. "I'm intrigued. What have you collected?"

"Just my family heirloom."

"Which is?"

"It's a mini replica of the Jules Rimet World Cup trophy England won in 1966."

"I'm sure you just spoke English to me, but I didn't understand a word you said. I heard England, so are you British?" he asks in the worst London accent.

I roll my eyes. "My father is. I was born here in the States."

"Damn. You were almost cool."

"Sorry to get your hopes up."

He laughs. "You are quick hetero. Is that your entire collection, seriously? Do you never have memorable moments in your life?"

Only the ones that haunt me. "I guess not," I say, a deflated tone carrying my words.

"Fair enough." Javi turns around and reexamines his crate.

Javi gasps. "Wow, I can't believe this is here!" He pulls out a red and white vinyl record. "And only fifteen dollars, that's a steal!"

"Who is that?"

His face falls.

"Undoubtedly one of the greatest pop stars of all time. This album is her magnum opus and my all time favorite."

I shake my head. "I still do not know who you are talking about."

His mouth gapes open. "It's Rihanna!"

I tilt my head. "Is that a new album?"

"Kinda. It's the newest album, but it's almost ten years old."

"Does she not make any music anymore?"

"Who knows, but at least she made us this gem. It's a timeless classic that serves as a constant source of inspiration, motivating me to aspire to create impactful music one day."

"Then you should."

"What should I do?" Javi asks, looking at me.

"Make an album. You talk about it like I talk about soccer. I hear it in your voice."

"I won't say you are wrong," he says. "Music has been a part of my life since I can remember. I joined the musical theater in high school and wanted to study music and the arts, but my G-mom was hell-bent on me getting a degree and working a high-paying job since she couldn't. She didn't care what it was as long as it paid well." Javi finishes his thought, keeping his finger on the record sleeves, when I look up. "I can't stop thinking about making music, but I am not sure about a concept yet."

"I'm sure you will find one." I smile while I flip two records over and stumble on an unwrapped vinyl of my current favorite album, "You Should Be Here." The vinyl shoots up as I hold it up and show Javi, unaware of his marveling glances. "I love this album," I say.

Javi raises an eyebrow. "You like Kehlani too?"

"I've started listening to her more because of this album."

"Really? What's your favorite song?"

My lips twitch into a frown. "The Letter."

Javi opens his mouth, ready to question me further, but stops himself. My reason dawns on him without me saying a word. He takes the vinyl in his hands. "I understand what it's like to lose someone. Music fills the void sometimes." Javi looks at me with heavy eyes, not with pity but with empathy. He tucks both vinyls under his right armpit.

"What are you doing?" I ask.

"Adding a new memento to your collection," Javi says, puffing his chest out.

"I can't allow you to do that."

"Yes, you can! It's the least I can do after today. Plus, we would do each other a favor. I need more people to buy vinyl before it dies off, and you need a new memento to remember this happy day."

"Are you sure?" I ask.

Javi walks over to the line by the cashier. "I'm not doing this out of pity. I think you're a nice hetero."

I smile.

"You think I'm a nice hetero?"

"Don't push it."

His eyes flutter as he looks into his satchel. "Headass," he whispers. Once the customer ahead of us starts checkout, Javi immediately dives into his bag and retrieves his credit card. "Are you excited to listen to it when you get home?" Javi asks.

"I will once I save up for a player. I'm sure it will be great."

Javi walks up to the table and sets the vinyl down.

"Anything else for you today?" the cashier asks.

"I will take that," Javi says, pointing at the record turntable in the clearance bin. My eyes bulge out of my head as he turns to me. "Why wait?"

Infectious smiles creep across our faces and stay there.

Chapter 16

October 5, 2025

I ignore Romero's acknowledging glance with every passing second while we sit in silence the entire drive. His smug
demeanor from earlier still lingers, and I can't help but stew.
Who does he think he is? Treating my friends like that. The
whole situation is uncanny. To add insult to injury, only Javi
serenades us in the Uber. The song is directed toward me, an
additional stressor to an already nauseating headache. If I had
the choice, I'd prefer Javi in this car over Romero, but only
to give him a piece of my mind. How dare he put me in this
situation?

I hate how I ended us, and he knows that. But his method of
coping is extreme. The least he could do is give me a heads-up
before he spills all the details of our relationship for fame. But
I believe karma exists. He makes money from our love story.
I struggle through my current situationship with my almost
repeat hookup. That same hookup bumps my arm while he
retrieves a couple of pills from his pocket and swallows a gulp
of water provided by the driver. Weird how he can take his
meds after drinking.

The Uber pulls up in front of the closed front gate at the

apartment complex and lets us out by the leasing office. I don't hesitate, bolting toward the gate by the mailboxes, even though I stammer with every step.

"Where are you going?" Romero asks, jogging over to my side.

"I'm going home," I say, brushing past him and marching to my apartment across the courtyard.

Romero trails behind me, pleading, yet I ignore him. It's what I should have done when he messaged me on that stupid app. There is no doubt I will delete D&D. If not tonight, then tomorrow for sure. I'm nearly at my front door when Romero wraps his hand around my arm.

"We need to talk."

I grimace as I shake my head, the alcohol inhibiting my filter. "About what?"

"You need to listen to me."

"Why would I need to listen to you? You barely speak to me unless you're horny."

"Caleb just let me explain…"

"Explain what? You just tried to blackmail my friends into talking to me. That's so unhinged. There is no way to explain that away."

"Would you prefer me to be honest with your friends and reveal everything about us?"

I glare at him, but say nothing.

He sways his finger between us. "This is beneficial for both of us."

"Beneficial how?"

"Well, for one, we don't out ourselves to your friends."

"Machi already knows."

"About me too?" His eyes widen in fear.

"Relax. I keep you from Machi because you are still in the closet. Unlike you, I am a decent human being."

"Don't say that. You know I'm good to you."

"Whatever. We can talk tomorrow." I turn to face my door and turn the knob. The realization that Romero has Machi's key hits when the door to the apartment doesn't budge. I press my forehead to the door as he jingles the keys behind me.

"I promise these are yours once we are done."

I furrow my brow and turn around before I let out a heavy sigh. "Fine." I cross my arms and lean on the exterior apartment wall.

He seizes his opportunity and steps forward. "I think about what's happening between us all the time. You came into my life when I wasn't sure what I wanted. On one hand, Angelica and I were exploring our feelings, testing our connection. We never materialized into anything beyond a routine of posting on social media and public displays of affection. In private, we hardly acknowledge each other's existence. It's all a show. But with you everything is different."

I say nothing, but he creeps forward. A wicked grin curves below his nostrils.

"You, more than anyone else, understand how hard this is. We project one image publicly, yet hide everything else privately. Our true selves. You get me, and that's why I can't quit you." He trespasses further on my personal space while he rubs my dress shirt. "I wanted you the moment I slid my fingers underneath that waistband, forcing myself to restrain while you lay on the bed."

He kisses my neck, and I close my eyes, remembering the

night. How intense we were together. How ferociously the lust unfolded. A faint moan escapes my lips. Thinking about it some more, I don't remember him restraining his desire at all. I pull away and narrow my eyes, unaware of what he's referring to. "What are you talking about?"

He has a deer in headlights moment, but quickly recovers his swagger. "Remember Chucky at your initiation?"

I stare at him, completely still. My jaw clenches, and I can tell he's uncomfortable when he deflates his chest.

"I was the one shaking my head at you before Duncan's wet towel lashing."

I point my index finger toward him, a bitter taste in my mouth. The blood flows like lava through me, and I'm about to erupt. "What the actual fuck?"

"Caleb, I did you a favor. It was worse before the football team got suspended. A wet towel was the least of your concerns, but I convinced Duncan to go easy on you. I didn't want what happened to the rest of us to happen to you."

I eye him. "Then why so moody toward me during the game, at the bar, and at Angelica's house?"

"Because I was a little jealous. It took me forever to get as far as you did in one game. My mind is off, medicated or not. Sometimes I just can't keep my mind straight. I struggle to see who is there for me and not. But just know that I am here for you. Believe me."

"I don't believe you."

"If I could have it my way, I would be with you. We would love openly and be like Angelica and me, but something more real. A love story everyone roots for. Teammates to lovers. We could do that if we just lived anywhere else. If I had known, I would have transferred to USE and played there. But we can't have something here in University Hills or SESU. This is just the way life is here." He pulls my body close to his, his face warm and inviting. "But I still want to try."

He leans in for a kiss, but I pull away.

"What's wrong?" he asks.

"It's not any easier at USE."

He cocks his head. "What do you mean?"

"The USE environment is part of the reason I ruined my last relationship."

His eyes widen. "You've dated a guy before?"

"Yes."

"Is that why you came here?"

"No. I came here for soccer. The homophobic environment would force me to prioritize my goals over guys. Focus on a dream over a heartbreak. That's why I chose SESU."

He looks down as if he's pondering his next words carefully. "I see."

Romero straightens himself and retrieves the key to the door. Without breaking a stare, he reaches around me and unlocks the door. "Let's go inside. Probably better for us to share this in private."

I nod and step back, Romero following me into the apartment. What I hoped would start as a tepid conversation soon would unravel into another drunken mistake. I am sure none of my neighbors saw us walk in together, but feel less confident they didn't hear how the rest of our night unfolded.

Chapter 17

October 5, 2025

The sunlight through my window startles me awake the next morning. My duvet slides off my torso as I attempt to sit up, but the merciless blend of muscle soreness, post-coital fatigue, and a throbbing hangover makes the motion unbearable. The smell of vodka and chlorine sickens me to the point to never want to drink again. Thank God there is no practice today because I'm immobile to leave this bed. I turn my head to the right and watch Romero stick his head through his shirt, covering the best parts of last night. The memory flushes my cheeks a bright red.

"Morning," I say, stretching my arms over my head.

"Morning," he responds and flashes me a wicked grin.

"That was hot last night." A smug smile pinches my cheeks.

"We need to make this a regular thing." He winks at me.

"I'm sure we could work something out."

He rises off the bed, with only a T-shirt and underwear on, and walks over to retrieve his jeans in the furthest corner of the room. I watch each of his slow and jagged steps, and I can't help but smirk because of his subtle limp.

"I have been meaning to ask you something," he says.

The duvet rustles as I sit up. "Sure. What's up?"

"What's your beef with Roger?"

"What?" I ask, shaking my head. I send a whimsical stare to him, but he returns me a more curious one.

He slides his pants up his legs and reattaches his belt. "You can't tell me there is no animosity between you and the guy who shoved you into a hot tub last night. Everyone in the world knows there is mutual hatred there. Look at the comments on Reeltime."

My stomach flips when he mentions the social media app. "What are you talking about?"

"This." He saunters over to his boots on the edge of the bed and turns his phone to face me. The video looks like it was taken from someone sitting in the hot tub based on the angle. The clip replays me crashing into the water and abruptly ends with a shot of Roger folding his arms with a satisfied smirk on his face. I exhale as he pulls the phone back to his face. "The comments are brutal. Mostly toward Roger, but a few people commented about you. It ignites recent interest in the USE-SESU rivalry."

He throws his phone on the bed, and his eyes pin me to my spot. "But you still haven't answered my question."

I play coy while I tilt my head. "What do you mean?"

He scrunches his face. "You know what I mean," he says. His demeanor matches his posture, where his arms are under his chin after he belly-flops onto my bed. Romero's heel taps his butt as we wait for my answer. His playfulness has me folding a bit.

"It's complicated."

He narrows his eyes. "Complicated how?"

I shake my head. "You wouldn't get it."

He studies me for a prolonged moment. His features are unmoved by my avoidance. "You think my situation is easy?"

"It's not the same. It's more complex than you and Angelica."

"More complex than navigating Angelica's impossible standards while appeasing her father, who's not a fan of me."

"I can't imagine why," I deadpan. We share a wry smile before I clear my throat. "But why be with her at all?"

"She holds the keys to the doors I want to unlock. My skills aren't enough to make it, so I need some external forces on my side." He slides his hand onto mine. "If I had it my way, things would become simpler."

My skin flushes.

"But since we are in this predicament," he says while shaking my hand. "I look for any opportunity to see you. Now that you are a model, our schedules align better."

His hand releases mine, and his finger travels up my arm before he grips my biceps, rubbing it in a sensual motion. "Which means more of last night."

I flex in his hand, which he squeezes.

"And I promise to be better around you. I did not handle Vince and Machi well, so let me make it up to you by helping with this Roger thing."

I look at him, not convinced that I should involve him. "It's not worth it."

"Please. Let me help." There is a softness in his eyes that convinces me he's telling the truth. I hesitate for a moment, but there is no use debating myself. No point in changing a convinced mind.

"My ex-boyfriend and I broke up because of Roger." Labeling Javi an ex for the first time is unnerving, and I'm stunned how easily the label left my lips.

Romero's expression mirrors my surprise. "Roger broke y'all up?"

I nod.

Romero looks as surprised as a man who discovered he fathered a child. "There is so much to unpack there. I didn't realize you actually dated the guy you mentioned before. But I am more surprised by Roger. I never clocked him as…"

My neck cracks as I whip my head from side to side. "No, it's not like that. Roger is not like that."

Romero laughs. "Oh, that makes more sense."

"Roger found out, and I felt it was best to leave. Broke a heart in the end."

Romero pecks my lips. "Well at least it worked out for us in the end. It would have been nice if you were fit at the beginning of the season. The sparks would have flown much earlier if it weren't for your injury."

"I guess karma gave me a broken leg for breaking a heart."

He smiles as he rubs the lump in the bed covering my healed leg. When I think he's about to pull me in close again, he rises to his feet.

"Where are you going?" I ask.

"I have a lunch date with Angelica at Gretta's Grill."

"Oh," I say, leaning back in the bed as he walks toward the bedroom door.

"I'm sorry, but I need to go home and change first. I didn't expect to stay the night." He turns around with another grin that weakens me. "But thanks for the dessert."

I flinch at his joke. "Goodbye!" I toss my pillow at him, and he playfully ducks out of the way, winking before he turns and heads for the front door.

The clicking of his boots on the hardwood grows more distant by the time I finally roll out of bed. My midterms are this week, so I need to study. If Romero is telling the truth about the modeling gig becoming a second job, then I will need to switch my courses to asynchronous online.

The university allows this for student athletes if they have a passing midterm grade before the change. I am fine right now, but all it takes is a horrible midterm to tank everything. I slam one foot to the ground but recoil when I feel hard plastic rather than hard floor. A prescription bottle rolls beneath my bed. It looks like Romero's meds.

"Hey Romero!" I call out.

I half assume he left when I hear silence, but the faint click of a boot heel crescendos until he reappears in my doorway. I swoop down, retrieve the pill bottle, and shake it at him.

"Forget something?"

"Oh yeah. Good looking out again."

"For sure," I say with a smile. I extend the bottle out in his direction and glimpse at the label. The prescription is in his brother's name. Confusion dawns on me because I swear these are the pills he took in the Uber home. "Did you have these last night?"

Romero pulls the bottle out of my grasp and slides it down his right breastplate pocket. "Yeah, these are my meds," he says.

I furrow my brow. "The Adderall is for your brother though."

"I know, but we share medications."

"Is that allowed?"

He shrugs. "It saves my family money."

"You can't get caught with this Romero. This could get you into trouble."

Romero sighs. "I know, but Andres and I struggled to pay attention growing up. When Andres got injured last year, doctors diagnosed him with ADHD and prescribed him Adderall."

"But why are you taking them?"

"Because my parents never took us to a doctor. They don't trust them. Andres and I microdose his pills. You can judge me for it. The pills help me."

"But Romero, if you are drug tested…"

He lifts his hand. "We have never been drug tested since I have been here. Not once. The school uses it to scare people, and they never follow through." Romero's phone vibrates, and he pulls it out of his pocket. Angelica's picture illuminates his screen, so he turns and exits the room. "I'm running late. We'll talk later."

He leaves the apartment when another hangover headache pierces my skull as I process all that unfolded. I worry about Romero. It's one thing to use Angelica to promote his image, but using his brother's medication? A throbbing sensation pounds my head, thinking of all the repercussions. He's playing a dangerous game, and I hope he doesn't get caught. I can't imagine what would happen. I lay down again and stretch out my arm toward the nightstand and lift my phone to view my home screen. It's littered with hundreds of unread notifications.

Machi: *Let me know when you get home, my silly Oshawott!*

Of course, she still calls me that.

Machi: *I am spending the night with Vince and his family since I have not heard from you. Please message me soon.*

Vince: *I hope you're alive. Just checking in for Machi. Tell us you are safe.*

Jesus I am an asshole. I should have responded last night, but Romero can be quite distracting.

Caleb: *I'm home. So sorry about last night.*

Machi's response arrives faster than lightning.

Machi: *Oh thank God. I was about to call the police.*

Caleb: *That seems excessive.*

Machi: *When Romero's involved, I'm always nervous. I don't trust him at all. He didn't blackmail you or anything?*

Caleb: *No not at all. Should I be concerned?*

Machi: *I have my reasons. He has an agenda.*

I raise an eyebrow. Machi has never spoken about Romero before. I wonder why he rubs her the wrong way. I was about ready to type out everything about Romero and me, but now I'm conflicted.

Machi: *Don't let his words and good looks seduce you. He's bad news.*

Too late for that.

Caleb: *Don't worry I won't. And you've spent the night with Vince?*

Machi: *That's a long story too. Fill each other in later?*

I send her a thumbs-up emoji and scroll down to find an unread message from my dad. He usually texts me once a week, offering dry updates about his life. However, today was different.

Officer Thomas: *I saw the livestream yesterday. Sorry I could not come to the match. Those were some goals you scored yesterday. Proud of you.*

I smile, but I don't feel my father's warmth radiating from his message. It feels hollow. If everything were as it was, he and my mom would make the hour journey to watch the games. I understand he struggles with grief still, but my brother and I are all the family we have left.

Caleb: *Thank you! I hope you can come to the next one.*

To my surprise, he answers.

Officer Thomas: *You know my schedule has always been busy. I will call later when I am free!*

Caleb: *I understand. Also wanted to let you know I finally got a sponsorship deal. One step closer to the pros.*

Officer Thomas: *Your mother would be proud.*

I tap the heart icon on my phone screen, place it back on the polished wooden nightstand, and stare up at the ceiling. Just the mention of her name has me reminiscing about her. How her messages were novels compared to my father's. How detailed and sweet they were until the end. I hope she is still watching over me and sees me where I am at. Not the problem child she thought I was. I tried my best, and it's not her fault what happened. I just wish I knew how she felt about the situation. Maybe then we could have healed together.

I rub my hands on my face, trying to snap out of this dangerous line of thinking. As I regain my composure, my eyes wander around my bedroom. The three-tier bookshelf situated to the right of my well-organized mini desk catches my attention. I take in the sight of my book collection, neatly arranged from left to right on the top shelf. The vibrant covers of Mesut Özil's and Arsene Wenger's biographies pop against the backdrop of the hazy room.

Further along the shelf, Starr Carter and Simon Spier stand as fictional heroes, their spines displaying stories that feel similar to mine. At the far end, the last complete picture of my family acts as a bookend. We looked so happy together two Christmases ago.

My mom's luscious blonde hair blowing in the fall air as she wraps my brother and me in her favorite white sweater. It's striking how similar we look, from the square faces, blue eyes, and even the pigment of our skin. My brother reincarnates into my father in his youth, with his broad frame and signature curly hair pulling everyone's attention.

What I would give to have another moment like this again.

Descending to the next level, my eyes land on a display of gleaming medals and soccer trophies, each award a symbol of the perseverance and triumph I experienced. I lower my gaze to the bottom shelf and fixate on my prized vinyl collection. The sight of my tiny assorted records captures my attention. The covers of "You Should Be Here" and "Anti" vinyls safeguard the precious melodies hidden within their grooves and the memories in my mind. I never played them, preferring them to stand as placeholders in time. I will if I am ever ready to revisit my past, but I never am.

However, the exposed Javi vinyl hits me the hardest. My eyes meet Javi's piercing gaze, which leaves me feeling more exposed, sending shivers down my spine. He exudes an air of nonchalance as he poses in a hazel-colored T-shirt adorned with studded earrings. The soft glow of the room's ambient light dances on Javi's curly highlights and a glimmering gold chain around his caramel-toned skin.

Yet, his shaded face conceals the stubble slightly disconnected from his goatee.

I stare at the autographed cardboard cover that envelopes a large plastic disk until tears form under my eyelids. I remember when I took this photo. Memories flood my mind, and I can almost hear the silky timbre of Javi's voice again.

CHAPTER 18

March 9, 2025

Falls

"How do I look?" Javi asks, eyes fixed on me.

I adjust the lens's focus knob until Javi appeared crystal clear. "You look good." My cheeks burn as I glance into the Polaroid camera. I tap the button in the far-right corner, ejecting a miniature picture at the bottom of Javi's camera.

Javi takes a few steps closer, retrieving the photo and swaying it in the air. We peer down at the developing photo until an image appears after a few minutes. "This is a keeper. I should hire you as my personal photographer. You always highlight my best qualities."

He tilts the picture in my direction. "Here. Take it."

"What's this for?"

"Just something to remember me by when I become famous," he teases.

"Oh really?" I say.

"Don't you think I will be famous?"

"I think you will. I'm just offended you didn't sign it first."

Javi smacks his forehead. "Of course. How could I forget?"

He pulls a Sharpie out of his pocket and signs the white base beneath the photo. He slides the photo into my pocket just before yanking my arm toward him. "C'mon. Follow me."

Javi charges ahead, his eyes sparkling with excitement as he gestures toward the trail. The delicate scent of spring foliage lingers as his lengthy body begins the arduous uphill ascent on the smooth pavement. I follow close behind, my footsteps crunching the wild grass below. We veer off onto the loose caliche path a few yards after conquering the steep incline.

Javi and I navigate through a maze of majestic oak trees and fragrant mountain cedars until we stumbled upon what we were searching for. The secluded lookout tower stands on four amber wooden pegs that rise from the ground, with an L-shaped staircase hanging down its side. With some convincing on Javi's part, we ascend the creaking staircase. Each step sends a jolt of anxiety through me, but I take solace in the deck's sturdiness beneath my feet. Javi's reassuring words about the deck's ability to withstand thunderstorms and high winds provide a sense of comfort, even though I remain skeptical of his reassurance.

The observation deck's potential danger turns into an afterthought as I meet Javi at the railing, staring east at the panorama view of the University Hills tucked into the valley. Forest green vegetation and exposed limestone litter the landscape between me and the Baptist church steeple. The sunset slowly paints the sky with warm oranges and pinks above us. Scattered homes and faint hymns of nature complete the rural fantasy with dulcet harmonies perfect for meditation.

"Thoughts?" Javi asks, staring at the horizon.

I positioned myself at the railing right of Javi. The scenery hypnotizes me. This is the most gorgeous view I have ever seen. "It's beautiful."

Javi fixes his amorous glances on me. "I just find it more peaceful here."

"How did you find this place?"

"I took the wrong road home for Christmas break and stumbled across this gem. It's now my nature therapy retreat when I need a break from school. Not that I would ever recommend anything near SESU, but this is my exception." He retrieves his Polaroid camera from me and presses it against his face. He turns and angles it, capturing the stunning sunset.

I turn to face him. "How often do you come here?"

"When I see myself falling."

I furrow my brow. "Falling?"

He nods.

"Like how Carl Jung describes falling or how Alicia Keys sings it?" I ask.

We both crack a smile.

Javi exhales deeply before pausing, almost as if he's contemplating how he wants to answer this. "Most days, I come here to escape the world when I sense my self-worth crumbling." A pleasant chuckle sneaks out of Javi as he steps closer. "But today, I don't need to escape this feeling. I guess you could say I'm falling more like Alicia."

My smile splits my face in half. It stays there for as long as I can while we both stand in silence, experiencing our surroundings. Javi breaks the silence as he steps forward and kisses me as if we were lovers in a past life reunited once again. His gentle lips trace mine, sparking fresh electricity through my brain.

If it weren't for the wind chill, we would have continued for hours. We readjust ourselves before we face the town. The faint sounds of crickets and cicadas ring in my ears while the sun unleashes blood oranges around the skyline. The scene is stunning, and its beauty offers the calming serenity that makes me feel safe. I understand why Javi drives here when he's falling. I'm glad he's closer to Alicia Keys right now.

"I think I'm falling too." I say.

"In what way?" Javi asks, his gaze still fixed on the distance.

"I think both."

"What do you mean?"

I prolong an exhale. "Before I came here, I was unbreakable. Nothing would keep my life off track. Until last summer inflicted the worst pain imaginable. Soccer served only as a distraction from the brokenness my family shared. But then my mom passed away at the end of the season, and I spiraled out of control. I was falling hard last semester, and I nearly hit my bottom." I want to cry, but I hold back my tears, recoiling when Javi's hand slides down my back.

He flinches. "I'm sorry I didn't mean…"

"No, it's okay. It's a bad reflex." I brush off my shirt and notice a dazed expression on his face.

To soften him up, I reclaim my spot next to him and lean in. "But then you came into my life and showed me something different. I almost skipped that day when we went to that café. When I first saw you, I wasn't sure what to think. You were the first guy I met who owned his identity. You weren't trying to conceal who you are like other guys. And that was so attractive to me. I was so drawn to you from the first moment, and I knew I wanted to spend time with you. The more time I spent with you, the more I wanted to be with you. Call it God, fate, or the universe, but it brought us together in a class and made us project partners."

"That project was a joke, but at least we got an A." I see Javi's eyes start to redden.

I laugh again, but his remark cannot deflect the thought popping into my head. "Maybe sharing a project was our start to something more?"

Javi's lip twitches as he opens his mouth. "What are you saying, Caleb?"

"I want you to be my boyfriend, Javi."

Javi wheezes for a second, and he looks like he's going to fall apart. "You do not know how long I have been waiting for you to ask me."

We share a sweet kiss before he buries his head in my shoulder. I feel some tears soaking into the fabric. "I have never felt the way I feel about you," he whispers. The shirt muffles his voice. "And no one ever makes me feel this way." He stares into my eyes, but there is a look of terror in his. A conflicted gaze between being scared to fall in love or being heartbroken.

He squeezes my hand. "We can keep this private, too. I know this would complicate things for you, and I don't want your life to be more stressful than it already is. I enjoy that I have this with you. It's nobody's business but ours."

"I love you, Javi."

My first *I love you*. Ever. The moment slams into me before I realize what I said. Much to my relief, Javi wraps his hands around my neck, pressing his forehead into mine. "I love you too."

The kiss before is child's play compared to this one. I pull him in so tight that I am afraid I will lose him. The passion swells between us like a river about to burst through a dam. Our tongues collide, and we continue until the point we almost suffocate. By the time we finish, we breathe so heavily you would think we ran a marathon.

"Should we get a picture together? Savor the moment?"

I nod.

Javi leans his head on my shoulder and closes his eyes, shutting out the visual chaos of the world. I take a deep breath, inhaling the crisp air and Javi's sweet scent that provides a blanket of relief. I feel Javi adjusting himself.

We share intimate stares as intense as our bond before Javi retracts his vintage Sun 660 instant camera. He extends his hand out with the camera facing us, capturing the setting sun and skyline behind us. Just before he presses down on the flash button, Javi's soft lips press against my cheek. A tingling warmth trickles through my body, and the corners of my mouth tick upward, revealing the first genuine and effortless love in a long time.

Part 2

Chapter 19

November 8, 2025

I knew something would change my life today.

There was no sign from God, or my mother as my guardian angel, but I am on a lucky streak this past month, so I know something is coming. I can feel it. The moment my phone rings in my seat, I throw my navy Vicuña blazer back around my shoulders and leap off the lime green stage. The cameraman halts the photoshoot as I sway across the set to the back corner of the warehouse.

I answer my phone when Coach Ramsey's contact appears on the screen. "Hello?"

"Caleb, this is crucial. My old pal, Matthew Evans, will reach out to you any moment now. Please be available to answer the call," Coach Ramsey says.

"Not a problem, Coach. Anything you need from me?" I ask.

"Nothing at all. I've already discussed this with our compliance officer and received conditional approval. I will see you at training in a couple of hours. Also, take Romero with you to training so he's not late again."

Coach Ramsey hangs up before I peel the phone from my

ear. I turn back around and see Romero walk onto the set, donning an identical suit to my own. He smiles and winks at me before he strikes his pose. It's the most we communicate in public, but we can't keep our hands off each other in private.

For this photoshoot, the producer had us share a changing room, which we wasted no time exploiting the first opportunity we had. Even our away trips have become sexual rendezvous more than the intended business trips. The past month with him has been more of a gay fantasy than anything serious.

An unknown number flashes on my screen this time. "Hello?"

A man with a hoarse Welsh accent screams into the phone. "Caleb, hello! How's it going?"

"I'm good," I say, turning to my left and admiring my reflection.

"It's great to chat with you. I'm Matthew Evans, an agent for Emerging Football Talents, and I wanted to discuss something with you. I've already spoken to your coach about the reason for my call, and he's on board."

"He called me just before you did. He shared nothing with me."

He laughs. "That sounds like him. He's always been quite elusive for the twenty years I have known him. I could talk for hours about our friendship, but I won't waste your time, Caleb. Let's get straight to it. Have you heard of Emerging Football Talents before?"

"No, sir."

"Allow me to provide you with an overview. Emerging Football Talents is an agency dedicated to representing top-notch players. Especially the ones that will help us pay our bills down the line." He laughs at his own joke. "I tease about that last part, but I am serious about our talented network of scouts and coaches recommending the best players at the collegiate level to us. We offer p remium r epresentation i n o ffering players to professional teams and to leverage your image and likeness to your advantage. How does this proposition sound to you?"

I smirk at the question and turn my back on the photoshoot, cupping my hands over my mouth to whisper, "That would be amazing!"

"And that's not all! Playing as you have this season, teams in the country are showing interest. Scouts have mentioned your name as an invitee for the upcoming MLS Combine. As long as you keep playing well on the pitch, I'll handle the business side."

My mind dances amidst a whirlwind of thoughts. Walking up to the combine dressed in the fancy clothes from my modeling session is the first idea to form. In the next, I grasp my first professional jersey outside the stadium that would later embrace me. Chills surge through me, their raw power catalyzing a shiver.

"Are you still there?" Mr. Evans asks, breaking my line of thought.

"Yes, I am," I say, still forcing a calm tone on the phone.

"Good. Jack praises you, and I believe you're a perfect match for this agency. Please review the contract I will soon send. It's a written record of everything I have covered on this phone call. Take some time to decide, but the sooner I hear a response from you, the better."

"Sounds good. I will let you know soon."

"Good lad. Cheers!" Matthew Evans concludes my life-altering phone call, and I am so overcome with emotion that I can't move. I almost forgot to breathe. My body is about to contort into an uncoordinated happy dance, but another phone call interrupts me. This one with a surprising caller ID.

"Hello," I say.

"Hey, son! I just wanted to check in with you," Officer Thomas says, the most animated he's been this entire year. "Am I interrupting anything?"

"Not at all. I'm almost done here, and was actually about to call you."

"Oh? Well, I am so glad I reached out. What's going on?"

"So I got an important phone call today. Matthew Evans of Emerging Football Talents called me, asking to represent me as an agent."

My fathers animated tone becomes interrogative. "An agent talked to you? What's he saying?"

"Yeah, he is a friend of Coach Ramsey. He said he would help market me to sponsors and set up pro-trials. I informed him of my interest in his services. He sent me the contract already."

"Did you sign it?"

"No, I haven't. He told me…"

His exhale crackles on the phone. "Oh, thank fuck. Send me that contract as soon as you can."

"Oh ok. Is something wrong?"

"Nothing. These agents are clever with these contracts to help line their pockets. He might have tricked you without someone looking over it."

"I don't think that's the scenario here."

"For fuck's sake, Caleb, send me the fucking contract!"

I stand there in stunned silence. It takes everything in me not to travel back in time to the moment I caught him standing over her. The veins in his head bulged as he gripped the countertop. He swore he never hit her, but just breathing that toxic air traumatized me in more ways than one. I managed those tough days the same as a young boy to a young man, blind submission to another belligerent tantrum.

Today would be no different.

"Okay then…sent."

The phone jostles around until his voice reappears. "All agents weasel in their agenda. I'm not saying that this man is a con man, but I just don't want you to get burned. Believe it or not, I am overjoyed for you."

"Doesn't seem that way." I face the crew taking apart the set.

"I know I have been absent for the last year, but I want to atone with you. The last thing I need is to lose you too, with all the success you have built. Please let me be a better father to you."

"I understand and appreciate your help," I say.

He clears his throat. "Your mom would be proud."

A smile appears on my face. "I think so, too. I'll talk to you soon."

I hang up the phone, my lips curving downward on my face in the mirror. He's right about my mom being proud, and it stings a broken spot in my heart. I'm about to shed a tear when I see movement behind me. I turn around and find Romero in his chair next to mine, staring at me, and I recoil backward.

"Hey," Romero says.

"Hey," I say, diverting my eyes away from him.

"How's everything?"

"Good. You?" I raise an eyebrow.

This is a strange series of questions from Romero, especially since he never asks personal questions. It's usually the normal sinister glance, and the clothes fly off, or some plan he has in his head to improve our situation. There is never any wholesome conversation.

"I'm good. Angelica wants us to film the rest of our Reeltime series for her profile. She's calling it 'Love Story: Angelica's Version.' For our first episode, we performed the 'NO LAughing matter' challenge. Since the challenge revolves around recreating the spontaneous kiss with a scenic view described in the chorus, I came up with splicing clips of our sunset drive to her family's ranch. Just before the chorus, we walk hand in hand to her family's red maple tree. I remove my cowboy hat and plant a romantic kiss on her lips as Javi sings in the background. I think we killed it, and our profiles will generate significant traffic with an increase in followers."

"Wow. It sounds like it's serious between you two," I say.

It's the one thought that constantly lingers in my mind. He talks as if they are not in a relationship, but Angelica's reels paint a different picture. They appear to do a couple of activities together, like going to local coffee shops, attending festivals, eating at Gretta's Grill, and making appearances at Buster's Run on the weekends. Then there are the Reeltime posts showing how they do everything together. It's one addi-tional layer that makes our relationship, if you can even call it that, more complicated.

Romero sees the seriousness in my tone and cocks his head. "Angelica and I? Please. Like I said before, it's all just a show. Angelica needs me to amplify her status as a content creator. She's moving into singing next, so she will be busy with her music. I get more attention from all the sexy fans sliding into my DMs than she does. We are not serious. I have more important people to please, especially tomorrow night." He rubs my arm up and down, but I narrow my eyes at him. "You are still going to the party at the mansion tomorrow, right?"

"I don't think so."

He narrows his gaze. "Why?"

I shrug. "I just think it would be better for me to skip."

"What's wrong?" he asks.

"Nothing, just a lot on my mind." I avoid eye contact as I walk around him to grab a water bottle on the table behind him.

"About?"

I sip from my water bottle, still unsure if I should share the news. This is not something we talk about with each other. And since my father hasn't given me the okay yet, it's best I stay silent on it. "It's a long story."

"Don't overthink about Angelica. I don't feel the same about her as I do about you. She's just a meal ticket. Besides, I would hate it if you shared your dick with a new loser," he whispers, chuckling as he stands.

When he pats me on the shoulder, I flinch. "What?"

"I just want you all to myself, and to prevent you from getting all those diseases."

I wince while sticking my index finger in my chest. "Prevent me? Are you serious?"

"Caleb, you are more used to stuff like this than I am. I have only been with one guy. I'm not sure who you are with when I'm not around."

What the actual fuck? Does he seriously think I am a whore? It takes everything in me not to punch him right in the mouth. Witnesses still cleaning up the set is the only thing keeping me in check. It would be a terrible look to start a fight here. It will take one word from the producer to Angelica's mom, and I am out of a job.

I instead take a deep, jagged breath. "First, you make me feel like a paramour, and now you are calling me a whore. What's the matter with you?"

He put his hands up in surrender. "My bad. I didn't realize you were sensitive. I'm just making sure I still get my fix when I need it."

"Which one?"

Now it's Romero's turn to furrow his brows. "What are you talking about?"

"Hookups or your other habit? But don't forget, only your brother can help with the latter."

Romero grimaces. "What the fuck is your problem?"

I stare at him, still raging over his disease comment.

"Are you upset that we are both candidates for Player of the Year?"

I roll my eyes. "God, you're insufferable."

"Really? Because it sounds like you are too insecure to share the spotlight with someone you share a bed with."

What is he talking about? I couldn't care less about the accolade at the moment. I won't lie by saying I don't fantasize about winning it because it is essential for me to win to go pro. But that's not the main reason. The conference also nominated Roger with us, and nothing would give me more joy than beating him. It would be my greatest achievement to wipe his smug smile off his rich and preppy face, and I'm confident in my ranking among the three of us.

"Don't project your insecurities onto me. It's not a good look." I move forward, ready to leave him behind, but Romero confronts me with a feral expression.

"Insecurities? Wow, you are fucking big time now! Next, you are going to tell me you called Coach Ramsey, asking for the superstar treatment. Is he offering you a room to yourself on road games now?"

His rambling catches me off guard. "What the hell are you talking about?"

"I'm talking about the call you just made with Coach Ramsey."

I stare at him slack-jawed.

"Don't play stupid. I know it was him you were sending some contract to," he says.

"Are you tweaking out on your brother's pills or something?"

"You are a piece of work. I thought we were partners here. Sticking up for each other, covering our backs. I didn't realize you would knife me in the back."

"I was talking to my father."

Romero stares at me as if he identified the enemy. "I know what I heard. You said 'agent' on the phone and something about Coach Ramsey's friend."

I suck in a breath and hesitate, prolonging Romero's agitation. "You heard correctly. I have a new agent, and I was sharing the news with my father."

He tenses in his spot, but doesn't unleash the anger I'm sure he is storing. Instead, he chuckles and massages his brow with his fingers. I don't expect any congratulations from him, but I also don't expect this. Romero looks up at me and gives a thumbs-up. "I am guessing an agent from Emerging Talents, right?"

I nod.

"Well, I guess congratulations are in order. Emerging Talents is huge. That's a big win for you."

My voice pinches as I look him over, not sure of what game he's playing here. "Thanks," I say.

"I mean, anyone on the team would kill for that. They are ultra-selective when they sign a player. I have been trying for years to sign with them. An agent representing you there would take you to new heights. I'm just surprised they chose you."

The steam leaking out of my ears could fill a sauna. I clench my fist down by my right side while gritting my teeth. "Coach Ramsey made the introduction to Matthew Evans on my behalf. He said I was the only person from our team to be represented and promoted by Emerging Talents."

"I'm sure he did. And I bet Mommy and Daddy were just jumping for joy." He says this with so much vitriol.

I try to mask my irritation, but the words leave my mouth pointed. "It was just my father on the phone."

"Why? Your mom needs a break from you?"

The words fly out before I stop myself. "My mom is dead, you piece of shit."

The warehouse hushes to ghost-quiet. Romero freezes, staring at me. My breath has slowed, but my flaring nostrils convey my desire to punch him. I don't, to my surprise, and shove down all the rage deep inside me. We don't utter a single syllable, collectively holding our breath in anticipation of the other.

Romero makes the first move. "I didn't know," he whispers.

"Well, now you do."

He bobs his head, appearing satisfied with his thoughts. Without uttering another word, Romero bumps into my shoulder, and I watch him storm off past the deconstructed set.

It's in this moment, as he walks away, that a tsunami of irritation crashes into me. There was no reason to belittle me for earning an opportunity I worked hard for. Nor was there reason to involve my parents in the heat of the moment. I regret telling him about my mom, but he pushed the last button before all the tension spilled out. Romero's mask slips, and I'm embarrassed that I focused on his body to see that earlier.

That's the price I pay when I see someone naked before I see his naked truths.

Chapter 20

November 10, 2025

"If the results hold in tonight's conference games, we will secure a spot in the championship. What's your opinion on finishing in the top two this season?" The interviewer absentmindedly brushes her curly, bronze hair away from her right ear, revealing the school emblem on her neatly pressed black school polo.

Even on the computer screen, I see the school reporter forcing a smile before adjusting her microphone to Duncan's face, left of my pixilated self. "Sweetheart, this team's having its best season yet, and it's incredibly deserved!"

Machi moves her hand onto the mouse pad and pauses the video. "He is gross," she says, standing to my left. Her hand presses on the desk while she grimaces. "How is he the captain?"

I shrug. "Coach probably felt he was the best for the job, especially since he played for the Celtic Youth Academy in Scotland. I know he's an alpha male, but he's a good leader on the field."

"I think Vince is better, honestly."

"I don't disagree, but is that based on merit or because he's your boyfriend?"

Machi burns a shade of cherry red. "It still sounds surreal when you say it."

"Is it going well? Nothing for me to worry about?" I ask in a teasing tone. I know Vince is treating Machi well. He speaks only respectfully about her in the locker room, ignoring Duncan's baiting every time.

"Don't worry. He's a perfect gentleman."

"He proves he's nothing less in the locker room." My finger taps the mouse pad, and I hit play on the interview.

"I could not agree more," the interviewer says. "With the recent suspension of the football team, the soccer team inherited new fans on campus. Myself included. I must say that watching the team play the game has been an enjoyable experience. Was developing an exciting style of play a tactic to recruit new soccer fans for the season?"

Duncan leans into the microphone this time. "When Coach Ramsey introduced us to his philosophy last year, we knew it would take some time for the team to adjust. But from the first day of preseason, we knew what to expect. This team worked incredibly hard to meet Coach's expectations and play the style of football he envisioned for the program. We're witnessing the results of the process. We stumbled at the beginning, but we are unstoppable now that we have found form. One of my best seasons, especially with my two Defensive Player of the Week awards."

The reporter nods. "The process has contributed to the visible sophomore stride in Coach Ramsey's tenure. And it's hard not to give credit to you and the best transfer in the conference next to you. It takes new players to adjust to a system and their surroundings, but Caleb, you have made it look so easy after recovering from an injury. Could you tell us about how you settled in?"

The microphone tilts from the interviewer's lips toward mine.

"Well, Coach Ramsey's guidance aided my recovery and smooth transition here. He understands me as a player, and it reduces the pressure on me to play well here. As the captain noted, trusting the process is crucial."

"It works for you, too, Caleb. I know last season with USE, you won Freshman of the Year. This season, your stats have been even more incredible since you recovered from that injury. With this continued consistency, where do you envision yourself by season's end?"

"Hopefully, as conference champions in the most competitive nationwide conference." I beam my best million-dollar smile at her.

"Do you think you will beat your old teammate, Roger Astor, for Player of the Year?"

I turn to Machi, still looking at the screen. "If I were still at USE, he wouldn't be playing."

I face the computer again, where my digital self rubs the back of his neck. "My sole focus is on the next game. That's all I can control right now." I force myself to keep that smile on my face.

"I understand. Gentlemen, thank you for your time. Well, Rottweiler Nation, the men's soccer team will play for the conference championship this Sunday at 8 p.m., so come out and support our team. And of course, go Rottis."

I click off the interview and close my laptop. "Any thoughts on my interview?"

"It wasn't bad. Everything sounded crisp until they mentioned your nemesis's name. I forgot you won Freshman of the Year last year," Machi says, twirling my desk chair so I face her.

"Yeah, I did."

"Yet you still left USE?"

"Yep."

"Roger really fucked you over."

"He gets what he wants, and that means getting rid of me. He manipulated me and exploited a difficult situation. But luckily, that doesn't matter anymore."

"What do you mean?"

"We could beat them Sunday to win the championship. It would mark this program's first major trophy. It's more memorable than another championship at USE."

"How do you feel about it?"

"I feel good about our chances. If we win, it's another feather in my cap on my way to signing a professional contract."

"Oh, that's so exciting! You got this. Also, did you see that link I sent you?"

"Which one?"

"The one about Javi and his album release this Friday."

"Oh, right. I watched that video."

Machi's link opened a video of Javi's interview on late-night TV. He poured his heart out about the muse that inspired the album. How 'this person' inspired the most special love he has experienced. The host begged him to rec-reate the "NO LAughing matter" challenge, but he declined, insisting he would perform the challenge with someone 'special.' Whatever that means. He instead blew a kiss to the female host dramatically in front of a blue screen, alternating between various settings. The clip went viral on Reeltime. He finished his appearance by singing his number one hit to a crowd of adoring fans.

"I think it's romantic that he's reaching out to someone through his album, and saving his own challenge for that special person. I hope this person loves him back."

"Being in a relationship has turned you into a romantic optimist, huh?"

"All I am saying is, I hope 'that person' realizes how special they are and reaches out to Javi soon. I think Javi deserves to post his challenge with the inspiration behind the song, not just a late-night TV host. It's poetic, I think."

I shrug. "I guess we will see."

Machi studies me for a long minute before she wanders around my room. "Are you doing anything today?" she asks.

I rotate back toward my desk. "I'll study here for a bit until training later today."

"Today? You played yesterday."

"Since we will have a day off later this week, we needed to train today. Luckily, it's just a pool recovery session."

Machi walks over to my closet and scratches my hangers across the bar out of view. "So, you swim and heal yourself? What stupid idea is that?"

"It's more like stretching on the pool's shallow end and then treading water in the deep end."

She pokes her head out. "Tread water?"

"It is where we stay above water using only our feet."

"But you suck at swimming," she says, looking confused.

"Yeah, I drown."

She blinks as if she witnessed an unexplainable event and turns away. "So you drown to heal your body. I will never understand soccer players." She removes a T-shirt from the hanger and lays it over her shoulder. "I need to borrow the shirt I bought you for work because I forgot about the laundry. Before I leave, do you need anything?" She emerged from the closet, a Third Place Roaster shirt in one hand, a blanket in the other.

My eyebrow arches. "Where are you going?"

"Third Place."

"Why?"

"I have a shift later today."

I cock my head. "I thought you said you quit."

"I wrote my notice, but I haven't submitted it yet. I just haven't gotten around to it," she admits.

"You don't have to work anymore with my sponsorship deal. As I promised you, I would pay for everything since you helped me settle in. That, and you are an amazing friend. You deserve the extra free time for studying and Vince."

"I know, but can I be honest with you?"

I raise an eyebrow. "Is everything good between you and Vince?"

She gawks at me. "What? Yes, Vince and I are great. I feel like I am having a mid-college crisis."

"Are you okay?" I sit up straight in my chair.

"Yeah, I'm good. I have just been feeling this way about school for a while. My classes, plan, and academic life are nothing how I imagined they would be."

"I'm sorry, Machi."

"It's okay. It started after my freshman year sucked for me.

I enrolled in a major that my parents approved of for me and took stupidly hard courses I didn't enjoy and killed myself to get all A's. I have no friends in the engineering department, and my classes ate away at my free time."

"You still got me though," I say.

Machi smiles, but drops her head. "I know, but we spend so little time together. That's my fault."

"It's not your fault, Machi. You had to work after your parents stopped sending money. Your job at Third Place Coffee had to pay the bills. But now I can afford your bills, and would love to take that stress away from you. It's the least I could do for you."

"And I love you for that, but I have to confess something."

I furrow my brow. "What's up?"

"Is it bad that I'm glad Shane's wrongful death payouts stopped coming because I enjoy working there more than I study for classes?"

"Really? You always talk about the stress it brings you. I just figured you hated it."

"But I thrive under that stress. I enjoy making compli-cated lattes during a Monday rush. It's like I'm my Pokémon, continuing to level up with every challenge. It was something to look forward to. And part of me envisions a future in the coffee business."

"So you want to work at Third Place forever?"

"Of course not! But I think I want to open my own shop one day. It's the first choice I made about the future, and I feel good about it. Maybe I will create a Taiwanese coffee shop."

"Oh, Machi. That's exciting. I am so happy for you."

"Me too. I plan to finish the semester out and then officially switch majors for the next semester."

"Have you told your parents?"

"No, I haven't, but I will call them here soon."

"I understand." I nod. "Do you care if I play music to study?"

"I don't mind, but every music streaming service is down right now."

I frown when I confirm Machi's story on my phone. "Well, do you care if I play the vinyl player?"

"Sure. I vote for everyone's favorite new album. I think it's great for studying." Machi's grin remains on her face as she exits the room.

"I'll think about it. I appreciate your advice."

I stretch out my body before reopening my laptop, and I pull up a new Google Chrome tab, clicking my book-marked university portal page. My screen illuminates with my Motivation Psychology assignment, which I continue to lose motivation for. However, I won't have much time after practice to finish, so I grab my textbook instead and open it to the last chapter we discussed in class.

Given that vinyl is my only source of music, I roll my chair to my bookcase and remove my shiny turntable from the shelf before placing the record player on the ground. I retrieve a pouch dangling from the top rod of the bookcase and lean over in my chair to operate my player. While holding the tone arm away from the turntable, I pull out a carbon fiber tooth-brush and wipe it front-to-back, following the instructions I received on the day I got it. After eight front-to-back move-ments, I wipe my cloth over the turntable and record player surface, removing moisture and all signs of previous use.

As I finish my initial setup, I look up at Javi's vinyl again. I still can't believe he sent me his album before the release date. One that even Pitchfork expected as this fall's most anticipated album release. "NO LAughing matter" became an internet sensation, catalyzing the biggest explosion of couples showing off their romance as spontaneous scenic kisses. The same one I planted during Mardi Gras, not so long ago.

It hits me how little I appreciate Javi's intent in his gesture. He knew how excited I was to hear his project, so he sent me his first album on vinyl as a throwback to our first date. I feel foolish for mistaking a romantic gift for a curse. It's not his fault things ended between us. It's mine. If anyone should avoid anyone, it should be him to me. Instead, he reached out in the way only Javi could pull off, showing he cared.

I pull off the sleeve, exposing the dark and baby blue color-melt record, and set it on the record player. I lay the tonearm on the outermost groove and sit back, waiting for his familiar voice to ring in my ears. It doesn't take long to recall all the memories. The nostalgia slams into me. Hard.

Chapter 21

March 23, 2025

Queen of caves

When Javi told me we were going to the city's hottest gay club, I never expected we would party in a bunker. A skinny walkway is barely visible through the hazy, smoke-filled air that stretches out in front of me. In a few hurried paces, I step onto the worn-out dance floor, the faint whisper of sneakers squeaking, stilettos clicking, and Sperry's scuffling adding to the pulsating beats from the Queens of Pop playlist ringing in my ears.

Rainbow laser lights adorn the dusky space, casting an ethereal glow that dances off the disco ball above. The air is heavy with hints of alcohol and sweat, mingling with the diverse array of fabrics and fragrances worn by the massive crowd. I navigate my way around the bar, running my hand along the chips and cracks of the concrete walls, the rough and uneven texture pricking my fingertips.

A wrap around walkway surrounds the bar, bathed in a soft neon glow, and two staircases beckon patrons to explore on each side. One staircase provides outside access. The second staircase leads to a door next to the DJ. The music blares from the speakers placed in every corner, drowning out any conversation and immersing me in the energetic atmosphere. Massive flat screens positioned across three walls display videos of dancers bursting with neon spandex that syncs with the rhythm, captivating the crowd and drawing them closer to the DJ booth.

A fresh wave of pulsating energy crashes onto the dance-floor when Lady Gaga's infectious music video "Rain on Me" illuminates the TV screens while the music booms from the speakers, causing all flamboyant fems, burly bears, and every gay male subtype imaginable to flood the dance floor. Their presence is palpable as they lock arms and lips, creating a colorful whirlwind around me.

In the bar area, the chatter of silver-haired gays mixes with the laughter of beautiful lipstick and butch lesbians. I exchange awkward glances with some onlookers shuffling by me, most brushing up against me. Weary of being unwittingly targeted for a third time, I lean on the empty dancer's cage, scanning the crowd's movement.

My discomfort is difficult to hide, but I don't want it to ruin my first time at a gay club. Javi raved about this place, and I want to enjoy it. Just as I relax, a third touch lands on my lower back. A ragged breath leaves my lips when I turn around, but I'm relieved when I see it's Javi, clad in a black mesh top and leather pants, holding a couple of cherry vodka sours.

"So, what do you think?" he asks, sipping his drink.

"This is…different," I say, looking around.

He tilts his head to the side. "What do you mean?"

"A place like this. It's different."

"You've never been to a gay bar or club?"

"That and I have never been to an underground bar in the middle of nowhere, let alone one requiring a cave entrance and paying a homeless guy change."

Javi smiles before snorting. "That's The Cove for you, the best gay secret in the South. The person standing outside the entrance is the security personnel, responsible for collecting the entrance tokens. If you don't pay, he'll scare you away."

"Are those homeless people security in disguise?"

"No, they're homeless, but they're cool. The owner of the complex takes care of them, and they guard our hidden rave."

"Talk about being hidden, especially having to take a special party bus to get here. Also, where is the restroom? I didn't see a bathroom anywhere."

Javi laughs again. "Well. Bathrooms in gay clubs are not the cleanest nor safest places, if you get what I mean. We have to use the complex bathrooms upstairs by the concession stands."

"It must be bad if they're making us return to the surface to use the bathrooms."

"That's one way to put it."

I smirk, but remain subdued.

"Are you sure you are okay with all this?" Javi asks, grabbing my arm.

"I'll be fine."

"I know, but I just want you to be comfortable and enjoy this place." He wraps his arms around my neck.

I reciprocate the gesture around his waist. "I enjoy being with you."

Javi and I kiss more subtly than I did in New Orleans. I open my eyes and smile at him, but shudder from the raking stares of eavesdropping spectators. It unsettles me, and Javi notices as he looks around himself.

"I will make sure nothing bad happens. I promise. None of the USE gays come here, so no one will out you."

I nod, but the reassurance doesn't cool my apprehension. More men stare, assessing every detail of my body.

"Trust me!" Javi nods and reaches down for my hand.

I wrap my hand in his. My heartbeat quickens its pace, sending a rush of blood coursing through my veins. A warmth spreads throughout my body, tingling in my fingertips and radiating from my core. With every step forward, Javi pulls me close into his orbit, peeling away my cool exterior until I'm exposed and raw.

The moment is exhilarating, but I feel out of my element. Men gaze hard at me, violating the little personal space I have with their eyes. It transports me to the darkest chapter of my life, one even darker than losing my mother. The longer they stare, the more my stomach drops.

I'm on the verge of telling Javi about the anxiety crawling up my spine when the roar of the crowd drowns out all other sounds, including the rest of my thoughts. The track cuts off, and the roar of artificial thunderstorms and high-tempo drum and bass blares from the speakers above. A raspy Eastern European voice fills the room over the top of the bass.

"Y'all ready to misbehave in this cave?"

Everyone cheers and applauds.

"Oh yes, baby. It sounds like time to get this show started!"

A harmonious blend of synth and simple techno replaces

the thunderstorms, creating the EDM equivalent of elevator music.

"We have a great show for the Queen's Feens tonight. We have some lovely newcomers to drag who are blessing our stage. Joining us from University Hills, give it up for our local gems…"

I turn to Javi and shout over the introductions. "What is going on?"

Javi glances at me as if I had just asked a stupid question. "Are you sure you aren't straight?" His answer comes out as a cacophony of vowels and consonants.

I wrap my hand around my ear. "What?"
Javi leans into my ear. "It's Postojna DeVayne's drag show. Are you sure you're gay?"

"Who is Postojna Devayne?"

The speaker's voice echoes across the venue. "Show some love for all our queens tonight!"

On cue, the crowd breaks into a frenzy. "Tonight, the rules are long and blunt. Just like me!"

The crowd whistles.
"Just kidding! I'm a cheap queen, so get plenty of drinks to confuse me as Ms. Fenty. And those drinks taste as cheap as me, so don't be a whore! Grab more! Get your phones out, honey! You will want to remember this so you can touch yourself to them later. Hehe."

"Scream for the queen's feens. It's brave to tuck your treasures and sync your lips with the lyrics, so admire this beauty. Honey, it's not just about the wig and dresses to be this stunning. This Ukrainian queen aspires to rule the world.

And she is your dream girl. One more important rule. My inspirational drag mother always created a kind and positive vibe, so this space is our dedication to her. She believed that your origin doesn't limit your potential. Don't be ashamed of your walk or talk because it's crucial to your identity. And that's the tea. Tonight we came ready, so all of you better stay ready. Now…let the good times roll!"

The music changes to the intro of Flo Rida's "Let It Roll" in the background. The beat energizes the crowd, encouraging them to clap in rhythm while spotlights flash around. All lights converge on the door by the DJ's box. A male voice screams from the speakers.

"Please welcome your host, the Queen of Caves herself, Postojna DeVayne!"

As Postojna DeVayne swings the door open, the room erupts into a symphony of thunderous applause, shaking the air and sending surges of electric energy into the crowd. She struts to the balcony, waving at us as if she were greeting her subjects. Her mocha skin glows, radiating a natural beauty that captivates all who lay eyes upon her. As she approaches the edge of the balcony, the crowd serenades her arrival. The sight of her gown, adorned with a mehndi-designed pattern woven into the sapphire lace, catches the light and sparkles like stars in the night sky. The puffy Juliet sleeves envelop her arms, exposing her delicate clavicle and shoulders.

She saunters down the staircase as she balances her weight against the rail, our eyes momentarily blinded by the dazzling glare emanating from her eight-row rhinestone bracelet. A crown of stalagmites rests upon her head, its jagged edges contrasting with the softness of her curly black hair, which seems to float in the air as if defying gravity. In her hand, she holds a stalactite scepter, its yellow ribbons fluttering in the breeze. The touch of the ribbons against her skin is delicate, adding an element of whimsy to her regal presence.

As she nears the floor, a staff member rushes over, exchanging her royal staff for a microphone. The crowd holds its breath, eagerly awaiting her first words as she prepares to cap-tivate them with her regal voice.

"How y'all doing tonight?" she asks.

The crowd erupts into a prolonged shriek of joy.

"This crowd has some wild energy tonight. It feels like you all have held in that sound for a week. Those heteros giving you trouble again?"

Javi laughs with the crowd while I sneak a grin.

Postojna greets the bar regulars and some of her generous tippers. "I love meeting all you beautiful people, and this crowd is very sexy tonight. I understand why you horn dogs just can't control yourselves." Postojna twirls in her spot, the ends of her gown floating above the ground. She moves her right hand down her body, palm facing up. "What y'all think? Is this something you would feast on?"

The crowd erupts with whistles and catcalls when she puck-ers her lips. She stops twirling when she sees me and struts over. "What about you, hot stuff?"

My throat goes dry as I lock eyes with Postojna. The entire bar stares at me, and it freezes me in my spot. It's not the glances that bother me, since sizable crowds watch my games at the USE stadium. But those fans don't look at me like I'm meat in a lion's den. Javi wraps his arms around me, and his touch soothes me despite the scrutinizing gazes of the other patrons. I lean into Javi, hoping Postojna instead taunts another member of the crowd. This doesn't happen, and she beams back at him, her salacious smile remains unfazed.

"Somebody loves playing hard to get. We'll meet in the bathroom later."

The crowd laughs.

"It's funny because we don't do that here. But I see this white boy likes his Latin blood, so I digress. For now, at least…" Postojna DeVayne walks over to the base of the staircase and begins her introduction. "Tonight, I have a special treat for my feens. The House of DeVayne is hosting an epic three-way showdown extravaganza against two legendary houses in the region. Since you all love threesomes…"

The crowd erupts in applause.

"I figured you would love that. Now go grab yourself a wonderful cocktail from our fabulous bartenders, who are serving our famous Blueberry Lemon Moskal and Palestine Power Punch tonight. And if you cheap hoes hate the prices, just remember we donate to charity. In the meantime, is the audience ready for my opening act?"

Cheers echo across the bar once again.
"Allow me to perform first from the House of DeVayne, bringing all the femme queen realness on the runway. I dedicate this one to you, handsome." She points at me before the spotlight dims. Even from my limited view, men flank the Queen of Caves as she ascends the steps to the balcony. A run of electric piano keys plays on a loop in the background.

By the time the lights turn back on, Postojna transforms into someone unrecognizable from moments ago. She mesmerizes me as she coolly takes her first steps in jet-black pumps into the spotlight, revealing her new bejeweled satin sapphire sheath. The crowd gapes at her gorgeous ensemble, leaving the bar room in anticipation.

One hand on the railing, the other in her new long, straight blonde hair, Postojna maintains a dignified pose. She closes her eyes, posing as if she's on the cover of Vogue, while descending the stairs. A couple of seconds later, Rihanna's voice sings the introduction of "Where Have You Been?" Postojna's lips move in sync with Rihanna's voice, and she stretches her right arm out while angling her hand down at a right angle while maintaining her catwalk. She brings her other arm out and twists her shoulder in, angling the other hand at ninety degrees, creating the first of many flawless camera lines. Her eyes lock on the emcee, the corners of her lips tilting upward. The emcee's voice booms from the speakers.

"Everybody make some noise!"

The crowd erupts in thunderous admiration, and for once, I celebrate with them. It's a breath of fresh air watching someone perform without fear of a coach making sissy remarks. No shame in a parent demonizing your sexuality. She owns her autonomy, and I can't help but feel envious.

Staying in sync with the song, she wraps her right arm over the back of her head and touches her left shoulder once she hits the bottom floor. Postojna's left hand connects her right elbow before bringing her left arm down to her hip, finishing her first rotation. The crowd burst into a drunken frenzy. She's the center of their universe, and many patrons stretch out a tip in admiration.

She stops her dancing once she hits the floor, holding in place for the spotlight and audience to fixate on her. She moves her lips during the pre-chorus to mimic the song's intensity. Once the tempo builds up, she holds onto her dress while performing a couple of stanky legs on the beat, almost identical to a performance by Rihanna herself. But as the beat is about to drop, Postojna pulls off her dress and her long blonde wig. Postojna takes off in a series of coordinated dance moves in a dazzling pink jumpsuit and cherry red bob cut wig. The song changes to the chorus of "S&M."

Postojna encompasses Rihanna, mimicking her walk and her dancing with precision. Her performance oozes elegance personified, and the audience agrees. If her lineage placed her among the blue collars in the crowd, tonight was Postojna's coronation ceremony. Everyone loses their minds in the crowd at the performance we are witnessing. Postojna grabs a younger and masculine male from the crowd and pushes her butt on top of his chest, sliding into the splits. She bounces her crotch up and down, pointing at me while mouthing the lyrics.

I hold out a few singles, joining the others. Postojna dances over to me, scanning me while the music plays. She grabs the dollar between my fingers, pulls me in, and presses her lipstick-soaked lips on my cheek. She peels off me and collects the rest of her tips, leaving a fresh stain for Javi to laugh at. Javi pulls his Polaroid camera out of his purse, capturing the unforgettable memory.

Javi and I climb the spiral staircase after the show ends. We push through the crowd in the skinny, claustrophobic hallway until I push open the heavy stone swing door, revealing the cave that acts as a foyer of the club. We turn left, avoiding the sprawling crowd and the deep groans to our right. As we approach the cave's opening, we slide down the drop-off, hop the fence, and walk toward the sparse crowd of patrons sitting at picnic tables under the sporting complex lights overhead.

My gaze sweeps over the scattered picnic tables as we walk closer, their surfaces worn and weathered, illuminated by the faint glow of the flood lights. A short line forms in front of the concession stand, transformed into an impromptu bar on the right side of my field of vision. I forget we are standing on top of a bar still in full party mode because all I hear is faint conversations, the pop of bottle caps, and the crackle of a radio.

We walk over to the concession stand to order a few sodas before we found an unoccupied table just to the left of the pavilion. Even with the roughness of the bench digging into my pants, I'm relieved to sit down. The stiffness is my leg hardened into concrete. It's also refreshing to take a few swigs of my Sprite without the heat of vodka. I'm taking in my surroundings until I see Javi staring at me, as if he's expecting an answer from me.

"Did you say something?"

Javi cups his mouth. "What did you think of the show?"

"Oh, right." I shrug until my shoulders touch my ears. "It was not at all what I expected."

Javi raises an eyebrow.

"Is that a good thing or a bad thing?"

"It was an experience, for sure." I grab the damp napkin underneath my bottle and wipe my cheek, remembering the lipstick stain.

"Well, at least now we can say you have experienced a drag

show at The Cove. We never have to return if it was too trau-
matizing. I know the queens can be extra sometimes."

"It's not that." I tap the wooden table with my fingertips.

Javi sits up. "What's wrong?"

I catch a lump in my throat and exhale deeply. "It was the
crowd and how they were."

Javi's bright aura dims at my words.

"What do you mean by that?" Javi asks, folding his arms
across his chest.

"It's not because they were gay."

Javi relaxes. "Then what was it?"

I lean my torso over the picnic table.

"The way they were staring just as if they had violated me,
especially the older guys."

"Caleb. All men do that. Hetero and non-hetero. I bet
thousands of women can relate to you."

"I don't think so."

Javi furrows his brow.

I clear my throat. "Awful things happened to me in the
past, from older men who stared at me the same way. Except
they violated me differently."

Javi gasps as the realization sinks in. "Caleb. I'm so sorry. If
I had known, I would never have put you through that."

"You didn't know."

"Yes, but I still would never put you in a triggering position. I don't want you to suffer again."

"I know." I look up at him as he reaches out his hand. I
place mine in his, feeling his finger wrap it. He squeezes gently
as he looks at me with more care than any man has shown me.
It's his next words that break me.

"I love you, Caleb."

I sniffle through my words. "I love you too, Javi."

A small tear trickles down Javi's face before a mist of red floods his cheeks. "You don't have to worry about that ever again. We move forward and heal together."

A full-toothed smile stretches across my face. "Deal."

Javi squeezes my hand a final time before releasing it. He pulls his phone out of his pocket, scans it for a brief second, and slaps his hand a few times on the table. "Our Uber is here, so we can escape all these creeps making my man uncomfortable."

He rises from his seat and walks around the table until he towers behind me, proceeding to give me the most comforting bear hug. We untangle ourselves and share a long, loving kiss. But as each second passes, the kiss evolves into something more intense. I know Javi feels the same because he has the same glazed expression as me when we pull away.

"Let's get out of here," he whispers.

I grin as I stand, and we race to the Uber with only one thought in our minds.

CHAPTER 22

March 24, 2025

In love

The sexual tension is killing me. I have never had to muster this level of willpower to behave in this car since we left The Cove. I'm tempted to yank Javi across the third row and press my lips to his for the most intense kiss we have ever shared. Probably would have already if our eavesdropping driver hadn't forced us into silence. We settled for lingering glances that ended in smirks instead. When what feels like an eternity passes, the Uber drops us off at our resort-style student housing complex. We thank the driver, exchange pleasantries, and head into the dormitory with our exchanged glances and stares persisting.

We walk halfway down the hallway before we step inside Javi's room in the quad apartment. He shuffles me across the bare living room to his assigned room in the far-right corner. Posters cover all the walls in the standard room, each corner chosen to display musical inspirations. Lauryn Hill's Grammy ensemble hangs above the desk, the black cropped top and multicolored tulle maxi skirt catching the light, their textures begging to be touched. The air carries a faint scent of paper and ink, remnants of the poster's creation. Rihanna's presence commands attention above the dresser, her solid chrome hearts slip dress and microprint robe framing her like a work of art.

I stare face-to-face with Frank Ocean looming above the bed. Frank's expression is one of contemplation, especially his face partially hidden as he clutches it. The sight of his muscular torso and vibrant lime green hair adds an unexpected touch of intensity to the room.

Javi sets his speaker onto his vinyl player above the dresser, and the slow and sensual beats of Rihanna's "Love on the Brain" flow from the nightstand speaker, the melodic rhythm wrapping around the space.

If I measure our wealth in the time we have to share, we're millionaires. And there is nothing I want more than to savor this moment. I recline on his bed, my attention fixed on Javi as he saunters toward me. He slowly peels off his mesh shirt, exposing his toned upper body. I strip off my shirt, trying my best to disguise my excitement with coolness. Javi steps closer to me, his lips an agonizing few inches away.

"Are you sure?" he whispers.

My lips twitch into a faint smile. "I'm sure."

"I guess that makes two of us," Javi says.

The kiss sends a gentle warmth through me. The finesse of his lips controls the moment's pace, starting and building with intensity as we maintain our position. His tongue, however, tastes sweet and adventurous. I lay down as soon as the duvet hits my back, stretching my hands above my head. Javi unbuckles his leather pants, revealing a bulge more pronounced in tight red mesh underwear. I follow his lead, unzipping my dress pants, mirroring the same excitement poking into my slick boxer briefs.

Our tongues slide between our mouths as I slide on top of him, my body aching with a longing so deep I can barely breathe. Javi contorts and moans as I press my lips against his neck. I cling tightly to Javi, trying desperately to hold on to the remaining warmth in a harsh world.

Our bodies sway effortlessly, each movement in sync with the sensual beats echoing from the speakers. Each touch sends a wave of warmth through me, a tingling delight that plays with my senses. I turn over, and Javi's lips leave a trail down my body, forcing a satisfied moan to leave my throat. I flinch back as the sensation ignites a welcome tingling. He pauses and stares deep into my eyes. I nod to the unsaid question and close my eyes, waiting for the next sensation. He peels back my boxer briefs until they dangle from my ankles, and he steals a breath.

The friction Javi applies to my body sends goosebumps across my skin. I clutch the cotton sheets as I gasp, my body quivering as his tongue sends a wave of tingling heat across my skin. My mind drifts into another dimension with each sensual movement from him, and I caress the base of his jaw with my hands. His tongue slides across the head of my dick, and it takes everything in me not to spasm with satisfaction. The pain tingles like pleasure, but the pleasure builds so quickly that I fear I am about to finish too early. I slide my hand down his jawline, saving me from an early detonation. Javi, unmoved by my deflection, moves up my body and presses his lips onto my hips and then to my lips. I wrap my hands around his face and share a slow, passionate kiss only lovers could share. He moves toward my neck and whispers in a hushed tone. "Take me."

I stare down at him as he slides his underwear down his slender hips. His physique doesn't match the athletic fantasy I envisioned, but he's perfect for my first time. He's all I dream about now. I trace his sun-kissed outline with my fingers, drifting from his shoulders to his hips before I wrap around his round butt. Just the feel of him has every drop of blood rushing down to my legs. Javi slips in between my knees and finishes his preparation before hovering around my pronounced manhood. He smirks at me and moves his body down onto me, claiming the last moments of my virginity.

He slides down and fractures my past perception of intimacy. For years, my concept of sex swung on the pendulum of traditional masculinity, swaying between the sides of religious precedent and patriarchal benchmarks. But this sensation contradicts everything, and it's so liberating. I crave Javi more with every careful stroke of my pelvic bone, shedding a layer of my former self.

I clasp Javi between my two hands, the rhythm of my pounding heart a steady drumbeat matching my hip thrusts. His head lolls back, and his groans become more pronounced as he presses against me, leading him to encircle his arms under my shoulders. His nails dig into my upper back, the pressure building with each breath, a harsh, high-pitched sigh escaping his lips. I'm beyond infatuated, and I lose myself.

But my lack of experience shows in my stamina, because I squeeze Javi tight to my chest and wheeze as I explode. He pants as my thrust slows, and leans forward onto my chest, his breathing still heavy. I fixate on the ceiling above me, allowing endorphins and rational thinking to cool the firing passion that raged minutes prior.

"That was your first time?" Javi utters as he spreads himself all over my naked body.

"Yeah. Why?" I whisper.

"I feel amazing."

A smile curves onto my face. "Not bad for a hetero?"

Javi nibbles on my collarbone. "You fulfilled my straight fantasy."

His long bookcase catches my attention, especially the catalog of vinyl albums, all organized by color. The Rihanna vinyl from the farmers' market leans against the back wall of the bookcase, its cover matching the poster above the bed. The album's last song, "Close to You," echoes from the speaker.

"Wow. That collection you have is intense," I say. "Like I said, I love the sound of vinyl. Did the sex make you forget?" Javi says. He shifts his body and crawls under the blanket. I pull him close, pressing my chest against his back, and wrap my arms over his shoulders. I trace my fingers along Javi's chest gap, lying in blissful contentment.

"Are you excited for Rihanna's new music?"

Javi lifts his head. "What kind of question is that? Of course I am! I've been ready since her Super Bowl performance. I hope this time she actually means it."

"I can't believe she has released nothing since 2016."

"Don't remind me of the torture. If I had known I would only enjoy her music career during my childhood, I would have begged my G-mom to take me to her concert. I'm not giving up hope for that ninth album, though. At least she's keeping us pretty in the meantime."

"You are a glutton for punishment, aren't you? Waiting all that time for an album that's not coming," I tease.

He glares at me. "Don't test me."

I throw up my hands in protest. "Fair enough. What's your favorite album?"

"Anti, remember? Her 'timeless classic' we still enjoy while we patiently wait for its successor. Have you listened to her music yet?"

"To be honest, my mom listened to her. I like Kehlani."

"Oh right, duh. Have you listened to your vinyl yet?"

"Not yet."

"Why not?"

"Because I don't know how to work a turntable."

Javi smacks his forehead. "What am I going to do with you?"

Javi turns off his speaker and peels back the covers, exposing my bare skin to the cool air, causing goosebumps to rise on my arms. He walks over to the bookcase and, squatting down, examines his collection. He grabs the "Anti" album and the record player before he saunters back to the bed. Javi sets the nightstand lamp on the floor and positions the turntable so the speaker faces toward us. With a glint in his eyes, he slides back under the duvet and places the album on my chest.

"Here," he says.

I lay silent, rubbing my fingers across the center panel. "What are you doing?"

"I am going to show you how to enjoy this as much as I do."

There is such anticipation in his eyes that I can't help but crack a smile. I indulge him and pull out one of the cherry red records up to the light. Goosebumps rush up my skin as he returns the contents together. "It's so nice."

"It's part of her Rih-Issue collection. She turned all her albums into vinyl, each one with a uniquely colored record. I collected the entire set after she released them."

"So, what do I do?"

Javi tilts his head so his eyes can see mine. He takes a deep breath without breaking his gaze. He pulls my arm until we are both standing naked by the nightstand. Javi swaddles my athletic build as best as his skinny frame can contain. He pokes his head around my right bicep, and I peer down at him.

"What now?"

"Line up the record on the turntable."

I do as he instructs.

"Now turn the right dial to the first click."

I turn the dial until the first click, and the record rotates in place. Javi reaches into the nightstand and pulls out what looks like an eraser for dry-erase markers. He places it in my hand.

"What's this for?"

"It's for cleaning the vinyl before we play it."

"How does that work?"

Javi sends me a teasing grin. "I will show you if you let me."

I nod, and he takes my hand while I clutch the tool. He positions my hand to hover above the record.

"Now gently press down."

We lower our hands together, a faint anticipation lingering in the air. The vinyl cleaner bar connects with the vinyl, similar to an airplane landing, jagged at first but smoothing itself out.

Javi lifts my arm when he's satisfied with my work. "Now for the magic."

He steps to the side of me to grab the sidearm and lays the pointed end with a gentle touch. A blast of static precedes the powerful sound of "Same Ol' Mistakes" from the stereo.

Javi turns me around and holds out his hand to me. "Care to dance?"

A laugh escapes me as I intertwine my hands in his. He pulls my naked body close to his. We waltz across his dorm room, swaying our bodies to the beat.

"Not bad on your feet hetero."

"Occupational hazard."

He smiles and lays his head on my chest. I rub my nose through his curly hair, but his uneven breath tells me something is wrong.

"Are you okay?" I whisper.

"Yeah. Just a lot of thoughts popping into my head."

"Like?"

"Well, it's kind of personal. Is that okay?" Javi asks.

"Sure."

"Do you miss your mom?"

I stop tracing his chest and look at him, my brows furrowing. "Why do you ask?"

He pauses. "Her death is the only thing you've mentioned about her since the coffee shop."

I take a deep breath in, and I lay my chin on his head.

He clears his throat. "We don't have to talk about it if you don't want to."

"It's complicated," I whisper, stroking my fingertips against his smooth skin.

"I understand. I wasn't trying to make you uncomfortable. It's just…I have a complicated relationship with my mother, too."

"You do?" I whisper.

"I mean, if you even call it a relationship. The last time I talked to my mother was the day I came out, which went about as badly as I imagined it would go. Long story short, my parents never sent me a return flight ticket to come home after music camp in New Orleans, and I lived with my G-mom until I went to college."

"I'm sorry, Javi."

Javi peels off my skin to look at me. "Don't be. I was just curious how close you were to your mom. I don't know what it feels like for a parent to pass, but I understand losing my mom. You don't have to suffer alone."

I nod. Javi's love wraps me in a blanket of oxytocin, a love so comforting I feel safe enough to blurt out my next words. "I lost my mom to suicide."

Javi stares at me like I said his mom was dead. "What?"

"And I never talk about her because I hate how she left us." I cut off Javi before he could utter a syllable. The words tumble out more icy than before. "It wasn't fair. The whole thing. She promised I could come to her with anything, and she would help. I guess I found out the hard way how untrue that was. I should have just suffered in silence."

"Caleb, that's not true."

"I know it was. The one problem I needed help with the most and it broke her. Her death fractured my family. My father traveled so far for his extra work assignments with the state police that I never saw him until the funeral, leaving me alone all winter break. I'm not surprised my brother left after that. Actually, I'm jealous he found a new family." My breaths fly out fast and sharp, and I take a beat to reset.

Javi rubs my chest. "I'm sorry. I didn't mean to upset you."

"It's not your fault my father left me to wallow in my grief."

"Where was he?"

"The southern border."

Javi gasps. "Why is he at the border?"

"He was part of a group of state troopers who signed up for border patrol. He never told me why he went, nor saw past the irony in wanting that job."

Javi stays mute, and it strikes me as odd.

"What's wrong?" I ask.

Javi releases me and straightens. "Where is he?"

"I think Laredo."

The color drains from Javi's face. "I'm from Laredo."

I look at him, puzzled.

"I thought you were from New Orleans."

"My mom grew up in New Orleans before she went to a conference in Laredo and met my father. She got pregnant with me and tried to move him to New Orleans, but he couldn't. She moved to be with him." His eyes darken with every word, and it hit me how shitty my statement sounded.

I wave my hands frantically. "I wasn't saying that being from Laredo is a problem. You just talk about New Orleans so much, I didn't realize you were born in Laredo."

"It's not that, Caleb."

I furrow my brow.

"My dad didn't have enough money to pay a hospital bill, so they left for Nuevo Laredo to have me."

I open my mouth to say something, but stop myself as I try to fit the pieces of the puzzle together. It hits me like a slap, and I look at him, horrified by what he's revealing.

"Just protect my secret. Please. You are the only person I have ever told, and I can't have anyone find out. I don't know what would happen if immigration found me."

I nod. So many questions race through my head, and I'm on the verge of asking them. But I hesitate because nothing good will come of my asking. It's not worth bringing down the mood any further. Javi's shoulders drop before we lie down on the bed again. This time, he buries his head in my chest.

"I'm sorry. I didn't mean to unload trauma like that on you."

I pull Javi in for an embrace of comfort to offset the heavy conversation. "It's okay. I didn't mean to stress you."

We touch our foreheads while our breathing subsides. I hold him here for minutes and still cultivate the strongest intimacy I have ever felt. I scan my closed-eyed lover, admiring every perfection within Javi's imperfections. Every chip in his armor resulted from every battle he faced. All his habits result from life lessons I never witnessed.

"I will never tell a soul. Because I love you, Javi. And I will do anything to protect you."

Javi's eyes soften at my response. I press my lips to his, the taste of passionfruit tingling my senses again. "I don't deserve you, honestly. But now that I have you, I can't lose you," I say, twirling his curls with my finger.

He takes my jawline in both hands. "That's too bad because

you are everything I've dreamed of."

I wrap my arms around him in a bear hug, pulling him closer. "A closet case like me?"

"I even find a nice outfit every once in a while."

"You have such a way with words." He smirks at me.

"If only I could send you the song lyrics I write about you."

"You are writing songs about me now?"

He peels off me and stares me down like he's mulling over my response. "I told you I would make an album like this one day. All I needed was a muse. And I think it's only fair if you see the lyrics for yourself."

"Well, I hope you'll share them with me when you're ready."

"They are still in my notes on my phone. I would text them to you, but I don't want the messages to expose you."

That realization dawns on me. "Oh shit, you're right."

A lightbulb goes off in Javi's head, and he gives me an incredulous look. "Have you ever heard of D&D?"

CHAPTER 23

November 10, 2025

The static crackles for what feels like an eternity while I sit at my desk, staring into a now black computer screen. Javi created a musical treat for all who listen; each song oozes a rich blend of R&B and art pop while coated in my most private memories. It's a sweet musical masterpiece, but like any other dessert, I overindulge to the point of sickness.

A wave of nausea hits me after Javi sings his last chord, and I fight the urge to throw up. Why didn't I listen to this sooner, and why did I refuse to reach out to him after he sent me this? Some songs conceal me well enough, but "The church" is too specific. The lyrics explain all my secrets and the fallout. His description of my mom in the stories I told, my deepest, darkest secret, and the final chapter of our romantic tragedy all intertwined in this bloated rollercoaster of a song. All it will take is one internet sleuth from USE, and details of my whole personal life will explode on Reeltime.

I scramble for my phone, hoping that I can throw an irrational Hail Mary to delay his album release or remove "The church." It's not uncommon for artists to delay and alter their albums. SZA's *SOS* took forever to create with multiple delays, but still received universal acclaim. I'm not asking Javi to postpone his album for five years, but I can't have my most vulnerable moment hitting radio waves.

I scroll through my home screen, contemplating what to do next. Since I don't have his phone number, I'm left with two options. I could reach out on his official Reeltime account, but I doubt I will reach him. A social media team monitors his account, for all I know. That would leave Discreet and Delete. I click on the app icon and scroll to the favorites pin. Two profiles still appear on my screen. The green dot on Romero's profile is active, which raises my eyebrows. That's for another time. I click on Javi's profile, the scenic overlook from that day in the park.

My phone vibrates in my hand, and I see Romero's profile on the screen again, but this time with an unread message.

Mister E: WE NEED TO TALK!

The phone buzzes again.

Mister E: It's an emergency!

No, Romero. I'm having an emergency. I can't talk to him right now, but send him a quick text message anyway.

CT no E: I'm busy.

Mister E: I am serious. We need to talk. Like now!

CT no E: I'm sorry, but I will text you later.

I click on Javi's profile and type out a message to him. Just before I'm ready to press send, I nearly leap out of my seat when a silhouette appears behind my blinds and bangs on the window.

"Caleb. I need to talk to you now!" Romero pounds the glass so hard it sounds close to shattering. If I hadn't recognized his voice, I would have feared for my life. I still sit stunned in my seat.

"What do you want?" I shout.

"I need to talk to you inside."

I roll my eyes. "Fine," I say, more afraid of the consequences of saying no.

I walk out of my bedroom and dash down the hallway to the front door. Instead of standing in front of the door, Romero presses himself against my bedroom window, as if he's planning to burglarize it later. I clear my throat, causing Romero to peel himself off my window.

"Is your roommate here?"

"No, she's at the library."

He gives me a quick head nod as he walks past me, as if nothing awkward had unfolded. I close the door and watch Romero throw himself onto the couch, looking the most disheveled I have ever seen him.

"Is this going to take long? I have things to do," I say.

I walk over to the loveseat next to him across the living room. He buries his face in his hands as I sit down, muffling the next words out of his mouth.

"Something happened," he says.

"What do you mean, something happened?" I sit more alarmed.

He exhales deeply and throws his hands to his thighs. "The party got crazy. Angelica and her girls came through, and everyone started having a good time. An amazing time. Good drinks and music started flowing, and everybody was sharing good vibes. Later that night, Andres opened our weed stash and rolled blunts for everyone. I hit it twice, setting everything off in a blaze."

"I don't understand why you are telling me this. Are you recapping everything I missed?"

Romero folds his arms, his glance now toward the floor. "We're all enjoying ourselves, high as shit, having some beers, until the police roll onto the property, guns blazing, and ruin our party."

"Ok. Cops ruin parties all the time." I conceal my irritation about his urgency to tell me this story, all the while I have my own crisis to address.

"Yes, but these cops charged everyone with possession of a controlled substance, providing alcohol to minors, failure to prevent underage drinking, and some other bullshit charges."

I sit back, a little concerned. "Oh shit. How many people were there?"

"It was just me, Andres, Angelica, and a few of her friends when the police rolled up, but the underage girls caused all the problems."

"That sucks but I'm sorry, Romero."

"I'm sorry to you too."

I raise an eyebrow. "Sorry to me," I say, my thumb retracted back toward me.

He nods.

"There is nothing to apologize to me for."

"See, that's where you're wrong."

"What the hell are you talking about?"

"You just didn't let me explain the whole situation. So the cops would call to give me a case number. They haven't notified Coach yet about last night's events, but it won't last. Angelica's dad came home thirty minutes after the incident and took her away from the cops. He threatened us with a drug test this week as he was showing us out."

"Are we all getting tested?"

"Does it matter? I'm still screwed."

"I'm sure you'll be fine."

"Have you not been listening?" He looks exasperated at me.

"You told me you only took a couple of puffs. I'm sure it will be out of your system in no time."

"Not that!" His outburst echoes across the room, stunning me into silence. I have never seen him so angry before. I furrow my brow until faint recognition creeps back into my mind. His brother's Adderall.

"Romero I…am sorry."

"I should have seen this coming. I can't believe this would happen to me."

I let out a frustrated sigh. "Romero, I warned you this could happen."

I instantly regret the words as they leave my mouth, and Romero allows no time for damage control. His face contorts into a mask of anger.

"So are you gloating?"

I flinch.

"What is your problem?"

Romero grins, to my surprise. "How could I forget you are so big time now?" Romero stretches his arms and moves them away like a man with a bright idea. I wince at the sight. "Mr. Caleb Thomas, the face of University Hills. The highest-selling soccer jersey in the University Store's history, and the pre-destined conference MVP. I'm not surprised you're acting this smug."

My mouth gapes open. "Excuse me?"

"It has me thinking that we should rethink our situation."

I shake my head, raising my arms and my vocal volume. "What do you mean, rethink our situation?"

"I mean…we need to change our dynamic. At least level the playing field."

"Level the playing field? What are you talking about?"

"I'm saying you are going to save me from this."

I blow a raspberry before laughing. "And how am I going to do that? Give you my piss? If that is your plan, I guess you forgot they watch us take a leak."

"I'm aware, Caleb. I have two ways that you can help me." Romero's tone unsettles me, but I sit stoic and unfazed.

"Which are?"

"First, persuade Coach to waive the drug test."

My jaw slackens as I throw my hands up. "Romero, how the fuck do you think I will convince our coach to postpone a drug test?"

"Because you're Coach's favorite right now. Just look at how he got your agency deal. You have him bowing down at your feet, and I imagine he will obey any order."

"Is this a joke?"

"Not at all. You have that power."

"Romero, I can't convince Coach of anything. He runs the program. I don't. On top of that, Angelica's father coordinates the drug tests. Why don't you get your girlfriend to convince her dad?"

"She's not interested in helping me right now."

"And I can't help but relate to her."

"Well, you and her don't share similar predicaments."

"Is that so?"

"Yes, which leads me to my backup plan if you can't convince Coach Ramsey. "

"Which is?" I ask, failing to conceal my agitation.

"The cops who busted the party were the state police. And given your dad's position on the force…"

I almost burst out laughing. "There is no way I can convince a police department to remove your charges, Romero. That is not up to my father. And if he could, I would never ask him to break the law."

"I think he would if you asked," Romero says.

"My father would never."

"I think you could convince him."

"I will never jeopardize him, so fuck you for even asking!" The words leave me like venom the moment I rise out of my chair. The adrenaline courses through so fast that I pace back and forth in the kitchen. My heart bashes against my chest so hard I have to grip the counter. I drop my head down, trying to compose myself.

He laughs as he watches me. "I hope he helps for your sake because you won't like the alternative."

"What's that supposed to mean?"

He grins wickedly. "I talked to Roger Astor last night."

My heart sinks at the mention of his name. I raise my head and see Romero smiling, almost pleased with himself. "What?" I ask.

"I invited Roger after you said you weren't attending our party," Romero says, readjusting his position on the couch

"Why?"

"I wanted the company. Someone to commiserate my

downfall with at your expense. I figured he would understand since we both will eventually lose the conference MVP to you. But he surprised me. That Ken doll told me a bombshell about you."

I swallow a lump in my throat. "What did he say?"

Romero shows his full-toothed grin before pulling his phone from his pocket. He taps on his screen twice before he sets it on the coffee table. "Check the app."

I pull out my phone and scroll to our message board on D&D. Multiple screenshots of text messages fill my screen as I return to my seat in the living room. I slump into it more than I read every line. The surrounding air becomes paper-thin. My heart cracks with every word slamming into me like a sledgehammer. It's all here. All of my darkest secrets. My mom's suicide note, my relationship with Javi, and the real reason I left USE.

Tears pool at the base of my eyelids, whether because of shame of the truth of the events or being played by a scumbag, I'm not sure. Part of me knew a deal with Roger was a deal with the devil, but I thought he guaranteed his silence. It doesn't take gravity long to complete my anguish. Romero just looks at me, mesmerized by my capitulation.

"So it is true."

I wipe my tears while Romero takes me in, as if he's reveling in the moment. He rises and heads for the exit.

"Given that we understand each other better, I will let you decide how you want to proceed. I would hate for all your personal baggage to come out on Reeltime's biggest gossip blog."

I grip his arm before he takes his first step, burrowing my fingers as far as I can. If it's a fraction of what I feel now, I hope he feels some pain. "Why are you doing this to me?"

He jerks his arm out of my grip and leans in close. His eyes tear into me while he grinds his teeth. His mask finally slips off his face. "Like you, I have dreams. Unlike you, I never received the agent, the most lucrative NIL deals, the accolades, or any of the special treatment I deserved."

I sit motionless, affronted by his reasoning.

"I knew I was in trouble when Coach bragged about how you would change the team's trajectory. He was confident you would guide us to the championship, even with your injured leg. Did you know he told me the same thing this past spring?"

I stare at him, too stunned to respond.

"I never realized he baited me to stay until after the transfer portal closed and you had signed with us. So, for my last year of eligibility, I swore to take what is due to me. Since Coach Ramsey would not help build my exposure, I had to create a new plan. Angelica was perfect."

"So you used her fame to market yourself?" I ask.

"She caught her ex in a cheating scandal, and it gave me my opportunity to become her new muse. It was you I couldn't figure out how to stop."

"Stop me?" I blurt out.

"Playing well in your position was the original plan, but it was useless given that we lost every game. Your speedy recovery didn't help my case, so the night of the retreat was my first chance to rattle you."

"You mean my initiation?" I ask. My breath was uneven between my words.

He tilts his head back and bellows a sinister laugh. "Duncan hesitated when I pitched the idea, but a quick reminder of how

I ruined his love life convinced him. He sent your performance to my phone, just so I had the embarrassing material to hold over you. I wanted to plan everything in the shower until you ripped off my towel."

I swallow, regretting that moment more than anything in the world. I'm even contemplating selling my soul at this point to spare me the torture of the memory. "So you used sex to get to me?"

He nods. "I would have saved myself the trouble if I had texted Roger earlier."

I flare my nostrils while Romero walks over to the door before eyeing me.

"So here we are, finally. For once, I have you right where I need you, and now you can experience how I felt ever since you arrived." Romero turns and walks to the door, turning as he opens it. "At least I'm generous enough to extend a lifeline to save yourself by saving me. If you can't...well...you will wish you had never come here. Good luck, Caleb."

Romero slams the door of the apartment.

I throw my phone across the room and convulse in my seat, shouting unintelligible profanity as if an angry hive of hornets were attacking me. My emotions shift from anger to sadness to confusion as my tantrum finishes, and I try to understand how I could accomplish any of this.

Machi was right about Romero, and now I'm stuck figuring out how to save myself from spiraling to my inevitable doom. But there is a tinge of hope available, and I have to cling to it. I rise from my seat to find m y p hone n ear t he d oorway a nd type out a message to Coach Ramsey.

Chapter 24

November 12, 2025

I can't stop picturing my downfall. Romero takes his drug test soon, one that will inevitably end his college career. His response is to blackmail me with personal information so damaging, you'd think it's fiction. Sadly, it is a truth I have lived with for the past year, and now Romero wields it as leverage to solve his impossible problem. Knowing I will probably fail, he found the anchor that will sink us both. But I still cling to the delusional hope that somehow, I will accomplish this. Pulling off some miracle to save myself this time after failing at USE. I rub my forehead raw until it looks like a sunburn.

It takes a good fifteen minutes to trudge across campus to the entrance of the library. With my phone already glued to my hand, I dial Coach Ramsey's phone number while scanning the area. It's a miracle he was on campus today, and I was relieved he was available for a last-minute meeting. The dial tone rings repeatedly while I scan the vast first floor.

It's hard to see him through the sea of college kids, either pushing each other through a congested walkway, conversing at the conference tables, typing on the desktop keyboards, or waiting in line for coffee from the overwhelmed coffee stand. The call goes to voicemail, but I see Coach Ramsey shift from clicking on his laptop to writing in his notebook at one of the round tables to the right of the coffee bodega. Our eyes meet, and he beckons me in his direction.

"Hey Coach," I say as I pull the free chair and Coach Ramsey's attention away from his screen.

"Caleb, my boy. Good to see you."

"Are you busy?"

"I'm actually wrapping this up now. I spliced important clips together from previous USE matches for you boys to watch before the match."

"I'll look at them tonight."

"I know you will. Are you buzzing about the championship match?"

"It will be an exciting game."

Coach Ramsey nods sagely. "So what do you need to talk to me about?"

My mind paces as I try to explain the point of this conversation. The plan is simple. I ask Coach about the drug tests and convince him to allow me to take the test instead of Romero. But how I will deliver this idea is difficult. How do I approach my coach about drug testing that is not public knowledge?

For all I know, I could open my mouth and reveal some unofficial information before the athletic director did. This would throw suspicion on me and implicate me in something I'm not involved in. With this thought flying in my mind, I catch my tongue and sit petrified in front of my coach.

"Are you okay?" Coach Ramsey asks, studying me.

"I um…need to talk about something…"

"Caleb, what's going on? You look unwell."

"Um…yeah. I've had a lot on my mind."

"Are you struggling with burnout?" he asks. "Take training off if you must, because I want you as fresh as possible."

"I appreciate that, but it's not burnout."

"I see." Coach Ramsey slurps his coffee and scans me as he places his mug back on the table. His stoic look never wavers, and it unsettles me. Before I can explain, he presses his hands together in a CEO fashion. "I may just be your coach, but I treat all my players like they're my sons. It concerns me if something's distressing you. Are you in some kind of trouble? Is something happening in your personal life?"

"Yes, it is."

"Okay, that's a start."

"It's difficult to put into words for you."

Coach Ramsey smirks and relaxes in his chair. "Believe me. Having been around young men, I've heard just about every-thing. Nothing surprises me anymore."

I rub my hands back and forth across my thighs, stumbling over my words to stay vague. "So I got into an argument with someone…I guess you could say a person I was seeing…and now we are in a tough situation…something that is spiraling out of control."

Coach Ramsey looks unfazed. "Caleb, son. Stress happens to players, even someone with your talent. Maybe it's not as bad as it seems."

"What do you mean?" I ask.

"Well, have you been doing illegal drugs?"

"No."

"Are you using steroids or banned substances that the NCAA says we can't use?"

"No."

"Drinking in the dorms?"

"I don't live in the dorms."

His eyes narrow at my response, but he brushes it off in a second. "Stolen anything?"

"No."

"That's all and good. Have you made an inappropriate pass at a girl?"

"No."

"Were you sexually inappropriate with a woman?"

"No."

"Have you fathered a child?"

"No."

"Ok. You have nothing to worry about. If you're being honest with me, I think I can help." Coach Ramsey answers the phone, vibrating on the table. "Oh, excuse me for one second."

He steps away from me. I can't hear his conversation over some of the chatter. Coach Ramsey's demeanor is more irritated when he walks back to his seat. My legs bounce faster under the table as he gathers himself. "Well, speak of the devil. One of your teammates is in some serious trouble, which is a major blow before the big game."

"That's not good," I say, trying my best to remain still and composed. Sweat percolates between my clasped palms in my lap, the longer his silence stretches. This can't be happening. I need to say something, but Coach interrupts me before I can.

"Yep. Looks like the athletic department is already intervening. We've seen the wrath of this athletic director after how he tore the football team apart. They opened an internal investigation and ordered a drug test for the player. Not a great look right now."

The anxiety drowns me to the point where my body trembles, and my cotton shirt soaks up the sweat droplets under my arms.

"What does that mean?" I ask.

"It means I will have to gather all the facts, wait on the results of the drug test, and decide what happens to that player based on my findings."

My throat goes dry while Coach Ramsey rises from his chair.

"I'm sorry. I have to cut this meeting short, but the athletic director called me into his office. Whatever it is, I am sure it will be fine. For once, just relax for a bit. Stop putting pressure on yourself and look at all the good you have accomplished. You have everything going for you, but we can schedule something later if you need." Coach Ramsey pats me on the shoulder as he walks by. "But I think you're going to be okay. There is nothing you can't handle."

He leaves the library, taking my chance of saving myself with him.

Chapter 25

November 13, 2025

The training session plan sails over my head just before I follow my teammates to the weight room. You could duct tape Coach Ramsey's plans across my eyes, and my brain still couldn't absorb the information by the time I walked into the stadium gym. How could I? My brain is so busy catastrophizing how my future will transpire. Romero's drug test is tomorrow, and I have not saved him from his mess. I'm running out of time and options. I try to calm my nerves and ignore it, but Romero walks right in front of me, sending an already spin-ning brain into hyperdrive.

A series of dumbbells and exercise bands lay across the floor with a circuit workout written on the board. Coach Ramsey walks us through light soccer-related workouts on the quads and hamstrings, focusing on dynamic movements. I wrap a large rubber band around my legs, squeeze my thighs together, and squat. My focus wavers the second I catch Romero's glance, and a shot of cortisol flushes m y body. H e 's on the verge of immediate suspension from the team while exposing me in the most petty way possible. Yet, he looks as cool and collected as ever, not a hint of stress on him.

I don't know what's worse, but both infuriate me. He strolls over in my direction, and I think he's coming to talk to me. But I should have known better since he blocked me on D&D after visiting me. He slams his shoulder into my chest instead and walks past me with a smug swagger. I recoil and reach for his arm, but he slithers out of my grip. He walks over to the dumbbells and performs a couple of lunges, avoiding my forced eye contact. I'm about ready to trail him, but a hand presses on my shoulder.

"Don't," Vince says. He balances himself as he stretches his right quadriceps.

My shoulders tense.

"He's not worth it. Just another inflated ego, jealous of your success."

I relax and return to my station.

Vince trails close behind. "Are you okay?"

"I'm fine. Just a lot on my mind." I lift my weights off the floor and stretch out my left leg. A jolt of pain shoots up my body after hitting the ground. I return to standing and repeat with my right leg.

"Are you sure? Machi is worried about your erratic behavior today."

I ignore him and grunt throughout the rest of my set.

"Is she right?" Vince persists.

I slam my weights into the ground, gritting my teeth. My leg tingles with pain, but I ignore it. "I'm fine," I say through my clenched jaw.

I reach for my water bottle and watch Duncan and Andres walk over to the space between Romero and me, a mischievous grin etched onto their faces.

"Check out this conference superstar!" Andres says, wrapping his arm around his brother. Duncan gazes at me and joins the mocking fest, patting Romero on the chest.

"How do you feel about the conference championship banquet, Romero?"

Romero lifts his dumbbells and begins his second set. His eyes fall on me, and a smug smile forms. "I think an unexpected surprise is in store."

I blow a soft raspberry.

"Oh yeah? What makes you so sure?" Duncan asks, projecting his question loud enough for everyone to hear.

I continue my workout, pretending not to listen.

Romero drops his weights to the floor and wipes away the sweat percolating on his brow. "Just a feeling."

Duncan shrieks with laughter. "He's riling you up, Thomas."

My blood boils, but I take deep breaths to restrain myself. Duncan remains relentless and refuses to grant me peace. "He's got you on the ropes!"

I roll my eyes and start my dumbbell squats. Duncan rotates his head back and says something inaudible to Romero. Romero nods, but his eyes never leave me. Coach Ramsey calls Vince, Andres, and Duncan away a few moments later, leaving Romero and me alone with an awkward space between us. To my surprise, Romero gravitates toward me.

"You seem on edge," Romero says in the most arrogant tone.

"Gee, I wonder why?" I say mid-squat.

"Oh, come on, Caleb. You know I'm just teasing. I'm more confident in you winning than me." Romero looks around before stepping closer. "I'm just curious if you will receive it with your dignity intact."

I push out a breath and remain silent.

"I take it you didn't have success with Coach."

My lips press into a thin line. "He said there was nothing he could do."

"Well, that's too bad. I guess that means you have to turn to your police dad to save you."

I glare at him. "Like I said, I doubt he can help us."

"Have you talked to him yet?" There is an edge in his voice now, more panicked than threatening.

I texted my father this morning, but I didn't explain the situation. I asked him to join me for his dinner break at Gretta's Grill. His patrol routes are close to me today, so I thought it was my best chance to see him. We have never had dinner together since Mom died, and he's yet to see University Hills. He hasn't responded to my text, and I'll keep that information to myself.

"Have you?" Romero asks. His question is sharp as it leaves his lips.

"What difference does it make? This desperate plan will never work."

"It needs to work," he says through gritted teeth.

"Why don't you just realize your situation and accept it? That way, we put each other out of our misery."

Romero shows a stiff smile. "Don't forget how we got into this mess."

My nostrils flare at his implication, and I inch closer to him. The tension brews into a bitter confrontation. "Because a narcissistic asshole let his ego blind him to his own stupidity."

Romero flinches. Our teammates notice the smile that

drops off Romero's face and circle around us like a schoolyard brawl ready to start. "Watch yourself, Caleb. Don't let karma catch up to you."

"Are you referring to your own experience?"

He minimizes the distance between our faces so that only a sheet of paper could pass through. It's funny that I would fight the urge to kiss him not too long ago. Now I resist the urge to punch him. A faint whisper escapes his lips. "Big mistake, Caleb."

"It doesn't matter now. You're on borrowed time anyway."

He smirks and brushes his nose with his thumb. He surveys the surrounding crowd, taking in every detail. Romero draws a long breath and clears his throat. He unleashes his venom in two syllables. "Faggot."

The following events unfold too fast to comprehend. The gym becomes a blur, and I register only the brief pause between my inhale and exhale in my breath. A pause with enough time for my right fist to connect with Romero's left cheekbone. I don't feel the impact, nor do I see my teammates' faces change as the event unfolded. Their voices sound distant and incomprehensible. It's as if I'm trapped in a hazy dream, desperately trying to grasp onto something real. My clenched fist dangles to my side, and the throbbing in my knuckles returns me to reality.

Vince wakes me from my trance and peels me away from Romero as Andres restrains Romero. The rest of the team gathers in awe at the unfolding events. I clutch my throbbing knuckles, and Romero swears multiple profanities, clutching his face. "You fucking bitch!"

Coach Ramsey breaks up the crowd and pulls us away from

everyone by our collars. He drags us out the exit before shoving us onto the sidewalk. "Sort that shit out somewhere else! Don't come back until you do. I will not have any distractions while we have a championship to win."

The door slams shut behind me, completing my embarrassment. I try to calm down by smoothing my clothes, but it's useless. My blood is boiling. There is no point in resolving my Romero issue. He's so hell-bent on ruining me, so I don't regret punching him. It's a relief, even if I go down in flames. And I'm believing it wouldn't be so bad if I did. I could discredit Romero by outing him in the same way he outs me. He implicates himself as my fling, diminishing any power over the public he held over me. It could turn my public shaming into a messy social media breakup. Not ideal, but better.

A shove from behind knocks me out of my thinking and off my balance. By the time I center myself, I turn around and see Romero rubbing his jaw in front of the parking lot.

"Fuck you, Romero!"

"I'm so sick of you, Thomas. I should have ruined you the first chance I had," he says, trudging toward me.

I stand my ground, expecting a counterpunch he never threw in the gym. Romero throws his shoulder back, and I put up my fists, ready to defend myself. I flinch when his arm moves forward, but he doesn't make contact. He stops in front of my face, holding his phone up for me to see. A veil of rage still covers his features, but he acts like a tattletale instead of a brawler.

"What is that?"

"Look at it!"

I scan Romero like this is some prank, but he's serious. The same screenshots he sent me on D&D appear on the screen, but they are miniature in his phone messages. It's a rough draft of a text with the words 'for your next post' beneath them. My blood runs cold when the receiver's contact info becomes clear. I forgot about Angelica and her ability to ruin people with her gossip posts. Panic creeps into me, and I see Romero registering it with a sinister smile. "Now that you're done over-inflating your self-worth, it's time to stop fucking around. Call your dad now, or I'll send this to Angelica."

"He's on patrol and probably won't respond."

"I don't give a fuck. Either call him or…"

"I texted him this morning," I blurt out.

Romero appears unconvinced as he studies me. "You're lying."

"I am not, I swear. My phone is inside, but I can text you a screenshot."

"What did you say?"

I told him everything, reassuring him my father would visit even though I was not confident. He takes a long moment to process everything, mulling over the details. Then, he looks down at his phone and deletes his draft to Angelica.

"My test is tomorrow morning. Fix this!"

Romero barges past me back into the stadium, this time without driving his shoulder into my body. I place my hands on the back of my head, trying my best to steady an unsteady breath. I'm praying my father will come through for me. For him to put aside the issues we share since Mom left and step in to save me. It would be a miracle if I got a response in time.

To my relief, his response does appear.

CHAPTER 26

November 13, 2025

"I guess I will take the shrimp carbonara," Officer Thomas says, handing the menu back to the waiter. He pulls his reading glasses off his worn face, heavy bags drooping under his eyes. He massages his five o'clock shadow before he pushes a loose strand of his thinning hair above his receding hairline. His prim uniform is the only part of him that is well-kept.

"Feeling fancy for a dinner break?" I ask, trying to lift the mood at the table, which is currently on life support.

"Gretta's Grill has a generous first responder discount. I usually eat here when visiting University Hills. Many officers eat here and grab a drink next door."

"That's nice." I want to ask how many times he's stopped in town without reaching out, but I let it go. No point in starting another argument now, given the circumstances.

"I'm actually glad you texted me. I wanted to see you before your big game."

I raise my eyebrow. "You did?" I squirm in my seat while looking at my father. His admission is sweet if it came from a normal father invested in his son. But in this case, it's more unsettling than comforting.

"I got a promotion at work."

I breathe a sigh of relief and lean back in my chair. "Congratulations."

"Thank you. The extra hours out on patrol paid off."

"Have you told Joshua?" I ask.

His face darkens. "I called him, but he never picked up. So I left him a voicemail." The corner of his lips ticks downward.

"He'll come around," I whisper.

He laughs me off. "I doubt it. He rambled about everything during his mother's eulogy. Your brother's outbursts and the casket laying are the last things I remember before my Christmas bender." He takes a swig of his water, but I know he wishes it were bourbon. If he weren't working, I would probably drive him home afterward.

I sip my water and clear my throat. "He was just hurting."

"I guess he is still hurting. It's so bad he fucked off and moved in with his girlfriend's family."

Palpable tension fills the space for what feels like an eternity, and I can't help but rearrange my silverware to ignore it. The waiter refills our glasses before my father clears his throat.

"So, Caleb, my boy, any news from that agent of yours?" His voice shifts from soft to stern.

"What do you mean?"

"Well, what has he been up to since the Soldano sponsorship deal? Any progress on trials or professional contracts?"

I readjust my position in the chair. "Nothing yet, but we haven't spoken since I've been busy. Trying to calm my mind for this weekend."

"Well, that makes sense. Winning the first cup in the school's history tomorrow is a massive opportunity to be scouted."

"Yeah, for sure," I say, tracing the base of the water glass with my finger.

He looks up, analyzing me. "Is your leg okay?"

"Minor discomfort mostly, but nothing I can't handle."

He nods. "Grades good?"

"A's and B's, but I'm thriving in my psychology courses."

"That's great. She would be proud."

It's my turn to nod. "Are you?" My words catch both of us off guard, but his face contorts before I can take back the question.

"Of course, I am. Why would you ask that?"

"Because I don't know you anymore," I say.

"What's that supposed to mean?"

My subconscious is screaming at me to change the subject. But his dumbfounded expression on his face strikes a nerve in me, and I choose to bite the bullet. "It means you've been so distant this past year, it feels like you're punishing me for her death."

He leans back in his chair, looking aghast. It's the most emotion he's expressed in a while. "What are you talking about? I have reached out when I can, but you know I am busy."

"You were never this busy when she was alive. It seems all you care about is work now, while you abandoned the rest of your family."

"I was trying to cope with losing my wife. It's something you would not understand."

"You are not the only one who lost her. I suffered and needed my father to help me navigate through that."

"Caleb, you went back to university after the funeral, and Josh moved out of the house. You both left me to grieve on my own."

"Only because you told me to go back, even when I wasn't ready."

He scoffs. "Why are you bringing the past up now?"

"Because I need you now. The same way I did then!" My voice carries as it silences the entire restaurant. We wait for casual talk to resume, affording me time to rehearse. This will be difficult to explain, but now I fear this is my only opportunity. I draw in a long breath. "There's something happening to me."

He crosses his arms and leans forward. "Like what?"

"Someone knows about Mom's death and has been harassing me about it," I say.

"Caleb everybody knows about her. It's public knowledge at this point. Anybody can just look up…"

"He found out about her suicide note."

My father furrows his brow. "What note?" He leans forward, gripping the table. "What note are you talking about? The official report never mentioned a note. I scanned every single page multiple times."

"I found it next to her when I came home."

He looks at me, confusion morphing into something much angrier. "You mean to tell me my wife left me a note? After all this time. Do you know I almost lost my job arguing with the medical examiner when he ruled her death a suicide? Why wouldn't you tell me this?"

"Because she addressed it to me!" I rub my thighs under the table. "Why do you think I came home that day?" I whisper.

His mouth opens, a sorrowful whisper leaving his lips. "Because it was your birthday."

"She messaged me for the first time all semester to invite me home. She said she had a gift for me." I fight the urge to cry as much as I did then. There is a pause between us, and I use every second to regain what's left of my composure.

"What did she say?"

I tell him everything, sparing no detail. I provide context for the camp she sent me to the summer before, and the aftermath when I returned. It hurts that I have to reveal I'm gay while explaining my mom's last words. It feels more repressive this way, like I'm delivering the bad news that he lost his job and his house at the same time. With Mom, it felt like a relief admitting I was gay to her. But she didn't take my news well, exploding into a biblical fit. Once she calmed down, she created a plan to 'fix' me, one we hid from my dad. I followed everything she asked, but look where that got us.

I stare at my father now, who has sat motionless while I spoke. The stillness stretches for a minute before he reaches for his napkin. He wipes at his mouth before pressing it to his face quickly. If I hadn't been staring, I would have missed it. He tosses it to the side before he adjusts himself in his chair and clears his throat. My heart clatters into my ribcage like a wrecking ball while I wait for his first syllable.

"I don't know what to say." His hushed tone feels like the edge of a serrated knife.

"I know it's a lot, but I really need your help." He remains quiet. I proceed anyway, unable to read him. "A teammate I slept with found out from Roger. Now he's blackmailing me to save him from a drug test he'll fail. And I don't know what to do."

He draws a long breath. I dangle on the edge of my seat, holding mine as I wait for his first word. "I can't help you."

I catch myself before I fall out of the chair. "I'm not asking you to…"

He shakes a finger to silence me. "Stop. I said I can't help you. There is too much to process."

I open my mouth, but my father interrupts before I can rebuttal.

"You knew my wife's death was a suicide after you saw me fight the medical examiner on his opinion. I con-vinced myself it was my fault, and all this time, you withheld that information from me. On top of that, you're gay, but you told your mom and hid it from me. That she hid it from me hurts, since we told each other everything."

"She promised me she wouldn't say anything. We wanted to tell you when we fixed it," I say with a crack in my voice.

"And when exactly was that supposed to be?" My father glares at me with so much intensity that my inhale feels shallower.

"After that camp, I don't think I ever will be."

"All of that, and now your mother is dead."

"I didn't want any of this to happen…"

"Stop!" he shouts, slamming the table. The whole restau-rant pauses its conversations and turns toward us. An awkward silence lasts for a minute before the crowd returns to their faint conversations. He rises to his feet when the restaurant returns to normal.

"Please, Dad. I need your help through this," I say.

My father pulls out his wallet and sprinkles a few bills on

top of the bill, adjusting his trooper hat on his head as his frigid gaze freezes me in my seat. His words are an avalanche, swallowing me into cold despair. "I'm gutted, Caleb. You absolutely mugged me off. My wife is dead, and for a year, I blamed myself. Your brother estranged me from his life, thinking I was the reason for losing her. I take the piss, ignoring the emptiness when I walk into my empty home after work. My life is an ongoing attempt to numb the pain through a series of patrol shifts."

He leans in close to deliver the final blow. "I don't care that you like geezers, not in the way your mother did. I might have reasoned with her to find another way to handle this. What happened to you at camp is bloody awful, but I am miffed that you hid it from me. You chose this chaos. You put yourself into this situation with your teammate. This is your mess to clean. I will not sacrifice what's left of my life for someone who left my life in shambles. This is your problem, and I want nothing to do with it."

Only the whispers of Javi's album in the speaker are the only thing that registers when the last word leaves his lips. I struggle to breathe the paper-thin air. How can I? I feel like my hurting father stabbed me in the heart. I thought I would come clean and we would heal together, but I was horribly wrong. He takes one last long look at me, pushes in his chair, and leaves the restaurant without uttering another syllable.

Chapter 27

May 6, 2025

For once

"How far away are you?" Javi asks, his voice a low hum in the speaker.

"I'm walking over now. I just finished my exam."

"Ok."

"How long until you leave for the airport?" I ask.

Javi grunts to clear his throat. "My flight doesn't leave for another couple of hours. We'll have some time."

"Ok. Thank you for staying longer."

He says nothing and hangs up the phone. I'm not surprised by this since I broke the news that I was leaving USE a few days ago. We have spent little time together, nor have we had a long conversation. And I don't fault him for it. I would be heartbroken too if my love left me. It's something I'm used to. I'm just glad he delayed his flight to spend a little time together before the inevitable goodbyes.

Once I descend down the steps in the courtyard, I walk toward the setting sun across the campus. An empty, manicured meadow swallows my every footstep as the library trails further behind me. A bath of warm oranges and reds fights to stay in the sky before the darkness consumes them. The resort-style dorms appear just a short distance across the intramural fields, and I pace down the street, driven by our Uber after our night at The Cove. There is nothing I wouldn't do to relive that experience. I would even break my leg if I had to.

I rush over to his dorm building, hoping to milk more time. I stop before Javi's room and knock. A few seconds pass before footsteps approach on the opposite side. The door creaks open enough to see half of Javi's face. A thin line appears on his lips, and his dark eyes look puffy and red as he stares at me.

There is a pause, almost as if he's contemplating whether to let me in. He steps aside and leads me into his room. Javi stripped his intricately decorated room down to the standard university mattress, bed frame, nightstand, dresser, desk, and chair. He pulls out the chair before he sits on the mattress. He motions for me to sit on the chair, and I oblige. The silence fills the air while our gazes avoid each other.

I clear my throat. "Thanks for staying longer," I say.

"My flight got canceled yesterday, so I didn't really have a choice," he says with a sharpness I'd never heard before.

"Oh. Where is the rest of your stuff?"

"My cousins already came and picked up my stuff. They are holding everything while G-mom gets my room ready. I'll pick up my stuff later after their bar shows."

"Ok." I scratch the back of my neck. I struggle in these situations, and I'm scared to relive the same conversation with my mother again. Since then, I've learned how to soften the blow when giving bad news.

"I don't have a lot of time, Caleb," Javi says. "Just tell me what you need to do."

"I just wanted to tell you in person everything before you go."

"What more is there to tell? Out of the blue, you tell me you're leaving over text."

"I know, and I'm sorry I did that. I was dealing with exams while trying to coordinate with my dad. It was a mess, but I should have done a better job telling you."

"Yeah, I agree," he says, folding his arms.

"I'm sorry." I drop my head and look at my palms in my lap.

"It's whatever." He releases a deep breath. I look up to Javi, rubbing his eyes. "Where are you going?"

"I'm not sure yet. I just entered the transfer portal."

His lips purse tight before making a popping noise. I think he's about to ask a question, but his lip quivers. Tears flow in an instant, and he falls apart. I dash across the bedroom to his bed. My arms wrap around him, closing the distance between us. At first, he resists, but then leans into me. His eyes linger on my T-shirt around my shoulder.

"Why do you have to leave me?"

I swallow hard while I rub his back. My chest tightens as I search for the right words to soften the blow. The full truth is off the table because it would hurt him. Especially in forced situations where I lost, no matter the decision. I was brutally honest before, and look what happened. I love Javi too much for the truth to take him too. He'll be okay, and that's all that matters. "It was a decision beyond my control."

Javi sniffles aggressively, and I rest my head on top of his. My shirt muffles his voice. "But you were one of the best players this year. Why are you leaving the team?"

"I just wasn't a good fit anymore." I want to say Roger, but I hide that fact.

Javi's limp arms cross behind my back, and we embrace each other for what feels like a lifetime. His tears dry up, and his breath eases a bit, so he pulls away and looks at me for the first time since I arrived. His gaze resembles a puppy caught in the rain looking into a stranger's home.

"I think I'm going to withdraw my attendance for next semester," he says, wiping his face.

I raise an eyebrow. "Really?"

"There's no point in staying. Only you kept me at this school if I am honest."

A deep exhale escapes me when he reveals this. Roger can't threaten him now. "What are you going to do?"

Now he takes a deep breath. "I'm not sure yet. G-mom will force me to get a job if I won't go to classes. I want to pursue music, though."

"Maybe you could make that album you mentioned."

He furrows his brow. "What album?"

"The one you talked about at that farmer's market."

He cocks his head and holds it for a few seconds. But he slowly pieces together the memory recall until he sees the moment in his head. "I wasn't serious in that tent. I know I wrote those songs, but I couldn't actually make music."

"It can't hurt to try."

He considers this for a moment. "But what if I make some-thing terrible?"

I rub my neck. "Go again. It's like trying to find a new team when things don't work out."

A brief laugh escapes him, a welcome relief from the tone of our encounter. "I guess you're right."

I smile when we lock eyes, but he doesn't return the gesture. The special bond between us is hanging on by a thread. My heart rattles against my chest while we play this staring game of chicken, both waiting for the first move. Like opposite ends of a magnet getting stronger as the distance closes, we both lean close. Our lips meet in the middle, but the sparks don't fly like before. This feels desperate, like the last breaths in a room without air. We press our lips together for as long as we can, trying to salvage whatever is here. As he pulls away, his lips quiver, but the corner of his mouth twitches upwards. He's on the verge of speaking, but his phone buzzes in his pocket. He reaches down and reads the screen. "My Uber is here."

"Of course," I say. A grimace forms on my face. Javi looks at me for a long second before a familiar smile creeps onto his face. He pulls his backpack out from under the bed.

"Here," he says. He unzips the top zipper and reaches into his bag. He wrestles out his Rihanna vinyl a few moments later and hands it to me.

"Take it," he says.

I shake my head. "I can't," I say, putting my hands in the air. "You love that vinyl."

"I know, but I want to lend it to you."

I cock my head. "What do you mean?"

He sighs as if I should know the answer. "If I give it to you, I live with the possibility of never seeing you again. But if I lend it to you…" Javi gives me a sly look as he lays the breadcrumbs in my mind. I pick each one up and smile. "I would have to see you again."

He smiles as he extends the vinyl until the cardboard pokes my chest. I grab each end and stare down at the record. I'm about to utter my thanks, but I hear his backpack zipper again. Javi jumps off the bed and walks toward the door. He looks back at me. "I hope to see you soon."

Chapter 28

November 15, 2025

Reeltime sends me the second-worst possible notification from the school news account. I click the link, and an action picture of Romero fills my screen with the headline below:

Athletic Department Suspends Men's Soccer Player Romero Ramirez Following Failed Drug Test.

I squirm in my chair at one of the designated SESU tables, trying to loosen the now asphyxiating bright tan tie around my neck. I knew this moment would come, but it's a different dread living it. Romero has been radio silent since the news broke. His social media accounts are quiet. No messages from him in the group chat before Coach Ramsey removed his phone number. What's even more nerve-racking is the absence of his threatened retaliation post toward me, at least that I'm aware of. The thought steals the air away from me. I shove my phone back into my pocket before I even start doomscrolling.

Vince walks toward me with a buffet plate in the President's Banquet Hall. The hall has a Renaissance Palazzo style with rich wood panels, marble floors, and brass details. Antique candle chandeliers divide the room. My teammates and I dress in white shirts, black tuxedos, and our signature colored ties on one side. The USE players are on the other side in navy blue suits and sky blue ties. It's tradition for both teams to attend the championship banquet on the eve of the match. We won a home-field advantage because we beat them earlier in the season, so we're hosting the event. Vince pats me on the shoulder and leans in once he reaches his seat next to me.

"Bro, you good?" Vince asks. "You look like hell."

"I'm just processing the news," I say with some edge to my voice.

"Man, I feel you. That shit with Romero is crazy. It sucks to be suspended before the biggest match in our team's history. I wonder how he's holding up."

"Who knows?" I shrug, but the tension in my body makes it barely noticeable.

"I imagine Romero's not taking it well. It's unlucky that of all the people the conference could have chosen, it had to be Romero. Rumor has it he begged the administrator to delay the test, but it apparently didn't make a difference. Dude failed his drug test real bad."

"You're telling me," I mutter under my breath.

Vince continues with a piece of chicken skewered onto his fork. "But he was reckless for doping up. This happens when you get caught." I let out a sigh while he chews his food. Vince takes a minute and analyzes me. "Bro, what is up with you?"

"It's pointless to talk about it."

Vince cocks his head. "What does that mean?"

"It's nothing. Just leave it," I say in a flat tone.

Vince studies me for a second before he shrugs, pulls up his napkin, and dabs his face.

I rub my palms on my face.

"Well, in the spirit of changing the subject, do you know anything about Machi's friend who is visiting?"

I raise an eyebrow. "What are you talking about?"

"Machi mentioned she's inviting an important friend down for the weekend. I figured this person was staying with you. Did she say something to you?"

"I know nothing about that."

To be fair, Machi has never mentioned a friend from her past. Maybe I have been so off my game that I ignored her by accident. Jesus I'm a lousy friend.

Vince rolls his eyes, but the tiniest smirk forms on his face. "You two are a mysterious duo. Now you both are hiding stuff from each other."

I shake my head. "I haven't seen her around for a couple of days. I figured she was with you."

"The same thought crossed my mind, but with you."

"I'll text her here in a second."

"Don't worry about it, Caleb. You look tense. Maybe grabbing some food can help you relax for a second."

"I don't know if I can eat right now."

Vince squeezes my shoulder. "You got to eat. We need you tomorrow at your best. Put aside whatever's fucking with your mental right now, and go take care of yourself. If you don't, I will feed you like my baby sister."

At first, I don't budge, but the moment Vince grabs his fork and makes baby coos, I leap to my feet. My stomach growls the moment I migrate toward the sizzling bell peppers and chicken. Fresh-made tortillas, beans, and dirty rice brush my nose, and my hunger instantly distracts me from Romero.

I line up behind the chatty USE players. The orchestral music in the background deafens their conversations, and I feast my eyes up and down the buffet bar. I grab my plate and start piling it with a small scoop of the stuffed chicken pasta before I make a chicken taco. My stomach growls at the sight of all the food options. I'm about ready to bolt toward my table when I smell a whiff of pungent cologne.

"Fancy seeing you here, Thomas."

That voice is pretentious and arrogant. I turn and see Roger with a sinister smile, standing in front of me as he hands me the utensil for the next tray.

"I mean, it's the pre-championship game award banquet, Roger. No shit, I would be here."

Roger smirks. "Forgot how unpleasant you are."

"Only my best for you, Roger."

"Lighten up, Thomas. Your situation improved after you left."

"You mean after you blackmailed me to leave?" I hiss.

"We made a deal for my silence about your situation, and by the looks of it, you are succeeding at this struggling school. You should thank me."

"That's a load of shit. Your big mouth forgot about that once you and Romero started talking." Roger shows all his bright veneers in a sinister smile. "Romero had a lot to say about you, and a lot more to offer than you. I couldn't resist spilling a few secrets here and there for the right price, but I did not expect him to unload everything."

"He told you everything?"

Roger nods, and my stomach does a somersault. His smile grows at the sight of this. "I had my suspicions about him for a long time, but I would never have pegged you two together. Given your track record, I should have realized the possibility sooner. I'm sorry the two of you didn't work out."

I clutch my shaking fist to my side. He looks down and shakes his head, while Javi's "NO LAughing matter" plays through the speaker.

"It seems I'm not the only one spilling your secrets. How's Javi doing, by the way? Is he still around or did he have to leave too?"

My eyes darken as a bolt of rage strikes me. I slam my full plate on the floor and horse-collar Roger. "Listen, you fucking entitled shit!"

We clink our heads together as we grab a fistful of each other's blazers. We shove each other back and forth, bumping into the buffet table. Before I say another syllable or swing my fist, players from both teams rush toward our scuffle. Vince rushes in and breaks my grip on Roger, pushing us apart before a fight breaks out.

"We're good here." He turns to face me. "We're good!"

The school executives from both schools watch the commotion while Coach Ramsey approaches us. He yanks my arm toward the dinner table.

"What the hell has gotten into you?" His voice is a low growl.

"He's a bastard and deserves worse."

"I don't care! He could be a pedophilic priest for all I care. You don't make a scene in front of the athletic director and the conference executives. This is the first time we get to host an event like this. We can't make a scene. You of all people can't make a scene."

"Yeah, but Coach…"

"But what? What has gotten into you?"

"It's just him. We have an ugly history."

"So? You are a better player than he is, and with a brighter future ahead. Why get into a fight over shit in the past?"

"Believe me, he deserves much worse."

"And why is that?" Coach folds his arms across his chest.

I'm on the verge of regurgitating the word salad of this past year, but I hesitate. I grit my teeth instead. Every time I want to talk to this man, my brain short-circuits. It's probably because I treat him like a deity, and I'm suffering from theophobia. My stare wavers from his, and we stand in an uncomfortable silence for a beat. Coach Ramsey stands there, unmoved. He looks like he's on the verge of scolding me, but softens his tone.

"It's not worth it, Caleb. He's only trying to get in your head to pull you down to his level. It's the only way he can beat you."

I exhale a frustrated breath, but ultimately reason with him. "You're right, Coach."

He smiles, and his facial features morph from English mobster into a teddy bear. "Good lad. I'm glad you came to your senses. Tomorrow night is your fight to win. Just remember not to make it fair for pretentious kids like him. They are not used to the struggle for success."

He pats me on my back and sends me back to his table. The glares from both my current and former teammates send an uncomfortable tingle down my spine as I sit back down at my spot.

Vince trails behind me and taps my shoulder. "What was

that about?"

"A year of stewing finally spilling out," I say. My thumb and index finger pinch my forehead, massaging away an aggressive headache. There is a brief pause until a plate slides toward me.

Vince smiles as he gestures down at the plate. "I figured this might help with that headache."

I ease up and can't resist a smirk. "Thanks. You didn't need to make me a plate."

He shakes his head. "I didn't make you a plate." Now it's his turn to smirk. "I stole Roger's plate after your brief altercation finished."

My smirk transforms into a full-toothed grin. I nod a silent thank you before I dig into my meal. Even though the food came from the same buffet, this meal tastes better stolen from a privileged fuck like Roger. One who always gets his way. After a few bites, the SESU athletic director walks up to the podium with a handful of envelopes, passing the award plaques on the table to his left. He taps the microphone, causing quick thuds loud enough to silence the room.

"Good evening. Thank you all for joining us. We will begin today by bowing our heads in prayer…"

Vince taps my shoulder and whispers, "Would it make you happier if I told you your name is in the Player of the Year envelope?"

I suppress a chuckle, but look over and whisper to him, "Do you have secret telepathic powers or something?"

"No. I only asked if it would bring you joy. Don't tell me this stupid award show would make you happy."

"It wouldn't hurt," I whisper.

"You white people and your trophies."

Thank God the prayer was over because I couldn't suppress this laugh. He smiles at me with a glint in his eye, almost like satisfaction in a job well done. If his goal was to distract me, it was a successful mission. It makes me appreciate him more.

We both shift our attention to the podium.

"Welcome to the first-ever American South Conference Men's Soccer banquet. My name is Bill Soldano, and I'm the Athletic Director of Southeastern State University. On behalf of the university, it is an honor to welcome the Conference Commissioner and board members to this inaugural award ceremony for men's soccer. SESU thanks you for the opportunity to be a foundational block of this growing conference. We knew this day would come when we would celebrate our men's soccer team at the conference championship game, and we are fortunate to share this glorious historical moment with our greatest collegiate rivals. We welcome the University of Southeastern members to our campus and wish you all the luck our traditions allow us to."

Another forced laugh echoes across the dining hall.

"I know everyone in attendance is eager for the exciting game tomorrow! I pray everyone does well, stays free of injury, and gives everything tomorrow. But I know everyone is just as excited to learn the winners of tonight's most coveted awards. So without further ado, let's get to the exciting part of the event this evening."

He stacks envelopes to his left and slides the first one in front of him. "The conference coaches came together this past weekend and assessed every player in all squads. I will announce the individual conference winners in a few minutes."

"First, we will read the team of the year selections."

The First Team All-Conference team comprises SESU and USE players, with a few exceptions. The SESU logo appears to the left of Marshall, Duncan, Andres, and me on the projection screen behind the athletic director. Vince pats me on the back, and I can't help but feel overwhelmed with joy. It's rewarding to be recognized for playing well this year, and now I can only hope that this is not the only honor with my name on it.

"Congrats, bro," Vince says.

I'm about to repeat the phrase back, but stop myself, remembering he's not on the board. "Thanks, but I'm sorry…"

He waves his hand to cut me off. "Don't apologize. Like I said, these award shows are pointless. Still happy for you."

"I understand. I still appreciate you." I look back at the screen, ready to take in the recognition again. But when I see Roger on the board next to me, my stomach turns enough that anxiety replaces the joy.

"Congratulations to all team selection winners in attendance and watching from home."

The crowd applauds.

Bill Soldano moves the top envelope to the center and opens the tab on its back. "Now, for the individual award winners, beginning with Coach of the Year."

He pauses for dramatic effect.

"And the winner is…Jack Ramsey of Southeastern State University."

Our side of the hall burst into celebration, as it would throughout the night. Coach Ramsey walks to the stage, a smile breaking through his typical stone facade. A similar smirk curves on my face when he tips his head toward my flustered old coach, flashing his plaque. My old teammates look unamused, much to my delight. Bill Soldano and Coach Ramsey smile and pose for a picture before he returns to his chair for some final applause. Our athletic director repeats his process for the rest of the award ceremony. His voice pitch changes when announcing SESU winners.

"Goalkeeper of the Year…Marshall Bailey of Southeastern State University…Defensive Player of the Year…Duncan Robertson of Southeastern State University!"

When Duncan returns to his seat, only two plaques remain on the table, but Bill Soldano retrieves the last remaining golden envelope and slides it across the podium.

"Ladies and gentlemen, it's my honor to announce that the voting members have selected this next player as the American South Conference's Midfielder of the Year and the Most Valuable Player of the Year."

My heart pounds against my chest as Bill Soldano breaks the conference seal on the envelope. A trickle of sweat forms around my hairline. I grip the edge of my seat, desperate for my name to be read.

"And the winner is…Roger Astor of the University of Southeastern."

My ears cease to function the moment Rogers's name is called. At first, I'm sure I misheard our AD, but the realization of my reality hits when he stands and adjusts his suit. A faint ringing in my ears drowns out the applause from USE members. I sit in disassociated silence, failing to register Vince's compassion and my old teammates' vindicated joy. I feel like I'm dreaming a nightmare, and somehow, I will wake up in the next moment, gasping for air. But I'm firmly awake.

I trace Roger's steps to the stage as the last drops of faith leak from my soul. Bewildered, I sit until disillusionment saturates me when Roger claims the night's highest honor, the Player of the Year Award, watching him flash his expensive smile and wave toward the crowd. He masquerades his pompous narcissism with a diplomatic disposition for the room. Every ounce of me wants to scream the truth about him and how he set himself up for success at my expense. Reveal all his threats toward me during my last days at USE. But even if I had the courage, this moment reminds me that he always gets what he desires. He always has.

Roger walks off the stage as he did the locker room that day, his chin held high at all he has accomplished at my expense. I rub my fingers across my forehead, hoping I disguise my displeasure, but Roger's smile stretches to his ears as he sees right through me.

Vince taps my shoulder. "Caleb," he whispers.

"Not now Vince."

"Caleb. It's important!"

"Vince, I'm not in the mood."

"Look!" he says, with more bite in his tone. Vince frowns when I pull my hand away from my face. His brow knit together as he passes the phone to me. A frozen Angelica illuminates his screen. "I'm so sorry Caleb."

I hit play and dread the next minute of my life.

"Hello, my angel babies. Here once again with some explosive tea you will crave to sip on." She clasps her hands together in a prayer position. "So, no surprise we discovered controversy in our athletic department at SESU again, but this time, the men's soccer team finds itself in the spotlight. Let's unpack all the details."

The color drains from my skin when the screen cuts to Angelica's face in the corner with an action shot of me as her background.

"A confidential informant leaked new information about Caleb Thomas to me, and it will blow your minds."

What unfolds next catches me off guard.

Angelica describes parts of my relationship with Javi at first, but then blends in my hookups with Romero without mentioning his name. She refers to him as "Sideboy," and explains that he is ironically also dating a woman. She suggests I had cheated on Javi with Sideboy after I discovered he was an illegal and that he was getting deported.

Angelica says my mom had found out about my alleged situation randomly and became distraught about my sex life. My alleged scandal damaged my mom's upstanding reputation in her church community, and she felt increasingly isolated from everyone.

The one part she got right was my mom sending me to reparative therapy, but it wasn't as a last-ditch effort to save her image. The whole thing sounds ridiculous, but my blood runs cold when Angelica mentions my mom's suicide. She implies that my unwillingness to change causes unbearable grief, and reads just the ending line of my mom's suicide note to sell this point. Word by word. But when she finishes, she emphasizes the same conclusion I came to after my first read-through.

That she died because of me.

Chapter 29

November 15, 2025

I want to run away. Vanish. Transport to another dimension. Anything to escape the hell I find myself in. The video spread like a virus, another phone lighting up seconds after the one next to it. The dumbfounded stares in my direction became the most notable symptom. I darted out of that dining hall five seconds after the banquet ended, just when the stares were unbearable.

The darkness outside greets me like an old friend and camouflages me from the rest of the recipients. I depart across the campus toward my apartment, the route identical to the one I took after my first training session. How crazy fate can shift in two months. From the moment I stepped to my mark for that Yo-Yo Test, I convinced myself this was my redemption story. This was my starting point on my journey toward my wildest dreams. That hard work and perseverance would alter fate in my favor.

Instead, I drew the rare three death cards that cause a tarotist to shudder. The death of a parent. The death of my first relationship. And now, the death of everything I worked for. The feeling intensifies the closer I approach the exit.

As soon as I cross the street to Spoiled Rotten, I sprint as fast as I can to my apartment. My body slams into the front door before I reach for my key. My hand shakes violently as I unlock the door. The moment the door swings open, I tumble into the ghostly quiet apartment, lit only by the soft moonlight from outside the window. I slam the door shut and stagger into my room, holding myself together by the adrenaline saturating my nervous system.

The moment my bedroom door shuts, I surrender to grav-ity by trickling toward the floor while my hands cover my face. My fingers rake through tangled hair as brief, silent seconds before my anger obliterates my self-control into dust. Nothing but hell breaks loose.

"Son of a bitch!"

Everyone and God are tuning in. I rise and kick the side of the rolling chair, sending it crashing into the stand. The lamp shatters across the floor before I jerk the bookcase, allowing my favorite novels and memoirs to tumble to the floor. Th e desk becomes my next victim as I flail my arms across its sur-face, sliding papers, projects, and the rest of its contents off like windshield wipers in a heavy rainstorm. Chargers and desk toys tumble across the floor like raindrops. In a swift second, I lift my desk like a wrestling opponent and launch it across the room. Hate devours me as if it skipped a meal.

My miniature trophy tumbles out of the unzipped head-phone pocket on my soccer bag. I reach down, pick it up, and hold it close, as I had many times before. Passive aggressively passed down to the firstborn for several generations, I treasured the gift unlike my predecessors before me. But now, the sight of it only triggers more rage.

I turn and launch the trophy toward the back wall. It connects with my favorite childhood Mesut Özil poster. The trophy shatters the glass frame and knocks it off the poster hinge. The childhood poster crashes to the floor beneath it, scattering glass shards all over the hardwood floor. I collapse to the floor and wail for what feels like an eternity.

I lie in the fetal position on the cold laminate floor, my right hand pushing the glass debris back and forth. My cheek presses hard to the ground as I stare at my door, while gloomy thoughts cluster like thunderclouds in my mind. The first thought is my father's crestfallen look after I revealed Mom's suicide note. I feel awful hiding it from him, but it's what Mom wanted. She explicitly asked this in her note. I owed that to her after how the depression destroyed her.

A depression I didn't mean to cause.

I did everything she asked. I went to church every Sunday, attended ministry groups for gay men, and went on that retreat she requested. Neither one of us knew what conversion therapy was, but we were desperate. I didn't know how awful that camp would be, and what it would do to me. She didn't understand, and from there, I lost her.

My second thought crashes into my head. One last promise I swore to keep. That I would be the man she envisioned. One that turns his dreams into realities and resolves the gay panic. That promise weighs heavily on me as I close my eyes, dwelling on how I failed miserably. Javi, SESU, Romero… all rapid thoughts replaying in quick succession.

"Caleb!"

Machi's high-pitched screech yanks me back into the present moment. The fear in her pitch complements her disturbed gaze when our eyes meet. Her pale complexion resembles a ghost as she hovers in the doorway, waiting for my response. She combs her fingers through her trimmed bob cut, attempting to process everything in front of her. My voice cracks under the weight of my emotions.

"Machi…I am so sorry."

"What's wrong? Please tell me." She tiptoes over me, squatting down to meet me at eye level.

"I just can't do it anymore," I say while fresh tears spill down my face. "I can't do this anymore."

Her hand brushes up my back, stroking me like a cat. "What are you talking about?"

"I can't live anymore," I choke.

She gasps. "Caleb, don't say that!"

"I can't anymore." My voice aches more with every syllable.

"No, no. It's going to be okay. I don't want you to leave."

"I can't…" I try to string a few more words together, but the tears gush out of my eyes. Machi pulls my head in, and I weep into her collarbone, while her hands stroke the top of my head.

"No, Caleb. You are not going anywhere, and I'm staying right here," she whispers. Before I protest, Machi cranes her neck toward the hallway. "Vince! Can you come in here for a second?"

Almost on cue, Vince enters the room seconds after she calls him. The outline of Vince's muscular frame shines in the moonlight beside the situation. His dark complexion contrasts with the white dress shirt compressing his build. He scans the room, processing the events unfolding in front of him. "Jesus, man," he whispers. "What happened?"

My nose inhales a ragged breath, and I stumble through my response. "I just…I don't…I can't…"

Machi summons Vince over. He squats down as she leans into his ear and whispers something inaudible. He turns his head toward her and nods, looking back at me.

I gaze blankly at them, my energy depleting well past empty. "Please, both of you, just go."

"Caleb, we can't do that," Machi whispers.

"Just let me be, and I promise I will be quiet."

Machi is about to speak when Vince lays his hand on her back, nodding again.

"Do you mind if we chill with you for a minute?" he asks.

I shake my head, but with no genuine conviction.

"What if we just stay for a minute, and if you still aren't up to it, then Machi and I will leave you be?"

Machi stares daggers at Vince, but he brushes it off.

"What do you say, man? Let's vibe for a second, and we'll let you be afterwards."

My nose sniffs before I nod. "It doesn't matter. Everything's dead. There is no point anymore."

"What do you mean by that?" Vince asks, sitting down on the floor.

"Angelica summed it up essentially."

"She's a bitch for discussing your private life on Reeltime," Machi says through gritted teeth.

"The gay part is true, though." Tears slide across my face.

"There's nothing wrong with that," Vince says.

"What?" I ask. Genuine confusion distorts my facial features.

"There's nothing to be ashamed of. I knew you were gay," he says. His tone, firm yet comforting, takes me aback. I peer at Machi, searching for confirmation, but Vince cuts in.

"I never told Machi this, but you reminded me of my cousin Lemarcus when I first met you. He helped raise me after my father left us when I was a boy. Lemarcus acted guarded, like you, in public. He always exercised caution around everyone and removed himself from situations when he sensed danger. But in his safe spaces, he was his flamboyant and outgoing self. When he wasn't dancing, he would babysit my sisters and me. Lemarcus would play with dolls with my sisters and help me with my homework. He also showed me how to talk to girls, kept me looking my best, and helped me stay true to myself. He was the male role model I needed, even if he didn't fit the mold."

I sniffle. "He sounds like someone who could offer me sage advice about this."

"He could if he were still around," Vince says, lowering his voice and staring at the floor. Machi strokes his back.

"What do you mean?"

Vince takes a deep breath. "He died when I was 14, stabbed to death when he walked home from his dance school."

Machi rubs his back as she looks at Vince the same way she looks when reminiscing on her brother—on the brink of tears.

"It still hurts." Vince leans on Machi. The memory seems to knock the wind out of him.

The tears return to me, but they belong to Vince this time.

He clears his throat. "I swore to be an ally from that day on."

"Thank you for being that ally," I say, my sadness shedding off my body.

Vince's smile radiates back at me, one as rare as drawing a jackpot-winning lottery ticket. "It feels like he brought us together in heaven to help us heal."

"All of them did. Him, your mom, and Shane. They are the bond that holds us together," Machi says. She fights her own tears. Vince gives her a soft kiss on the cheek before he maneuvers around the broken furniture and glass shards. He reaches down to pick up an unharmed vinyl before sitting on the floor.

"Are you listening to him, too?" Vince asks as he studies Javi's vinyl cover.

"Somewhat." I sit up as he examines the record.

"Where did you get this?"

"It's complicated."

"How complicated? I haven't been able to find one. These have sold out everywhere," Vince says.

"You wouldn't understand."

"Try me."

His kind eyes pulsate through me as every second passes, soothing my hyperactive amygdala. Vince clears a spot on the floor and sits cross-legged on the ground. Machi cozies up next to Vince, and she rests her head on his shoulder, as he wraps his arm around her.

I pull myself off the ground and mimic their posture. "I'm the inspiration behind *NO LAughing matter*," I whisper.

Machi and Vince exchange knowing glances, but there is no surprise in their expressions.

I figured they don't believe me, so I continue explaining.

"Javi's album is about our relationship at USE before I transferred here," I say.

Vince and Machi look back with sympathy.

"Oh, Caleb," she whispers.

"We met a month after my mom's funeral to work on a group assignment, but then I caught feelings. We kissed after our date during Mardi Gras, and he was the guy I had my first time with after The Cove."

"Caleb, man," Vince says.

I cut him off before he utters another word. "He gave me a Polaroid picture of us on the observation tower in University City, which he uses now for his album cover. I took that picture of him and kept it in the Kehlani vinyl on my shelf. But then everything happened…"

"Caleb. We know," Machi says.

I freeze and turn to them.

"How do you know?"

"Caleb. Don't take this the wrong way. We have been friends for a long time, and I know when you are hiding something."

"What are you talking about?"

"I know how the vinyl showed up, but I was surprised how paranoid you became. I was concerned after you threw it in the trash."

"You threw this in the trash?" Vince asks, holding the vinyl.

Machi nods. "He did! So I picked it out of the trash and kept it around as promised. I knew he hadn't released his album yet, and read he lived in New Orleans and went to USE. This could not have been a coincidence."

"I'm sorry," I said, replaying those memories as I see everything more clearly.

"Relax. I didn't want to force it on you, especially since it was heartbreaking. But once I read about him, I knew you two shared some history."

I turn to Vince. "How did you know?"

He points at Machi. "She told me everything after I called her. We worried about you."

"Did you ever reach out to him?" Machi asks.

I drop my shoulders and huff out a breath. "No, I didn't. I figured he didn't want to talk to me again. Especially after the way we left things. He probably hates me."

"I doubt it. He dedicated his whole album to you." She unwraps Vince's arms around her and stands.

"Or he's punishing me. He got mad when I tried to explain everything to him."

"Maybe he was just hurting at that moment. He might have healed while creating this project," Vince says.

"How?"

"He sings about the love of his life on his album, and he harbors no hard feelings toward that person. Only continued affection. I believe Machi when she says that it's you he loves."

I consider this for a minute. "I don't know."

Machi pulls out her phone when it buzzes in her pocket. After a quick glance, she walks toward the hallway. "Maybe someone else could convince you."

I look at Machi. "Who are you talking about?"

Machi walks out of the room, but his voice echoes in the hallway. "A friend I invited over."

"What friend?"

Now a smile creeps onto Vince's face. "That friend I told you about at the banquet."

A bewildered expression contorts my facial features. "What are you talking about? You asked me if I knew anything about that."

"Yeah true, but she said you would know who it is."

"But I don't! I have no clue what's going on." My breath paces.

Machi pokes her head back into the bedroom. "You'll remember him when you see him."

"Him?" I ask.

There is no time to process when Machi walks into the room, her hand gripping the jacket of the man trailing close behind her. My breath hitches when his silhouette steps into the dim moonlight trickling in from the window. My heart pounds against my chest the moment Javi's cocoa eyes lock with mine. He looks as nervous to see me as I am to see him.

"Hey Caleb," he whispers.

Chapter 30

June 1, 2025

The church

Leave it to me to feel a chill in God's house in the summer. It's my first time since my mom's funeral that I stepped foot into a church, and it's an awkward homecoming. It feels like coming home for Christmas break from college and reuniting with high school friends who never left. Their lives are stuck in time, while I moved on. As I sit in the front pew alone in this empty chapel, I reflect on my regrets from my past.

Javi's my freshest regret. We split less than a month ago, and I'm debating what feels worse: the crippling pain on Javi's face when I told him I was leaving, or the hope in his eyes without me disclosing the full truth about my exit. Both remind me of the moment he slipped from my fingers, and that's enough sadness to fill a lake. It's pathetic. I thought I would save him from Roger's scheme, but I can't tell if I made a difference. He could spill all my secrets to some stranger, whether I left or stayed. Roger never fails to amaze me.

But keeping secrets from Javi made me feel as grimy as Roger. Javi deserves to know the truth, and I'm ready to come clean. So I sit alone in the church pew, focusing ahead at the altar, and struggle with how to handle what happens next. I rake my fingers through my hair, trying to grasp my thoughts. I reached out to Javi a few weeks ago, hoping we could reconnect as I had promised. To my relief, he had a break from recording his music, and he picked a church to meet in.

The door swings open from the side, echoing with a booming thud throughout the chapel. My hands clasp behind me on the pew as I take in the striking man entering. His sharp white tank top peeks out from an unbuttoned lace dress shirt, which hovers over tailored dress pants. Javi hesitates for a moment but walks toward the pew, genuflecting before sitting to the left of me.

"Thanks for coming," he whispers.

"I'm glad you saw my message on the app because I was afraid you deleted it. However, I had to double-check our meeting location. Why are we at this church?"

Javi adjusts his gold necklace. "Do you remember our first night here?"

"When we almost got shot?"

He laughs. "Yes, but do you remember after we escaped Bourbon Street? The spot we stopped at?" His eyes glint as he stretches his arm to an unstained window. "That's where we shared our first kiss," Javi says, pointing to the exact spot for the moment mentioned.

His finger points to a group of people walking around the perimeter of the property before they disappear into the crowds beyond. We watch a couple stay behind with a tall young man embracing his girlfriend in front of the gate. Realization dawns on me then, as I watch them, a flicker of sparks crackles in my mind, reminiscing this for a sweet second.

"Feels like fate offering a subtle reminder," Javi sighs.

"Wow, we have come full circle, haven't we?"

Javi turns his head and raises an eyebrow. "Full circle? What do you mean by that?"

"Another moment to reveal myself to you."

Javi stiffens his posture. "What are you talking about?"

My throat bobs for a second, but I swallow my pride. "I haven't been as open with you as I should have been."

Javi smiles as he searches my face like a detective looking for clues. "You are so overdramatic. What are you holding back from me?"

I open my mouth, but only air whispers out.

Javi tenses as the playful demeanor dissipates into the surrounding air. He scans around the empty church before he leans in close. "Oh, you are serious."

"It was killing me not telling you," I say, scratching my elbow, avoiding eye contact.

"Ok, well, what do you need to say?"

I shake my head as I readjust my body, my palms rubbing the denim of my jeans.

"Caleb, you are making me nervous."

"I'm sorry, it's just a lot."

He flinches at my answer, and I draw out a prolonged, uneasy breath with an ounce of doubt flowing through me. "I haven't been fully honest with you."

"Ok. What do you have to say?"

My parched throat struggles to swallow my saliva. "I should

have been more open about everything in my life, especially with my feelings toward my mom's death."

He nods but says nothing, watching me as I clear my throat.

"This entire problem started when I was twelve."

"Twelve?" Javi crosses his arms. "What problem has manifested itself since you were twelve?"

"Puberty," I whisper.

Javi's mouth twitches, ready to form another question, but the light bulb goes off in his brain, and his face softens as I explain further. "What did you do?" Javi asks.

"At first, I tried ignoring it. When that didn't work, I tried praying the gay away. I attended extra church masses, practiced reconciliation with priests, and volunteered at Life Teen. I tried everything, but it just wasn't working. So I panicked and finally told my mom last summer."

"What happened then?"

"Everything but what I expected."

Javi tilts his head. "What do you mean?"

I swallow hard again. "Growing up, I went to my mom for everything because she solved every problem while tending to our needs with gentle care. But this ended up being the exception. It was as if I had spooked her. Her usual calm tone had more edge to it. Her words were more uneven than usual. It was as if I were talking to an imposter."

"What did she say?"

My breath hitches for a beat. "She panicked and rambled to herself, and asked me all these humiliating questions about my nonexistent sex life. If I watched porn, masturbated, or had sex with any guys. She asked me what guys were triggering a sexual response."

"That's horrible, Caleb. I'm so sorry."

"Once she finished questioning me, she put the fear of God into me, hurling biblical verses to drive her point home. She agreed to help me, but we kept it between us."

"What did she do?"

"She started routine check-ins with me the next day and continued through most of the summer. She also sent me resources on guiding me through my same-sex attractions. But it felt hopeless since I couldn't feel any progress, so she recommended I sign up for our parish's Journey into Manhood weekend retreat."

"What is that?"

"It's a peer-run conversion therapy retreat."

Javi moves his hands across his face. A faint gasp escapes his lips. "Isn't conversion therapy illegal?"

I shrug. "The organizers advertised it as talk therapy, and the retreat is technically an 'experiential experience' run by guides and volunteers."

Javi gives me a suspicious glance. "That's sus."

I nod. "I wish the alarm bells had gone off when I arrived, but Mom and I were desperate. The moment she dropped me off in front of the camp's minivan, I knew the weekend would become more traumatic than transformative."

My voice becomes more frantic as I recount this memory. "First, we walked around a campfire in the woods in our underwear and talked about gay experiences. Some guys confessed to cheating on their wives, having sex with close friends, and watching gay porn. It was weird. But then we discussed how certain feminine products related to our mommy issues. My guide interrogated me about my mom, whether she was needy or controlling, or if she inappropriately nurtured my feelings to the point where I can't love women. If I didn't fix it, I would only develop an attraction by forcing myself on them. The whole interaction was more violating than comforting."

"What the fuck?" Javi whispers while shaking his head.

"I wish that was the worst of it. We had to role-play traumatic interactions with our parents in a taped-off rectangle. I wish I had made something up looking back now."

"What happened?"

"I shared the story when my mom and dad were having a typical argument after he arrived home one night from a shift. To be honest, I don't even remember why they were fighting. But it escalated into a screaming match, with them exchanging insults with one another. I ignored it until I heard shattering and a thud. I ran into the kitchen and remembered seeing my mother squatting on the ground, holding onto the fridge door. A small trail of blood streamed down her forehead. She looked terrified. I saw my father standing over her and the broken blender above the fridge."

I wipe my face and feel Javi's arm rub my shoulder. "Did he hit her with it?" Javi asks.

"I don't know. They both said it fell from the top of the fridge after my father punched it, and the blender had hit my mother before I walked in. But that was after I jumped on my father to restrain him. He threw me off his back, and I crushed my side into the countertop before falling to the floor. I couldn't breathe, and I just lay there until help arrived."

I inhale deeply.

"The lead guide, in his late twenties, said something like, 'You were a boy trying to save your mother. Do you know what you received instead? He said you were worthless and could not help her. You never stood up from the kitchen floor, did you? You've been lying there all your life.' The oldest guide that played my father said, 'You're worthless, weak, and a pathetic faggot.' They put a dummy between me and a guide, and handed me a baseball bat and instructed me to seek a new father and release myself from this one. At first, I thought this was a joke, but then everyone was screaming at me. The guides were in my face, just yelling at me until it disoriented me. I panicked and just took the bat and…"

Mortification washes over Javi. "Please don't tell me you…"

My breathing speeds up as I act out my response.

"I took the bat, lifted it over my head, and swung down. But after I hit the dummy, they just kept yelling at me to hit it while I screamed for what felt like an hour. After several rounds of me wailing away, one guide crouched close to the floor, and in a blood-curdling shout, the youngest guide screamed, 'Finish him!' And in one swing, it was over. The guide representing my dad lay there motionless next to the dummy. Then, the guide from the church, representing my new 'dad,' stands with his arms open. He said, 'I love you, son. I care about you.' He approached me and wrapped his arms around me. But the worst part was the healing touch technique at the end of the retreat."

Javi appears mortified by every detail, but still straightens in his spot. "What more could they possibly have done to you?"

"Well, the guides organized a group of six people, all in our underwear, and led us into a dim, humid space that held only a couple of candle lanterns and a faraway speaker. Sitting on the carpet, we waited for the phone to connect to the speaker. The guide volunteered to give me a healing touch."

"What is that?"

"It's this reparative technique that is supposed to help men remedy their same-sex attraction caused by the lack of a 'healthy' non-sexual masculine connection. I sat between the guide's legs, leaning my back against their chest during the healing touch. The giver would wrap his arms around me for the entire session. I was terrified and didn't want to do it at all, but he assured me everything would be okay. Once the Christian song "Oceans" started, I moved between his thighs and leaned back while he wrapped his arms around me. Men from the group touched my arms, legs, and chest. But at the song's beginning, I felt his…him on my back."

Javi's eyes redden.

"And he just kept massaging and rubbing himself on me. He said, 'You used to be the golden child. Your life was wonderful before someone hurt you, and you built walls to protect yourself. It's time to bring down those walls. You wouldn't want your mother to find out about you now, would you?' Once no one was looking, he slid his hand underneath my underwear. I closed my eyes to endure it…and I'm glad my eyes were closed…because I couldn't…"

The last memory cripples me. A waterfall of tears cascades down my face. My head crashes into Javi's chest, mimicking the image of Jesus with his disciples in the stained glass window next to them.

"I'm so sorry this happened to you," Javi whispers. He

strokes my hair while I smear my tears into his shirt. "What did you do?" Javi asks.

I pull away, inhaling with a stuffy nose. "Nothing. I was silent after she picked me up, but I was hysterical internally. I isolated myself from everyone for days after it happened."

Javi rubs his forehead. "Why are you telling me all of this?"

I look ahead at the crucifix and wipe a tear away. "Because a week later, I told my mom, and my whole life fell apart." My voice cracks as I rub my eyes and clear my throat. "She came into my room almost a week before I left for USE. I ignored her questions about the sessions at first, but she kept pestering me. Asked me about the camp, my progress, and whether I had sinned. She wore me down to the bone before she broke me. I spilled everything and spared her nothing."

"What did she say?"

"She just stood there. Completely speechless. It's like her entire demeanor drained out of her, leaving a hollow entity in her place. She just covered her mouth and closed the door. From that day on, she was never the same."

"Did you both ever talk again?"

"I tried when I was leaving, but she didn't want to talk to me about it. She said that she had failed. I didn't know what she meant by that, and never asked her. During the season, she had developed a deep depression and never showed up for games. She took antidepressants for a while to go to work, but she didn't improve. She still suffered. Then on my birthday, she reached out to me. She said she wanted me to come home to see her. I was so excited that I drove home that night to see her. But the moment I walked into that house, I knew something was wrong. And I couldn't believe what I saw."

Javi rubs my back again, the one gesture holding me together before I admit the moment my life changed.

"There was no response when I entered the house. I called out for her, and I heard her phone ringing in her bedroom upstairs. The last thing I remember that day was wailing after touching her unconscious body, lying still in her bed. I think a neighbor came by and found me before calling the police. My father came home shortly after that."

I sob so hard that I don't even try to control my tears this time. I feel Javi wrap his arms around me and hold me close. He attempts to soothe me, but it's useless. The sadness floods my system to the point where I drown.

"You can't blame yourself for that, Caleb," Javi says.

"But it is my fault." I reach into my pocket and retrieve a folded piece of paper. I hand it to him, my face still buried in his shirt.

"What is this?" Javi asks as he takes the paper.

"Her last words." I peer up to watch Javi unfold the note.

"Dear Caleb," he says, clearing his throat.

By the time you read this, I will be gone. I never saw this end for myself, but it's one I deserved, given how I have committed the biggest crime as a mother.

As a mother, you do anything to protect your child. So when you told me about your sexuality, I invested everything I could into helping you. Your struggles became my struggles. The last thing I wanted was for these urges to consume you and derail everything you have worked hard for. So when I found that camp, I figured we had found the answer to our problems. A blessing in response to my prayers. When you told me what happened, an overwhelming wave of guilt consumed me.

I failed as a mother by sending you into the clutches of evil, which I was trying to defend against. I put sin in your heart and tainted your soul. Because I pushed so hard for you to get the help you needed, you got hurt instead. No matter what happens next, I carry that shame that I indirectly harmed my child. No amount of pills will fix what's broken inside me.

This whole predicament with you has killed me, and there is nothing more I can do to change that.

Javi drops the page onto his thigh. "Oh my God."

"I blame myself. Every day."

"Caleb, you can't blame yourself for this. This is not your fault. None of this is." He rubs my back while I rest my head on his shoulder. Then he kisses my forehead before pressing his lips to mine. "Why would you tell me all of this now?" he whispers.

"Because I was never fully honest with you about what happened."

"But it doesn't matter now. You don't need to explain. I understand how distressing this is."

"I owe you an explanation, especially since it affected everything."

"I don't think it did…"

"It affected why I left."

Javi stops stroking my back. "I thought you left because your coach cut you from the team."

The warmth vanishes in his eyes as he glances at me, forcing me to look at the tabernacle. Even all the celestial angels in the stained glass see me crack in my seat. I wipe my eyes. "Roger forced me off the team."

"Roger? How did Roger force you off the team? And be

honest, especially since we are in a church," Javi says, his face pinched. His expression leaves me exposed. Never did I expect Javi to discomfort me, but I was wrong. A little ring of sweat gathers along my hairline.

I release a deep sigh and let the full truth out, something I will regret later. "He blackmailed me."

Javi looks taken aback. "Blackmailed you how?"

"He walked up to me in the locker room after practice and handed me a note. It shocked me when I realized it was my mom's letter. He threatened to send pictures of the letter to everyone and frame me as the gay son who killed his mother."

"How did he find this?"

"He was my roommate last year. He said he found it cleaning out our dorm room, but I knew that was bullshit because I kept it hidden in the Kehlani vinyl you got me."

"But why would he do this?"

"He hated me."

"Why, though?"

"At first, he complained I was a terrible roommate because I didn't follow his rules or put up with his bullshit. But the coach moved me into his role when the team wasn't playing well, which set him off. This aggrieved him so much that he felt getting rid of me was the only option. He said the coaches promised him a starting position when he signed for the team, and I was destroying his legacy at USE. Whatever that meant."

"So you left so he wouldn't expose you?"

"Sort of. I ignored his threats until he mentioned you."

Javi's eyes widen. "Me?" he says, pointing at his chest.

I nod.

"What did he say about me?"

"After I refused his one-sided offer, he gave me this." I pull out the Polaroid with his signature on it from my pocket. The tension builds to an unbearable pressure, and all I see is Javi's skin becoming pale. "It was in the other flap of the vinyl. He threatened to call ICE on you if I didn't leave."

Javi sits still, but I see the steam blowing out of his ears. He sits and stews for a few moments, each second adding an unbearable layer of stress. I cave when it becomes too much.

"Please say something."

"I can't believe this." Javi snatches the photo and leaps to his feet, storming toward the exit.

I follow close behind. "Javi! Wait a second!" I lunge and stretch for his flailing left arm, tugging him so he spins around.

"Let me go," he scowls.

I release his arm and slowly back a step away. "Javi. I did this to protect you. I did this for…"

"Why would you hide this from me? Why didn't you say something?" His words echo against the vaulted ceiling. My feet anchor to my spot, not daring to step any closer. I stand in front of him, crestfallen.

"I believed Roger when he said he would get you deported. The last thing I wanted was for me to hurt you. I failed my mom, but I will not fail you."

"Caleb, are you stupid? Roger says racist shit like that to all Latino students on campus. He's threatened ICE on me multiple times as a twisted joke, but now you confirmed it as truth." He buries his face in his hands, trying to conceal that he's on the verge of tears. "All I ever did was love and protect you from danger. I kept us a secret to protect you from your teammates. How could I be so stupid to think you would do the same for me?"

"I didn't know he was lying."

Javi rubs his face, swatting away the tears before he paces in place.

"Now I have to drop out to save myself."

My feet spring to life, and I rush to him. "I'm transferring to SESU next semester. Come with me, and I can protect you."

Javi shakes his head while he wheezes. "You broke my heart, lied to me, and then sold me out. I can't believe I ever loved you." He bolts toward the exit with me in hot pursuit.

"I made a horrible decision because I thought it would keep you safe. Javi, I'm so sorry, but please let me fix this. I love you. I don't want to lose you, too."

I reach for him again, this time placing my right hand on his shoulder. Javi wastes no time yanking my hand off him and turns to face me. In one fluid motion, he pulls his right foot back and swings into my left leg. A snap reverberates in my ear, and I collapse to the floor in agony.

Javi stares, too stunned to say anything. He backs away slowly before sprinting out the door. I wrap my leg in my hands, but it's useless to soothe the true, raw, unbearable pain. This is the worst physical feeling I have ever experienced as I lay on the church floor alone, moaning in agony. I knew then no one could ever repair this physical, emotional, and spiritual fissure, ripping me apart.

Chapter 31

November 15, 2025

"Caleb?" Javi says. A confused look spreads across his face.

I wonder if it's because of the shock on mine. I'm convinced this is a hallucination. A symptom of my panic attacks. But here is Javi standing in front of me. His voice sends chills down my spine to hear the haunting sweetness in it.

Javi comes closer and emerges under the moonlight, his silhouette evolving into a man looking as stunning as I remember. His sun-kissed curls still shine even in the darkness, and his glowing baby face is more eye-catching in his outfit identical to the one he wore on our first date. The same formula that captured my attention then works perfectly now.

I open my mouth, but my words catch in the back of my throat.

"Are you good?" Vince asks. He steals a glance at Javi, who now looks uncomfortable with each ticking second, and then glances back at me.

"But how?" I ask, my voice catching before I can ask more.

Machi walks forward. "Javi was my surprise friend staying over the weekend."

I cock my head at her. "But how do you know each other?"

"We met online a month ago, but in person today," Machi says.

My confusion must be plastered on my face because Javi cuts in next. "Machi reached out again earlier this week. She told me you were in trouble and needed my help."

I stare at my best friend. My wonderful best friend. "Thank you, Machi. I don't know how you brought him here, but I owe you big time for this."

Machi pulls away and shakes her head. "I didn't fly him in." She passes Javi a knowing look as she walks to me. Machi then rubs my shoulder as she scans my confused face.

"Vince and I will leave so you two can catch up." Vince and Machi hold each other's hands before turning toward the living room. Javi hugs Machi and shakes Vince's hand before he focuses back on me.

"Hey," Javi says, his steps closing the distance.

His sultry voice matches the one buried in my memory. Each syllable warms me like lying next to the fire on this bitter night. I'm convinced that I'm delusional, but my disillusion becomes a reality the moment we stand inches from one another.

"About that video, please know I never said…" I say, but he interrupts me.

"It's ok. I know it's bullshit," he says.

I nod as we stand in an uncomfortable silence.

His eyes trail down to my leg. "How's your leg?"

"It's fine. Healed mostly."

"It didn't set you back much, did it?"

"Just a few months, but I recovered quickly. Getting back to my best."

"That's good."

"How did…how is this possible?"

"Your friend is very caring. I reached out to her over a month ago to send the vinyl. She did the rest."

"But she said she didn't fly you out."

"She didn't. I called my manager and said I needed to fly here to help a friend. I hope you don't mind me just showing up unannounced."

"Not at all. I wanted to reach out again, but I figured you still hated me."

"Why?"

"Because we ended on horrible terms."

Javi purses his lips before he looks down toward the ground, my vinyl collection in his line of view. He walks over and squats down at the records. "They're all here," he says.

I walk over and squat next to him. "I couldn't get rid of them. You know that."

Javi pulls his own album out. "Not even this one?"

"I would be lying if I said I didn't try."

He shoots me a look. "You tried?"

"Machi fished it out of the trash," I say.

He looks back down. "After all the coordination between Machi and me to send you the vinyl, you still never listened to it?"

"I didn't say that, but it just took me forever to have the courage to listen."

"Why?"

"Because I was afraid of what I might hear, and would have to force myself to relive the same experiences I had moved on from. I didn't want to go through that again."

Javi averts his eyes down at his own album and traces the corners. Tension suffocates our conversation for a beat while we sit in silence, looking down at the records. I exhale once the guilt finally overcomes me.

"I'm sorry," I whisper.

"For what?" he asks.

"For snapping at you just now," I say to ease the mood a bit. "But also for my part in how we ended."

Javi turns his gaze back to me. "What do you mean?"

"I wanted to protect you, but I'm also guilty for hiding the entire truth from you. It was eating me alive after we said goodbye at USE."

Javi nods but says nothing.

"Are you still mad?" I ask.

"Not anymore," he admits. "It felt like you stabbed me in the back at first. I thought you poured everything on me just to soften my reaction towards you. It took some time, but I realized you were just trying to be vulnerable."

"But won't you still be in danger?"

He squeezes my shoulder and leans in. "I got a work visa through my record label."

"I'm glad."

I smile and stare at his face on the album cover again, for maybe the millionth time, watching it shift in Javi's arms. He removes the vinyl from its sleeve, before opening the hood of the record player and setting the vinyl on the turntable.

"What are you doing?" I ask.

"Helping you clean the room."

"What? Why?" I ask.

"I figured you would need the help," he says, his tone more playful than before. He flips the switch, and the melted dark and baby blue rotate until it's a uniform cerulean. "Besides, I'm not staying in this pigsty while I'm visiting."

"Are you staying here?"

Javi smiles as he nods. "Machi agreed to let me stay here."

I rub my face. "Of course she did."

"Yeah, forgot to mention that." He places the wand on the record, and the introduction to 'Falls' booms from the speaker. He saunters over to the bed and picks up the pillows. "She also said you would stay in her room."

"We might need to switch bedrooms tonight. Honestly, you don't need to clean. You're probably tired from traveling."

"I don't mind, but it would go faster with your help."

"Ok."

I retrieve the broom from my closet and sweep the glass into a pile. We move in silence for a few songs with the record player playing in the background, but not loud enough to wake a sleeping complex. I sweep away the debris into a trash bag while Javi reorganizes the unbroken items he deemed salvageable. After I throw away my last contents in my dustpan, I study Javi as he leans my poster against a wall, and his facial profile sends a shiver down my spine. His beauty is effortless, and it pulls my attention like the earth pulls the moon. Old feelings bubble inside me, and I can't help but take him in. Javi notices my stare and turns toward me. We gaze into each other's eyes, the tension palpable between us.

"What's wrong?" he asks.

"Nothing. I'm just not sure about something."

"Which is?"

"What does this mean?" I ask. My finger sways in the space between us.

"What do you mean?" he whispers.

"I mean, where does this leave us? What are we doing here?"

"I'm just helping clean your room."

"No, not that. I'm just confused about what's happening now."

"Because I wanted to come here?"

"But why come here after all this time? After all that happened?"

He says nothing, but takes a step further. Standing a stoic foot away, his striking eyes invite me in closer. "What do you think?"

My breath loses control while my heart crashes into my chest. I want to resist my next move, mostly because I'm afraid of what he will do. But with all my hesitation, some invisible force pulls me in. I close ninety percent of the distance, making sure I read his body language. He doesn't protest. Near his face, I hesitate, my mind wrestling with the decision. Half of me feels like a selfish prick if I go further. The other half is desperate to feel a spark with him again.

Luckily, Javi covers the last ten percent of the distance. His lips crash onto mine, evoking all the mental stimulation I craved. I receive his soft lips on mine and increase the intensity in increments. A tsunami of dopamine floods my mind as I clutch his jawline in my hands, the feel of moisturized skin grazing my own. His cologne entrances me like a love potion, and I can't pull myself away from him. We reignite the intense bond between us, stitching the love once destroyed back together.

He pulls away and looks at me with sympathy, before tapping my chest and regaining his breath. "You need to get some sleep. You have a game to win tomorrow. We'll address this later."

I nod, even though I would stay up all night with him to rekindle whatever we have in the moment. But I'm glad he pulled away when he did. He was right. I needed sleep for tomorrow. The game would be the least of my problems.

Chapter 32

November 16, 2025

Nerves jolt through me as we wait for the referees to lead us to the field under a growling Rottweiler's Den. The energy transports from the stands into the tunnel as the school band hypes up the sold out crowd. The athletic department's social media littered Reeltime with posts highlighting the match programs on every seat and handing out free bright tan and black shirts to all attendees.

The social media team hoped to create the atmosphere to match the occasion for SESU's first conference championship. An explosion of cheers above me suggests their efforts paid off. Under any other circumstances, I would be buzzing for this type of atmosphere. Just not at this moment, thanks to Angelica's Reeltime post. I'm not even sure what to expect tonight. Machi warned me about my situation trending on Reeltime and suggested avoiding looking at it on my phone. It didn't take much to convince me. I know there is a sea of bright tan and black in the stands, but how many will be supporting me?

I push the thought away for the moment while my current

teammates and I stand next to our sworn enemy for the second time this season. All USE players puff their chests out and keep their heads up, the same intimidation factor I used to perform when I played for them. But the intimidation feels meek right now, especially given our previous win against them. Only Roger stands out in attention as he studies me, a contemptuous smile etched across his face.

I imagine he's worn that smile all day since I have been trending on social media. Now the entire world knows my deep, dark secret, and he's relishing the moment. I stare back undeterred, but secretly plot a scenario where I could escape a red card for a reckless challenge on him. It's been a long time coming.

Duncan's shouting interrupts my stewing, and he leads us onto the pitch behind the referee. My cleats press onto the vibrant grass as we walk out, and a thick vapor dissipates into the overcast sky as I blow heated breaths into my icy hands. I leave last out of the tunnel behind Vince, where the largest crowd all season welcomes us with bedlam.

I look across the field at the jumbo screen on the scoreboard. The screen lags a second, which gives me enough time to watch myself appear in clear high definition. It takes a heartbeat for thundering applause to deteriorate into some raspy jeers that mute Vince's shouts.

We walk out to the center circle and turn to face the crowd. The noise softens, but the tension remains palpable. The crowd burns its stares toward me with such visceral intensity that I'm convinced I am standing trial for a heinous crime. I guess I might as well be. Angelica's post has cultivated a court of public opinion, and her aggressively homophobic fans are the prosecutors. They even sent a letter to Coach Ramsey demanding my removal from the team or threatening consequences.

I can't imagine they have any power on campus, so the threat didn't faze me. But showing up in a black 'Justice for Janet' shirt with my mother's face in the front row is another level of vile I'm barely stomaching. It's a fucking circus act using my mom's death as some battle cry. And they found the gay son to demonize for their cause.

If my mother were alive to see this, she would be appalled. I am convinced she would walk right up to them in the most ridiculous church dress and scold them for their behavior. Once she accomplished her motherly mission, she would walk back to my family and wrap herself in endless blankets, smiling and hugging my brother, where he would wave toward me.

To her left, my father would stand next to her, completing the picture of my supportive family. But this is an impossible picture to paint. I only blame myself for it, and I can't take anything back. Matthew Evans, in his Baker Boys cap, is the first face I recognize, forcing a half smile and shaking a thumbs up in my direction when our gazes meet.

Machi catches my eye as she swats away at phones invading her immediate space in the bottom right corner of the stands. She hates unwanted attention, but as she swats those phones as if they were mosquitoes, a smile forms on my lips. The past twenty-four hours have wound me so tight I almost snapped like a twig if it weren't for her and the man she attempts to protect from a photo ambush. Javi locks eyes with me, the same gleam in his eyes as when we first met. I never expected him to show up in the dramatic fashion he did, but I am grateful that he did. Even more grateful that he stayed to help me through the circus. We spoke a little after the kiss and agreed to sleep in separate beds to prepare for today.

Seeing him up in the stands boosts my energy more than any of Machi's pregame lattes. I nod in his direction as he remains oblivious to the swarm of fans screaming for his attention. His manager, fearful for his artist's safety in traveling here, according to Javi, taps his shoulder before he whispers something in his ear. Javi only nods, but his focus never wavers from me.

The crowd erupts in cheers when three men in identical black suits emerge from the tunnel in a triangular formation. I watch as the man in front holds a banner displaying each school's logos and colors, and the two schools' athletic directors behind him hold the conference trophy. Tonight's biggest prize.

"And now, please stand for the national anthem."

Two SESU ROTC cadets walk out halfway between the players and the touchline and present a standard American flag. Angelica strides out of the tunnel behind them in her Jimmy Choo winter boots. There is little time for me to register the smugness on her face because I am staring at her 'Justice for Janet' tee peeking out of her denim jacket, identical to the jeans hugging her curves. Her bright white smile deceives the embracing crowd, unaccustomed to her bullshit.

Our eyes meet when she scans my body with a condescending eye as she walks over to the microphone stand. The audacity of this privileged socialite.

I scowl back at her, but she diverts her attention toward the microphone. It's interesting how the band assumed responsibility for playing the national anthem for the entire season until a rumor about the attendance of a rising star in the music industry and his manager caused the athletic director to have his daughter perform the number solo. No point in stressing about it now. I have other problems to focus on.

She clutches the microphone between her fuzzy gloves, with enough fur to cover a Sphynx cat, and bellows her first notes, trying to recreate Whitney Houston in Tampa during the Super Bowl. She embellishes her grief and sorrow in the anthem, investing more in the performance's theatrics rather than the patriotism the song calls for. Most fans in the stadium hold their hats or hands to their hearts, if not clutching their kids.

Everyone's focus unravels the moment Angelica reaches for a high note as she stretches out the "land of the free." The note is an octave outside her range because instead of sparking the crowd's energy with a powerful delivery, her voice falls flat, and everyone in the stadium winces as they turn to look at her. It's as if her singing cracked the silicon coating that encapsulated the wickedness within her, and now it leaks out for everyone to see.

I conceal my smile at first until I see Javi wince in the stadium with his manager rubbing his temples. Machi nearly falls out of her bleacher seat laughing.

The crowd forces a round of applause before the announcer attempts to salvage the energy that is rapidly slipping out of the stadium. He reads the names off the starting lineup for each team. It takes a few minutes before he reads my name, but when the announcer does, the reception is as icy as the light precipitation. Three factions of fans have formed in the stadium attendance: SESU fans, USE fans, and everyone who hates me.

I do a quick burst of sprints to warm up the muscles in my legs before I meet everyone just outside the 18-yard box. My teammates watch me as I jog over, a thicker sense of tension over camaraderie filling the air. I slot in next to Vince and wrap my arm around his shoulder in the huddle. He does the same.

Duncan stands next to me and eyes me warily, which puts me off enough that I keep my right arm close to my side. Everyone else eyes one another as if a lengthy debate had just concluded, and now they are expecting my next move.

Duncan clears his throat as he turns to address everyone. "All right, lads. Let's get our heads right. Tonight is the most important day of our lives. We have to block out all the noise that's trying to mess with us."

There is a long enough pause for everyone to look in my direction before Duncan continues on his somewhat inspirational rant.

Vince leans in close. "Are you sure about this? I mean, about playing today," he whispers.

"I need to play today. It's the best way to get past everything."

"Hey, Harry and Megan, what the fuck could you blokes be talking about?" Duncan asks. The disgust oozes from his tone. "I don't know if you fucking noticed, but we're playing in a fucking championship game. I'm trying to get us focused, since your drama dragged the circus in."

"What do you want me to say?" I snap back.

Vince squeezes my shoulder, but I ignore him.

"Nothing would be a start! If you can't figure that out, I will happily batter you into silence," Duncan hisses.

Vince stretches his arm across my body like a protective parent shielding a child from danger, breaking the huddle. He clears his throat, and a smooth yet stern tone silences the whispers among everyone else. "What's your deal? You have been on a tirade ever since you entered the locker room, rambling about drama that's none of your business."

"I think knowing how a teammate handles his mother's death is my business!"

"Why can't you be a teammate and help a man out when he's down? What happened to the unity you preach about?"

"What unity do we have when an actual faggot from those faggot foxes snuck into this team and dragged us into his mess?"

A red mist descends on me, and I'm ready to lunge at Duncan, but Vince stops me. "Watch yourself," Vince growls.

"It's true. I'm especially uncomfortable knowing he watched us get naked all the time and said nothing. I want to be around real men like Romero, shaggers with ladies, and a baller with the boys. It's violating knowing a guy like him stares at you like a piece of meat."

"Looking at you, Duncan, there's not much to be excited about," Vince says. This gets a laugh out of some boys, but Duncan clenches his jaw and grits his teeth.

"I would watch how you talk to me, Vince."

The two stand in a heated standstill as the frosty drizzle falls to the ground.

"Do you really want to know?" I ask.

Duncan turns to me, annoyance seared onto his face. "Enlighten me," he says.

I look at Vince, whose tough-guy demeanor has melted into a comforting smile. I take a deep breath before saying, "I'm a gay man who lost my mom to suicide."

The group hushes to a dead silence.

"The same gay man whose ex-boyfriend created an album based on our relationship, including a 'NO LAughing matter' challenge I'm sure everyone has done," I continue.

Everyone turns away as I look at them. Only Duncan's gaze never wavers, so I reciprocate by looking into his eyes.

"And had a gossip influencer twist the worst moments of my life against me to boost her following. What that reel doesn't reveal is that scumbag Player of the Year threatened to have Javi deported if I didn't leave the program. And I couldn't live with that and my mother's death for one lifetime. So I came here to protect him. I broke his heart, so he broke my leg."

I close the distance until I'm painfully close. My finger presses into Duncan's chest. "And through it all, I'm still here. For once, I'm not running from my past. I'm here playing the game I do best, and don't give a shit what you think of me for it."

Everyone is mute. I stare down at a defenseless Duncan, who stands rooted to his spot.

His breathing is uneasy, and he darts his gaze away from mine. I retract my hand, seeing the uselessness of the action, but an unsuspecting arm wraps around Duncan and me. Coach Ramsey walks us back into the huddle, linking our team together again.

"And that's how we will win," Coach Ramsey says. "The smallest detail that makes all the difference. Personal Courage. We've been cautious instead of cocky. We seemed scared to face a team we had already defeated, careful with our passes in the warm up, and lacking the bravery to face this match. Life offers fleeting moments, and Caleb used one to speak when he didn't need to. Now it is your turn to follow his lead. This is our fucking championship game. You may never get this moment again."

The shrill of the referee's whistle interrupts Coach Ramsey's uplifting speech, but he keeps talking, pointing his forceful finger at several players.

"Don't miss this chance to express yourself in the game of life. A single brave moment can change everything. Play in the moment. Play football that knows no limits. You all know the style of play. You all know the system. But now take all of that and use it to help play the game you love on the biggest stage of your fucking lives. Come on, boys! Get up for it!"

The team erupts in roars of excitement after a flush of adrenaline as Coach Ramsey smacks Duncan and me on the back. He centers himself, heels down, slapping the ground rhythmically to make the group sway.

"One team..."

Coach shouts.

"... for eternity!" we respond.

"One dream..."

"...win a champion's ring!"

"One dream..."

"...win a champion's ring!""One theme..."

"... leave a legacy!"

WOOF, WOOF, WOOF, WOOF, WOOF.

We break out in bursts of excitement and anticipation, ready for whatever USE throws at us. Duncan walks in my direction, sizing me up once again. But this time, he offers his hand, and I clasp his with mine. He nods before he pulls away, and I almost let him leave, but I can't miss my opportunity to correct him.

"If it means anything, I never got excited when I saw you naked in the locker room."

I can't help but laugh as I watch the color drain from Duncan's already pale face.

CHAPTER 33

November 16, 2025

Even with the momentum from Coach Ramsey's speech, USE bullies us on the pitch after the whistle blows. The Foxes dominate us by passing the ball in intricate patterns between themselves, demonstrating their death-by-possession tactics seconds after kickoff. White and sky blue flash past everyone in bright tan and black with quick one-touch and two-touch passing. Marshall saves us from trailing early on with multiple acrobatic stops that seem to defy gravity. Another strike shaved the post before crashing into the stands just seconds later. As soon as we find some rhythm in the game, the Foxes hunt us down in packs and win back possession.

Despite this, I still pose a threat to USE. My control of the ball looks easy, even under pressure. I have no trouble finding dangerous spaces to operate in. My problem is my lack of chemistry with Andres, which hinders us in attack. We both operate as strikers in our new 4-4-2 to accommodate Romero's suspension, a more challenging position for me compared to my preferred central attacking midfielder role in our traditional 4-3-3 formation. Our struggles compound about fifteen minutes into the game while breaking on a promising counterattack.

I intercept a misplaced pass and drive twenty yards toward the USE goal. Andres and I make eye contact outside the eighteen-yard box, and I position myself to play a splitting pass between the defenders. Just when I expect him to cut in and sprint past his defender, I chip a pass to land before the penalty spot for him to shoot on his first touch. However, Andres checks toward me, and the ball rolls out of play for a goal kick. A fresh round of boos and sarcastic cheers ring out, reminding me that anything less than perfection wouldn't cut it today.

I would not have to wait long for a chance at redemption. Vince plays a diagonal pass in my direction, and I beat my defender, settling the ball with my left foot and a drop of my right shoulder. Andres jerks his body weight forward, pulling the defender in before stepping into the space behind. Anticipating Andres's run to the back post, I wrap my foot around the stitching of the match ball and curl a cross into the free space.

With two elongated strides, Andres launches himself into the air and connects his head with the ball. The ball pivots toward the top corner of the goal, but the power of Andres's header keeps the ball airborne until it crashes into the stands. The crowd roars and applauds our first attacks with less jeering toward me. I accept that even scoring ten goals would satisfy no one here today.

The USE goalkeeper takes the proceeding goal kick, which causes the outfield players to shift toward the ball's trajectory. Vince leaps for the header, colliding with Roger mid-air. The ball bounces off Roger's head before deflecting off Vince, a kind bounce towards me as it rolls inches closer.

I shuffle my feet over, ready to pass on my first touch, but another body collides into mine and I thrash forward before touching the ball. An elbow strikes my lower ribcage as I try to regain balance, which sends me gliding across the frozen pitch.

"Ref!" I say, throwing my arms in the air.

The referee spreads his arms in and out twice. "No foul! Play on!"

"Justice for Janet," Roger says as he dribbles away.

He thinks he's outdone me, but he ran only a few feet away before a couple of SESU Rottweilers hunt him down, mirroring the breed's genuine spirit when one of their own gets hurt.

Vince slides his built frame on the ground in front of Roger's path, aiming more for Roger than the ball. Vince's coordinated slide tackle trips Roger's leg, but the ball ricochets back into Roger's running path. Roger stumbles forward, waving his arms back and forth as he sprints toward the ball.

Roger almost finds his footing again until a feral Duncan body-slams him to the ground. The referee almost swallows his whistle as he marches to Duncan, brandishing another yellow card for Duncan's disciplinary collection.

"You don't fucking touch him, you faggot," Duncan says before casting saliva on the ground near him.

As he walks back, he glances over at me while I rise back to my feet. I notice the tiniest twitch in his lips as Duncan shuffles backward to his spot. Even with his crudeness, I smirk as I retreat to my defensive position for the free kick. But before I take my first stride, a rush of heat shoots to the back of my head as a cold, blunt object strikes me.

My hand jerks back to the point of impact, and a little throbbing taps my fingertips.

"What the fuck?" I shout, jerking my head back toward the crowd, where I find a swath of hecklers desperate for my attention.

"Over here, faggot!"

I see a USE fan wearing a Javi mask in a black robe, swinging a dildo attached to his shorts back and forth. The surrounding fans are wearing a shirt that says "Make a pass if you take it up the ass" in Rotti colors, with soccer balls covering only the last two letters of the slur. The masked fan points at me.

"Hey, Thomas. Come take a little taste."

Some SESU fans interject. "Quit encouraging him. Your mom may not survive if he meets her. Hide her!"

Both groups erupt in laughter and point at me. I am about to lash out at them when I glance over to Machi and Javi, steam coming out of both their ears. Machi almost flies over her seat, but Javi holds her back. A wave of calm comes over all of us as we exchange knowing glances, a reassurance that we can get through this. I nod at them before I turn to the SESU fan section.

"No need. He's too small for me anyway," I say before turning to face the ball, unconcerned with only faint whispers behind me.

The free kick materializes into a wasted opportunity, but USE regains their dominance over us. They possess the ball for longer periods, inflating their confidence. A dangerous cross flew in from the winger moments later, cutting through the space between Duncan and Vince. The outstretched forward throws his leg into the ball's pathway and makes the faintest of contact, redirecting his shot that shaves a millimeter off the post before crashing into the stands. USE bombards us with similar attacks as the end of the half ticks closer. My body needs a break as I try to conserve enough energy for one more play, ignoring the slow-burning pain building at the back of my skull.

In one moment of reprieve, Duncan intercepts a cross with composed chest control. The ball bounces a few feet forward, and he takes two large strides right behind it. Seconds after Duncan launches his right leg through the ball, I sprint into the space behind the USE right-back. I bend my run to beat the offside trap and stick out my foot without altering my stride. My right cleat is magnetic as I caress the ball, and swiftly bypass the right-back, moving closer to a scoring position.

As I cross the perimeter and set my feet to strike, I connect my instep to the inner stitching of the ball. It curves across the field and travels toward the far post. The keeper dives as a courtesy, given that his body weight could not send him to the floor fast enough. The trajectory of the goal from the ball saves him because the ball sails wide of the post, forcing the stadium to gasp. It was a welcome break from the booing. But as I jog back into position, the pounding in my head worsens. A percussionist beating his drum looks gentler than the rate at which my blood vessels dilate in the back of my head. I need an ice pack, but I'd rather stick it out for these last seconds instead of calling for a substitution.

How I would come to regret this a moment later.

Roger notices our unaware left-back ball watching his keeper's long pass, and maneuvers around our defender undetected. Our left-back, caught out of position, lets the ball travel over his head, which lands at Roger's feet. Roger redirects the ball with his first touch into our 18-yard box. On instinct, I sprint at my top speed to recover for my teammate to stop Roger's attack, pushing through the head thumping and quick twitch of pain shoots up my leg from my healed leg break, but I would rather break my leg again rather than let Roger score a goal.

Roger notices me and hesitates, as if he's baiting me in, before he pushes the ball just a few inches ahead of him. He drops his shoulder to shield the ball apathetically from me, and I don't realize what he's doing until it's too late. I run as fast as possible toward him, closing the distance at top speed, but the adrenaline flushes through my veins and prevents me from slowing down. I don't adjust my feet to remain in control, and my upper thigh connects with his left hip, sending Roger tumbling onto the pitch. He clutches his leg and rolls multiple times to exaggerate the impact. To the horror of everyone wearing bright tan and black, the referee whistles and points to the penalty spot.

"Fuck's sake," I mutter.

If my head was pounding before, it was assaulting me now. I watch as the referee holds up a yellow card in my direction, before Duncan, Vince, and Marshall confront the referee, shouting in a rapid, unintelligible manner. The referee takes a few minutes talking to a furious Coach Ramsey and calming the players down. He directs the rest of us to our spots while Roger takes the ball and centers it on the spot. The referee points at the goal line as he instructs Marshall where his feet should be before the penalty kick. He faces the penalty taker, points at the whistle, and then jogs back to the players.

"Stay behind the line and wait for the kick! This will be the last play of the half," the referee shouts, swinging his arm back and forth. He blows the whistle before semi-squatting and focusing on the players.

I stand behind the semicircle, praying the worst doesn't happen. The whistle rings in my ear, but I remain in place with everyone else, waiting for Roger. Facing the ball, he runs and then moves laterally to his right. Roger performs a few quick steps before a short run-up and takes a sharp lunge just before whipping his left foot around the ball. I take off in a full sprint forward, anticipating a rebound.

But instead of a save from Marshall, I watch him dive in the opposite direction of the ball that rolls into the bottom right corner of the goal. USE players ran into the far corner to celebrate with their traveling fans. Feeling stranded on a deserted island in the middle of the ocean during a hurricane is the only thought rushing through my head as I walk with the team to the lockers for halftime.

...

I slump over in my chair, one hand holding the ice pack to my head, the other holding my face. Vince pats me on the back without saying a word, but I ignore it. I'm too busy living in my head, thinking how stupid I was not to see Roger baiting me into drawing a foul. I should have noticed he could have just driven forward and shot before I could even catch him. By slowing down, he wanted to engage me so he could later embarrass me. He succeeded.

How could I have missed that minor detail?

All I want is to disappear somehow so I don't suffer

through the tongue-lashing I will receive from Coach Ramsey. My head throbs with pain, and can only take so much. The ice pack is helping at least with the pain from whatever was thrown in my direction. I peel my hand away from my face and now see the mood I had been sensing. Everyone either slumps in their chairs, staring at the ground, or leans back searching for something on the ceiling.

Duncan and a few other players poison the mood further with shouts of frustration and finger-pointing a t everyone who is not performing well. His last remark crucifies me for my mistake that put us in this current losing position. I guess I ran out of brownie points with him.

The door swings open, and we all snap into position, sitting up straight in our chairs. I expect a frustrated tirade from Coach Ramsey the moment he walks in, but his demeanor catches us off guard. He claps as he walks over to the whiteboard.

"Fantastic boys! Fantastic! We were unlucky with the penalty, but this game is anyone's for the taking. Even when we struggle to play our game, our qualities will give us the edge in this championship match. Remember, boys, we are only down by a goal. The opportunities will come if you keep working hard."

We stare at him, dumbfounded, everyone trying to process what is unfolding in front of us. Coach Ramsey writes one word on the board: persevere.

"Persevere. What does that mean to you, boys?"

Nobody says a word.

"Caleb. What does this mean to you?" Coach Ramsey asks in an optimistic tone.

Everyone turns their attention to me. My eyes dart around

as my heart leaps out of my chest. I find Coach Ramsey standing there, almost restraining himself from sharing the answer before I say anything.

"To…um…survive?" I answer.

"Close. It means to overcome. Surviving implies that you let life's forces defeat you and leave you to perish. Preserving means you stand up to those forces to achieve the ultimate success. That you rise to the occasion and win at life when life thinks it has beaten you. You persevere when life steals everything of meaning from you, and you are on the verge of despair."

A tight smile appears on my face when I realize the implied meaning.

"Let's be honest with ourselves here. We didn't play our best that half. There were a few chances, but overall we were second-best. We struggled to keep up with the opposing team in that half on our home field. They won every major duel out there. Marshall looks like he's in a shooting drill rather than a championship match, and we're passing the ball around like we walked out of the pub an hour ago. The stat keepers gave us possession stats out of pity."

This gets a faint chuckle out of us.

"If you all want to survive, keep performing as you are. The match concludes in forty-five minutes, and we can focus the rest of the semester on having fun with family and friends. But I know this team. You all want more than that. I know you boys can persevere through anything. I see the desire in your eyes. This team won't back down or give up. The whole conference expected you to lose this year. They predicted you'd finish last in the conference, but you all took that and threw it in their faces. This group will take on anyone without fear. That includes USE, an opponent with a five-year winning streak over us, which you all beat like they stole something."

He paces in front of the whiteboard.

"Despite the drama off the field, our goal stays the same. We made it here to win, not just to show up. This group has surpassed all previous teams in its history, but we still have more history to write."

Coach Ramsey turns and circles the word. "Don't leave this room focused only on survival. Leave here, knowing this is your chance to exceed expectations. Walk out of here prepared to win the game."

I lean forward and nod.

Coach Ramsey scribbles new tactics for us to follow in the second half. After he's done explaining, a fresh wave of eagerness sprinkles across the locker room. His choices are bold, but I think they could work.

...

Riding an emotional wave pumps us up for the first ten minutes. Duncan and Vince boost the defensive effort by diving into challenges. Their tenacity increases the physicality, shifting the game from possession to a strength battle. Our fouls outnumber successful passes, leaving them with more stains on their white shorts.

Coach Ramsey shifts an extra player into midfield, creating a 3-4-3 formation to focus on scoring. Andres moves to the center as a lone striker while I shift over to the left-forward position. Our new strategy challenges USE's defense with a trio of attackers, something we struggled to do in the first half.

In addition, this formation allows the wing-backs to push forward and deliver the ball to the attackers, further increasing our offensive advantage. However, we become susceptible to counterattacks because of fewer defenders at the back. But given how well Duncan and Vince held down the back line in the first half, it's a risk we will take.

The risks seem to pay off early because our new dynamic catches USE scrambling as I drive the ball forward into the attack. An ill-advised back pass from their right winger sends Melvin gallivanting toward an exposed USE back line. He finds Andres, who pins the center-back, pushing off his back. I outrun the unaware center-back, matching the far-side right-back's poor positioning.

Melvin plays the ball with his first touch ahead of me, just outside the 18-yard box. I close the space between me and the ball, facing the goalkeeper, racing toward the ball as well. The goalkeeper charges toward me, closing the gap between us to leave me only seconds to decide my next move. I chip the ball over the keeper as he goes to the ground, and my left ankle connects with the outstretched glove of the goalkeeper.

I somersault into the penalty area, but peer up to see the ball bouncing toward the net. But moments before I can cel-ebrate, the ball kisses the center of the far post and rolls back out toward the outer perimeter of the six-yard box. The crowd gasps a second after the contact, and I bury my head in my arms once the defender clears the ball. I lift myself, but I feel an increasing pain forming below my knee. Slightly limping, I return to my position, ignoring the pain.

Composure should have been the second word on the dry-erase board, because a more contentious fifteen minutes of aggressive challenges built tension between the team benches. The spark that ignites a blaze starts with Roger spinning away from Duncan toward an acre of space ahead of him. As he sprints away, Duncan lunges outward and wraps his legs around his shins, sending my nemesis to the floor like a tree being chopped down in the forest. Players swarm the referee after his whistle, but before the referee can address the situation, a massive confrontation explodes.

Duncan sizes himself up against a couple of furious USE players. The fury boils over onto the sideline as Coach Ramsey exchanges heated arguments with the USE coaching staff, forcing an assistant referee to separate them. I join multiple teammates and rush to Duncan to pull him away from a likely fight while the referees de-escalate everyone. The referee shows yellow cards to multiple players and coaches on both sides.

However, the referee walks over to show Duncan a red card and points to the stands, ejecting him from the game. His incoherent rants fall on deaf ears, and he walks over to the bench at Coach Ramsey's shouting requests. The fans scream their grievances on the opposite side of the stadium.

"What the fuck is that, ref?"

"What game are you watching?"

"Get off your knees, ref, you're blowing the game!"

Amidst the chaos, I feel temporary relief as the ref becomes the target of abuse, but the daunting task in the last fifteen minutes erodes my joy. We need a goal to extend our season, but this must happen with ten men on the field instead of eleven.

USE wastes no time reasserting its dominance with its new numerical advantage on the field and controls the rest of the second half as it did in the first. Their possession dissects our defensive formation, and they suffocate us for extended periods, forcing all ten of us behind the ball to stop the attacks. This only plays into their hands. The longer they have the ball, the less time we have to score.

The only positive is that USE has wasted every chance they created. A center-back heads an uncontested cross over the bar. A first-time shot curled away from Marshall's near post. Their inability to score provides a bright spot for us, especially with Roger losing his cool with everyone.

USE lays siege to our half for most of the remaining time, but their sloppiness creeps back as the game ticks toward its finish. I know I have to try something if we are going to score a goal. So with less than a minute left, I gamble with a press on the center-backs. Since Duncan's sending off, I moved into central midfield, playing as an auxiliary striker and attacking midfielder, expected to adapt depending on how the game presents itself. I've led the first line of defense against USE since then, hoping to find the right moment to apply pressure to their players. And as Roger remains out of position behind me, not supporting his center backs in possession, I know my time to press is now.

Anticipating a pass to the center-back in front of me, I sprint toward him. The center-back's first touch is dreadful, and the ball rolls forward into my path. The center-back attempts to compensate for his mistake by diving toward the ball, foot first, but I lift the ball over the challenge and sprint into the grass ahead. I hold the ball close to my foot, exerting the last drops of energy I possess.

While isolated outside the box with no teammates in

support, I withstand the strength of the recovering right back, doing all he can to unbalance me. I use my quick agility to weasel away and roll the ball with the sole of my left foot to my right foot, dodging the right-back's tackle. While I turn and maneuver the ball past the defenders, I pull my leg back as if I am shooting, but tap the ball between the legs of the other center-back, hoping the center-back tackles his own teammate. He does, which gives me crucial space to fire a shot toward the goal before the left-back crashes into me outside the box. The ball swerves in the air as the goalkeeper stays mounted in place, watching the ball sail past him. But to the goalkeeper's relief, the ball rattled off the crossbar.

The crowd gasps at the point of contact, but I can't hear them over the crunch in my leg when I land on my body. The grueling, bone-breaking pain flares in my leg, the same unbearable pain I felt in New Orleans. I fight to stand up, but I can't fight the sharp stabbing attacking my body.

With an agonizing breath, I push my head to the floor, on the brink of tears, knowing that my game is over. All I can do is let out an agonizing scream. The cries were so deafening that I didn't hear the referee blow his whistle to end it all seconds later.

Chapter 34

November 17, 2025

"How do you feel?" Matthew Evans asks, his voice crackling in the phone pushed up to my ear.

I walk towards the blue BMW purring in my apartment parking lot. My eyes stare down at the boot constricting my fragile leg, making any short walk feel like a marathon.

"I've had better days," I say.

"You and I both. What did the doctor say last night?"

"He said I have a stress fracture in my lower leg, and that I'll probably be out for eight weeks."

"That's rough, lad. It's such bad luck that you got injured in the last moments of the season. I had been receiving positive reports from the scouts in attendance up to that point. There hasn't been a lot of communication since."

"I don't think many pro teams want to sign an injured rookie right out of college."

"No, they don't. But the good news is that no one lost interest in you joining their squads in the future. They will just monitor your recovery closely."

"Even with the whole 'Justice for Janet' protests and Javi drama?"

A long exhale crackles in my ear. "That was difficult to explain away, so I described it as social media garbage designed to distract you during a match of huge significance. I would advise releasing a counter-story to control the narrative, though, just in case negative publicity spills out. I think waiting another year will benefit you in the long run."

"So I guess I have to repeat everything I did this season. Recover from an injury, rehab with SESU doctors, and then play well under Coach Ramsey. At least I know what to do, right?"

"Well, not exactly."

My breath slows as I hear the faint tapping of keys in the background.

"The athletic director informed me this morning that he is suspending you and opening an investigation into the allegations of foul play brought forth against you."

"I'm suspended! Because of allegations of foul play? From who?" I say while gritting my teeth.

"An anonymous source."

I want to scream, 'probably his fucking daughter' out loud, but Matthew Evans steals all the time for my outburst.

"Before you react, Jack and I saw this coming already, Caleb."

I rub the back of my neck at this revelation. "What do you mean?"

"Jack got a call from the athletic director, who applied pressure on Jack to remove you from the team after your teammate got suspended. He threatened to withhold NIL funds, scholarships, and anything else he could think of if you played last night."

"Did he say why?"

"Jack said no. It was completely random. But UCLA had already approached Jack to become their next head coach. He wanted to take some time to think about it, but after that mess of a conversation, he'd already accepted the position. He sent his letter of resignation this morning."

"Wow," I say, grabbing my forehead between my fingertips. I lose a bit of balance processing all this information. "So I guess I'm off the team here as well."

The prolonged silence is enough of an answer for me.

"Well, I have good news at least. I'm putting the finishing touches on your next deal, so you can close this chapter here and start anew. Jack is already working on incoming transfers for UCLA. I let him know you will be in the portal by this afternoon and eligible to play in the spring semester. We'll finish your transfer by the book with your blessing, but I can't imagine you would turn down playing in Los Angeles rather than stay in University Hills without football."

"You're not wrong," I say. A full-toothed smile plastered on my face.

"Good. And I almost forgot. Regarding your rehabilitation…"

My back straightens at the remark. "What about it?"

"SESU will not process any potential hospital claims under their insurance because the athletic department suspended you. On top of that, UCLA will not cover your rehab either until you become a student-athlete with them the next calendar year."

"What does that mean?"

Matthew Evans draws a long breath. "It means you are on

the hook for all the medical bills out of pocket."

I almost faint in the parking lot. "How am I supposed to pay for all that?"

"Just take a breath. I know it's a lot to process, but Jack worked his magic for you again."

"How?"

"We have an old teammate from uni who is an orthopedic surgeon specializing in sports medicine. Jack talked with him over the phone last night about your situation, and he agreed to help us."

My mouth gapes open. There is no way I am one of the luckiest people in the world right now. "Is he doing it for free or something?"

"Christ, no! He agreed to make a generous payment plan with us based on your current NIL deal with SESU. Once UCLA completes the deal, we will adjust the plan to help him out. He's essentially taking a tremendous loss helping us up front before we make it right after the fact."

"But why would he want to help me?"

"Well, partially because Jack was the nicest teammate to him in college, and they remained good friends after that. Jack even visited him and his husband just before the season started."

I remain silent while the understanding fills my brain.

"The other part being, well, you know. He probably understands your struggles the best."

"Yeah, I get what you mean."

"The only other caveat is that his practice is in New Orleans."

It's at this moment that Javi moves two large duffel bags to the trunk of the car. I questioned all morning why Javi had so much luggage with him if he was only staying for a couple of days. Now I'm wondering if there is something else unfolding that I'm not aware of.

"Is that okay?" Matthew Evans asks in a less confident tone. "Do you know anyone in the area?"

"I know someone."

Javi's eyes meet mine in a way that melts me to the floor. He tilts his head upward before slamming the trunk shut.

"Good. You won't need to worry about attending classes either. Given your situation, the university prefers that you finish the semester online. So you are free to head over there whenever, but I would travel sooner rather than later so we know the full extent of the injury. Is that okay?"

"Yeah, I'm good with that."

"I hope this wasn't too much information, but everything moved lightning-fast. Is there anything else you need from me?"

"No, I'm good. Thank you for all the help."

"Of course! You are still a promising talent. There is time to make a star out of you. I'll be in touch."

The phone call goes dead as I pull the phone away from my ear. Javi leans on the passenger side door, arms crossed, looking like he's been waiting an eternity for me. It feels like I have waited just as long. The palm of a hand rubbing my back startles me out of my daze, and Machi walks up beside me.

"Look at my wounded warrior," Machi says, wrapping her hand around my shoulder and pulling me into a side hug.

Vince trails behind her. "How are you feeling?" he asks.

"Sore," I say. "But luckily, I have a long break ahead."

"I mean you deserve it after all the shit you've been through." Machi peels off me and leans into Vince.

"Do you know what you're going to do?" Javi peels off the car door and walks over to us.

"I think you all figured that out for me."

They all share confused expressions until I give them all a wry look.

"I know you all concocted this plan for me to go to New Orleans."

Vince clears his throat. "I mean there weren't any alternatives the way Coach described it. So we all got together last night to figure out how to help."

Javi approaches and places his hand on my shoulder. "And my G-mom said it would be cool if you stayed with her while you're recovering, so you don't have to find a place."

"She doesn't have to do that. I don't want her to feel uncomfortable with a stranger in her house," I say.

Javi waves me off. "Don't worry. I will be there too. We need to catch up, since we didn't really get the chance while I was here. That was the whole point after all."

"Are you sure?"

His hands slide down my arm and into mine.

"I want you there," he whispers. My skin flushes as I gaze into his twinkling eyes. "You will be as good as new when you come back here."

My smile drops the second he says this, and he recognizes it instantly.

"What's wrong?"

"I won't be coming back here next semester."

Javi looks aghast as he distances himself. He glances at

Machi and Vince, both staring at me, confused by this revelation. These reactions catch me off guard, like this might be the first bit of breaking news they were genuinely unaware of.

"You're leaving me again?" Machi asks, this time with her hands on her hips.

"You guys didn't know?"

"Coach didn't mention that to me. When did this happen?" Vince asks.

I recount my conversation with Matthew Evans regarding my suspension with all three of them, each with a unique reaction to my story.

Vince looks the most perplexed. "Why is the athletic director suspending you at all? What is there to investigate?"

Javi explodes. "He can't fucking do that. It's illegal for him to remove you without actual proof you did something wrong!"

Machi lifts her phone, her voice so calm and even that it unsettles me. "Maybe retaliation for this?"

Vince, Javi, and I stare at the phone screen. A series of comments float on top of Angelica's revealing post about me on Reeltime, most comments on a hyperlink under the words:

Social Media Sweetheart Swooned by Bisexual Bilker

I scroll through some comments.

@Reeltimetea: "Wow, Angelica in love with a con man? Probably the best she can do tbh."

@Davethemachoman: "Karma's a bitch, ain't it? That's toughhhhhhhh!!!!!!"

@AmyvanHolland: "I can tell you as a close friend, Romero was her source for all drama related to athletics. Romero lied to her about my relationship with Duncan, exaggerated what

happened with the football team, and lied about his relationship with Caleb. So glad these two monsters were put in their place!"

@DamienT_15: "Romero and I secretly hooked up in high school after practice for about a year. One day he told me his aunt was sick with cancer and needed the money for treatment. I sent him the money, but he ghosted me afterward. A genuine piece of shit."

@MariaGomez: "*@DamienT_15* same here…"

@RottiRoundUp: "Feeling terrible for Caleb Thomas right about now. He was used as a distraction for this. I wonder if she lied about him too."

@DamienT_15: "*@RottiRoundUp* I wouldn't be surprised if she made the majority of it up."

The stories continue for days with people highlighting Romero's history of swindling and gossiping about University Hill's biggest gossip. The same way she does in all her videos. It's the reason I feel no remorse for the brutality in some comments.

"It looks like it's backfiring," I say.

"I guess the world has a funny way of working itself out. Too bad her national anthem performance didn't pan out," Machi says, turning her phone away.

"My manager and I talked about that this morning. Apparently, she messaged him through the app, trying to reach out after the performance. He said she wanted to talk about the next steps for a contract and that her dad could pay him more to sign her. He blocked her right after that," Javi says.

Machi laughs. "I don't blame him. I would do the same if she didn't know where I worked. She's psycho when she's thinking of revenge."

"It's probably better that you're leaving. Where are you heading?" Vince asks.

"UCLA," I say.

"No way," Javi says. His eyes narrow at me, but the coy smile stays put.

"Yeah, I'll travel there to play again once I've healed."

"I have an apartment just blocks away from campus, right next to my recording studio."

"You don't say?" I say.

We both freeze in place, a gushing wind of thought flying through my head. I hope he's thinking the same thing I am. The change in color on his face suggests we might be on the same page.

"Well, you lovebirds got a lot to catch up on," Vince says, smiling. "But I think you guys need to hit the road if you want to make it to New Orleans while the sun is up." He extends his hand, and I clasp it before we wrap each other in a bear hug. "It was a pleasure kicking it with you, Thomas."

"Mine too. I'm sorry we won't be able to play together again."

"Don't stress. I'm out of eligibility anyway. I just have graduation to look forward to."

"And I promise to attend."

We exchange smiles before a disgruntled Machi looks me over and pulls me into a hug.

"I'm going to miss you," I whisper in her ear.

"Good," she asserts. We laugh as we pull away. "Oh, wait! I almost forgot. I spent a couple of hours packing the rest of your personal effects." She smiles and reaches down for the box at her feet. "I might have added something else too."

"What do you mean?"

"Open up and see."

I peel off the lid and gasp at its contents. "You bought a Nintendo Switch?"

She nods as I set the box down and retrieve the game console. "I thought we could play together like we used to."

"I would love that."

"Good, because I expect you to play every night now. Since you're leaving me again."

I pull her into another hug. "Thank you. I promise I will," I whisper. I reach into the box and pull out the World Cup trophy I left on my nightstand, dropping it into her cupped hands. "I want you to have it."

"Why? It's your lucky trophy."

"And luck should be with you on your new journey. I don't need it anymore." I roll her fingertips over the trophy before wrapping my hands around her. "I'm going to miss you. Thank you for everything." A few tears form at my tear ducts.

Machi rubs my back as she pulls away.

I sort through the rest of the contents, checking off a mental checklist of everything in my room. I pull out the Kehlani vinyl and reach into the flap, but can't find the note I always tuck behind the vinyl. Instead, I pull out Javi's old autographed Polaroid, the first time I have seen it since the summer. "Where is my mom's note?"

Javi approaches the group, his hands in his pockets. "I switched out the note with the photo. I just wanted you to have the fresh start you wanted."

"I put it in a safe place for now," Machi says. "We felt you should remember your mom for all the good times you shared. It is time to heal from her death and let go of what happened. Your mom loved you, and she would hate to see you beating yourself up for this."

Javi wraps his hands around my waist. "You deserve happiness, Caleb. Let us help you feel that again."

My cheeks flush when I stare at the best people around me. They are right. Maybe I need to heal more than just my body for the next couple of months. I won't have much else to do.

Javi acts as my crutch as I hobble over to the passenger side. Vince and Machi trail behind me, each carrying my final belongings. Javi waits by the door like a valet about to open my door for me. The moment he does, the familiar tune of "NO LAughing matter" dances around my ears.

"Wait!" Machi says.

We all turn to look at her.

"You haven't done your challenge yet," she says.

I follow her finger as she points to the left of me toward a very confused R&B singer.

"What?" Javi asks.

"You haven't posted a 'NO LAughing matter' challenge yet, and now's your chance!"

Javi's bewildered look flips to a shrewd one.

"Oh, come on. The song's about him. Who's better to be a part of it than him?" she says, retrieving her phone.

We exchange glances with each other. "You want to?" I ask.

"I'm good with it. Are you okay with breaking the internet?" Javi asks.

I shrug with a grin. "It can't be any worse than the dumpster fire I set earlier."

He laughs and nods his head toward Machi. "Hurry before you miss the chorus!"

Machi directs Javi as he scrambles to the opposite side of me, leaning on the car door. Vince rushes over to adjust my position in the video frame before he darts behind Machi. Javi takes my hand and tugs me over to him so only inches separate us, the same distance between us when we created an unintentional social media trend. But that thought never crossed our minds. It was as real as love could feel in that moment. Nothing forced or enhanced with filters.

We wait a handful of seconds as the chorus approaches, as Machi counts down with her hand. I take my mark, ready for what comes next.

Acknowledgements

In soccer, a foul in open play refers to an unfair and illegal act by a player against another while the ball is in play. I felt this was the perfect title for a story that mirrors my own in so many ways, whether playing the sport or just simply existing. I dedicated my life to soccer growing up, hoping that I would become a professional soccer player. It made sense, given I am the son of a French immigrant and I was born in 1998. From then on, my childhood comprised school and soccer, including practices and games every week leading up to summer. I attended multiple college camps, trying to impress scouts to one day sign me to their youth academies, college, and professional teams. I loved nothing more in the world than playing the sport, so I believed it was destiny.

What I didn't expect was how intense my internal struggles would develop as I got older. I lived in rural Texas, one of the many hostile areas for gay minors in the country. I didn't have a role model to look up to, and I knew better than to use my parents' computer to search the internet for solutions to something I wrongly deemed a problem. It wasn't until Robbie Rogers came out that I saw an out professional soccer player with my own eyes. His story was captivating, and it sparked some hope in me I hadn't felt before. What should have been a moment of acceptance devolved into deep self-loathing and depression. My classmates and teammates scowled at the news of his coming out with such visceral hatred that it scared me into silence out of fear I would receive a similar reaction or worse. I even turned to religion and conversion therapy to change. Even though I never lived through the trauma Caleb experienced, I left those sessions more broken than healed every single time.

It wasn't until I arrived at St. Mary's University in San Antonio, Texas when I couldn't hide anymore. We had a history-making season where we won our first conference championship. I had one of my best seasons of my career, and I felt so depressed. I felt so numb to one of the biggest moments of my life. Something broke in me, and from that moment on, I stopped trying to change who I was. With the help of a psychologist and a priest, we worked together to help me come to terms with who I am. Step by step, I slowly embraced who I was, and came out to groups of people at a time. My college coach was a massive supporter, which was more than I could have hoped for. To become captain my senior year is still one of the biggest honors I have ever received. My team-mates' reactions were mixed, but there was powerful support from the guys that I played with since my first day on campus. I never expected that from them, but it still warms my heart to this day.

I never achieved my childhood dream after college and ended up attending graduate school. However, I am at peace that I found writing to help me heal. There are so many people I want to thank who made a lasting impact on this book's journey. First, I want to thank Dr. Eric Howerton for accepting me into your writing seminar so many years ago. You gave me the tools to start a writing career I am growing to love more and more each day. You are the closest thing to formal training I have, and I am forever grateful for it. Thank you to Frankie, my editor at Olive Press Publishing, for cleaning up my messy writing and elevating this story to another level. You were as big a cheerleader of this work as I was, and it was my pleasure to work with someone who connected with the story the way you did. It was also a joy to work with someone who shares a mutual suffering of supporting Arsenal. I am so glad the Olive Press Publishing social media team reached out when I was searching for an editor. If there is a writer looking to publish their work reading this, I highly encourage you to check them out. Thank you to Sofie for designing this amazing book cover and book interior. You created a cover better than I could imagine, and designed a book that I love and cherish so much. I can't thank you enough. Another special thank you goes to Antoine for producing this audiobook. Your magic touch transforms a novel into a sensory experience, and I am so grateful I had the opportunity to work with you. Thank you for making this dream a reality. Thank you to Jordan for an unforgettable performance as Caleb. You are such a talented narrator, and I am so glad you were a part of this project.

I want to say a massive thank you to an elite group of women who supported me by taking the time to read this story. Thank you to Erin, Megan, Remy, Divina, Mikayla, and Brittany for your honest feedback that helps improve my writing every day. I'm forever grateful. Thank you to the ARC readers for your time in reading this book. A massive thank you goes to my family for being everything opposite of Caleb's. It is still the minority to have parents and a brother that have not shut me out from the family, and still cherish the relationship we have. I love you guys. Finally, a big thank you to my partner, Bryce. You were on the front lines of all my struggles, and I cannot thank you enough for your unconditional love and support. You are amazing and I love you. I also want to thank the fur babies Jack, Wilshere, and Brady for always providing the emotional support and the escape when I get overwhelmed by life. I know they can't read this, but let this be the written promise for more belly rubs and head scratches.

Lastly, and most importantly, thank you to you, the reader. You are the most essential part of any author's journey. Thank you for spending your valuable time exploring this world with me. It means the world to me to share my story with you. Southeastern State University is a dark, fictional setting for queer people's existence, but it is also the perfect place to write about the LGBTQ+ community's most resilient members. It may have driven away Caleb and Javi, but there are still characters that I can't wait to introduce you to. Stay tuned.

About the Author

Patrick Voss is a full-time chemist specializing in toxicology. Outside of writing, he is a marathon runner, an R&B fanatic, a thriller girlie novel connoisseur (thrillers written by women) and an avid Arsenal fan. He currently lives in Dallas with his partner, their two dogs, Brady and Jack, and their cat Wilshere. This is his first published work. You can find him on the following social media sites and website below:

Website: www.patvosswrites.com
Instagram:@patvosswrites
Threads: @patvosswrites
Goodreads: www.goodreads.com/patrick_voss